The Epilogue of August

Based on a True Story, Subject to the Whims of Fiction

By Jennifer Milder

Part 1: 1967

Chapter 1: Recounting

Pop Gray's makes the "Best Ice Cream in the State." That fact is confirmed by a white wooden sign that's propped in the corner of the store's front window.

Sometimes, after he clocks out at noon, Billy likes to sit on his bike for a while, there on the corner of the Seaville town square, watching as a line forms out the front door of the ice cream parlor. On a hot day like today, it would snake around the block, well past the Dixie. Billy, who's always looking for another job to help his momma make ends meet, won't look for work at the Dixie. Word has it the owner, Mr. Robinson, doesn't like colored folks.

Pop Gray's, though, is the best job he's ever had. Inside, they've got a brand-new icebox, humming the tune of deep freeze, and a churner that cranks beside it (with the peculiar *whip-loosh, whip-loosh* sound it makes), swirling in rhythms of color and flavor.

The countertops are always gleaming—Billy sees to that—everything trimmed in chrome, and those red leather stools tucked beneath have just the right amount of swivel. The curved malt glasses and scalloped sundae cups that line the shelves behind the counter are the real glass kind, and they shatter hard when dropped. Billy should know. He's always having to clean up after somebody's mess. The silverware also sparkles like treasure, polished by those Sundae Girls to Mrs. Gray's highest standard of shine.

Today, however, as Billy sits on the corner, Pop Gray's isn't open, and nobody is in line. Because Something Terrible happened there last night.

Uncle Joe came over with the news first thing this morning. There was blood everywhere, he said, and while Billy hasn't been inside himself to see it, the idea alone makes him shudder. He hopes no one asks him to bring in his mop.

Police cars drive in slow procession around the town square, and a man in blues and his search dog scour the green expanse, the dog sniffing eagerly at everything that moves, poking and prodding through the Something Terrible. Billy can hear the muted crackle of the officer's walkie-talkie, but he's too far away to make out what they're saying.

A small wisp of a man approaches Billy's bike, a pencil tucked behind his ear, and he clutches tight to a wide-ruled notepad, its pages flapping in the warm wind.

"'Scuse me, son," the little man says to Billy. "You got a minute to talk to me about what went on here?"

"Who, me?" Billy does a double take. "Sorry, sir. I don't know nothin' 'bout it. I only work in the mornin', so I wasn't there last night."

"Ahhh, so you're telling me that you *work* at Pop Grays?" the man asks, a small smile brightening his serious face. He has a paper badge tucked into the rim of his hat that reads "Press."

Billy nods. "Yessir, that's right."

"Hmmm…how old are you, boy?" The man with the "Press" badge pulls a pencil out from behind his ear.

Billy squirms on the seat of his bike. He runs his fingers nervously over the rusty handlebars. "I'm fifteen, sir."

"What's your name, son?"

"Billy Jackson, sir."

"Well, Billy," the man continues, scribbling on his notepad, "I'm Len Garvey from the Wilmington Star News. Pleased to meet ya."

"Well, likewise," Billy responds, slightly bewildered but comforted by the man's smooth transition to kindness.

"Mind if I ask ya a few questions?"

Billy shakes his head, uncertain if he has a choice in the matter. The reporter rolls on.

"What was it you said you do over there at Pop Gray's?"

"I's the janitor, sir."

"Aha." Len Garvey scribbles down a note. "And tell me, what are your duties there at Pop Gray's as janitor?"

"Well, sir…" Billy begins, thinking the duties of a janitor must be pretty obvious. "I arrive first thing in the mornin'. I clean up whatever mess is there from the night before, and I take care of the garbage, the bathrooms, the floors, you know…"

Billy's favorite part of the job is helping Mrs. Gray open up because that's when he gets to see it all come together. Denny's the one who makes the ice cream, and Billy will watch as he pours this in, dumps that in, then mixes it all up. The creamy batches he makes in those huge steel basins get frothed up good inside that new Whitehouse steel churner.

Pop Gray's kitchen is separated from the storefront by burnished metal swinging doors, so most folks don't get a chance to see this magic being created. But Billy does, it's one of the perks of the job.

Sometimes, Denny offers him a taste. "Say, Billy, what do you think about this here butterscotch cream?" Denny would ask, and it makes Billy feel like he's part of something bigger, more than just the mopping and cleaning.

On a good morning, while Billy is finishing up the floor, and Denny is whisking and mixing, Mrs. Gray will crank up the jukebox that sits over in the corner. She likes to pick and choose the tunes herself, and she favors that high-brow music—the big bands and the Lawrence Welk stuff. None of that rock and roll the kids keep asking for.

Before Pop Gray's opens, Billy double-checks that the crimson leather booths that line the storefront windows are clean and crumb-free, then he exits out the side door as the Sundae Girls roll in the front with their pink aprons and practiced smiles, ready to serve up soda creams and chocolate malts.

The reporter scratches on his notepad, wiggling his nose in thought before shifting his line of questioning. "So, Billy, did you know the two girls that got shot?"

Across the square, two police officers duck under the police tape that has cordoned off Pop Gray's and head inside the store. The street is solemn, and the roar of the ocean can be heard in the distance. The scent of greasy breakfast foods fried up at Grady's Café wafts down the block.

"Nossir," Billy answers. "Not really. I mean, I seen all the Sundae Girls, and I knows their names, but I ain't ever really talked to those two."

"I see," Len says. "You from around here, son? Live on the island?"

"Yessir." Billy nods. "My family's lived up on Shell Beach for years, and my granddaddy, he helped 'em build up the boardwalk back in the twenties."

Billy is proud of his roots here in Seaville, and he leans forward on his handlebars and smiles. Shell Beach is nothing but sand and shanties now, but there are pieces of its past still scattered in the sand—some splinters of wood from the old boardwalk and the burnt-out foundation that used to be the Shell.

Billy lives with his momma in a weather-beaten cottage beside the sea. They've got good neighbors all around, and folks can keep to their own up there, keep to their ways. There are Sundays of grand picnics, swimming, and fishing, mercifully free from the stare of white people's suspicious eyes.

"Shell Beach? You don't say?" the reporter responds, hungry for more.

Billy continues, his jangled nerves easing. "You know much 'bout Shell Beach, sir?" He steps off his bike and props it against a lamppost, turning to the reporter with his full attention.

"Well, I know about the big fire…"

There was once a grand resort built on Billy's end of the island. They called it the Shell, a thirty-room hotel framed by dunes with wild red daisies growing at the base of the curves. Billy's momma said it was something to see—its pavilion brimming with jazz music, and the boardwalk bustling with hustlers and hope. Momma and Uncle Joe would spend Friday nights at the concession because they sold cold beer, popcorn, and grease-fired hushpuppies.

"Yessir, the colored folks had it pretty good up on Shell Beach, at least for a few years," Billy says. "Until that fire wiped 'em all out in '36. Uncle Joe says no blame was ever laid for that fire, but as I heard it, the white men saw it all going too good for the colored, and they took it on themselves to set things right."

"You think the white men burned down the colored resort?" Len asks, somewhat speculative.

Billy shrugs. "And then, a few years later, like a part of the white God's master plan, the water left the inlet that divided the two islands, and Shell Beach and Seaville merged into one."

"Huh," Len says. "Kind of like forced desegregation."

Billy nods. "Not much left up north after all that. That's why I come down here and over the bridge, lookin' for work."

"You're mighty young to be working a tough job like janitor…"

Billy puffs up his chest with pride. "It ain't my first hard labor, sir. I's been working at some odd job or another since I was twelve. First, Uncle Joe helped me find work mowing lawns and cleaning out gutters. You know, for the rich folk who lived across the bridge. Didn't pay much but enough change to buy me a cold Co' Cola every now and again."

The reporter nods, but he'd stopped taking notes.

"Then, when I's old enough to drop out of school, I'd hop on the beach car and take it down past Airlie where an open bed truck was waiting to take me inland to pick corn and cut down tobacco."

His focus drifting, Len looks over Billy's shoulder at the police activity on the corner.

"But when that work nearly broke my back," Billy continues, unaware as a fifteen-year-old would be he was losing Len's interest, "Momma said a more sensible choice would be taking up the janitorial arts. And that's how I landed right here at Pop Gray's."

Len pulls his focus back to the subject of his interview, digging for something he could use. "You like your job, Billy? People are nice?"

"I do." Billy nods, making a list in his mind of all the things he likes about his work. Well, there's the ice cream, for one. He doesn't have a lot of spending money, but it seems his spare change is always enough to buy a cone. And Denny is always nice to Billy. They call Denny "The Confectioner," which Billy thinks is kind of a silly name, but that's the way it works at Pop Gray's. Denny also happens to be Pop's oldest son, and as many of the girls would say, Seaville's answer to Elvis Presley.

Billy is the only colored person who works there, and truth be told, most of the customers are white, too. So, he always makes sure he enters and leaves through the old colored entrance, even though that's not the law anymore.

Billy may not have much of an education, but he's no fool. It's plain to see that fists still grip tightly to the ways of the old South in Seaville. The men drinking coffee at Grady's Café just shake their heads when the colored kids walk by. You ask them, and they'd say it feels like it's all slipping through their fingers, much like the sand that lines these very shores. Folks here are set in their ways, with their bad teeth, farmer's tans, the dirt under their fingernails that tells the story of an honest day's work.

"Yessir, the people at Pop's are nice to me. They treat me right. I sure do feel bad that this terrible thing happened. Couldn't hardly believe somebody could get killed here in Seaville. Things just ain't how they used to be, I guess."

Billy's mind wanders back to the Something Terrible that went down inside Pop Gray's, and he knows that things around here are never going to be the same. He can feel it, the change rolling in, and it won't be denied. It's as relentless as the tide.

"How so?" the reporter asks, his pencil interested again.

"Well, sir, you see, when they started bringin' the beach car over from the mainland, the island just opened up, and now there's all sorta people comin' and goin'. But as Uncle Joe says, even after good ol' LBJ pushed through his desegregation, the beaches here, well, sir, they got they own set of rules…"

"You're talking about the white beach down at Lumina and the colored beach up at Shell?"

Billy nodded. The imaginary color line—who is allowed where in God's greatest playground of white and green and blue—is drawn down the middle of the island by Mercer's Pier, which juts into the sea like a rampart.

"Yessir," he answers, pulling a handkerchief from his brow and wiping sweat from his forehead. The noontime sun in the spring there shows no mercy. "Progress happens real slow 'round here. Like that drawbridge there they put in a few years back. To some folk on this island, well, that bridge is a traitor. It lets in the new, the different, the other. And a place like Seaville…Well, folk here have a hard time reckoning with change. They call it sin and shame and pray against it in Sunday church."

The reporter is surprised a boy like Billy could be so well-spoken, and he looks long and hard, perhaps even with admiration, at his subject before furiously jotting some more notes.

"I reckon that folks here are thankful for the money the 'others' spend on the island," Billy continues, staring across the green into the darkened windows of Pop Gray's. "Well, really they counting on these waters to keep the change at bay and to keep their way of life—the way things always been—from rushing out with the tide."

The sun glints off the chrome of Billy's bike, and the reporter squints as he thanks the boy and turns back toward Pop Gray's. The afternoon is going to be a hot one, and Billy thinks he'll bike on back to Shell Beach and take a long dip in the cold, blue sea.

Chapter 2: Yearning

Eileen Conway, with her impeccable white teeth and tumble of sleek brown curls, squeezes Aggie's elbow, excitement sparking from her fingertips like sugared candy. The two girls dance together out the front door of Pop Gray's, waving their pink aprons in the air victoriously, their hard-won conquests. Dogwood petals flutter and fall, pink confetti scattering the sidewalk in solidarity with the celebration.

The girls had just landed the summer job every teen on this island covets. They were chosen to be one of Pop Gray's Sundae Girls, and their first shift would begin tomorrow morning.

Fred Gray took care to account for all aspects of the success of Pop Gray's, including the shape and size of the girls who wore his aprons. He'd measured Aggie's waist with his yellow sewing tape, pinched his dour face, and looked her up, down, and over.

"You will *almost* do," he said, scratching his clean-shaven chin, his eyes weighing, assessing. "The red hair is good, though. We could use that here…" He took the liberty of fingering the tip of Aggie's ponytail, measuring for silk and softness.

Everyone in Seaville knows the Sundae Girls have to be pretty and petite, all-American but also enticing sweethearts and temptresses. Fred Gray fiercely protects the reputation of his brand, and the store his father had opened twenty years ago. The Sundae Girls he selects have to fit the part.

He'd sighed with resignation as he handed Aggie the uniform, and before he could change his mind, she'd dashed out the front door with a thanks and half a wave tossed back over her shoulder. Eileen was there waiting for her, squealing with glee when she saw Aggie's white-knuckled fists clutching the same pink apron she had carefully folded into the palm of her own hand.

The pair skip together down the sidewalk, giddy, dodging the shoppers who are laden with grocery bags and curious glances. At the corner of Main and Tarboro streets, Eileen gives Aggie a hug. It's the real kind, full of anticipation, hope and a hint of brighter tomorrows.

"See you in the morning," Eileen promises. She smells like lavender soap, and Aggie inhales deeply, absorbing the scent into her very skin, letting it linger. She watches Eileen walk away, the bounce and sway of her step causing her amber curls to escape her ponytail, and they blow like coiled paper streamers in the warming March wind.

Turning onto Chestnut Street toward home, Aggie slows her stride, savoring this moment of acceptance and possibility for just a bit longer. On the front porch, a pair of white rocking chairs challenge the wind. The sweeping, old oak tree in the backyard spills its shade across the small house and its lawn, laying a dark blanket over the young grass that's just beginning to sprout in every shade of green envy.

She ambles up her front steps, admiring Mama's carefully clipped azaleas, her pride and joy, which seem to be taunting her with their beauty, boastful in magenta and mauve. At full bloom, Mama's garden is a sight to behold. Tulips and irises in the spring, swaying proudly on their tall stalks, and lilies arriving closer to summer, orange and red exclamations curling toward the sun. And in the winter, just when you thought the show was over, the camellia bush by the front steps, its waxy limbs bare of flowers now, will drip with snow-white flowers.

Sometimes, though, it seems to Aggie this garden is all Mama really cares about. She takes up the rake and the spade every morning the sun shines, negotiating with its rays, weeding, cutting, planting, adjusting this, and arranging that. Mama says a good garden tells the story of the family who keeps it. It lets neighbors know who *belongs* there, the cottage beside the mansion.

Their house is the leanest and oldest on the block. Though Mama tries, it's just the two of them working to keep things up. Sometimes, if she can find extra money, Mama hires Billy, a colored boy who lives on the south end of the island. He comes on his bike with his ladder strapped to his back to clean out the gutters or cut away oak limbs that dangle too close to the roof.

It doesn't really matter to Aggie she and Mama aren't like the other families who live there in the neighborhood. We *are* different, Mama says. Better, for the struggle of it all.

The screen door swings open, and Patricia's broad frame fills the doorway.

"Well? Why're you standing out here lollygagging? How'd it go?" she asks, wiping her wet hands on a dishcloth. Her mouth is set in a grim, disapproving line, braced for bad news.

Aggie clutches the pink apron in a tight fist behind her back, and bounding up the porch steps two at a time, she whips out her prized possession, waving it like a flag of victory.

Finally, Mama will have some good news to share with the other ladies at Bridge Club. Aggie knows she'll casually slide the news into whatever conversation is being had while stirring sugar in their tea or dealing out the cards. Her voice will convey pride, but just enough so they can't call it gloating. Mama has a way of making sure she is *heard*, a little bit of boast and bluster yet achingly polite. And to be sure, no one will make the mistake of underestimating the Littletons again.

"That's right. Pop Gray's. Right. Fred Gray's place. Mm-hmm, August will be working there this summer," Aggie can hear her mother's linen-clipped drawl announce into the phone receiver as she gallops upstairs like a wild horse.

"Mm-hmm, you don't say? The Neal sisters, too?"

Aggie pauses, mid-prance, panic throwing a wet blanket over her swagger. *The Neal sisters, too?* She groans and slumps down against the frame of her bedroom door until she's a crumpled heap on the floor, the forgotten uniform squashed beneath the weight of her thighs.

Goddamn it! The Neal sisters walk around like they own this town. Now they're Sundae Girls?

Aggie had worked too hard for this, spending all winter skipping sweets and washing her face with rosewater to clear up her complexion. She had brushed her long red hair one hundred strokes each night until it shone like Mama's newly waxed kitchen floor.

The Neal sisters. Oh, I can't stand them! They're always prissing about in those stupid pink bows. Their daddy has some big job down at the bank, and word is he bought the older sister, the tall one, the title crown in the Hanover County teen pageant. She still wears her satin sash to school. *To school*! Who does such a thing?

Those girls have never been kind to Aggie. She hears the giggles and whispers as she passes in the hall, and she knows what they are laughing about. That cutting word—*bastard*—serrated as it was with cold truth, sliced open every old wound carved into her childhood. Their gossip stung like salt, poured into the crevice representing all the things she would never have.

Aggie, who keeps anger locked up inside her like an unlit pilot light in an old gas stove, is ready to ignite. She feels the flame now, flickering high, teasing the temperature of her fury.

But no! she scolds herself (and this is the voice she's learned to listen to), tossing her thick red hair behind her shoulders. *Forget about the Neals.*

Aggie dreams about being a movie star one day, and she knows the road to Hollywood is going to be paved with adversity, everyone working against her. If she wants to succeed, there will be a million more Neal sisters in her path, and she's going to have to learn how to step right over them. She unfolds her body from the floor, creasing out the wrinkles in the uniform, and then she slides the pinafore over her freckled shoulders. She marches into the hallway bathroom and forces a smile in the stained vanity mirror, happy with the way the frock fits, snugly on all her curves. Yeah, she could look the part. She brushes her hair up into a fiery-high ponytail, rummages through a drawer to find her own pink ribbon, and ties a bow into the flames. She could be all that, too.

It will be all right, Aggie, she tells herself. *This could still work out. Don't forget, you have Eileen.* The thought brings light back into the face reflected in the tattered old mirror.

Mama taught her well, and she knows she can handle the Neal sisters. She'll be the best damn Sundae Girl Pop Gray's has ever seen. And she'll make sure everyone in Seaville *knows* about the gifts August Littleton has to offer, all the red, round, rolling parts of her. Tied with a pink bow on top.

Chapter 3: Striving

Winter has been strong and stormy, volatile for these parts of the Carolina coast, and the first of April swoops into Seaville like a weather-worn seagull, bruised but unbowed. Gray morning fog lifts and evaporates, revealing a sky of unsettling blue. Peals of laughter escape through open windows, and morning laundry is hung out to dry. A few colorful umbrellas find their stakes in the sand, and the hardware store lines the sidewalk with a brand-new stock of plastic shovels and sand pails. April is a time for celebration in Seaville, as the island has turned its cheek on another winter, and every year, it promises the seasonal opening of Pop Gray's.

Mama insists on driving Aggie to work on her first day, her shift beginning promptly at ten o'clock. Aggie makes her mother stop the coughing and sputtering old sedan just outside the town square. She wants to walk the last few blocks in her new pink uniform to let all those prying eyes get a good look at her.

As she approaches the polished glass doors of Pop Gray's, she sees the Neal sisters and Eileen crossing from the other side of the square. Together. Laughing and carrying on. The anxious anger begins its quiet pulse beneath her temples. She'll be *damned* if she's going to let them have Eileen, too.

The tall sister, the pageant queen, is pretty, for sure, but Aggie has noticed when she forgets to put on her airs, a thin veneer of contempt tweaks the corners of her eyes and droops and tugs at the pouting slope of her lips. She wears her beauty like a mask, the truth seeping out at the edges.

Short and thick, the younger sister, Louise, boasts a broad face and button nose that resembles a rabbit. Even now, she burrows her little bunny nose into her sister's ear as they spot Aggie walking up Main Street.

"Look, Kimberlee, here comes Raggedy Ann…" says Louise.

The slight floats across the distance, carried on the undercurrents of the thin April air. Aggie knows the insult well. It seems her bright-red hair emboldens others to label her as one of three things: a doll, a witch, or somebody's stepchild.

The sisters dissolve into nudges and giggles at their own joke. Eileen tries her best to shrug off the awkward moment, then she deferentially drops behind the two girls to let them pass through the front door before her.

Deflated, but determined not to show it, Aggie smooths her pink apron and offers Eileen, who still holds the open door, a grateful smile.

Wafting aromas of vanilla bean and burnt sugar consume the air in Pop Gray's, and Aggie's bitterness softens. The jukebox hums a tune by Connie Francis in the corner, and sunlight streams through the store windows, bathing everything in warm yellow light. *This is the magic of Pop Gray's,* Aggie thinks. *It's always somebody's respite from something.*

Mrs. Gray greets the girls, wearing a red-checkered dress and her own frilly apron, though hers has scalloped edges and a satin bow that ties with a flourish at her back.

"Welcome, my Sundae Girls. Welcome," she intones. Her manicured nails beckon them to follow her through the swinging chrome doors that divide the store from the kitchen. "You may put your coats and your purses here." She gestures to a small closet beside a side door. A worn sign hangs by a single nail above the threshold, stating it's the "Colored Entrance."

"Excuse me, Mrs. Gray," Louise asks, raising her hand but not waiting for acknowledgement. "You don't want us to use that door to come and go, do you?"

"Well, Louise, are you a colored girl?" she responds with an arch of her brow. Aggie chokes back her laughter with a quiet cough.

Louise's bunny cheeks puff up in offense. "Well, no, obviously not." She holds her bare arms in front of her so that all can take note they are, indeed, a pristine white.

"Well then, you may use the front door to arrive and depart, dear," Mrs. Gray continues. "And, in fact, since they just changed the state laws, I'm afraid we have to let *all* our customers come and go through the front door of our establishment."

Kimberlee, the older sister, leers forward with large, frightened eyes. "Even the colored ones?" She gasps, blinking her long eyelashes in startled succession.

"Yes, I'm afraid so, dear." Mrs. Gray gathers a stack of paper napkins that had tumbled out of order on the shiny chrome counter. "We must keep everything nice and neat for our Opening Day." Effectively shutting down the sisters' objections to the new state of civil rights, she says, "Now, shall we get started with our first day of training?"

The sisters exchange knowing glances, then they gather the rough edges of their disgrace to answer the call of the rapid *click-click-click* of Mrs. Gray's kitten heels as she leads her gaggle into the store's small walk-in freezer.

"It is a tiny freezer, yes," Mrs. Gray explains. "But it is also our most important stock room."

The freezer space is indeed tight, with a ceiling so low that even the teenage girls have to stoop to enter. There's not nearly enough space for all five of them to fit inside. Eileen and Aggie, bringing up the rear, hold back, hovering just outside the walk-in.

Aggie takes the opportunity to snatch a silky slice of Eileen's elbow, pulling her closer. She whispers, "Those sisters are the most stuck-up, bigoted, bunch of bi—"

Eileen thrusts her slender finger to Aggie's lips. With alarmed eyes, she gestures toward the inside of the freezer and the lecture that's supposed to be commanding their attention.

"And so, we will *always* have a supply of delicious vanilla here in the freezer, ladies, even if we run out of *all* of our other flavors," Mrs. Gray concludes, framing the word "vanilla" in the air like fine art etched in gold. She parts the Neal sisters with a magician's flourish and steps toward the freezer's threshold so she's standing in the middle of their shivering circle. "The freezer door opens by turning this handle, like so." She looks around. "Now, pay attention, girls, this handle is tricky, and you don't want to accidentally get stuck in here."

The scold is directed at Aggie, who's fidgeting and shuffling her feet in an obvious demonstration she has lost patience with the tutorial. Done learning, Aggie wants to *perform* and begin her new role as a Pop Gray's Sundae Girl.

Mrs. Gray moves the group over to the serving counter, where tubs of flavors lay in wait for hungry customers. She sinks a sparkling ice cream scoop into a frothy vat of peach confection, and her surprisingly strong biceps flash beneath the capped sleeves of her checkered dress as she demonstrates the "proper" scooping technique. The girls then line up behind the counter, silver scoops in hand.

"Dig from the elbow, girls. A nice well-rounded globe of ice cream," she says. "Pile it high here in the dessert dish. Yes, just like that." She slowly passes down the line of trainees, each positioned behind a tub of ice cream, digging, mounding, sculpting, and adjusting an elbow here or a wrist there. Mrs. Gray's pupils attempt to present their dish as a work of art, a masterpiece of color and cold.

"Our customers may also choose a sugar cone, and those are displayed at the end of the counter. The scooping is the same either way." Like a salesman displaying a prized model, Mrs. Gray showcases the golden triangle cones that are stacked by the dozen beside the colorful chest of ice cream tubs.

Mrs. Gray bustles them to the very back of the store where two large steel churners sit beside a deep industrial sink and the tall drum of a dishwasher.

"You all know Denny, I presume?" she asks, breezing past her son. Standing beside one of the tall churners, presumably supervising the bubbles and foam, he gives the Sundae Girls a wink and a sly smile. "Here at Pop Gray's, Denny is known as the Confectioner, and that is what you should call him while you are on the job."

"But after work, you can call me anything you want, ladies," Denny adds, prompting his mother to swat him on the arm.

Mrs. Gray proceeds to demonstrate the mechanics of the dishwasher, which each girl should load or unload, depending on the dish cycle, before completing her shift.

"Our work area must also stay spotless, clean as a whistle," she continues, spraying the counter with liquid from a tall plastic bottle and wiping the droplets away with a white cloth. "Just a splash of vinegar will—"

"Mrs. Gray," Louise interrupts. "Is it really necessary that we *all* need to do the cleaning tasks? I mean, the dishwashing and the spraying and all…" She motions to herself and her sister. "Couldn't *some* of us *just* take the customer's order?"

The cold drumbeat of indignation grows louder inside Aggie's crowded mind. Her eyes burn, yet she feels certain her dam of ire will hold back the tears. She digs the heels of her soft-soled shoes into the black-and-white linoleum floor and her bitten thumbnail into the soft flesh of her palm, steeling herself with the small rush of pain.

The damn Neal sisters would *not* be her undoing. Not today, not tomorrow, not ever. No, August Littleton would rise to the top like the whipped cream on those damn sundaes. She would be better than any of these other girls, better than any girl who had *ever* worked at Pop Gray's.

"Oh, yes, the customer's order," Mrs. Gray responds, without actually answering Louise's question. She consults the clock on the wall hanging over the entrance and ceases her demonstration on the scouring of counter stains. "I suppose we do need to move onto that. It's almost time to open up the front door to welcome our guests."

Aggie takes a deep breath, willing the blood to drain from her face. She consoles herself with the thought of the hours she'll spend working side by side with the lovely Eileen.

She studies the profile of her friend. Her high cheekbones and cascade of curls that refused to be tamed. Those tinted lips hiding that shy smile of hers…

"So, ladies, the most important part of this job is to accurately take the customer's order, then serve that order with a smile," Mrs. Gray continues, neatly folding the clean dishrag she's been using for demonstration. She then leads the group back to the front of the store.

Mrs. Gray explains it all, but she does it far too quickly: jot the customer orders on a small yellow pad, use that to create the checks, then reconcile everything with the store's new state-of-the-art electronic cash register. She taps her long nails, like red commas, over the clunky keys of the register, and with a shrill ring, the machine's door pops open to display crisp bills and silver coins inside.

"And then, girls, you *must* remember, at the end of the night, all the cartons of ice cream need to be moved from the front display freezer to the deep freeze walk-in. That is *critical*, girls, so we don't ruin our product. After all, that is what the people are coming for—not your precious smiles but the best ice cream in the state."

Concluding her instruction at precisely one minute until noon, Mrs. Gray clips her kitten heels to the front of the store, and with a certain ceremonial grace, she flips a hanging sign on the door from "Closed" to "Open." She then turns one last time to her pupils.

"Ready?" she asks. The nervous bob of four ponytails answers her. She turns the deadbolt and throws open the front door, expertly wedging a doorstop beneath it with the pointy toe of her shoe.

And so, on that first day of April, the Sundae Girls set to work.

The shop grows busy quickly, and as expected, a line swells out the door within the hour. Aggie lets her anger dissolve into a studied smile, and for a while, she finds she's able to forget all about the Neal sisters.

However, the Sundae Girls' first day does not go smoothly. Poor Aggie, who paid little attention to the instructions, fumbles through her tasks. After mistaking vanilla ice cream for lemon, misplacing checks, forgetting to scour, and dropping a tray full of spoons on the floor that draws everyone's attention, she knows she's failing at her new job.

Mrs. Gray spends the day in a corner booth, sipping her seemingly bottomless cup of coffee and surveying the girls. There's a newspaper spread on the table before her, but she doesn't look at it. Not even once.

When the spoons clattered, Mrs. Gray snapped into action, daintily crouching to help gather them, the swirl of her checkered skirt like a picnic tablecloth spread out on the floor.

Her eyes meet Aggie's, thin slits of disapproval. "Don't let it happen again, Miss Littleton," she advises, handing her the last of the littered silverware.

Aggie's stomach roils as she realizes the spectacle she has just created. Slowly, she rises from her knees, brushing a bit of imaginary dust from her apron, but she's careful to keep her eyes affixed to the ground. Customers crane their necks awkwardly over the tops of the red booths and swivel to gawk from their chrome stools. Their idle chatter dulls to a whisper in response to the sympathy and shame of the moment.

When Aggie finally raises her head, she searches the room for Eileen and finds her behind the cash register, pecking out numbers. Eileen glances over at August, offering her a simple shrug and sheepish smile at the same moment Kimberlee passes by with a tray of sundaes. She's too close and grazes Aggie with her pointy elbow.

"Great first day on the job, Raggedy," Kimberlee mutters disdainfully before regaining her false charm and swooping away to deliver the desserts.

Through the large bay window of Pop Gray's, Aggie watches the sun begin its retreat behind the brick fortress of the Dixie. Feeling worn out and used up, she clutches tightly, like the dirty spoons still wrapped in her fist, to the pride that accompanied her down the sidewalk that morning.

She hears Eileen begin to profusely apologize. "I'm so sorry, sir. It's my first day, and well…I can't seem to get it to work." Behind the cash register, she stands with a puzzled expression, her brow knit and her fingertips pounding the keys with frustrated ferocity. Grumpy old Mr. Lewis, on the other side of the register, holds several dollars in one hand while impatiently drumming the fingers of his other hand on the countertop. Tears threaten the tops of Eileen's lower lids, but just as the situation seems to be bordering on hopelessness, Mrs. Gray swoops in for the rescue.

"Sorry about that, Mr. Lewis. We have to find new help every year," she says, nudging Eileen aside and retrieving change for the impatient customer. "Y'all have a good evening and come back and see us, you hear?"

Vicky Gray's smile, sweet as the strawberry syrup that graces her sundaes, dips into a wrinkled frown as soon as Mr. Lewis leaves, and she pivots on her heel to confront Eileen.

"Young lady, a smart girl like you should be able to figure this out. I expected more from a Conway." She sniffs the air as if something has turned foul and clips away in her sharp-toed shoes.

Blood rushes back to Aggie's cheeks, and she feels that sickening knot in her stomach again. Who does she think she is to speak to Eileen - sweet Eileen! - in such a way! She wants to run after Mrs. Gray, yank her back with her billowy bouffant, and show her what she could *expect* from a Littleton. But instead, Aggie remains resolute, an angry statue clenching dirty spoons. She can't do anything that would jeopardize this job. What would Mama say to the ladies at Bridge Club? And what about the Neal sisters? Oh, they would just be delighted to see her go.

Mrs. Gray retreats to her booth fortress, Eileen wipes away her tears, and Aggie finds a bussing tray for the dirty spoons. Silently, she vows vengeance. Someday, when she's made it, her star stamped into the Hollywood Walk of Fame, she'll come back to Seaville and rub their little upturned noses in it.

In the meantime, she thinks, maybe I'll find a way to borrow some money from that offending cash register.

Chapter 4: Appraising

Denny sighs with relief as he pours the last batch of peach cream into the churner and mops his brow with a dishrag. The kitchen can get hot, even this early in the season, and it's been a long opening week at Pop Gray's.

His father has been all over him, demanding more time, more work, and more ice cream. For the first time since he quit high school to come work at the store, he's starting to miss the calm rhythms of the classroom and the clatter of the school hallway. And, of course, the girls.

But working here ain't so bad, he reasons, stacking his tall mixing bowls in the sink. His parents gave him that cool title, the Confectioner. It makes him feel important when they make people call him that. Like he's amounted to something.

And it's pretty cool he gets his pick of the Sundae Girls. This year, they were all kinds of cute, so he had some deciding to do.

There was Kimberlee and her little sister, and of the two of them, he'd pick Kimberlee for sure. She had long legs and a sharp nose, but she was pretty. She'd won that beauty contest too, and that made her more attractive to Denny.

He liked the little one, Eileen, but she was too shy for his taste. And more like a girl than a woman, she probably wouldn't put out.

The one who would put out, Denny thinks, *is August. Man, she has curves in all the right places, and it's kinda hard to resist a redhead.* But something about her scares Denny, and besides, Kimberlee says August likes chicks. Which, truthfully, Denny finds kinda hot, but whatever. That one seems like too much work.

He unties his apron and peers through the small window embedded in the chrome swinging door that separates the kitchen from the store. He sees Kimberlee out there in her short pink skirt, bending over to scoop a cone. She ain't the sweetest girl, but man, he'd like to get her in his backseat.

Yeah, she's the one he'll pick this summer. She'll have to do.

It's almost the middle of September, but the heat has not let up, and Junior is sweaty, but Shep is positively saturated. Small pools form in the fatty crease between Shep's neck and back.

Luckily, they had enough change between the two of them to buy two Cokes at the corner store. Now, they sprawl across the sidewalk, flicking jacks back and forth, less a half-hearted game and more a way to pass the afternoon.

If Junior goes back home, Daddy will make him return to church. No sir, not again. He'd already done his time this morning, praying and repenting. Mama says they'll need extra church for a while since their family has a lot of sins to ask forgiveness for. That being the case, he reckons he'll stay out there in the heat with his best friend, soggy ol' Shep.

Junior finishes the last of the Coke in one long swallow and tips the curvy glass bottle on its side, giving it a spin. It lands on Shep, who jumps to his feet quicker than a buck trying to run from a shotgun.

"Stop it, man," Shep says, his voice cracking, somewhere between a kid's squeal and a man's objection.

"What do you want me to do, play spin the bottle with you?"

Junior laughs out loud and stretches his bare legs in the sunshine, picking at a scab on his knee. That's about when he notices the long shadow staining the sidewalk, the stretch of a figure who must be looming on the street corner just behind them.

Junior turns slowly, craning back over his shoulder, curious and cautious. The shadow belongs to that colored man, the one Chief arrested. Junior studies the man, who looks lost at a crossroads, his shoulders slumped and his face all pinched.

He swivels back to Shep, who's oblivious to the shadow and its owner, still trying to kick the offending soda bottle away from him and into the overgrown brush.

"Psst," Junior whispers. "That's him. That's the guy who killed those girls at Pop Gray's."

Shep stumbles mid-kick, his jaw dropping wide, and Junior watches as he takes a giant step backward, ready to jump into the cover of the brush. Shep drops the silver jack still in his hand, and it makes a quiet, tinny sound on the sidewalk.

"But I thought…Chief s-s-said they c-c-caught him," Shep stutters. He always stutters when he's scared, and it kind of drives Junior crazy.

"Naww, Chief *did* catch him, doofus," Junior says, low and defensive. "But then, somehow, the judge let him off the hook for no good reason. That's what my mama says, at least."

They warily watch the tall stranger for a moment as he fumbles through his coat pocket for something.

"He's going for a g-g-gun." Shep trembles, stepping closer to Junior, who's a whole five months older and the stronger of the two. Nelson McCready pulls out a crumpled pack of cigarettes, and Shep exhales loudly.

Junior crouches on the sidewalk and begins to gather the jacks, stuffing as many as he can into the pockets of his denim shorts.

"What're you doing?" Shep huffs as he debates whether or not to help Junior pick up.

"Getting outta here," Junior says, fist closing tight around the last remaining jack. "But first…" He laughs nervously, louder than he thought his wavering confidence would allow, and throws the spiky jack with all his might, aiming high and shouting as he runs, "Killer! Killer! He's on the loose, y'all!"

"Ouch," McCready says, slapping the back of his head against the sting of the flying jack.

Before they can be implicated, Junior and Shep turn on their heels and race around the far corner, leaving the dust of the town's scorn in their wake.

Chapter 6: Repenting

With all that legal business finally behind him, Nelson has to find a job. And fast. He's outstayed his welcome in the Tucker's attic. So kind of Mr. and Mrs. Tucker to take him in after all this mess. They're salt of the earth, as Momma would say.

As the only colored businessman in Seaville, Mr. Tucker probably felt it his duty to help, but Nelson remains grateful. Mr. Tucker had even let him stock shelves at his little store down on Shell Beach until it became clear Nelson's very presence was just too bad for business. Yes, best to lay low as Mr. Tucker instructed.

When Mr. Dorian, his court-appointed lawyer, shook his hand outside the front door of the courtroom last month, he told him, "Son, you've been given a second chance. I don't know what kind of dark cloud followed you around to land you here, but I say it's gone now. The county says you are free to go. Just keep yourself out of trouble, you hear?"

"Yes, sir," Nelson had replied. "I always have and intend to continue." He smiled that morning, finally released from his cinderblock cell, stretching his limbs and tasting the air in the full-throated freedom of the outside world. The equinox had come and gone. Leaves hung brown and limp on the trees, but it still felt hot as all hell.

"But you remember now," Dorian had said, a ring of sweat slowly spreading from the collar of his shirt, "Judge Bentley says you can't leave the county. Not yet. Not until they clear the pending charges from your record. You got that?"

Nelson understood the court orders, but he wanted so badly to head home to Roanoke Rapids to see Momma, sit at her kitchen table, and butter a slab of her cornbread. Let her brush the crumbs off his chin the way she did when he was just a kid in dirty overalls.

"Can't be too long for that, can it, Mr. Dorian? Don't they just need to sign some papers and get the matter settled?"

Dorian cleared his throat and loosened his tie. He had jiggly jowls and a paunchy belly, and even in the shade, he always looked on the verge of heatstroke. That day, sunshine radiated in unwelcome waves from the concrete sidewalk.

"I doubt they'll try to take it to court, son. No way they can win on a second murder charge after this acquittal on the first. If they do, you'll be appointed another attorney by the court. Won't be me. But I'm sure it won't come to that."

"Okay, okay." He nodded, the answer providing some relief to the worry still sitting heavy on his chest.

Four weeks later, and here he is, still pacing the bare boards in Mr. Tucker's attic and trying to decide what his next move should be.

He catches his reflection in the little oval mirror Mrs. Tucker hung on the wall above the wire-frame bed. Not bad looking, not bad at all, he decides. Tall enough. Maybe even *too* tall at six feet, five inches last time he measured. His clean-cropped hair had grown into a tight afro all those months in jail, giving him an extra inch or so in height. The afro is the new style over at the university anyway, and he touches it up with a small hair pick he keeps in his back pocket. His white T-shirt and slim gray pants, which land far too short, the hems riding up his shins, belong to Mr. Tucker's son who'd been drafted into the war. The bottoms also hang a little loose on him since he lost so much weight while incarcerated. Still, Nelson feels grateful for any clothes at all.

After shaking Dorian's hand outside the jail that day, Nelson had used the two dollars left in his pants pocket from the night he'd been arrested to hop on a beach car that would take him to the boarding house on the other side of the drawbridge. He'd rented a small room there for the semester. Though it held little more than schoolbooks and clothes, it provided him with a safe bed to sleep in.

The boarding house belonged to Ms. Senster, and as Nelson approached, she watched him from a gap in the curtains at the window. She then opened the front door with a scowl before he could even reach for the knob.

"What nerve you got showing up here," she seethed through the narrow slit. "Get off these premises before I call the po-lice!"

Her words landed like a punch to the gut, but the smell of chicken frying on the stove wafted out the open door, and Nelson just wanted a little rest in his lumpy boarding house bed.

"But Ms. Senster," Nelson objected, his hand braced on the front door so she couldn't close it all the way. "I was acquitted. See? They let me out of jail. I'm a free man."

"Boy, you may have been acquitted," she muttered through clenched teeth, "but that does not mean you are innocent. I *know* you did it. We *all* know that you killed those girls!" She slammed the door shut, Nelson pulling his fingers back just in time.

"No!" he shouted, pounding heavily on the door. "No! Ms. Senster! I didn't do it!"

He heard the click of the lock and contemplated banging on the door again, desperate to plead his case, when he caught sight of Lila and Kitty standing in the front window, staring out at him with wide, frightened eyes. Nelson considered the girls his friends. He and Kitty had even gone and gotten a soda together once.

"Lila! Kitty!" he shouted. "Can y'all get her to let me in?"

The girls whispered to each other nervously before Kitty snatched the curtains closed.

"Kitty? Ms. Senster?" he called out to the darkened window and closed door. "I didn't do it! I didn't!"

Silence seeped from the boarding house and stillness from the window, as if everyone were cowering from a monster that lurked on the stoop.

Nelson begrudgingly considered his options, scuffling his feet over the concrete and fighting the urge to break down the door.

"Ms. Senster! What about all my stuff?" He kicked the doorjamb in frustration and bruised his big toe.

A mumbled reply from the other side of the door told Nelson she must be standing close. He could almost hear her breathing, heavy and mean, her flapping nostrils the only sound escaping the anxious quiet. He thought he caught a whiff of greens cooked in bacon fat, creeping out and taunting him from the crack under the closed door.

"I can't hear you! Ms. Senster? My clothes? My books?"

The window that had framed Kitty and Lila cracked open, the curtain brushed aside.

"It's gone!" Ms. Senster shouted. "I threw it all out! Now get out of here, and don't come back, or I really will call the po-lice!"

The window snapped shut, so loud that paint chips crumbled off the peeling ledge. Dazed and uncertain, his toe throbbing, Nelson stumbled back down the walkway, scared to look one last time over his shoulder at the life he once lived.

No belongings, no money, save for forty cents leftover from his ride on the beach car, and nowhere to turn. Just him, his hungry bones, and his long shadow, which seemed to mock him from the steaming sidewalk, the dark parts of himself he could not lose.

So, he just began to walk.

Ms. Senster's place was about a half mile south of the drawbridge. Another two miles south and he'd reach the college. He could head over there to see if he remained enrolled. Nelson kicked a pebble down the street and watched it splash into a muddy puddle. Get real, he thought, you ain't gonna still be enrolled.

Instead, he headed north back toward the island, wondering if he could find a quiet spot on the sand down by Shell Beach. Someplace to sit and figure things out. He passed by the Piggly Wiggly, and his stomach rolled. Despite his hunger, he knew they didn't want him in there either. Plus, he thought, can't buy much for forty cents anymore.

He was stuck all right. Trapped in a cobweb, as Momma would say, like the helpless prey waiting for the spider. His toe ached through his thin-soled shoes as he marched across the bridge, sweltering. It was the kind of day where the heat just sat on his chest, and he could hardly breathe. His skin prickled with sweat, the pits of his white T-shirt stained.

An ocean breeze cooled his brow as he shuffled toward the island square, the scene where it all played out. The night his life as he knew it came to a screeching halt. It felt like a spell was drawing him back there, though he wasn't sure how or why. Maybe the need to try and make sense of it all, to look for his own clues, to find fragments of memory that could redeem him, to figure out how it all got upended.

The square sat empty at that hour—almost noon on a Saturday. Some kids played jacks on the sidewalk, and a girl walked her dog past the Dixie, pausing to read which shows the marquis advertised.

The storefront windows of Pop Gray's sparkled in the sunshine, and Nelson watched from his stance on a far corner as Mrs. Gray flipped her sign from closed to open. He then shifted his gaze to the phone booth, trying to remember the person he used to be camped out in there. Before everything turned sideways. There must be something he could recall. Something he had seen or heard that night that could help him out of this mess.

An old lady in a polka-dot dress waddled out from the butcher shop, carrying a roast wrapped in cellophane. She spied Nelson standing resolutely on the street corner, gasped, and nearly dropped the roast. She quickened her step into her waiting sedan.

Nelson heard the screen door at the hardware store creak open and then slam shut, the harsh twang of the spring. A man in a ball cap strode out of the store with an armful of lumber and clambered into his truck, wheezing and muttering under his breath. Normally, Nelson would have approached him, offered him a hand, and maybe asked him if he needed any hired help for whatever project he intended to work on. But not that day.

He would stay quiet, find a place to be still, and try to get to the other side of the island, down to Shell Beach, to the soothing waters of the sea. He just needed to sit and *think*. Breathe in the salt air, stretch his toes in the sand, and consider the path that lay before him.

But God almighty, he was hungry, and he couldn't stop envisioning that cornbread. He'd had nothing but prison food for a month. All he wanted was some of his Momma's salty greens and maybe some sweet tea.

He licked his lips just thinking about it then wondered if he had any cigarettes left in the old pack he'd found smashed up in his pants. He groped the back pocket until his fingers found the wadded-up container. One left. He patted all his pockets, desperate for a book of matches, cursing under his breath when he came up empty.

Over his shoulder, he heard a snicker. Something dull and metal ricocheted off the back of his neck.

"Ouch!" he shouted, slapping at the sting. A jack tumbled off his shoulder and fell at his feet. When he bent to pick it up, he felt a strong nudge from behind. Nelson's knees buckled and he went sprawling onto the hot pavement.

Two boys ran away, a blur of blond and denim.

"Killer! Killer!" they chanted, shrieking and chortling as they galloped down the street. "That colored man got free, y'all! Lock your doors!"

Up and down Main Street, all eyes pivoted to the street corner where Nelson lay splayed, eyes he didn't even know had been watching. Tall windows in the grand houses that lined the square flung open to check the commotion. On the nearest corner, he could see a couple seated at the window table in Grady's Café. They visibly recoiled from the danger that threatened outside, alarm on their faces as they stirred sugar into their coffee. A man seated on a park bench abandoned his newspaper to leer across the distance at the lanky Black man splattered on the sidewalk.

With scrapes across his hands and elbows and a small spit of blood running down his forearm, Nelson hauled himself to his knees and then slowed to stand.

So much for going unnoticed.

His limbs felt thick in those cobwebs, and he knew his Momma had been right. He was the prey.

Suddenly, the strike of twelve sang from the church bell. Church. Of course! Surely, this could be a place to retreat, though he hadn't been in a long, long time. Not since the days Momma dragged him every Sunday to the Smithtown Baptist Church with its cracked ceiling, low brown pews, and faded hymnals.

Nelson brushed the knees of his dirty trousers again and headed, with as much dignity as he could muster, toward the sound of the pealing bells. The God that Pastor Peterson at Smithtown had been preaching about all those years would show up for him now.

He walked slowly, his head hung low, the ache in his hip growing with each lumbering step. The weight of the white gazes, which followed him still, stooped his shoulders, and the drum of their whispers beat on his temples. He held his breath as he proceeded, anxious not to further offend.

After several blocks, the church sidewalk curled into a cool and quiet path before him, and Nelson exhaled. Old elms, draped with Spanish moss that smelled of earth, lined the path, and the shade — he wanted to gulp it down.

The double church doors —white, pure, and passionless — wouldn't budge when Nelson gave them a pull.. Blood dripped from his scraped palms and splattered in small sacrificial droplets on the front steps of the building. He closed his fists tightly over his wounds, wincing at the pain, and knocked on the thick oak slabs. Waiting a polite minute with no response, Nelson stubbornly banged again. As he rattled the large brass handles, he left a smear of blood behind.

The salvation they had all preached about at Smithtown Baptist—it was *inside* there, wasn't it? But the locked doors frowned in disapproval at his bloody violation and refused to extend their welcome.

Nelson slumped down heavily on the steps, cradling his head in his hands. For the first time since this whole business began, he felt the urge to cry, a heavy and hopeless weight building in his chest. What was all the ceremoniousness for then? All those years in his fits-too-tight, Sunday-best shirt and tie. All those prayers recited and blessings extended.

Nelson heard the clap of thick-soled dress shoes approach on the cobblestone pavement and hoped the man who wore them would arrive with some sort of deliverance. Still, he kept his head bowed and didn't look up until he felt a strong grip on his shoulder. As he raised his chin, Nelson met the unyielding eyes of the church pastor. He had his Bible clutched tightly beneath one arm.

"Son," the pastor said, his voice low, "I can't have you here. Not after the sins you have committed against your God and this community." His thick Southern drawl was laced with a moral authority that made Nelson's stomach turn. As the hot sun angled through the elms to cast an oily sheen on the pastor's balding head, the small gold cross on his neck glimmered.

"But, Pastor," Nelson mumbled through sniffles. "I didn't commit any sins. The court found me innocent. The Judge said I was free to go." He raised his palms to demonstrate he was, indeed, unshackled but also to plea for forgiveness for a crime he refused to own.

"You need to leave, son," the pastor seethed, unmoved by Nelson's argument. "You are not welcome here."

"But, sir, I got nowhere—"

"Well, you need to leave these premises. I don't care where you go. And do not come back here again, ya hear?" The beefy pastor tucked his elbows under Nelson's sweaty armpits, which caused the Bible to fall to the ground. He tried to haul Nelson to his feet, but he lacked strength. The old man could only lift him to his knees.

Nelson clasped his swollen palms together in a desperate prayer. "Please, sir, if I could just—"

"Get your nigger ass out of here *now*," the pastor interrupted, "before I go get my shotgun." His volcanic ire had erupted, spittle flying from the corners of his mouth.

Nelson felt dizzy from it all. The world seemed to turn sideways for a moment, twisting and tumbling. The air smelled of hot asphalt and rage, and he quickly lurched forward and vomited at the pastor's feet. Pieces of the boiled egg they had served that morning in jail came bubbling up his throat.

"That's it. I'm going to get my gun," the pastor shouted, turning and breaking into a heavy jog toward the rectory. The receding *clickety-clack* of church shoes told Nelson his escape, in fact, was his chance at pardon.

High in the colorful trees, sparrows sang the blues, and squirrels scurried and scolded. The world that surrounded him still appeared beautiful to Nelson, despite the danger unfolding. He knew if he stayed any longer on those church steps, however, that would be where he would die.

He wiped his mouth with the back of his hand and looked away from the egg and bile on the ground. Gazing up with something akin to yearning at the tall church spire, its pristine white cross perched on top, the word *forsaken* trembled on his lips. Nelson struggled to his feet, his hip aflame, toe screaming, throat stinging, and eyes watering. He stumbled down the shaded path away from the church and back into the low hum of a Saturday afternoon in Seaville. In the distance, he could hear someone mowing their lawn and the voices of little girls playing a game, perhaps jump rope, counting loudly.

"Five…six…seven…eight…"

He limped away from the church as quickly as his limbs would allow and did not look back to see if the pastor had cocked his gun, ready to fire. A fly entangled in the web, he continued to fight even as the spider came in for the kill, its hungry breath rising in the rancor of the afternoon.

He paused at the corner just across from the town library to pull himself together. Ms. Mavey, the librarian, maybe returning from her lunch break, slid a key into the big red doors of the library and flung them open wide. From the corner, Nelson could see inside—the sturdy walnut shelves and the colorful assortment of book jackets that lined the back walls.

Ms. Mavey, perhaps feeling his eyes on her, turned toward Nelson before entering. He could see from her profile she was pregnant and pretty far along. He braced himself for her scowl and the slamming of the red doors. But instead, she offered him a soft, careful smile. After propping both doors open with a stop, she walked into the library and out of sight.

Could she be offering him refuge?

Once again alone on the corner, blood dried in splotches on his shirt and pants streaked with dirt, he tried to collect his wits. He filled his lungs with the sticky September air and swallowed it like courage.

Tentatively, Nelson walked to the entrance, stopping just inside. Still on the threshold, he'd be able to pivot and run if he had misconstrued the invitation.

Ms. Mavey seemed to be alone inside—a white woman with child. A dangerous situation for a Black man with blood on his shirt, especially one just released from incarceration. His presence there alone would be enough for the pastor to follow him with his shotgun and finish him off, so he stood in the library lobby with considerable hesitation.

"Do come in, sir, and have a rest." The librarian's airy voice floated through the stale air. Nelson took a tentative step forward to find Ms. Mavey adjusting papers on a small metal desk, settling into her seat as best she could with her extended middle section.

"Yes, ma'am," he said, taking one more cautious step. "You're sure it's all right?"

"Yes, sir." She laughed lightly. "It's a public library open to all."

Nelson surveyed the empty building stacked floor to ceiling with books and a few small reading tables tucked in its center. The back wall led to a bathroom door framed by two water fountains, one labeled "White" and the other "Colored."

"Go on ahead and clean up," Ms. Mavey said, following his eyes while still rifling through the clutter on her desk.

Suddenly parched, he shuffle-limped toward the fountains and bent to drink from the "Colored" one. When he pressed the button to dispense the water, he found the machine dry.

"You can use the other one. The water supply has been shut off in that one," she explained. "They changed the law a few years ago, but this town is just a little slow in catching up with the times."

He bent to drink, grateful for the water and not really concerned about which fountain served it. Nelson stood and wiped the droplets that lingered on his dry lips.

"Much obliged, ma'am," he said as he turned to head into the restroom. Before he closed the door, he turned back to the kind librarian. "But…don't you know who I am?"

Ms. Mavey blinked in surprise, but she didn't look frightened. On the contrary, she smiled as she rose from her chair and walked slowly in Nelson's direction. Resting one hand on her large belly, she held a small white box in the other.

"I know who you are, Mr. McCready. I've been following that trial. I know that they found you innocent."

For the first time since shaking Mr. Dorian's hand outside the courthouse that morning, his stomach settled, and he managed a meek smile.

"Now get yourself cleaned up best you can before you scare folks 'round here any more than you already have." She pulled some gauze bandages from the box and handed them to Nelson.

In the restroom, he washed away the dirt, picked gravel from his wounds, and wrapped the palms of his hands with gauze. When he finished, he opened the bathroom door and found the library filled with the giggly whispers of small children. They sat in a circle in the center of the room, their picture books littering the floor and their mothers hovering. Nelson carefully looked the other way in an attempt to make himself invisible.

"Samantha, come over here right now!" snapped one of the mothers, diverting her pig-tailed daughter away from the mangled stranger's path.

Ms. Mavey waved Nelson back to the safe haven of her metal desk. "Never mind them," she said under her breath. "They come in here every Saturday afternoon, and trust me, you are not the only one in town they have a problem with. Those little kids are terrors, too."

Nelson wrinkled his brow and shifted his eyes to the bump on her abdomen.

The librarian laughed. "I know, I know…I'm going to have a terror of my own very soon. I may need to adjust my opinion of the small ones."

She motioned to a worn easy chair adjacent to her desk, and Nelson accepted the offer by collapsing into the seat. Ms. Mavey quietly pulled an apple and a crust of bread from her lunch sack and offered them to him.

"It's all I have left," she said, "but you look like you might be hungry."

"Oh…" he managed, still uncertain. "Much obliged, ma'am. But…is it…it's okay to eat in here?"

"It is if the librarian says it is," she replied with a wink.

He wolfed down the bread in two large bites and ate the fruit with abandon, his loud crunches seeming to echo throughout the hushed library. While he ate, Ms. Mavey politely set about her librarian business, organizing files and alphabetizing her stack of returns.

"Thank you," he said when finished, nibbling the last morsel off the apple core and tossing it in the garbage can beside the desk. He stood to leave, wary of any additional attention he might draw from the mothers in the circle still huddled protectively around their children.

"You don't need to leave, you know," Ms. Mavey said. "Do you even have any place to go?"

Nelson shook his head and picked at some dirt under his fingernail.

"Let me make a few calls," she said, reaching for the phone sitting at the top of the desk. "Why don't you look around? Maybe find something you want to check out?"

"Oh, I don't…" he muttered.

"What? You don't know how to read?"

"No, I can read…I go to the university. I mean, I went there…I just…I don't have a library card."

"Not a problem we can't fix," said Ms. Mavey with a laugh as she dialed on the rotary.

Nelson walked aimlessly through the library aisles, careful to steer clear of the jittery mothers. He hadn't been in a library in so long. Not since grade school.

The only books he had been reading were those passed out and required by the teachers.

Momma beamed with pride when he got accepted at the university. She jumped up and down, hands raised to the Lord, and cried out with such joy Mrs. Simpkins next door said she could hear her "Hallelujah, Jesus!" clean through the brick walls.

Nelson wandered into a section marked with big cardboard-cutout letters that read "World Literature." His fingers ran over the rows of dusty jackets, the quiet rustle comforting him. Based on the accumulation, it seemed not a lot of people checked out those books.

He stopped on a title he recognized, *Crime and Punishment*. He pulled it from the shelf, examined the height and heft of the book, and weighed it on his palms like Momma would do to a watermelon at the corner store. Maybe that was his book. The one that called to him on that very day of punishment. He wondered whose crime he'd been punished for as he balanced the old Russian novel on his fingertips.

"That's a good one," Ms. Mavey said, peeking over his shoulder. Startled, he dropped the book, causing a loud thud in the sanctuary of quiet. The mothers of the gaggle sighed and frowned at the clatter.

"Sorry, Mr. McCready," she said. "I didn't mean to scare you. I'm a librarian—tradecraft to be pretty quiet on our feet."

He stooped to retrieve the fallen book.

"I just talked to Maurice Tucker," she continued. "Do you know him?"

Nelson shook his head.

"Well, he has a fine family, and he owns the little grocery down on Shell Beach. You know which one I'm talking about?"

Nelson nodded. Mr. Tucker's store was the only one a colored man would shop in on the island, even after they changed the laws.

"Mr. Tucker said it would be all right for you to come and stay with him. At least for a little while."

Relief washed over Nelson like a cool bath in a desert, and tears sprang to his eyes again. One escaped and rolled down his cheek.

"Here's the address," she said, handing him a small slip of yellow paper scribbled with her writing.

Nelson wanted to embrace Ms. Mavey, the petite, pregnant white woman who may have just saved his life. But he couldn't, and he didn't.

"Much obliged, ma'am," he said instead. With a nod, he wiped away the stray tear.

"Now, let's get you a library card for that book," she said as she walked back to her desk, her halo trailing.

Above him, his God swept away the cobwebs.

Nelson thinks about the day he met Ms. Mavey, the day that brought him to his knees. And yet, also the day he learned about the healing power of compassion. He stares long and hard into the mirror glass before him and cracks his knuckles in determination. Mrs. Tucker told him over breakfast that morning that Ms. Mavey had just delivered her baby, down at Seaville General. He sure would like to take them some flowers, maybe a rattle for the little girl. But no, he didn't dare.

Part 2: 2017

Chapter 7: Responding

"Well, it looks like old August is finally on her way out." I throw my phone onto the sagging couch and head back into the kitchen to resume a vigorous chopping of celery.

"You gonna go down there, Jan?"

"No, John. Of course not. Tomorrow is Thanksgiving." I open a cupboard, frown, and close it with finality.

Reclined on the couch in my small apartment, John slowly sips his beer, darting a hesitant glance at the clanging in the kitchen. "Could be her last Thanksgiving, you know. This could be your last chance. She might finally give it up about your father…"

Pausing over the celery and a pile of reeking roughage, I pick up a whole onion and hurl it at John's head. I miss, of course. It lands by the dog, who sniffs it, wondering if it might be a chew toy, then wisely decides against chewing.

"You? You're trying to make me feel guilty about this? You can't stand my mother either!" I slam down a bottle of olive oil. "No. No way. I'm not going, so stop trying to make me feel like shit. Save it for your clients."

"Okay, okay…but technically, you *are* one of my clients," he replies. He then raises his hands in surrender and turns back the pre-game coverage.

I dice and hack, celery flying in bits and parts around the small kitchen. I'm ready to end the discussion, but John does not relent.

Like a hamster on an endless wheel of analysis, he needles me. "I guess I was just thinking that it might be kind of like the last chance. Life doesn't usually offer those up on a silver platter. But you're right…I mean, aren't you supposed to work at the TV station on Monday, anyway?" He doesn't dare look in my direction, likely fearful of being assaulted with another root vegetable. "Wouldn't want to mess up that gig…"

He's right, of course. I finally have a job that promises a paycheck. I hadn't worked in almost two years. Hadn't even been able to line up a decent audition. I'm riding on my high horse straight into middle age, and the mortgage on our apartment is chasing me with a cattle prod.

"Goddamn holidays," I mutter, tossing haggard chunks of roughage into a waiting bowl of breadcrumbs. I've hated the winter holidays for as long as I can remember, except maybe for those few short baby years of Laney's when her eyes twinkled in the glow of holiday lights and the vague promise of Santa had a temporary but tangible feel to it.

Thinking about two-year-old Laney ripping into her first Christmas present on an early winter morning, her lips already smeared with the syrupy juice of a candy cane, a smile finds its way out of my frustration.

I grab another onion from the crisper since the one I threw had tucked itself beneath the belly of John's dog. I peel the papery fragments from the outer layer, my eyes watering from the bulb's vapor. *My problem is like an onion*, I think. *Too many layers…*

The last time we had all been to visit August in North Carolina, Laney had barely earned her toddler legs, John and I were still married, and August had recently been diagnosed with congestive heart failure. We spent a sweltering July weekend confined to the old front porch, which had begun to fall into disrepair. The garden wilted, the cicadas screeched, and my mother wailed, giving voice to the weight of her impending death. Irritable and inconsolable, she focused so much on her own tragedies she barely noticed the three of us. She couldn't even remember Laney's name, calling her Luna, Lana, and Lacey.

"Jesus, August, for the fourth time today, her name is *Laney*," John would interject, exasperated. But she completely ignored him, treating him like a ghost she could walk right through. So, he would storm off, taking Laney with him on long walks down to the beach while my mother seized the opportunity to sharpen her claws on her only child.

"Ungrateful," August slurred. She mopped her brow with a scarf and sipped whatever sloshed around in her glass, which at a certain point in the afternoon, no longer contained iced tea. It had been record-breaking hot that summer, and I remember diverting my gaze to the front yard, riddled with brown patches and weeping weeds. I wistfully wished I too had a splash of bourbon in my glass.

"You've always been ungrateful, Janus. I brought you up when *I* had *nothing*. I gave you everything when *I* had *nothing*. I gave up my chance to make it big in Hollywood. Now, it's your turn to take care of me…"

An orange monarch fluttered by the porch steps, sensed the unrest, decided it unwise to come any closer, and flitted away.

John and I ended up leaving town two days early, and as I recall, we couldn't barrel up the interstate fast enough.

I hate my mother, though it's taken me years of therapy and miles of distance to understand that. It's a twisted, convoluted hate born of neglect and absent of aggression. Over time, I've tried to starve that bitterness, sweeten it with sympathy, even beat it into submission. I learned to be passive in my disdain—something like acceptance but also like denial. But I cannot deny that my mother *did* teach me one thing invaluable: the ways and means of the selfish. And selfishly, if the end looms…if this is my last chance to *know*…

"But John," I protest. "I told Laney she could invite that new boy to Thanksgiving, the one from the play. I can't just up and leave for North Carolina."

John and the dog are both immersed in an interview with the Eagles quarterback. So, I dice the onion, tears streaming now. I imagine August, curled and arthritic, sinking into a hospital mattress, tubes running from her veins, her nose, her long silver hair knotted at her shoulders. Would she wake up tomorrow, knowing Thanksgiving had arrived, and realize no one felt thankful she was still alive?

No! says the voice I had come to listen to. I push the pity into the pile of onion skin and dice with more ferocity. August has her own cruel intentions to keep her company for the holiday.

Only six months ago, I'd been rushing to make the L train in the name of some godforsaken audition when August had called, wheezing her way through words, telling me to come quickly, promising a quick death. She said she might not make it to nightfall.

I'd dropped everything—my plans to take Laney to Long Beach and the callback for that car commercial. Why? Because that's what one's supposed to do as the only child of a single parent who claims they have one foot in the grave. But when I rushed into her hospital room, August sat straight up in bed, greedily eating a ham sandwich, her hospital gown gaping in all the wrong places and mustard decorating her chin like a Jackson Pollock knockoff.

"What took you so long?" she asked me through the half-chewed sandwich.

I lean heavily against the counter. Blood rushes to my head, rivers of resentment, and my mind begins its hazy scramble, the dull pulsation that presages an emotional nosedive. I close my eyes to fight the scattering mental debris. Then, through the rubble of fleeting moments and regret, a tangible memory surfaces and gasps for air.

A smoky sun rising over the jagged apex of a distant mountain. Bitter desert air blasting in through an open car window. The glow of the sunrise—pink, then orange, then dandelion yellow—blooming across August's sharp profile. Her lips were set in something of a smile, as close as they'll ever get to a smile anyway (except when they part to pull on her cigarette or sing along to Joan Baez). She was beautiful to me then. All flame and smoke. She smelled like marijuana and lavender, and all I knew of home.

That morning, promise, like a wavy mirage, seemed to be sitting just on the other side of the horizon. Only eight years old, I snuggled in a blanket in the passenger seat of our orange VW van, my bruised knees a bed for my dirty doll. August drove wildly, crashing like a renegade against the odds stacked before us, past the majestic layers of red rock and sandstone, weathered temples formed by unrelenting waters and unforgiving wind.

Maybe, I thought, *my life—the good one where I am never sad or hungry or forgotten—was about to begin.* After all, we were headed toward Grandma Patty, and she would take care of me even if August couldn't. She would bake things that smelled like cinnamon and offer Band-Aids for cuts and scrapes. She'd buy me new socks and underwear, and she'd rip the tags out if I needed her to. But as quickly as it surfaced, the mirage disintegrated, shriveled in the desert heat. We'd pulled into a dirty truck stop somewhere in a red-ridged valley deep in the heart of Arizona for gas and smokes. August found a pay phone to call home to let Grandma Patty know we were on our way.

Reverend Brown from Grandma's church answered the call and told my mother Patty had passed. I watched August crumple to the floor of that phone booth like a reed taken down by a tornado, her mouth twisted in knots of sorrow and her fists clenched in rage.

After she pulled herself off the ground, August bought a bottle of whiskey and some saltines from the truck stop while I sat in the car fighting the flow of tears brimming in the corners of my eyes. We drove the rest of the evening in trembling silence. I watched the rolling tumbleweeds outside the car window until August became too blurred to drive anymore. We pulled the van alongside the road for a cold and fitful night's sleep.

In the morning, sun washed over me as I stretched myself awake on the dirty van floor. I woke alone with a half sleeve of saltines resting beside me, which I presumed to be my breakfast. I stumbled out of the van and looked around for any sign of my mother, feeling both relieved and afraid when I couldn't find her.

The lonely two-lane road we'd slept beside stretched through a yawning valley with striated cliffs etched into the cobalt background. To my right, and two hundred feet up in the air, I noticed three arched caves carved into the cliffside. I surveyed the sepia-toned landscape, and in the mouth of the middle cave, a lonely figure balanced on the edge of the cliff, pondering the long drop below. A flag of red hair whipped in the warm desert wind, and I knew, precisely and regretfully, that August was ready to jump. I watched as she raised one foot in the air and hovered there in hesitation. Grief, abandonment, and soul-crushing doubt raced with adrenaline from my head to my toes.

Paralyzed and dumbfounded on the roadside, I couldn't move or breathe. As I watched, August released her balance, stumbling backward into the darkness of the sandy cave, and I lost her figure in the jaw of its shadows.

Only then did I allow myself to exhale.

Moments later, I watched her slowly saunter down a dusty path worn into the side of the embankment, her head bowed but her defiant cadence proclaiming her unbroken. She climbed into the driver's seat, her eyes never meeting mine, and the engine rattled to life. We drove onward.

Here in my kitchen, I lean heavily on the cold granite of the countertop. I realize if I have any notion of reconciliation, any thirst left for the cold water of the past, that—

Behind me, broth boils furiously on the stove, sputtering over the top of the pot and splashing with a hiss on the burner. *Shame on you,* the stove bubbles with a *hiss, hiss* off admonishment.

This might really be it. I'd tossed and turned through so many fitful nights, dreams where August would almost reveal *his* name. But the vision always evaporated in the numb haze of the morning, a fool's errand.

"Damn it." I knock the knife into the sink with a clatter, startling both John and the dog. "I have to go back to Seaville."

From the flat world inside the TV, the crowd roars its approval.

Thanksgiving Day feels unseasonably warm and sunny in the boroughs of New York. John slept over on the couch, as he often did during holidays, letting us celebrate "as a family." For one day, we could pretend to be what we once were.

We drink bloody marys with breakfast and roast the turkey in the oven, and as the grand parade skirts by my apartment window, Laney snaps green beans, and I peel potatoes. As planned, Laney's new friend, Darren, arrives in time for lunch, and we savor our Hallmark moment. Pleasant small talk about the basketball team and the upcoming school play, and then please pass the stuffing, and maybe, just maybe, the teens are holding hands under the table.

I'm overwhelmed by the satisfying normalcy of the moment. With the scent of sage and oven-fresh apple pie consuming the apartment, I grab onto it and tuck it away into the small place in my mind where first kisses and surprise rainstorms live, the part that still feels full and functional and alive.

After lunch, Darren departs with a handshake for John, a friendly wave for me, and an awkward teenage hug for Laney. John settles back on the couch, and the cheering and crunching sounds of football once again become our background noise. Laney unexpectedly offers to help clear the dishes, a sure sign she has something on her mind.

"Why do you need to go down there, Mom?" she asks, handing me the empty tin that once held pumpkin pie. I plunge it into the warm sudsy sink and begin scrubbing with purpose. "She's not a kind person. You say so yourself all the time."

My teenage daughter, despite her tousled hair and tattered denim, has always been wise beyond her years. She favors John, with her dark hair and sullen ponder, but the angular beauty of her face comes from my side of the family. Though her eyes are hazel, sometimes they lean to green, and when they do, they remind me of August's.

I bite my lower lip and choke back every mother's instinctual fear of failing her child. I wonder, fleetingly, if that doubt had ever rested on August's shoulders.

"You're right," I agree, shaking suds off my hands and grabbing the ugly dishtowel embroidered with lemons, a Christmas gift from John's aunt. "But she's my mother. And I'm her only family. Just like you might be *my* only family someday." I paint a dot of dish soap on her nose.

Laney wipes the suds from her face but keeps her eyes locked on mine, letting me know she means business. At fourteen, she expects all life decisions to revolve around her. "I get it, Mom," she protests, "it's just…I have the kickoff tournament on Saturday, and I—"

"I know," I say, cutting her off. "And I would WAY rather be here with you. But this is something I have to do, and maybe one day, you'll understand." I artfully change the subject, trying my hand at distraction. "I like Darren, by the way. He's pretty cute. And very polite."

"Yeah," Laney agrees. "He's all right." Her sulking lips rise into a proud smile as she wipes her soapy hands across the front of her jeans.

After drying and putting away the dishes, I reluctantly search for my car keys, finding them hidden in the bottom of a drawer (because we walk everywhere in New York City). I then toss the overnight bag I'd packed over my shoulder.

"I'll be back by Sunday," I announce with considerable confidence. "But just in case, make sure Laney takes what she needs for school over to your place. And lock up when you leave."

"Give your mom our best," he shouts as I exit. I feel the extra weight of his gaze upon me, sensing his need to know I'm going to be okay. His concern stems not from the lover who once was but from the therapist who still is.

My car creeps out of a city calmed by the holiday, reaches the other end of the bridge, and quickens past the steel cranes and industrial machinery of portside New Jersey. When I finally find the open road, the sun starts to sink behind the highway horizon of northern pines and billboards. Fading light dilutes the orange and gold of late autumn trees, and I roll down the window to inhale the distant scent of wet leaves and wood smoke.

The same road carried me away so many years ago, armed against the insurgencies of the world unknown. I carried only a backpack with thirty dollars tucked inside. My ride to New York, wedged between the reams of fabric and garment bags that littered the backseat of Ms. Devere's station wagon, remains seared in my memory, a formative influence on the person I had become.

Ms. Devere, the home economics teacher at Lee High and a part-time costume designer in regional theater, had been heading to a fashion conference. She casually mentioned her upcoming trip while lecturing on the mechanics of threading a sewing machine. I'd quickly grown despondent with my tailoring assignment because an ache, as real and desperate as any I had ever felt, started to rise in my throat. The desperation I'd been choking on for years finally bubbled up like bile. After the bell released us from class, I decided to seize my opportunity.

"Whatever will you do in New York City, dear?" Ms. Devere asked when I suggested I tag along.

I wasn't sure what words would escape when I tried to answer.

"Acting, of course," I replied.

I'd never acted in my life, and in fact, I couldn't recall a time I'd ever performed in any way on any sort of stage—no debates, no student councils, no ballet recitals dressed in fluffy pink skirts. I thought of August and her lost aspirations to become a movie star, a dream that had died before it was born.

But at that moment, standing in front of Ms. Devere's sewing desk, nervously fidgeting with the gold locket that hung around my neck, "acting" seemed the obvious choice. A legitimate reason to run away from a small town, something people might accept when they questioned my disappearance, before moving along with their own business.

Ms. Devere squinted her eyes and lowered her glasses to the tip of her nose, surveying my motivation and authenticity, as if trying to determine from my just-tumbled-out-of-bed countenance if *this* girl before her in the faded T-shirt and lopsided ponytail could *actually* act.

"How old are you, dear?"

"Eighteen."

"Mm-hmm. And does your mother know you are leaving town?"

"She does," I lied again. "She's actually encouraging me to go."

"Hmm, we'll see…" Ms. Devere picked at her sewing needle and adjusted her thread. "If I have room in the car, you can ride with me. But I just have so many projects to take up there…" She started to sort through a pile of patterns, and I knew the conversation had ended. But I also knew I'd gotten the answer I wanted.

Three days later, Ms. Devere pulled up in her low silver station wagon, windows rolled down with Barbara Streisand blasting from the car radio.

August looked up from her bourbon glass as I stuffed a scarf into my overloaded backpack and headed to the door. "You're running away with *that*?"

Clutching the frame of the screen door in my trembling hands, I paused to look back at my mother, who had propped herself on the armrest of the couch. A cigarette burned low in one hand, and her green eyes smoldered with accusation.

I thought about turning back, maybe trying to offer a conciliatory hug, but the yawning pit of resentment that lay between us seemed too unrelenting to cross. A person could fall in there and be lost for years.

"Ms. Devere. She's a good person offering me a ride, August. And she said it was no problem to stay with her for a few days while she's at the conference."

My mother remained silent, her glower dimming for just a moment as she considered me with something that looked more like grief. Her long copper hair had begun to fade to gray, and the beauty of her past drooped and sagged, taunting her with its gravity. She inhaled the stub of her cigarette and looked out the window at the idling station wagon.

"And I'm not running away," I said, attempting a peaceable offering. "I'll be back after spring break."

"Sure, you will," August sneered, wrestling a fresh cigarette from the crumpled pack, pressing her forehead against the windowpane as if to inspect the tires on Devere's station wagon. "No one comes back here. Well, except for fools like me, and I shoulda known better. But I had you and nowhere else to go. Now you're leaving me, too." She dug into the back pocket of her too-tight jeans to fish out a lighter and sparked the cigarette to life with a deep, theatrical drag. "It's okay, they all do. They all leave. And for what? You're not going to make it on Broadway, girl, you don't have it in you."

Were those actual tears in my mother's eyes, threatening to betray her? I had never seen August cry, not even when she collapsed on the floor of the payphone the night Grandma Patty died. No, I must have been wrong. No tears fell in the arid wasteland she called a soul.

"What will people *say* about you skipping town, Janus?" August sneered. "They'll all talk. They always talk. They're talking already. And they're saying that you're not good enough." She took a laborious pull on her cigarette, coiling inward like a snake ready to strike.

Remorse and rebuke balanced in the air, trembling and uncertain.

I remained still, paralyzed on the precipice between the life I had known and the life I chased, like a unicorn with a brand-new horn. A long moment of indecision and consequence passed between us, ultimately broken by the sharp fangs of August's outburst.

"Just leave already, Janus, if you're going to leave! Just go!" The smoke she held in her lungs billowed from her lips and nostrils like poison seeping from the deep well of grievance within her.

So, I turned on my heel and ran, tore down the front porch steps, a creature escaped from the lair. I hurled my backpack and the body strapped to it into Ms. Devere's car and did not breathe again until the station wagon cleared the block, and Chestnut Street had suddenly become a piece of my past.

Ms. Devere tilted her rearview mirror, her spectacles seeking my eyes as she eased the station wagon onto Main Street. "Geesh, no wonder you wanted to get out of here." She craned her head back over her shoulder. "Has it always been like that?"

Porous in her backseat, I absorbed the question like a sponge. I must have managed a nod in response, but words largely failed me for the eight-hour drive. Streisand, her voice blaring from the wagon's speaker, worked overtime to fill the empty space. With each state we put behind us, my breathing came easier and the panic quelled.

Though even now, more than thirty years later, as daylight abandons the concrete contours of the same interstate, I can still feel my mother's venom, its residual toxins scratching and burning beneath my skin.

Chapter 8: Returning

The only exit off the highway that leads to Seaville can easily be overlooked, and I almost pass it by. My eyelids feel heavy from hours of driving and my mind numb from the drone of memory and the din of background talk radio.

Once off the interstate, the two-lane road seems incredibly dark. Country dark. With only a waning moon dodging the clouds and the beam of my headlights to keep me company.

I have about ten miles of farmland to pass through before the road curves toward the coast, where the arch of the drawbridge will greet me. Moonlight graces the tobacco fields, which have all been harvested for the season, and the livestock are in their pens for the night. The land is quiet and still on this unexpected Thanksgiving drive as my car cruises down the lonely road.

I crack my window. Damp ocean air curls its way into the car as I approach my old hometown. I deliberately drive past the wrought iron arches that frame Airlie Park and its dark grove of weeping willows, their boughs billowing tonight like beckoning fingers in the wind. Passing the turn into August's neighborhood, I keep going over the drawbridge.

From the crest of the bridge, the Seaville town square stretches before me, bathed in the watery evening light. A picture-perfect postcard. Old-fashioned gas lamps line the street strung with pine garland and satin bows for the holidays. An empty spruce sits in the center of the square, waiting for tinsel and lights and forced merriment. The neon letters on the Dixie's marquis glow brightly, illuminating the empty sidewalks, while "Closed" signs hang in all the darkened storefront windows.

Beyond the town square, Main Street continues toward the ocean, segmenting two rows of stately southern homes. As I drive past their tapered columns and moss-draped oaks, speed limit twenty-five, I can see their parlor lights glowing from within, families finishing their holiday feasts, clearing dishes, clinking glasses, and in the distance, someone is playing the piano. Its tinny notes drift out their open window and into mine.

I had never given it much thought before this moment—the portion and weight of a place that one carries with them. This place where I spent the latter half of my youth, accepted just enough to survive.

In hindsight, I had always been marked an outcast, the daughter of a witch. Even after I escaped, I felt this town, this burden of my past, dragging behind me like a roadkill carcass lodged in my back wheel.

But perhaps, another part of me actually *misses* Seaville. The part that feels *from* and *of* here.

I continue down Main Street, which ends at the beach right in front of Mercer's Pier. To the left, down Ocean Avenue, Shell Beach emerges, and to the right, Lumina Beach. Ocean Avenue itself remains a far cry from the regal homes of Main Street and their sated families. The homes here feel more like cottages, small boxes beaten by too many storms and abused by too many renters.

I drive past a tacky gift shop and a shuttered hot dog stand to where the road curves abruptly inland. It dead-ends in front of the tiny, concrete, rural hospital they call Seaville General. It's where August lays in wait for me. As I enter the lobby, a custodian mops the floor, trying to wrap things up for the night.

"Help you?" he asks.

"My mother…I'm here to see my mother, August Littleton."

He smiles with instant recognition. "You her daughter?"

I nod with some reluctance.

"She a feisty one…though not so much anymore." His voice turns conciliatory, his expression apologetic.

A familiar voice rises from the narrow corridor beyond the janitor. "Is that you, Jan?" Reena's warm, round face emerges from an office door behind the admittance desk.

"Reena!" Relief washes over me at the sight of her. "Thanks for calling me last night."

"Well, I just thought it was time. You know? Thanks, Bill, I can take it from here," she says before guiding me down the dim hallway. "She's holding on today, but I don't think it will be much longer, Jan. She seems to be in a lot of pain."

With each step that leads us closer to August's door, I can feel my anxiety tightening like a noose. I drop my eyes to the floor, where I proceed to study the hospital's linoleum, sympathizing with its cracks. Reena, who has always been that friend who knows just what I need even when I don't, leads me down the corridor without further conversation.

Reena was my first friend in North Carolina. Maybe my first friend ever. Though she had dark skin, and mine was light, it didn't phase me at the time. But I do recall August didn't seem too fond of our friendship, though maybe it had nothing to do with skin tone. Perhaps August envied the very *idea* of friendship, jealous I had found some level of acceptance that had eluded her most of her life.

I'd tried to stay connected with Reena after high school and through the years, but I lost touch recently as my aversion to our shared hometown grew, and the ties that bound us began to dissolve. Still, she was a constant amidst the chaos—smart and stabilizing. I'd never met anyone so aware of her own self-worth, of who she was and where she came from. I clung like a magnet to that confidence.

Standing outside August's hospital room, I muster the most authentic smile I can find.

"It'll be okay, girl. Good luck," she says with a wink. She then retreats down the dim hospital corridor, her shoes squeaking across the freshly cleaned floor.

The lights are off in August's room, but the gently parted curtains allow the moonlight to intrude. Instinctively, I move to the window and yank the drapes open wide. She would want the moon in here with her. Though she'd never been religious, my mother held solitary worship for the moon, marking her days by lunar cycles and planting her garden to the beat of its sacred rhythm.

As the streaming light floods the hospital room, August's wrinkled face illuminates, gray against a white pillow like dirt on snow. An oxygen mask rests over her mouth and nose, and she appears withered, whipped… thoroughly defeated. Her disease has danced victoriously over the cracked lines of her face. Her knuckles appear gnarled and her nails long, curving arcs like the talons of a hawk.

I carefully lift her chart from the end of the bed to survey its acronyms, abbreviations, and messy doctor signatures.

So, it's come to this, Mama. All these years you have been fighting everything and everyone. And now you've lost. It's just a chart and some tubes keeping you alive.

I pull a chair from the corner and slide it beside the bed. Silence mingles with the minutes, and I find myself exhausted. Resting my forehead on my crossed arms at the foot of the mattress, I quickly fall asleep.

I dream I'm climbing the old gray oak in August's backyard, scrambling for the highest branches, searching for something, seeking shelter in its limbs of golden leaves. I wake after several hours of fitful unrest. With my neck and shoulders throbbing, I check my fingernails for dirt and my hair for brambles before remembering I'm a grown woman, groggily yawning awake beside a hospital bed.

A glimmer of sunshine angles through the open curtains and slants across the foot of the bed. The monitors behind me beep steadily, humming and whirring as expected. The technology affirms August's life continues for another day.

"So, August, you made it through Thanksgiving," I whisper into the early morning silence. "Do you even *know* that I am here?"

*****

Oh, daughter of mine, I know you are here. I can smell the desperation wafting off of you like cheap perfume, even as I lay trapped in this lumpy hospital bed.

I knew Reena would call you up, just like she has before, and I knew you'd hightail it down here just so you could be here for it—my very last breath. It's my house that you're after, not my affection. That's what I know to be true.

Yes, I am ready to give up. I'm exhausted from fighting every day of my life. Fighting Mama, fighting you, and yes—fighting myself. All of my good and bad angels at war, weapons ready to fire.

And really, what was it all for? It sure as hell didn't turn out to be what I'd promised myself. This life of mine. I guess I'd always assumed there'd be some sort of logical relationship between the risk and the return. But maybe now it's clear I was just plain wrong.

Daughter, I have tried. These last few years, seems I'm always about to arrive but never quite get there. I've attempted to understand…the strain of these boundaries between the good and the bad…Well, they're all a blur now. Smoke and nonsense.

I know the end is near, and this is the end, isn't it? I've given myself permission to mourn the life I thought I'd have and the person I wanted to become.

I still miss Matty. Every single day. How we'd share coffee from a thermos while watching the sunset. And I haven't seen you, dear daughter, in months. We never talk. Not even a phone call. I'm certain it's my fault. It always is.

But the past is the past. It can't be doled out like spoonfuls of medicine. It just is. Lying there dead on the table.

Strange now…this feeling I'm having, this moment of reflection. I've made it this far alone, but it never felt like this. It's like there's an echo in my heart. I think it's my own voice, speaking words strange but true. Possibly more than I can bear to hear, this fading voice, this beckoning… I think it's the girl that I used to be, and somehow, she's survived the decay of time.

*****

A nurse bustles in with a bag of fluid and stops with sharp surprise when she sees me yawning at the foot of the bed.

"Oh, hello," she says in a thick, saccharine-sweet voice. "Are you family of Miss August?" She hangs up the fluid bag on the cart beside my mother.

I nod, standing to stretch my stiff back. "Her daughter."

"Oh, I didn't know she had any children," the nurse says. She places a finger on my mother's wrist, confirming a pulse. Her name tag reads Carol, and she doesn't look older than twenty-one. She takes out a blood pressure cuff, wraps it around August's withered bicep, and begins pumping.

Seems sort of pointless, all these monitors and charts. Either August is dead, or she's almost dead. The numbers in between don't really matter. Not to me, anyway.

"Is there a doctor on call this morning? Someone I can talk to?" I ask Nurse Carol.

She unfastens the cuff and says, "Um, yeah. Dr. Strickland will be doing rounds at about eight or nine this morning. Maybe a little later today…you know, the holiday and all." She keeps poking at August, punching on the machines, writing down notes, and measuring the level of fluids hanging beside the bed.

I look at the clock on the wall, and I'm surprised to find it isn't even seven yet. I need to find some coffee, so I slide on my shoes and grab my wallet from inside my overnight bag.

As I shuffle to the door, Carol pipes up again. "Um, sorry to interrupt you on your way out, but, um, did you know…did you know that your mom wanted a DNR?"

I stop with my hand on the doorknob. "DNR? What is that?"

"Do Not Resuscitate order."

"Oh," I say, though I remain confused. "Then why the life support?"

"Well, that's why I wanted to tell you," Carol says. "It's not really my place, and you can discuss it with Dr. Strickland when he comes around, but your mother, before she slipped unconscious, she said it…a few times…DNR, DNR."

I sigh with exasperation, and Carol fidgets uncomfortably. "You see, our patients usually have family around," she continues. "Someone we can discuss the order with before it becomes part of their chart. But with Miss August, no one was here, and we weren't sure if she was exactly…you know…" She uses her fingers to make air quotes. "'Of sound mind' when she was saying this. So, we didn't enact the order."

"Oh," I say again, not prepared for this discussion.

"Anyway, you should talk to the doctor about it."

"Ok, thanks. I will." I slip out of the room before Carol can emphasize any more expressions with air quotes.

The rising November sun warms my aching shoulders as I step out of the hospital. I can hear the dull thud of the ocean surf in the distance and decide to leave my car and walk the three blocks back to the town square. There, I settle into a small booth by a window at Grady's Café . Walloped with the scents of coffee and bacon, I decide to order both and push the laminated menu away, too tired to make any other commitments.

Elderly patrons fill the tables in the café, their brows furrowed as they pick through the morning paper or grumble about the coffee grounds lurking in the bottom of their cups. I wonder if August frequented Grady's, if she sat at the counter with the other blue hairs discussing bad news or the week's weather.

A DNR…Well then, she's ready to die. I hold the thought as something tangible, heavy, and certain. I close my burning eyes and lazily stir a packet of sugar into my coffee.

I really shouldn't be surprised. She's been fighting this illness off for years, and this time, it seems indifferent to medical intervention. She's been living all alone, holed up like a worm burrowed into a poison apple. *But alone by choice*, I remind myself.

She *chose* to reject those who could have found a way to love her. She *chose* to lace all conversations with cynicism and slurs. And she *chose* to drink away the isolation and reject simple overtures. Now she's choosing to die alone.

"Want a side of eggs with that bacon?" the waitress asks in a surly but not unkind manner. She sets down a plate of four greasy strips.

"No, this is fine," I reply without pleasantries. I then turn my attention away from the sleepy diner to the world outside the window, where the Seaville island square is beginning to show signs of life. A fickle wind tosses the golden heads of the elms that line the square, and their leaves, concluding their annual performance, cascade to the ground.

I watch an elderly couple wobble arm in arm from their car toward Robert's Grocery, the old man blotting his nose with a handkerchief. A man and woman sporting athletic windbreakers jog past the café, pushing a bright-orange stroller with a squirming toddler inside. Someone else throws a frisbee at their dog on the lawn that fills the expanse of the square.

Everything seems to be as it has always been—a simple place I've had to embrace and endure. At the same time, it feels foreign and contrived, a façade over the grit and grime I've learned to accept as life.

I feel an unexpected pang of pity for the young family jogging in tandem past the diner window. Maybe the life they've settled for here in this chosen small town is the only one they will ever know. Certainly, that kid under the hood of his stroller will find this sheltered existence to be as unfulfilling and confining as I have. One day, she may just jump into the back of somebody's station wagon to hitch a ride on out of here.

Munching on the last strip of bacon, its warm grease coating my lips like solace, I let myself imagine the life that would have been mine if I'd never smuggled myself away in Ms. Devere's backseat. Perhaps I, too, would have been a regular here at Grady's Café, its coffee stains and elevator oldies piped in from a corner speaker the backdrop of my day. If I'd never caught that ride to New York City, maybe I'd have graduated high school and gotten a job at the town library like my mother before me, finding faith and structure in filing and alphabetizing.

If I'd loped along here in Seaville until I found someone decent enough to marry, maybe it would be one of the square-jawed jocks from the football team, and maybe by now, we'd have sputtered along through four children and a mortgage his job at the car dealership just couldn't support.

No, Jan, I tell myself, dabbing the bacon grease from my lips. *That is not your given circumstance*. Mr. Leroy would say we rise to the challenge of our choices, and it determines who we become—more than the blood in our veins or the weight of our experience.

I am not from here, I reassure myself, sipping the last of my lukewarm coffee. *I am not one of these people, and this place is nothing more than a location marker in my history.*

Settling that, or at least setting it aside, I catch the eye of my grumpy waitress and request the check.

Returning to Seaville General, I find Dr. Strickland, young and portly, glasses perched on the tip of his nose, completing his morning rounds. After a briefing on August's condition (decidedly not good), I follow up on my conversation with Nurse Carol.

"Yes, a DNR is something we can help set up for your mother," he says, shifting his weight uncomfortably and clearing his throat. "But it's not something to be taken lightly, Ms. Littleton."

"Myers," I correct him. "Myers is my married name." After the divorce, I had seen no compelling reason, no roots pulling me, to return to using Littleton.

"Ah, yes, my apologies." The doctor inches his glasses up the bridge of his nose and struggles to find his bedside manner. "Your mother does not have a lot of time left, but there are some measures we can take to make her more comfortable, and perhaps…improve her quality of life for these last days."

"Days?" I seize onto the word. The timeline feels like a threat, a ransom note, staring down the barrel of a gun. Will I be here for *days*? This is only supposed to be a brief stopover, a pass-through, a drive-by.

"Er…or it could be weeks. We just don't always know in these situations." Dr. Strickland puffs up his big red cheeks, which are becoming redder as we continue our conversation, and blows out his hot breath in one long exhale. "Your mother cannot recover from this, Ms. Myers," he explains, misconstruing my rising panic. "With chronic heart failure, the weakened heart cannot pump out all the blood inside it. The blood backs up into the veins, and the body's tissues swell up like a sponge. The heart tries to keep up by beating even faster, and you can hear that your mother is having a problem breathing. Some patients with this condition say they feel like they are drowning. Eventually, this leads to organ failure, and there's not much we can do other than try to keep her comfortable."

"Yes, I see." I nod my head in understanding, but truthfully, I'm not paying close enough attention to really keep up.

"Why don't you spend these last few days with her," Dr. Strickland suggests, "and we can arrange some hospice care for her at your home?"

"My home in New York?" I ask with alarm. "Or do you mean *her* home?"

"Oh, your mother cannot travel, Ms. Myers. We need to keep her here in Seaville."

Nurse Carol reappears with another bag full of fluid, but she's careful to sidestep our conversation. I recall the DNR.

"So, if I take her home, and something happens…I *don't* call 9-1-1? We *don't* come back to the hospital?"

"Correct. If you wish, now that you're here, we can put the DNR in place right away. This means we would remove the ventilator that is helping her to breathe, and we would stop offering supplemental nutrition. Now, when we make these changes to her care, I cannot say what her chances are…but the will to live and to get back home is strong in some patients. Your mother strikes me as a strong-willed one."

Nurse Carol begins pressing buttons and rearranging cords. She smooths the pillow behind August's head and raises the bed to adjust my mother's shoestring body to something resembling a sitting position. The ascribed strong will does not stir.

"We could, of course, arrange for a hospice nurse to come and stay with you. But you, or someone in your family, would need to stay in the home."

Someone in my family? There's only me.

Cold and impossibly gloomy, the hospital room stands in stark contrast to the bright and vital world outside the window. It feels a million miles away.

"And Ms. Myers," he continues, lowering his voice to a hushed whisper. "Because your mother is in a good deal of pain, and, well, does not seem to be handling it well, I would recommend we explore a hospice option that can offer palliative sedation."

My brow knits. "What is that?"

"Palliative sedation is not euthanasia, but it is an end-of-life pain management protocol. You see, we can prescribe our terminal patients enough medicine—sedatives really—to, uh, cause unconsciousness. So they can rest instead of suffering…"

"Wow." I exhale. "I didn't know that was a thing." I hope he can't hear the relief leaking like a sieve from my voice. "So, you basically put her to sleep until she dies?"

"Well, not exactly." Dr. Strickland appears flustered. "We would explore a solution where sedatives could be provided as needed by your hospice caregiver. It is true that in some cases, after administering the sedatives, the patient, uh, never regains consciousness. But what we would hope for is to use as little medication as needed to achieve a peaceful sleep—to make her symptoms tolerable."

A quiet, peaceful August? Why wouldn't I want that?

"Okay. Yes, of course, that sounds reasonable," I agree.

"Very well, then," he says. "We can prepare the forms for the DNR, and I will get started with the hospice as well. Carol, can you call Gregor at County Hospice, and let him know we have a patient ready for his services? I gave his boss the heads up yesterday, so he should be ready to go."

Dr. Strickland leaves the room and choking back a rush of claustrophobia, I move impulsively to the window, fumbling with the latch and trying in vain to pry it open.

"Do these goddamn windows open?" I shout, slamming my palm against the cold glass.

Carol puts down her clipboard and offers a condescending smile as she moves to the window and opens it without effort.

My skin prickles with sweat, and my fingers and toes feel numb. The cool November air curls over the window ledge, down my cheeks, and over my shoulders. In the distance, I can hear the toll of the church bells, announcing the noon hour. *Ask not for whom the bell tolls...*

If August makes it out of this hospital alive…Well, I guess I haven't considered what would come next.

Nurse Carol suggests I head home to grab a shower before they remove the ventilator— "just in case." Her finger quotes really annoy me.

*****

I can tell you are bothered to be here, Janus. For all your acting skills, you sure don't hide that well. Maybe it's only fair, I never had much patience for you, like my Mama never had much for me. Oh, how I remember the things that got her going, like me always trying to skip church. She wouldn't hear of it. She already bought me a new dress, she'd say, though Lord knows where she got the money.

"These people need to know that I'm raising you right, August," she said to me, yanking a brush through my tangled red curls. "Today is the first baptism of the Matthews boy, and it won't do for you to sit at home sulking. No, ma'am, you'll need to dig your Bible out from whatever dirty drawer you've stashed it in, and you will march up to that church with me for the ten o'clock service. You hear me now?"

Mama got pretty strict when it came to anything having to do with pleasing others. It felt, to me at least, like she was always asking forgiveness for something. And if I had to guess, she wanted to find repentance for having me out of wedlock.

I had no interest in church or in seeing Junior baptized. I'd seen that boy act the fool and the devil on the farm, pissing in the haystacks because he was too lazy to go find a tree and scaring the horses with his loud BB gun right when I hoped to take ol' Jo out for a ride. That animal scattered so fast it was a miracle I didn't fall off and break my neck. Maybe he was jealous. Yeah, Junior had always been strung up I had a relationship with his Daddy, and he didn't.

But Mama, she was not one to be trifled with. I obliged, putting on the frilly dress, digging for my dog-eared Bible, and trudging along to church behind her. When we arrived, the place was full of whispers, and I was certain they were whispering about us. There goes Patricia Littleton and her lonely bastard child. *My shoes pinched, and my head throbbed. I could feel the bubble of anger rising in my throat. I hated that place and the people there in that church. I wanted to damn them all to Hell.*

"Real nice dress, Aggie." I heard the titter from behind me as I slid into the cold, hard pew. I knew

Kimberlee Neal's voice without needing to turn around. More giggles and laughter, and I knew her good-fornothing sister was sitting beside her, their hair tied up in those big pink bows they always liked to wear.

The Neal sisters teased relentlessly. If either spotted me just minding my own business, walking down the school hallway, or heading home from the library, their onslaught would begin. Bastard. Tramp. Queer. Homo. Fatty. Each day a different insult but always the same pinched and sneering pink bows bobbing behind them.

I tried to ignore it all, especially there at church where Mama said we're supposed to turn the other cheek. But honestly, it would burn me inside like hot, simmering coal. Pastor Brown would preach that we needed to follow the path of Jesus, forgiveness, and grace, but with each passing day I had to swallow down the Neal sisters' bubblegum brand of terror, I vowed to stray further and further from that path of grace.

And, Janus, it seems that is exactly what I have done.

*****

Grandma Patty's house is in the middle of Airlie Estates, a well-to-do sound front neighborhood with embedded estuaries and tall marsh grass at its border. When I pull in front, the afternoon sun begins its descent, the waning light drawing its long shadows across the dilapidated porch and bedraggled garden.

I haul my weary body out of the car and onto the sagging front steps, where I stand amidst the disrepair. The screen door hangs by a hinge while moss and ivy compete to corrupt the brick walls, foliage clearly intent on taking over the whole place. Tall weeds and terrible overgrowth seem to be having their way with Grandma's prized garden.

But it's the porch itself that decries all memories of its former sublimity, cluttered as it is with chairs of all types, shapes, and sizes. Rusted beach chairs with faded green and blue stripes, a splintered old rocker, and some crumbling version of a dining room chair upholstered in floral fabric. An old vacuum sits in the far corner, gathering dust and cobwebs. The porch speaks loudly of hoarding and hermitage, of the harrowed life of the one who lived inside.

"Holy shit," I mumble to myself. "Home sweet home."

It occurs to me, sadly, as I kick through the disarray—a spilled box of nails, a stack of yellowed newspapers sitting under a pile of bricks, a litter of used plastic water bottles—that a part of me counts on the inheritance of this old house to dig me out of my own money pit. My heart sinks as I realize each tattered square of this place screams of neglect. August's last middle finger to her hometown.

After finding the front door unlocked, I push forward into a dark, dusty living room that smells of mildew and bad habits. I sit down heavily on the old couch —*was it always a plastic slipcover?*—and close my eyes for a minute. Not long enough for that unsolicited army of lost memories to come marching back in. I feel a rumbling behind my temples, flickers and shadows of gray panic beneath my eyelids, the tightness rising in my chest.

No, not now. I scold my pain. *It's time to be functional and practical and work with the logistics on hand, the given circumstance. If August is actually being sent back home…if I am to play the role of caregiver and act the part of the loyal daughter…what needs to happen now? How does this storyline evolve?*

Fatigue drapes me like a worn-out robe, warm and knowing, yet my self-admonishment pulses with adrenaline, pulling me off the faded couch. I begin to forage the house like an intruder bent on finding treasure hidden in the rubble.

Under the kitchen sink, I find basic cleaning products, and in the bathroom, two spare rolls of toilet paper. Nearly bare cupboards reveal few edible items that meet the criteria of the main food groups. But all this would have to do because August could come home today.

I shower in the grimy tub, wondering when someone last cleaned it, but I'm thankful the water flows warm, and I change into clean clothes. The bathroom sockets are blown, but I find a working electrical outlet in the hallway to dry my hair. Though the hall sits bare of framed photos, stubs and holes in the wall identify where they once used to hang.

Gone is the old black-and-white portrait of a teenage Grandma Patty, her profile unlined and hopeful and ready to embark on life. The gold-framed photo of August has also disappeared. With her red hair aflame in the glare of the bright sun, she stood beside a white horse and a blue barn. I had endlessly studied that photo when I was a kid: the strain of her smile, her bare-fisted clutch on the horse's lead rope, and the awkward stance—shoulders slumped but chin high—like a girl instructed to pose. As her young daughter, yearning for something to love, I found my mother breathtakingly beautiful in that photo, a butterfly trapped in a glass jar.

With my hair half dry, I hurry into my old bedroom in search of shoes, pausing to give a silent salutation to the resolute old oak tree standing guard outside the window. "Can't climb you today, old friend," I tell the tree regretfully, zipping up my boots.

I glance into August's room to make sure it's fit to handle the throes of a dying woman. I see an unmade bed with a burgundy blanket rolled at its foot, the old box tv sitting on the dresser, unlikely to be operational, and a stack of folded laundry on the corner armchair. Books piled high beside the bed, a tattered writing journal perched on top, and a glass of water that surely had been there for days.

I race to the hospital, aware that time is of the essence. Winded from the hustle, I push through the door of patient room number two, and I can see August's breathing tube has already been removed. She's still alive, apparently. Nurse Carol stands beside her, adjusting fluids and punching machines.

"What in the hell?" I roll in, confrontational. "You took the tubes out while I was gone? What if she had… what if she couldn't breathe? You said, 'just in case'…" I quote my own air.

"Okay, just relax, ma'am," Carol replies in her lazy drawl. "Dr. Strickland said he had confidence your mother would have something left in her, and she needs to breathe on her own for twenty-four hours before we can release her to hospice. So, we had to get the ball rolling. And look here." Carol nods to her patient. "She's doing it all on her own."

Her labored breathing sounds like air escaping a balloon, but August's color has improved, and her skin seems less drawn. For a moment, I consider reaching out and laying a hand on her cheek, but I resist the impulse and instead sink with frustration into the bedside chair. *The waiting-for-death chair.*

*****

That's right, dear daughter, and you silly little nurse. I am still breathing!

You want me gone. You want to cash in on my assets. I make life hard, and you, dear daughter, were not made for a hard life. Your New York City illusions have failed you, and now you've come crawling back to claim what's mine!

So, I will show you all…I will just keep breathing. I will do it all myself like I always have.

Just like nobody in town thought I would ever be a Sundae Girl. They thought I wasn't good enough. They thought I didn't look the part. Not the right shape, they said, and her nose resembles neither a button nor a ski slope. She's from bad blood, they said, unrefined and unsavory.

And they were right. I was unrefined, and I didn't look the part. But no one paints August Littleton in a corner. I was the best damn Sundae Girl this town ever saw. And no one can ever take that away from me.

*****

I while away the next few hours, trying to occupy my hands and my mind, keeping company with the strained sounds of my mother's breathing. Carol offers me yesterday's copy of *The Star-News*, but I find it full of nonsense about school board improprieties and lawsuits at construction sites. I file my fingernails with an old file I find at the bottom of my purse. When I run out of distractions, I sit and stare blankly, for hours it seems, at my mother's sunken face half hidden beneath her oxygen mask, the tatters of a foe I've spent so many years fighting.

I feel nothing.

No, that's not true. I feel resentment.

From time to time, a low but perceptible groan emanates from August's chest, but she never awakens. Her breathing drones on like a hornet's nest, pained and agitated, and so I try to stay alert, ready for the sting. As night sets in, however, I nod off into stiff and merciful sleep, until I startle awake at the sound of my name.

I rouse from beneath a heavy blanket of exhaustion, summoned by the raspy voice repeating, with more authority this time, "Janus!" Weak moonlight from the open curtains spills across the hospital bed like a sacred shroud.

"August?" I whisper, disoriented, uncurling from the slouch in which I had slumbered. Clumsily, I reach out for her, and our hands collide, an unceremonial handshake, which she drops first.

She pins me with her blazing eyes. "Janus, did you *know* it was Thanksgiving?"

The kids at school used to say August had witch eyes, and even here in the hospital gloom, they continue to hold their power. They tell stories, unrelenting and complicated.

"Yes, I knew it was Thanksgiving, August. That's why I came." I fidget under the weight of my mother's stare, feeling unwelcome and out of place, like a cat trying to scamper across wet grass.

"Oh," she says, her expression like stone. "You didn't come because I am dying, then?"

"Well, that too." No point in beating around the bush.

The friendly janitor—Bill, was it?—steams the hallway floor, and the whir of the cleaner mercifully fills our silence. He waves as he passes my mother's open door.

August shivers. "It's cold in here."

"Oh, can I get you a blanket? A sweater?" I know I should be helpful. "Or do you want me to call the nurse?"

"No, just shut the window, Janus. I can feel that cold wind blowing in."

The window of her room appears shut tight, but I shrug and rise to close the curtains, blocking out the warm glow of the moonlight. The hospital room darkens, and I fumble with the switch of a fluorescent behind the metal bed rails.

"They say you can go home tomorrow, August."

"Huh," she grunts and attempts to raise her head, a failed effort that sends her crashing back into the pillow. "What in the…(*cough, cough*) holy *hell*? I can't go *home*!" Her agitation fuels her coughing fit, and several minutes pass until she can speak again. "Don't they know that I am *dying* here? Do you know what this feels like, Janus? I am (*cough, cough, cough*) choking on my own insides!" Her hands tremble, yet her voice lashes and whips off the stark hospital walls.

"I know, I know, August. But they will bring in hospice care. You can be at home. They can make you comfortable…" I trail off, unsure if honest words will irritate her further. "And I can stay for a few days, too. That is, if you want me to."

I watch as August's expression oscillates. She brightens, she broods, she considers her alternatives. And then, with a gravelly sigh, she relents.

"Yes, Janus. Of course, I want you to stay…but don't you have to work? Or are you still unemployed?" The drip of disapproval in my mother's tone settles like the sludge at the bottom of a river.

"You're not working, are you?" August needles, the question an indictment. "You're broke, then?"

"Well, in fact…" I begin with a deep breath, wondering how to explain the job at the TV station and if I'd even still *have* that job if I stayed in North Carolina past the weekend. I decide against answering at all, and I turn my face away to the closed curtains—a lovely floral pattern meant to distract from the antiseptic of the place.

"I told you that acting business was no good," August continues, funneling all her remaining energy into a froth of acrimony, its tide pulsing. "Well, then…(*cough, cough*) I suppose you'll be coming to me for handouts now. Is that why you're here? The real reason?"

Truthfully, I *am* bordering on bankruptcy. It's been over two years since I've had a paycheck, and I've refused to downsize my life, always convinced I will work again. The young girl who stumbled out of Mr. Leroy's class and straight into bit parts on Broadway would somehow keep rising to the occasion, even in my late forties. There have been no callbacks of late, though. No promising leads. So, I haven't *really* had a meaningful job since I filmed the soap commercial almost five years ago, and my savings account has dwindled to an unsustainable level.

August takes my silence as victory and resigns herself to the pillow, her eyes closed and satisfied. Her lip shows a thin upturn that borders on a smile.

I lean heavily on the hospital bed and fold my arms in frustration, studying the transformation of my mother's face as her happenstance smile fades to an open-mouthed snore.

*****

The welcome refuge of sleep, Behind closed eyes, I can let myself drift back in time, long before these sad hospital nights ….

I remember that I wasn't really sure where I was driving to as the tired beams of the old VW barreled ahead of me, punching the night and trying to dent the fog that had draped itself across the valley. Only six hours on the road, this screaming infant beside me, and all I wanted to do was turn around and go home. But Mama said I had to go, and when I got the money to buy the van, well…I guess everyone decided to agree.

Mama said we have family on the far side of Tennessee, but there was no way I could make it there tonight. I could hardly hold my eyes open, and the sun had just set, a furry blaze disappearing behind the rolling hills.

I pulled off into a truck stop and got out to stretch my legs. The girl continued to cry in her little bucket in the passenger seat, but I had to use the bathroom, and I really wanted a Coca-Cola. I let her scream her lungs out while I took care of my business, then I reluctantly climbed back into the van and picked up the little wailer.

I could feel her tense body relax as I eased her to my breast. Despite the darkness and the locked van doors, this still felt all wrong—cheap and tawdry tucked in the corner of this parking lot. As she nursed, I let my mind drift back to the morning and the difficult goodbye.

"I should've sent you away sooner," Mama said, "it's just...there were too many pieces to sort out." She cried, soft and ladylike, not the fat, sniffly sobs I tried to hold back. "I don't know why all this happened," she said. "But you've got yourself a new chance now. Go on out there in that big wide world and take it. Take that chance, Aggie."

I'd already lost so much it was like I wasn't scared of losing anymore. All the fear just disappeared right then and there. And in its place, I experienced a deep-seated anger, the kind that liked to sit and stay awhile. I took that anger and my milk-drunk baby into the back of the dark van, where Mama had helped me lay out a thin mattress and some pillows and blankets. A stash of peanut butter sandwiches and crackers rustled in their paper bag as I shifted the crumpled bedding to find a comfortable place for the baby and me to sleep.

These problems, I decided, could all wait till morning. I fell asleep clutching Janus's warm body, hoping and praying I'd find the holy path Pastor Brown kept talking about or, at least, a way to sleep through the night.

*****

I listen to August snore and I watch dreams flutter beneath her the curtains of her closed lids. I try to summon empathy. I wonder what performance she is staging for herself in the realm of sleep, I wonder what are the dreams of a dying woman? And do I play a part in them?

It was better n those early days, wasn't it? When it was just the two of us against the world? We had nowhere to be, no one to answer to. We just *were…*fearless nomads, tripping up and down the coast, hunting for starfish in the cold Oregon surf, wandering through tall California meadows. Curled up inside sleeping bags in the back of the VW, the stars blinking to life outside the dusty car window. I think that back then I must have felt safe and protected. Perhaps, even loved. We were making it work, August and I.

But once we arrived at Riverskeep, things began to change. Strange men with dusty bell bottoms and scruffy beards rolled into the picture, following August's scent, hungry for fresh meat, offering her drinks and drugs. Maybe she saw her path for survival and instinctively grabbed hold of it. And on her way to that wretched salvation, maybe she had to push me aside, discard me like ash in a tray.

Riverskeep flipped the coin for me, and I lost. Whatever bond August and I had was broken, and I had become nothing more than her unwanted and unworthy appendage.

These years remain damp and wilted memories. I'd turned into a scruffy, listless child who needed guidance, who needed a mother. But August shut down. She pulled away from me, and she continued to harden with the passage of time like hot volcanic lava turning slowly to impenetrable stone.

The move back east, the drinking, and the isolation all drained August's fire, crawling into her crevices and breaking her apart. Sadly, I was the only one there to pick up the pieces.

Chapter 9: Examining

As the hospital staff prepares August for her final discharge, I tuck into a dusty vinyl couch in the corner of the lobby to call John. I can hear the grog of a weekend nap in his voice and a televised hum in the background.

John, the therapist, is in fact, *my* therapist. Taboo, to be sure, but the attraction had been irresistible for both of us, at least at first. When I arrived in his office one late summer day, I sought an explanation for what I had become: panic-stricken, dependent, and self-absorbed. Another washed-up actress in her late twenties.

Dr. Myers turned out to be a skilled practitioner. As he tactfully held a mirror to my ego, I felt seen and realized. He gave all my headaches, the crying jags, and the compulsive need to escape into darkness alone—but still craving the attention and love of those standing just outside the door—a place to exist. They had a home. And in doing so, he gave me a door to step outside of that home.

"So, tell me, Jan, would you say that you have a history of unstable relationships?" he'd asked, pen in hand. A scratch tablet rested on one leg crossed over the other. So put together, so self-assured. He had a smooth gray suit, red tie, and sexy stubble, but the professional kind seen on menswear models. I found myself reacting to him, a balance of chemicals, a sponge absorbing its liquid life.

Entertaining the doctor's question, a parade of lost lovers marched through my mind. The small-town high school boys led the way, their sweaty brows streaking the backseats of cars. They were followed by the Manhattan men with their patronizing seduction of overpriced drinks inside crowded bars. They had all come and gone, tried and failed. Those I had conquered, and those who had conquered me.

"I mean, who doesn't have to deal with that kind of love in New York City, Dr. Myers?"

He had smirked, not in condescension but in agreement.

"You've told me about the anxiety and the depression that brought you in to see me, Jan," he said, remaining cool, even as he leaned in to take a bite out of me. "But what about anger? I'm wondering if you ever feel extreme hostility toward others in your life."

Surprised at the turn of the questions, I suddenly felt vulnerable and exposed. Dr. Myers had tucked me into bed and then ripped away the covers. Reflexively, I clawed for the locket on the chain around my neck before remembering it was long gone.

"Angry?" I asked. "Yes, I guess I get angry when I feel I've been done wrong. Again, don't we all?"

Therapy proved to be an expensive and unwelcome journey back through my regrets, moments I had buried beneath fanfare and alcohol and hoped to forget forever.

I recounted to Dr. Myers the time I'd tiptoed into Simon's dressing room in between takes, dressed only in a camisole and my flimsy silk robe. I wanted to make up after our most recent quarrel, though I couldn't remember what we had argued about. Simon wasn't there, but I found the note crumpled in a garbage can, the wad loose enough to draw my attention with the scribble of her name.

Lila,

Let's meet again tomorrow. Same time and place? I can't stop thinking about you.

-S.

I knew his handwriting and his penchant for signing notes with the single "S." Lila had just joined the cast, the darling ingenue, and she couldn't have been more than twenty. So, I didn't think twice. I didn't think at all, in fact. Rage had tunneled my vision to black, and all I could see were the matches sitting on the dressing table beside Simon's amber-scented candle. I struck one, burned the note, then lit the whole matchbook aflame. I dropped the licking ball of fire straight in the middle of Simon's overflowing garbage can and threw my robe on top to ensure a proper inferno. To leave my mark.

Dr. Myers took copious notes, wrinkling his forehead and pursing his lips before continuing his examination. "Jan, tell me how you feel about yourself now. Do you *like* yourself? Would you choose yourself as a friend, for instance?"

Well, I didn't have a ready answer to that one. I had made *something* of myself in that foolhardy city. Of that, yes, I was proud. Tumbling from Ms. Devere's Streisand-soaked station wagon into the bright lights, broken glass, and bleating car horns of the city that never slept had terrified, thrilled, and hardened me. It made my blood run hot and cold all at the same time.

And when Ms. Devere returned to North Carolina to finish her spring semester of home economics, I'd already made up my mind to stay back in New York. Her costume-designer friend owned a small walk-up on the lower east side that she rented to a young girl named Cher. Behind on rent and eager to sublet her couch and closet in her tiny studio apartment to make ends meet, Cher offered the space to me.

Cher struggled as an unemployed actress but employed waitress at the very upscale and overpriced Beauman's on Fifth Avenue. I had never waited tables before, but Beauman's was easy work, Cher said. She took drinks to the tables in a short black skirt, smiled at the ladies like their best friend, and winked at the men like she'd like to scribble her phone number on their checks.

So, within two weeks of arriving in New York City, I had a place to sleep and a job providing enough money coming in to make a meager trip to the grocery store. Jerry was a frequent and far-too-familiar customer at Beauman's. After serving him multiple martinis at the restaurant, I learned he worked as a casting director for an Off-Broadway theater company. Consequently, I had written my phone number on the back of his check, and a few days later, I earned my first audition.

I suppose I just got lucky. I didn't have talent or experience, and by Broadway standards, I didn't have a good enough face or body. But I got a part in Jerry's play —a small part, four lines—I deemed pivotal to the story. Of course, it didn't hurt I was waking up every morning in Jerry's brownstone.

The relationship didn't even last the full run of the play. Before long, I was back on Cher's couch, thumbing through the audition ads. But I was bitten by the acting bug, and I had a headshot, a resume, and a mindful of unlikely dreams. Something about the comfort of the darkened theater, the costumes that promised new identities, and stories that provided an escape to nowhere had sunk its teeth into my very core.

Over stale coffee one morning (so much worse than the espresso from the little Italian machine on Jerry's kitchen counter), Cher mentioned a method acting class at a local theater called the Round House. It would be a great way to network in the theatrical community, she said. We could go there together.

Slinking into the Round House that first morning, soft jazz jamming from stageside speakers, Cher and I struggled to stay awake after working the late shift at Beauman's. My eyes looked swollen from smoke and fatigue, and I could barely stifle my stretching and yawning, until Mr. Leroy strutted himself onto the stage, stepping in time to the drum's backbeat. I can picture him still, a tall flame of Jewish transvestite, auburn wig in the style of Bridget Bardot, long red nails, and a red pantsuit with angel wing sleeves.

"Welcome, friends. Those new and old," he said, his voice resonating from center stage, brawny and butterscotch. "Today, we are going to learn about embracing our characters, but more importantly, embracing our beings. Because how can we act—how can we portray—unless we understand? How can we act without *reacting* to one another and to the situation before us? Now please, let's go around the room. Introduce yourself, and tell us what brought me the pleasure of your company?"

Mr. Leroy had my undivided attention, and I rubbed the remaining sleep from my eyes and nervously grappled for the missing chain at my neck, waiting for my turn to speak. The introductions finally came my way, and I cleared my throat before speaking.

"Hello, everyone. My name is Jan, but I was born Janus…the god of beginnings and endings, the god who looks both ways, and the god of two faces…" I cleared the nervousness from my throat. "I guess that says it all. Why I'm here. I've spent my whole life trying to begin. Or end. Trying to invent my own character. I can't play the part of Janus, and I never really wanted to."

Mr. Leroy, who had been somewhat distracted examining his long red fingernails, glanced up at me in my seat at the end of row four and proceeded to look *inside* of me. Through my thin skin and oozing guts to the riotous emotions storming within. He then nodded his approval, which confirmed to me I would fit in quite nicely at the Round House.

Cher and I sat in the weathered theater seats of his class every Monday and Wednesday for six months. Each class would start with the sounds of Miles Davis or Coltrane, and every day, Mr. Leroy would find a new way to dance onto the stage—a shimmy, a shake, or a slide. A professed method teacher, he'd act out his favorite scenes, playing all the pertinent characters while waving his arms in despair or weeping in a corner as he called on his personal ghosts by way of demonstration.

"Stanislavsky," he announced one day, his voice booming around the small shoebox theater, "would want you to understand the difference between your 'given circumstance.'" He'd then pause for dramatic effect. "And the 'Magic If.'"

"If," Leroy continued. "The most powerful word in the English language. Conveying infinite possibility, disaster, or doom." He paced and pivoted across the stage, a unique and combustible blend of military march and runway strut. "The 'Magic If'…it should be applied liberally but with caution because it lets dreams out of the bottle and scatters whispers in the wind. Then they are gone, and you're left only with 'Then'—the consequence of chance."

I sat enraptured with the idea, reimagining the circumstances of my life. *If* we had stayed in California…

if Grandma Patty had lived through that spring…*if* I had known my father…

If. The word that begins miraculous recovery, spies the glimmer of new love, and opens a window offering the prisoner a chance of escape. It's that word one has in their back pocket as they navigate untold terrors, knowing there's always a way to compromise with fate.

"The actor or actress must always strive for inner truth. Do you understand the thoughts and emotions of the character? If not, how will you think and act as the character would in every scene of the play?"

I scribbled notes vigorously in the tiny spiral book I'd brought to class, hoping to buy some of what Mr. Leroy was selling. Sometimes, I'd get a nod and a wink from him, and I would feel validated in my efforts—like maybe I could swing the acting thing after all.

"By placing themselves in their character's situation," Leroy lectured to the room, where half of the students had nodded off, and others, like me, hoped to absorb, intake, and become. "You gain a better understanding of the *given circumstances* provided to the part. And by analyzing how you would respond if you, yourself, faced those same circumstances, your body and your voice will respond to be the part."

Given circumstance, I scribbled in my flimsy notebook. *Ask the If, be the part.*

"Why don't we see who can give it a go?" Leroy asked, nudging a guy drooling on himself in the front row awake. "So, the circumstance of the character is this: a young man heading off to join the military, scared and unsure. Now, go!"

The Ifs started flying in from the theater seats.

"What if his parents just kicked him out of the house?"

"What if he is actually a spy for the other side?"

"What if he's gay?"

"What if he was homeless and just looking at the army as a way to finally get a job?"

Leroy laughed. "Good, good…these are good. Why do I feel like some of you may have shared this given circumstance?"

I raised my hand, and Leroy smiled again. "Just shout it out, dear."

"What if," I started with trepidation, "he was abused as a boy? By his father. Who always told him he had to be a stronger man. And so he decided he would prove himself…to his father…by joining the war."

"Yes," Leroy said, snapping his long red fingernails and pointing at me. "That's it. That's what I'm talking about. See what I mean about imagining the backstory of the character? Really feeling what drives them, what motivates their actions and their words…Good work, Jan."

I beamed in row four.

"Children," Leroy continued, a term he used with both condescension and affection. "It's as simple as asking yourself these questions: Where am I? Where do I want to be? Am I comfortable or uncomfortable? What made me this way, and what can I change? The answer to these juxtapositions is how you form your character. And how your character forms you…"

I could almost hear the resonating clack of Mr. Leroy's high heels strutting across the stage as I came back to the present and struggled to find the right answer for Dr. Myers.

"I don't know," I said, drifting back to the therapist's original question. "I know who I *want* to be and who I *want* the world to see…and I like that person, I do. But I feel…Well, there may be some disconnect between the person I pretend to be and the person I think I truly *am*…Does that make any sense?"

"Perfect," Dr. Myers said, scribbling a few notes on his memo pad.

After a few more sessions, Dr. Myers had become "John," and my questions had become answers.

"Cyclothymia," John said. "It's a milder form of bipolar disorder, a condition many people have without ever realizing that they do. It presents as mood swings or a kind of panic attack, like you've been describing to me, but more in line with what we'd call 'emotional ups and downs' versus extreme outbursts."

Relieved my anxiety had a name, I hoped it also had a quick and convenient cure, like a pill to smooth out the rough edges or a potion to dissolve the angst. "Are you saying that you think I'm *bipolar*?"

"No. That's not what I'm saying. You are presenting with indications of something that is so common most people don't even seek treatment. If undiagnosed and untreated, yes, it can lead to further problems like bipolar disorder, but you are here, and you are already taking steps to manage the situation, Jan."

"So, you can cure me, then?"

"Well, I'm afraid that a condition like this is not necessarily something we can *cure*," John replied. "But we can work together to manage your symptoms. There are tools and coping mechanisms. Some psychotherapies have shown tremendous success in keeping this in check, as long as the patient buys in."

I understood the alternative to buying into John's professional advice would mean letting myself slide down that proverbial slippery slope, perhaps even following in my mother's footsteps. So, I came to John's office every week, and we identified triggers, practiced coping skills, and turned negatives—those damn *given circumstances*—into positives.

We worked on focused breathing to fight the panic, regulating moods through consistent sleep intervals, and introducing exercise into my day. I chose to take up running since the sweaty confines of New York City gyms revolted me. We worked on calling the triggers by their names: Neglect, Abuse, and Abuse.

At first, I was merely grateful for his help, but then gratefulness turned into affection and affection into lust. After a few months, John and I were completely entwined. We decided to get married after four drugstore tests proclaimed me undeniably pregnant. It just made things less complicated, we both agreed.

But ours was a scorched-earth kind of love— impetuous and irresponsible. We could have spent years flying by the seat of our pants, tumbling through toxic

West End parties and lovers' strolls through Central Park. But bringing a child into the world wound up sobering, a crash from our self-perceived societal grace. It felt like a slap in the face—to me, at least.

I crumbled. Too tired, too absorbed, and too fat to continue beating down the closed doors of my career, I instead committed to a new cause: providing Laney with the very things I had never known, like a mother's love and attention, a normal childhood, and a sense that everything would be all right.

I played the nurturer role well, at least for a while. I fed and bathed and embraced, I sang lullabies off-key, and I wrestled and prodded a stroller through the tiny inlets of New York City sidewalks and the small confines of its subways. I woke early and often for my baby girl, letting John sleep through the diapers and croup. I bought her books she couldn't read yet and tried to stimulate her growing mind with gender-neutral, STEM-inspired toys. I jogged every day uphill, both ways, trying to convince myself I was winning. That race. Every race. I just had to keep pushing.

But through it all, I could never really shake the sense it would eventually fall apart. I would be discovered as an imposter and exposed to the world as a fraud, and they would leave me because, as my mother taught me, they *all* leave. That fear of abandonment haunted me, worrying my daughter and husband would one day realize I was all wrong for the part, miscast, and walk off into the sunset of a better life.

There was a quake at the loose seams of this continent I had built on quicksand and hope. One day, the earth just cracked open, and danger and disarray slithered out like smoke, rising from the embers smoldering at my core.

Later, I'd find a name for this disquiet, harkening back to Mr. Leroy's lessons at the Round House. I described them to John as "If" episodes. Hours, even days, of lapses in judgment, feeling my reality tangibly implode, and my other self, my alter ego, inventing and inviting all types of welcome and unwelcome trouble. For as long as I could remember, I couldn't reason with my given circumstance. I had to disappear into a myriad of alternate scenarios that would allow me to cope with each day, each cruel slight, and the times I was forgotten and afraid.

Maybe the instinct of the actress took over, as I'd allow myself to slip into an unknown character, a crafted mask. The script…Well, that took me in whatever direction was opposite to the current. Anything impulsive would do.

Like the day I met Jared at the park on a cold, gray afternoon in the middle of winter. Pushing his own kid on a swing, he had a chiseled jaw and shoulders that could carry a load. I'd never noticed him at the park before, and on that particular day, we were the only two adults braving the elements. We laughed about our foolhardy decision as the wind whipped across the concrete play yard, sending my winter scarf flying into the bramble of some bare bushes. Jared picked patiently through the twigs and limbs to retrieve it while I kept two swings going. When he handed it back to me with a smile and suggested we go get coffee, my knees grew weak. My given circumstances, my wedding vows, and the diligent pursuit of normal, just crumbled to the ground.

We met again a few days later, this time at a bar uptown after I told John I planned to grab dinner with an old friend. Jared was married, too, and I didn't even ask what excuse he had offered his wife. We drank at the bar, flirting and telling old stories while cleverly avoiding our respective realities. That night, we both wore marriage like a new outfit we'd discarded on the dressing room floor.

It didn't last with Jared, but even though John never caught me red-handed, I knew something had to give. I tried to breathe through the panic and run out the remorse. I'd hug Laney harder and look for reasons to proclaim virtue in each new day of my married life. But the downward swings started coming hard and fast, and all the acting in the world wouldn't save me.

When one marries their therapist, sometimes one has to choose between having a husband and a shrink in their life. I absolutely knew which one I needed more.

So, all those issues that brought me into John's office in the first place, the turmoil that brought us together, tore us apart in the end. We saw a marriage counselor, of course, and laughed about it—a counselor needing a counselor. But in the time it took us to re-evaluate our love for each other, we realized our marriage was already over. It had crumbled like a sandcastle confronting the incoming tide.

John seemed to walk away from the carnage easily, and he remained my trusted therapist. I took the loss harder, proclaimed myself a failure at normal and struggled to regain my footing on the earth I had upturned.

I shake off the past and find myself in the hospital lobby, pulling at a loose seam on the dusty couch while John offers me his opinion.

"They call it a rally," he says on the other end of the line after I describe my night beside August's bed. "When people are close to the end, some get this brief period of energy where they almost seem like they're getting better. I remember it happening with my Uncle

Larry. My dad had called in the priest for the final rites, and when the priest showed up, Uncle Larry sat up and shook his hand and started telling his old war stories. Usually, it lasts a few days, then you can expect her to go pretty quickly. What does the doctor say?"

"You know," I reply, "they hate to give timelines. But she's having a lot of trouble breathing, and she seems to be on and off oxygen. She slept for hours on end, John, like *really* slept. From the time I arrived until she woke up in the middle of the night. Certainly, she *seems* like a dying woman."

"Want me to come down there, Jan?" John's offer sounds conciliatory and almost genuine. There's certainly no love lost between my ex-husband and my mother.

I ponder his proposal for a moment. How great would it be to have my therapist by my side right now? Reluctantly, I realize it would be easier to go forth alone because I'm so tired of making excuses for August— exhausted, actually. But if it's only August and I, slugging it out in her final days, perhaps I won't have to bear the burden of making excuses for her. A small slice of my conscience also whispers I *should* spend the time at her bedside. Didn't I need to find some way to reconcile, seek peace, learn my own truth…or something like that?

So, I tell John I'll be home in a few days, and I promise to call if anything changes, reminding him to wash Laney's basketball uniform before her game on Sunday. Because, well, life goes on.

Nurse Carol pushes August, slumped and stubborn in a wheelchair, to her waiting ambulance as Dr. Strickland approaches to shake my hand and bid us farewell.

"The hospice nurse should arrive at your mother's home by noon," he says. "Call back here if they don't." He does his best to offer me a reassuring smile, his big red cheeks puffed up like two beefsteak tomatoes.

"And how will I know what to do when…I mean *if*…something happens?" I trip over my question.

"Well, hospice will stay in your mother's home with her, and they will be her constant caregiver. You can let them guide you through it. And remember, she has a DNR now, so no life-saving procedures will be taken, and she should *not* be brought back to the hospital."

It's clear to me August has been a difficult patient, and I wonder if they're glad to be rid of her, glad she doesn't have to die on their watch.

Well, I let them off the hook. It's my watch now, and I can hear the hands of time ticking as loud as a telltale heart.

Chapter 10: Exploring

Gregor arrives promptly at noon, wearing yellow hospital scrubs and a nametag from Hospice America. His baggage includes an IV drip stand, a heart rate monitor on wheels, and a large duffel of medical supplies. He introduces himself to a fairly alert August, her adrenaline still pulsing from the excitement of the ambulance ride.

"Ms. August," he says. "Is it all right if I call you August?"

She nods, a curt, unwelcoming tip of the head.

Gregor is a slim Black man in his twenties with a small afro and a cross with colorful beads around his neck. Perhaps August wonders how a character like Gregor stands at the end of her bed at the end of her life.

"I will be setting up an IV drip just like they do in the hospital, Ms. August," he explains, his accent containing a subtle island twang. "But this one will be morphine. Just something to help with the pain." He unpacks a small medical bag. "So, one question I have for you now, and will ask again, is how is your pain? On a scale of one to ten, with ten being the worst pain imaginable and one being little or no pain, can you tell me your pain level right now?"

With a withering glance, she hisses, "Ten."

"Okay. Ten." Nonplussed, Gregor scribbles on a chart, then begins to rearrange stacks of books and other bedroom clutter to make way for the cumbersome rack of a heart monitor.

"Need any help?" I ask, unsure of my role in this new pseudo-hospital paradigm.

"No, thanks. I've got this. Is it okay if I place these things behind this chair in the corner so I can have access to the electric outlet here?" He picks up a stack of withered magazines and a frayed cardboard box that jiggles and clanks with the sound of empty bottles.

"Of course, of course," I say. "Sorry it's such a mess in here."

"I've seen worse," Gregor replies.

August coughs and clears her throat. "Why…" she croaks, her eyes thin and fixated on Gregor like a reptile sizing up its prey. "Why…are…you *here?*" Her words trail into the slim space that hovers between tension and anger in the room.

"August!" I scold, but the lids of her eyes just flop to a defiant close. I turn to Gregor with an embarrassed shrug. He just smiles reassuringly and continues organizing his supplies.

"It's all going to be okay, Ms. Myers. I am here to make her comfortable, and we will get to a place of trust. Or we won't. Either way, I can do my job."

"Please, if you don't mind, call me Jan."

"Okay then, Jan." He laughs. "It is good that she's been awake and talking, and that she has, shall we say, a devil in her soul?"

"Oh, Gregor, you have *no* idea."

"The pain…it makes them crazy," he says, but he adds quickly, "Not that your mother is crazy…"

"Oh no, she *is* crazy. It's okay. You won't find it in her charts, but I suspect she suffers from undiagnosed bipolar disorder."

"Undiagnosed and untreated? Her whole life?"

"I don't know for sure…but yes, I think so. It seems to run in the family."

"Okay…I see. Well, we will do what we can to keep her in the best state possible."

"So, about that…" I hedge. "When do we begin the…what do you call it? The sedation?"

"Palliative sedation," Gregor responds with a subtle arch of his eyebrow. "As I'm sure the doctor told you, that is sort of our, how do you put it, last resort? If we can manage your mother's pain and keep her comfortable and awake, that's what we will do for as long as we can. You can use that time to say your goodbyes."

Great, I think as I head to the kitchen in search of lunch. *A long, drawn-out goodbye for August. Just what I was hoping to avoid.*

I find a can of soup in August's bare cupboards, devour it, and head back to resume my obligatory bedside vigil. To my surprise, I find my mother awake and alert and lying in wait.

"So, August, the place looks good," I fib, eyeing the disheveled burgundy blanket that covers her and the layer of dust on the nightstand.

"No, it doesn't, Jan, but thanks for trying," she responds, her voice tired and raspy. "You don't have to be nice to me. Kindness won't cure me, you know."

"Well, it's been a while since I've been here, and I guess it could use some picking—"

"Why did you come?" August interrupts, her question punctuated with a hacking cough.

"Well," I begin, letting her coughing subside and choosing my words carefully. "I *am* your only family."

"Do you want us to be friends, is that it? So it can all go out on your terms? Make sure I leave you my money? My house?" Her ragged tone full of disdain, or perhaps disgust, she heaves and coughs, making sounds of an engine sputtering.

"What I *don't* want is to fight, August." I move purposefully from her bedside to the corner armchair and begin to fold a stack of clothes that had clearly once been folded.

What *did* I want? Love and acceptance from a person incapable of offering either? Answers? Ties for the trailing ends of my past? A red flag waves in my mind, flailing and flapping in a vicious tornado. *I want to know who my father is.*

With my back turned on my mother, a rush of silence drowns the room. As quickly as August's attack began, it subsides.

Wheeling around, I drop a wrinkled shirt on the floor as I search for the faint rise and fall of my mother's chest. To my relief, I find it, but her eyes have closed again, and she's asleep. Or pretending to be.

I catch my reflection in the mirror propped up on the dresser, and the sigh escaping my lower lip ruffles the slant of my bangs. Suddenly, I feel like a helpless eight-year-old all over again.

*****

I can hardly stay awake to even finish a fight anymore. I guess I'm gonna just let my dreams take me where they want to ....

The day I brought Janus back to this house, to my Mama's house, should have been a new beginning. I had been dragging that girl up and down the West Coast for years, and I felt right awful about it, I truly did.

When Mama died, I knew it meant we finally had a place to live, a home all paid up, and maybe something like the start of a fresh new life. But driving back into town shook me. It all came flooding back. Even seeing the sun shining on the water made me cringe. Then, I saw Mama's garden—a rightful mess. Everyone knew it was all she ever cared about. And there it stood, all awkward angles of weeds and sprouts and stones, and no one to fix it but little old me.

I tried, though. We settled in, and every day, I'd walk Janus over the bridge, and we'd set up down at the beach. We'd sit there for hours, me on the water's edge, watching the lope and curl of the green waves, and Janus digging in the sand. We'd sit until the moon rose from the sea. Even if only a sliver, it always made me feel better.

That ocean. I had forgotten how it terrified me so. I knew it was a force greater than me, and I made a point never to reckon with those. Mama told me once my daddy got taken by the sea. A wave came up too big for him to handle, and the ocean washed him away forever.

So, Mama raised me all on her own. She kept the house and the garden, and she got me through the hard things. And that's what I wanted to do for my little girl.

"Take care of the problem," Mama would say when I came home crying. Those other kids could be so cruel, finding all my weak spots and just digging in. Somehow, they knew the dark things I tried to keep hidden, and they'd tease me. They'd call me names, and they wouldn't let up.

Mama just wanted me to stand up for myself, to show them not to mess with the Littletons. And I wanted to teach Janus that, too. That's why I was always so hard on her. It just wouldn't do for them to see the Littletons in a state of weakness. It just would not do.

*****

Though I should be diving deep into the disrepair of the house, I decide instead to take a walk through the old neighborhood. Maybe I could get a little sea air to clear my mind. I grab an old umbrella that juts from the coat stand beside the front door, just in case the dark clouds that threaten from beyond the green marsh have a mind to roll in.

August's house sits in the middle of Chestnut Street, two blocks inland of the drawbridge. It's a modest craftsman, showing its wear and tear, tucked inside the well-established neighborhood of Airlie Downs. Chestnut dead-ends into Airlie Road, which runs in a curving arc bordered by the waters of the sound. It's lined with homes made of red brick or plantation white, all with expansive lawns that lead to feathered edges of marsh grass.

I stroll down Chestnut, the pristine sidewalk so contrary to the littered pathways throughout New York. On the corner of Chestnut and Airlie, I pass Sally Mavey's home, noticing she's hung a tinseled Christmas wreath on her front door already.

Sally, whom I've known since grade school, bossed all the kids in town around, but she also showed kindness and sought justice, never shying away from calling out the playground bully.

Sally, Reena, and I formed a threesome, whiling away our time swimming at the beach or roller skating across the bridge. My two best friends were completely different, opposites in many ways, and I had always been the glue holding them together.

After high school, Sally stayed in Seaville to care for her sick mother, and when her mother died, she used her inheritance to buy a large house in Airlie Downs, becoming a staple of the social fabric and earning a reputation for cranking the rumor mill. She enjoyed knowing everyone and everything. She favored her fashion in bright colors and tended to talk too loudly and too close. Folks around town may have found her to be too much, but I always had a soft spot for her brash perseverance.

On summer days, Reena and I used to follow Sal knee-deep into the waters of the sound, carrying nets tied to wooden sticks, hoping to catch blue crabs so that Ms. Mavey would fry up some crab cakes. Sal and Reena had grown up in the pluff mud and seashell treasures of this place, which made them like guides through a foreign land.

"Jan, there's a harvest moon tonight," Sally had said to me one day, her mouth full of sugar cone as we walked home from Pop Gray's. "You know what that means, don't ya, girl?"

"Uh-uh," I replied, licking aggressively at the globe of ice cream on my cone before it could melt.

"Well, the tide, you see…it's controlled by the moon. So, on a full moon like tonight, its pull is really powerful. And the moon, it draws the waterway so low that, girl, did you know that you can literally walk clear across to the other side just hopping from one sandbar to the next?"

I shook my head in disbelief and waved Sally off, certain she intended to pull my leg.

"Don't believe me?" she asked, wiping dribbles of vanilla from her lips. "I'll show you."

It'd been one of those sultry June days where a person could wring summer right from the sky, and we were sunburned and wind-tossed. Sal and I had spent the day sprawled on the beach, reading comics and bad paperbacks until the setting sun revealed the rise of the moon, huge and orange, like a peach bobbing in the ocean.

"C'mon, let's go. I'll buy you an ice cream on the way home," Sal had said, brushing sand off her knees as she headed over the dunes toward the island square.

Pop Gray's was busier than usual that evening, the heat of the day still unrelenting. A short line wiggled out the front door, and Lucy Gray stood at the counter taking orders.

Lucy, who used to babysit Sally, saw us standing in line and waved us to the front. "How you doin', Sal?" Petite and brassy, and a carbon copy of her mother, she'd taken over as the manager of Pop Gray's after graduating high school.

"Hi, Lucy. Denny here?" Sal asked hopefully. Sally had a mad crush on Denny, though inappropriately old for her, and despite his growing paunch and thinning locks, he remained the coveted catch in Seaville.

"Nah, he had a date. Just me and a few of the girls tonight." Lucy nodded over her shoulder as one of the Sundae Girls breezed by with a tray of ice creams covered in sauces.

The Sundae Girls, with their little pink dresses and perfect figures, bounced around Pop Gray's with confidence like celebrities gracing a small town.

Music played from the corner jukebox, something by the Bee Gees, and I leaned over the chrome countertop to peer into the frosted glass of the ice cream banquet, salivating at the choices. But without consulting me, Sally ordered us two vanilla cones.

With night upon us and the moon in full effect, we strolled toward the drawbridge, savoring each bite and catching the drips. The bridge was up, and a tall-masted boat struggled to pass through the shallow, sound waters.

"So. let me show you how it's done," Sal said, swallowing her last bite of cone and licking her fingers. "We don't need no stinkin' bridge," she shouted behind her as she raced ahead of me to where the water softly lapped the shore. She kicked off her sandals, and clutching them in one fist, she trudged into the water until waist deep. Then, she took a few steps further, up to her chest, the tips of her braids trailing in the water. "C'mon, all the kids 'round here know how this is done! You gotta trust me!"

I felt certain I would be too frightened to follow her, but when Sal made it across the deepest part of the channel and climbed up on a sandbar, her head still high and dry, I committed, plunging into the salty water and accepting the liberating baptism.

And it was always like that with Sal. She needed a friend who could handle her managerial tendencies, and I needed one who could show me the way.

I cross the street in front of Sal's house, which puts me on the corner where the old McCready house sits, dark and derelict, cobwebs in the shutters and furry moss climbing up the brick walls. An instinctual shiver crawls up my spine, though I'm far too old to still be haunted by the town's collective boogeyman.

From the corner, Airlie Road continues toward the hushed rumble of Main Street, where a stretch of old-money homes lay embellished with ivy-draped trellises and polished, white rockers. Through their street-facing windows, I can see chandeliers illuminating front parlors against the fall of evening light, the warm velvets and jewel tones glowing from within, telling the story of these grand homes and the genteel families who live inside.

At the foot of the drawbridge, the pink-hued dusk peeks behind the frayed edges of scattered clouds, and stars begin to punctuate the descending darkness. The curving sidewalk guides me over the bridge as streetlights flicker on with a quiet crackle.

A familiar pucker tickles the inside of my cheeks, and I realize my need for an evening walk might have been a psychological red herring. I hurry past Robert's Grocery in search of a drink—the good, stiff kind—but I pivot back when I remember I forgot to pack deodorant.

Robert's appears surprisingly crowded at this hour. Surfers, still in their wetsuits, jam the narrow aisles, six packs under their arms, accompanied by a few locals carrying small baskets of breakfast cereal and apples. While I browse the small selection of overpriced toiletries, a familiar voice pulls me from my intense decision-making.

"Jan Littleton, is that really you?"

An older version of high-school Brian stares across the aisle, now with glasses and a shopping basket full of antacids. Though I see some things have not changed, taking in his rumpled T-shirt, tousled hair, and the acne dotting his jawline. Throughout high school, I had dodged Brian's crush, convinced that we were meant to be great friends, but never anything more.

"Hey, Brian! Yep, it's me."

We share an awkward hug, his shopping basket of medicine a barrier between us.

"I saw you in that soap commercial. Did you move back into town? I heard your mom died. Are you staying in her house?" Brian has always been full of questions.

"No, no, and yes, for a short while."

It doesn't surprise me that folks in town think August has already died. My mother has never been the most sociable neighbor, even before she fell ill. Not a leader, not a follower, she has no real friends to speak of. Her existence in Seaville has always consisted of long working hours followed by short drinks alone.

Brian looks concerned with my disjointed answers, so I sigh and try to clarify.

"Okay, yes…I am staying with my mom for a bit. She's, uh, not well but still alive."

"I'm sorry to hear that, Jan. I mean, I'm not sorry she's still alive…" He shuffles uncomfortably, rearranging the bottles of antacids in his basket. "I meant to say I'm sorry about the whole situation." He clears his throat then shifts topics. "Hey, do you remember Tara Bradley?"

I nod, relieved at his diversion, and I do recall Tara, a pixie cheerleader with a thick accent and French braid.

"Okay, well, she's having her annual holiday party tomorrow night," he continues. "You should come. So many old high school friends will be there."

I bite my lip. "Uh, no, I don't think so. I wasn't invited, and it's been so long since I've seen Tara. Or any of you."

"Aw, come on. You can come with me. It will be fun." He leans in, his hand shielding his lips to deliver a loud secret. "Tara's husband is large, if you know what I'm saying. He likes to eat. There's always an insane spread at this party."

I laugh, and we exchange numbers and prepare to part ways. Behind his thick glasses, Brian's eyes dart briefly to my hands, which are bare of any rings. I head to the register with my stick of deodorant, hoping Brian doesn't assume we'd just made a date.

"Oh, Brian," I call back. "Is there a bar in town?"

He looks down at his antacid selection as if trying to weigh the wisdom of tagging along, then decides against it. "Try Clifford's. It's new. Just across the square."

Chapter 11: Drinking

Clifford's is a dimly lit corner café that smells of garlic and all things Italian. Sturdy walnut tables scatter across the dining room and a slim bar lines the far wall. The tables and barstools appear mostly empty at this hour, so I slide onto one and wait for a bartender, drumming my fingertips on the counter with impatience, as they taught me to do in New York City. Fleetingly, I wonder if August has woken up and if I should be heading home, but I reason I *deserve* a drink.

A man with midnight-black hair and peppered-gray sideburns emerges from the kitchen. Striking, he has a strong build that is less lumberjack, more biker. Wiping his hands on a crisp white towel tucked in the back pocket of his worn jeans, he smiles at me and steps behind the bar with casual authority. "What can I get you?"

I'm caught off guard for a moment, a fish on a hook. His eyes reflect deep pools of gray, framed dramatically with the weathered lines of a life well lived. I'm drawn to them with a strange, familiar fascination.

"I'll have a vodka soda with lime, please," I muster after an inappropriately long pause. Squirming off the hook, I avert my gaze. It's definitely not the right time to get lost in a stranger's eyes. I steady myself by watching his practiced pour, how he lets the vodka trickle down the glass. The fizz of club soda occupies the fluttering space in my mind. Yes, I deserve this drink. It's been far too long.

"Just visiting town for the night, or are you new here?" he asks, again with that damn smile. His voice sounds raw and gritty, and as he passes me my drink, I see his arm has been inked from the wrist up. The wing of a dragon escapes the cuffed roll of his shirt sleeves.

"Oh, well, I grew up here," I say, stirring once, preoccupied. I take a long sip as my nerves settle with the forbidden and familiar clink of the ice against the cocktail glass.

"Ah," he says. "A local, once removed—my favorite kind. I am, too, sort of. So, I bet you know all the good stories about this place."

"This restaurant?" I ask.

He laughs, wiping down the countertop with long, uncompromising strokes until the bar top glistens. "No. This town."

I nod in understanding, but I don't have an answer to his question. Seaville has always seemed like a non-committal place to me, with its buttoned-up bridge clubs, porch swings after Sunday dinner, and tourists foraging in the novelty shops. Not a lot of scandal earned its evolution into folklore around here.

"Name's Cliff," he says, tossing the towel over his shoulder and extending his hand.

"Jan," I reply, shaking it. An old familiar rhythm courses through my veins, the far-off drumbeat of possibility. He has a workman's grip with tough, warm hands, and his touch sets my nerves to racing. Our eyes lock again, and it feels significant and substantial, something I'm afraid I cannot handle, so I rip my gaze away for a second time. "Nice place you've got here." My voice escapes my lips like a breathless sigh.

"It's a little slow," Cliff says, following my eyes as they wander the restaurant, which now sits empty save for a couple sitting at a corner table holding hands, the dregs of a bottle of wine between them. "The holidays, you know…Did you come back to visit family for Thanksgiving?"

"Sort of. I actually haven't been here for quite a few years, and a lot has changed, without a doubt."

"But a lot has stayed the same?"

"Right," I answer with a laugh. "Sorry, you said you're from here, too? I don't recall ever seeing you around, and I think I'd remember."

"You wouldn't have. I was born here, but I moved away when I was just a kid. My parents split up, and I headed up to Boston with my mom. Grew up there, so I guess that's really my hometown. You?"

"Oh, I'm not sure where I'd actually call home. We moved back here when I was eight or nine, I guess. Before that, I lived on the West Coast. In a van."

Cliff raises his dark eyebrows in interest. "In a van? Now, this is something I've got to hear."

The vodka feels like a surge of confidence, and an energy is slowly growing between us, something pulsing and palpable. Fueled by the alcohol and rush of his attention, a blush spreads across my chest and up my neck, loosening the vise with its warm ascent. Impulsively, my hands flutter to my neck, seeking the locket, needing to twist the chain and twiddle the gold oval between my thumb and forefinger. However, it has long been gone, and so I rest my fidgety hands in my lap.

"Yeah, we, uh, we lived in the van…" And without even realizing it, I take my ripped, wrinkled, back-of-the-envelope life story out and begin to unfold it for this willing stranger standing behind the bar.

Chapter 12: Remembering

How did we end up *here,* I wondered as I kicked a rotting apple into the overgrown roadside brush. My worn sneaker scattered the earth, and a plume of dust rose before me like a genie from a bottle. *Could you grant my only wish?* I silently begged the fading apparition. *Get me the hell out of here.*

The Mutt brothers ran by, crossing too close with their chaos, and I could smell their sweaty armpits. One of them knocked me in the elbow, causing me to drop the sweet Macintosh I'd just picked and only half eaten.

"Hey!" I yelled. But they'd reached the pond already, wrestling each other over who got to string the worm on the fishing line. They wouldn't have taken the time to hear my objections anyway. Nobody at Riverskeep did.

My nose tingled as more dust kicked up behind me, and I heard the crunch of tires over gravel. I took a large step sideways, treading carefully at the edge of the brush. Snakes lived in there, I just knew it. I'd seen a twittering brown tail slink in there just the other day. And we'd all heard the story about that girl Brenna getting bit by a copper. She's definitely not right in the head anymore. I'd be sure to avoid the same fate.

As I picked my way along the fervid growth, my mother's orange VW van rambled by. The white roof was dirtied to a seasoned beige, and the faded paisley curtains that hung in the windows swayed back and forth as the vehicle bounced over the pitted road.

Until we landed in Riverskeep, the van had been my only home. August and I slept as nomads, curled up in borrowed sleeping bags on its floor, curtains pulled tight against the wind while wolves and wandering strangers lurked in the night. Sometimes, after days of driving, August would stop off at a campground. Maybe at a state park or river reserve. She knew which ones had the bathrooms with indoor plumbing, and we'd stay long enough for the park ranger to kick us out.

Inside our van, the upholstered seats were crunchy with spilled milk, and it smelled of mildew, gasoline, and rotted fruit. But August had her windows down, and the rock and roll cranked loud over the van's aching dashboard speaker. Mr. Fred sat in the passenger seat beside my mother, puffing on a thin, white cigarette, nodding his head to the music and blowing plumes of smoke past his wispy beard and out the open window.

"Hey there, sister," he said, flashing me the peace sign and a shifty grin as they passed by. August didn't offer a greeting. Instead, I get her slow, hypnotic nod. Her eyes looked heavy, and her face had that faraway look that told me she, too, had been smoking.

The orange van swerved to a stop in front of Mr. Fred's place, a grass-thatched yurt with a tall red clay roof. He had the largest yurt at Riverskeep, probably because he's the one in charge, and he let August and I stay with him, for a little while, at least. Mr. Fred's yurt was one circular room, with a bed, cordoned off from the rest of the room by yellow sheets hanging from the thatched roof. The bed was nothing more than a large mattress propped off the splintered floor by long wood planks, and my mother slept there with him.

Another small mattress, draped in scratchy blankets, tucked into a curve on the other side of the round room, and I slept there each night. When the sun set and the heat of the day receded, Mr. Fred opened all the windows, and the sounds of the surrounding forest—the chirping squirrels and caw of the crows—whispered to me as I try to ignore the other sounds coming from behind the yellow sheets.

"It's not even a real pillow," I whined to my mother one night, punching the stained pillowcase filled with wadded-up shirts and socks. "I can't sleep here anymore. It's weird, and it always stinks of smoke in here. I just…Mama, I just don't belong here!"

I begged August to let me sleep back in the van, but she wouldn't hear of it. Maybe she worried I'd be harassed by the Mutt brothers or their weird daddy.

"We will not be ungrateful to our host, who lets us stay on this farm for free. Do you hear me, lil' girl?" she'd said, grabbing both of my wrists with her long, strong fingers, her green eyes aflame. "What would people say if I let an eight-year-old girl sleep alone in a cold van? Why, there's gypsies out there…and bears…and all sorts of predators looking for prey!"

It had been clear to me even then August grasped for reasons. I wanted to reply *we* were the gypsies, and *she* was the predator. But I didn't. Instead, I huddled each night on the broken spring mattress with the sock-stuffed pillowcase, wondering how I'd ever survive those people and that place.

Each weekday morning, I rose early to the aroma of stovetop coffee and marijuana, and I got up to get ready for school. I took care to dress quickly, throwing on mismatched clothes from the small duffel bag I kept beside my mattress. It was only one room we shared after all, and even though no one paid any attention to me, I had no intention of being bare-skinned for longer than necessary.

The small schoolhouse, an old, abandoned barn, sat at the bottom of the orchard hill. All the children of

Riverskeep piled into the slanted structure, and the teachers, actual mothers who live on the farm and take their turn, passed out paper and pencils and sometimes stubby crayons for the younger kids. The lessons, loose and unreliable, were just another way to pass the time until I could be free of Riverskeep forever.

Each day at dismissal, the younger kids scrambled down to the pond, and if it was hot, they'd jump right in, wearing nothing but their underwear. Most of the teenagers worked after school, usually picking apples, climbing up the trees for the highest red orbs and tossing them gently into a waiting burlap sack or crate, effectively meeting their mark without bruising the fruit.

On Sundays, August and the other young mothers braided each other's hair, tucked daisies behind their ears, put on their best bell bottoms, and piled in the back of Mr. Fred's old Toyota pickup. They would head to the big farmer's market in the city, where they'd sell their apples to make money for food and supplies for the commune. Though kids could not join them, I yearned to see the city and to feel the wind in my hair in the back of that pickup.

Each day dissolved into another day with meditations to the moon and the thick haze of marijuana seeping into our pores. With no path forward but the winding dirt roads that cut through the orchard, I could feel myself growing sour like the vinegar from the apples left to rot on the ground. But after the last bushel of the summer crop was picked and carted away to market, I started to notice a restless shift in August. I'd seen it in her before, the fidget of the wanderer, the certain uncertainty that meant something new and dangerous brewed, ready to burst through my mother's thin skin at any moment.

It was a Tuesday afternoon, school has just been released, and a rainstorm had just cleared the valley. The Mutt brothers and all their scruffy friends had been cooped up inside too long, and they'd taken to swinging like monkeys through the bare branches of the apple trees.

On days such as these, I usually passed them by, feeling no affection for their shenanigans. But on this particular day, I decided I'd join them, kicking my tired sneakers off in the mud and clawing my bitten fingernails into the soft wood as I climbed. It was something to do amidst another day of nothing, and before I know it, I found myself high enough to see the little kids splashing in their skivvies down at the pond.

I could taste the air, the damp chill from the low clouds coating my throat. I felt empowered in my perch, and I decided it might be okay to smile. I was all alone, after all. The other kids didn't even notice I was hiding amongst them in the brown branches.

But just as my lips relaxed, beginning their careful curve over my teeth, I saw her coming. Agitated and angry, wobbly on her feet, like a lion left to starve. The wind caught the loose ends of my long red hair, giving away my hiding place, so I quickly tucked the curls behind my ears. I tried to contract my limbs to make myself smaller, nothing more than a bird on a branch. But it was too late. August spotted me and stood at the foot of my tree, rattling the trunk. Her unexplained fury rose like an earthquake to the highest limbs.

"Grandma Patty has fallen ill," she said. "Get your butt outta that tree, and stop actin' the fool. We've gotta get our shit together and fast. We leave in the morning. Now go pack your things."

I trembled in the limbs, the smile on my lips dissolving into a quiver. The idea of *North Carolina* seemed foreign and friendly and foreboding all at once. I'd heard August speak of it many times but never fondly. There were mosquitoes, she'd said. Bugs who sucked your blood. And the people there, they'd suck your blood, too. But Grandma Patty lived there.

A thousand miles into our journey east, we learned that Grandma had died of a stroke. Right about the same time our van chugged across the Mojave Desert. In an instant, our path forward careened, cartwheeled, and settled with a dull thud.

Grandma's house now belonged to us, and Seaville would be our new home.

I couldn't wait to sleep in a real house with a real bed and a real pillow. I did regret Grandma wouldn't be there because I thought she would be my protector. But honestly, I just couldn't wait to put my head on that fluffy pillow.

Chapter 13: Connecting

Across the dimly lit bar top, Cliff leans in and listens with intent, an audience for me alone in spite of the other patrons who have slipped in the front door for a Friday drink. The sound of their chatter, with its simple banality, pulls me back to the present, and I'm vaguely aware of a guy in a trucker cap at the other end of the bar hoping Cliff will pour him a drink.

"So, I take it you're no longer an apple farmer?" Cliff asks with something like a wink (but decidedly cooler). He dries the inside of a pint glass.

"No, my tree-climbing days are over."

Cliff drains the remains of a bottle of bourbon into a stubby glass, and without even looking in his direction, slides it down the bar to the impatient customer in the trucker hat.

"Quite a story," he says. "And now you live…?"

"In New York."

"Family there?"

"My daughter," I reply. "And John. He's my… well, he used to be my husband."

I feel like I'm tripping over my words, slightly boozy, afraid I have become a cliche, alone at a bar pouring my guts out to the guy pouring drinks. John used to joke bartenders were really therapists without degrees.

"Excuse me just a second," Cliff says, moving down the bar to grab an order. I watch him work efficiently, lining up the highball glasses. Then, precise shots into the cocktail tin, two or three commanding shakes, ending the production with a seamless pour. A sprig of mint from the array of mason jars lined up behind the bar and garnish.

He returns to me with an apologetic smile, and I take the opportunity to change the subject. "So, you own this place?"

"Yeah, I moved down from Boston about two years ago. Just kind of needed a change. My dad left me his house on the other side of the bridge when he passed, and I'd always had this foolhardy dream to own an Italian restaurant. My mom—she's the best Italian cook ever! So, here I am." He extends his arms wide, beaming around his restaurant. "It's been a totally new frontier for me. I was a cop back in Boston, worked the unsolved crimes desk. So, that's also one of the, I don't know, attractions of this town, I guess."

"Huh." I slide an ice cube onto my tongue and nibble it gently. "What do you mean?"

Cliff pours, swirls, and shakes. He doesn't miss a beat when he looks up in surprise. "The murders in '67?" he asks.

I take a moment to think, notion and recollection colliding and creating much like the ingredients in Cliff's cocktail shaker.

"Nelson McCready," he continues. "Accused and acquitted."

"Ahh. Pop Gray's?" I snatch the remnant of memory from the overgrowth of weeds in my mind.

"That's it," Cliff says, snapping his fingers. "Never solved. And in fact," he puts his elbows on the bar and leans down low and intimate, dish towel falling off his shoulder, "they never wanted to solve it, if you ask me."

"Hmmm," I muse, leaning back to evade his proximity. "I'm afraid I don't remember too much about it. But you seem to be the local expert."

"Nah, not an expert. Just interested, I guess. My dad was a cop, too. Worked for the county sheriff down here, not the Seaville Police. They didn't get along back in those days—the sheriff's office and the town force." Cliff scratched the gruff beginnings of his five o'clock shadow, lost in his recollection.

"But my pops always said there was something no good about the case. It frustrated him, y'know? That these innocent girls were dead. Biggest crime of the decade down in these parts. He said the sheriff's office was ousted from the investigation, and I guess it pained him that he was never in a position to help find out who did it. So, I don't know, I guess maybe there's something about a kid wanting to tackle his father's unfinished business."

I nod in understanding, though I don't really have one, never knowing a father whose business I needed to finish.

"But I know there's lots of folks around here who know a hell of a lot more than me," he continues. "I try to keep my ear to the ground, though. You never know when the ghosts are gonna rise from the grave…"

A timid rain begins to fall as I head home, and I curse myself for leaving my umbrella at the bar. I pull my jacket collar higher and worry about Cliff's story as I walk back to my mother's house, the cocktail easing the hunch in my shoulders and slowing my gait. I'd heard bits and pieces of the tale in the past, and it sat in my mind in layers, an onion I'd never cared to peel, rotting in the back of the pantry.

As a kid, I do remember lurking with others on the corner in front of McCready's house on Halloween night. Someone would point up to the dark windows, shouting something like, "It's him! I see him! Run, y'all! He's gonna get us!"

Racing away feverishly with the cloak of my witch's cape flapping behind me, I knew then McCready *supposedly* did something very bad, and I was *supposed* to be scared. All the kids had been told to stay away at all costs from the creaky, old house on the corner. Their parents taught them, and their peers taunted them until that lesson became good and ingrained.

Even years later, at the big bonfires at the end of the island, where the high school kids would smoke their first cigarettes and pass around bottles of sweet wine coolers, someone always had ghost stories to share. I'd heard the tale then, through the hissing, popping campfire haze, of the ghosts that haunted Pop Gray's. In the back of my teenage mind, dizzy with wine coolers, I must have known about the connection between McCready and the ghost girls, but I'd never given it too much time.

My stroll through the gentle rain brings me back home, and as I stand before August's hoarding porch, lit only by one dim bulb in a cracked sconce, I can distinctly remember being that young girl bumming a Marlboro Light beside the campfire. I can feel the tug of the town mystery. Suddenly longing for a cigarette, I collapse into the rickety old rocker.

Gregor emerges from the house, startling me with a loud crack of the hingeless screen door. "Oh, I'm sorry. I didn't know you were back," he says.

I smile up at him with doubtful hope. "Any chance you have a cigarette?"

"Nah." Gregor laughs. "And you should not smoke. Very bad for you," he says pointing at his chest.

"I know," I say with a sigh, "and it's been years since I've had one, anyway. It's just being back here, you know?"

"Yes," says Gregor. "It is hard to come home to this."

I exhale, relieved to have him standing here with me amidst the squalor of my mother's porch.

"Your mother's vitals remain stable. This is good news," he continues. "I have made her comfortable for the night, and I expect she will sleep. If she wakes in pain or takes a turn for the worse, we can reevaluate the situation."

Gregor will sleep on a rollaway cot set up in the dining room, keeping company with the old walnut table covered in dust, the peeling fleur-de-lis wallpaper, and the burnt-out bulbs in Grandma Patty's chandelier.

"I'm sorry we don't have an actual room for you to stay in," I say with a sheepish grin.

"Oh, it's okay, I'm used to it. It's part of the job. Also, I'm young, so I don't need much sleep."

"I've heard that about your generation. You think sleep is overrated, huh? What do you do all night, Gregor, when you're not with a patient, changing bedpans?"

He laughs. "Mostly dance. We go to the clubs. There are a few near the university."

I can picture Gregor in this other life, unbound and flying free, maybe a tattoo on his shoulder, dancing to a pulsing rhythm on a dark and smoky dance floor. I pity he's here with me instead.

"Well, good night, Miss Jan. Try to get some sleep yourself. No dancing for you." He wags a joking finger and chuckles as he heads back into the house.

With the dreaded knowledge I will need to eventually clean the corners and crevices of this old house, and since it seems unlikely I'll have the option of dancing tonight, I decide I might as well start the endeavor sooner rather than later. I grab the vacuum off the front porch, peeling away cobwebs, hopeful it still works. I put on a kettle to make some hot tea and find a pair of rubber gloves and some Formula 409 under the sink.

I start in my old bedroom, removing the top layer of grime that has settled after years of neglect. I strip the twin bed with its faded pink comforter, the same one I'd grown up with, then begin the search for clean sheets.

At the top of the bedroom closet, I find four or five boxes wedged tight on a high shelf. Wondering if any of them contain sheets, I pull them down and scatter them across the floor. One appears to hold linens, but as I start to dig through it, nothing resembles bedsheets. I see some frayed, white silk napkins from an old dinner set and two pairs of infant pajamas, withered and yellowed with time. These, I assume, had once been mine, when I'd been small and innocent enough to wear them.

I don't remember a mother who had cared enough to dress me in night clothes and cradle me in her arms. That rare connection we had once shared had been lost to time and rough-edged rancor.

"I named you Janus to mark my new beginnings," August had announced one night, stepping into this very room and setting down her bourbon. I can feel the very moment as if it were the present, the syrupy smell of my mother's breath and the rough brush of her fingers as she tried to help me unweave the twisted braid I'd attempted to tie in my long, curly hair.

"Janus was the god of time. Beginnings and endings. He has two faces, you see," she said with a hard yank of my hair. "He looks to the future and to the past."

"What were you beginning?" I'd asked as my red strands tumbled free from their captivity one by one. I sat there grateful for her calm attention.

August laughed at the question. "Why, I was beginning an end to all of this," she said, her arm sweeping the bedroom.

"Beginning and ending all at the same time," I whisper to myself now, standing in the doorway of this closet of forgotten things.

I dig into another box piled high with scraps and leftovers from my school days, my old yearbook from 1990 balanced on top. Dust powders the air as I flip the glossy pages, chock full of high school bands and hair-sprayed bangs. Heartfelt inscriptions from old friends read: "We will never be far apart," "you mean everything to me!", and "Best friends forever."

Right. I wonder briefly what had become of those kids, though truly, I suspect most of them still live somewhere down the block.

In this same box, I find the charcoal drawing I'd entered into a local art contest my junior year, which had surprisingly won second place and a fifty-dollar check. A horse and her foal grazing on green grass, a blue barn in the background.

"Why is the barn blue?" Reena had asked me in the high school cafeteria when I showed her what I planned to enter into the contest. "Aren't barns usually red?"

"Yeah, I guess so," I'd pondered. "I was trying to copy this picture hanging up at home. That one of August when she was a girl. She's standing in front of a blue barn like this. Pretty sappy, huh?"

"Nah," Reena contended. "It's cool."

I had no idea August had kept these tokens of the past—report cards, school portraits, and a newspaper clipping mentioning my art contest winnings. For such a cold-hearted woman, it is a surprising amount of prideful nostalgia.

Deeper in, I find my old mixtapes and a collection of albums that belonged to my mother. Gladys Knight, the

Beatles, and a few from the Bee Gees. I run my fingers down the spine of a Simon and Garfunkel album jacket, remembering "The Sounds of Silence" playing over and over again as I tried my best to stay submerged in a lukewarm bath, my mother's muffled crying behind her bedroom door.

At the very bottom of the cardboard box, beneath the albums, my fingers find a felty swatch of cloth. I pinch and pull to retrieve a squashed pink pillbox hat. I punch its insides to bully it back into shape when I notice a small "P" etched in the center in silky white thread. It smells of mildew as if it had been put away wet so many years ago.

The hat certainly had never been mine, and it looks nothing like a fashion August would have attempted, even back when she still cared about such things.

Grandma, it dawns on me. *Yes, Grandma Patty.* I laugh to myself, envisioning dowdy, pin-curled Grandma Patty in this flashy monogrammed hat, the haute couture of its day. Grandma P trying to pull off Jackie O.

I decide to try it on. Carefully, as if it's made of slivered glass, I position the wrinkled pink hat on my head just so before I realize the room has no mirror. I tiptoe into the hallway bath in disguise, holding the hat askew on my head. A sound, something between a rustle and a commotion, emanates from August's room. I flagrantly toss the treasured hat back into the waiting box and move toward the noise.

The shades are drawn, but in the dark room, I hear the unmistakable sound of crumpling paper, and it draws me closer. She's awake. I can see the outline of her gray head, barely raised above the pillow, her neck muscles straining, a small grunting sound smuggling its way out of her throat. As I watch, she rips pages from a book she holds firmly in the bony arches of her hand.

"August?" I ask, alarmed both at her struggle and her efficiency. I move in to take the offending book away, but my mother's strong grasp surprises me.

"Nooooo," she moans in response, leaking small guttural grunts.

As I try to maneuver what I can now determine is a journal out of her grasp, she manages to rip another few pages from its binding. She winces in pain with each jerking motion, and a weak flick of her wrist sends the pages scattering to the floor. The effort has drained her, and beads of sweat build on her brow. She collapses back into the pillow with a toss of her wild mane of greasy hair, moaning her displeasure.

"What is it, August? *What*?"

"This *thing* inside me…" August grumbles, her angry words slurred. She coughs, and a little spittle lands on her chin.

"I know, I know. There's fluid on your lungs…"

"What day is it?" August asks. "And what's the phase of the moon?" More coughing.

"Um, it's Saturday, I think." I lean in closer to try to peek inside the open journal. "And uh…almost full, I think?"

"No!" August retaliates. "The date, Janus. No…vember?" Her question starts strong but begins to dissolve in the stale air before fully realized.

"Oh, I don't know." I try to calculate the days since Thanksgiving, which I remember fell on November 23 this year. "I guess it would be the twenty-fifth."

"Uh-huh," August says in a thick whisper. "Riiiight. Full moon…tomorrow is your birfffdayyy."

"My *what*?" I lean in even closer, unsure if I've heard her correctly. "My birthday? No, August, my birthday is in December. Not for a few more weeks."

But she slips back into slumber, a small whimper that may have intended to be a word dying on her tongue.

Gregor appears bedside, rubbing the sleep from his own eyes.

"It's okay, Miss Jan," he says, "I can sit with her for a while." He checks the fluid level in her IV drip and her pulse, then takes a few notes on the chart he has clipped on the foot of her bed.

The journal pages are scattered among the crimson bedcovers and littering the floor. I gather them in the dark, then turn on a low lamp beside the armchair, trying to smooth and restructure them. I see August's handwriting, loopy and large, sprawled across every page.

Jan 18, 2017

There is nothing more to say on the subject of my death. It is not a question of will I live or will I die anymore. I will die. The doctors told me this morning. So, that is settled. I will not bemoan it here any longer.

There are some things I should set right. These are the holes in my loneliness.

I will call Janus, and I will call Geraldine.

I will make sure the cat who keeps coming around is okay. I can't keep feeding her.

I guess this is how it is supposed to be, how it is supposed to end.

I will get all I deserve, and the universe will have its way.

The house remains silent, save for the soft whir of the monitors beside August's bed. I squirm in the quietness. *Who is Geraldine? And what happened to the cat?*

The pages crumpled in my lap pull me with a force of their own, so I keep reading.

March 12, 2017

While I can still walk, I will go visit the farm and pay my respects. I don't know how I will get up there since I can't drive anymore. I haven't been in so many years. I'm not sure if I can even find it now.

I feel my mind slipping, but I have the memories— the good ones and the bad ones. I can't keep them in line, and it's making me so angry.

Yes, I am angry all the time now.

September 25, 2017

Ribbons and lace.

They made up my face.

Tear it apart.

Find your true heart.

So sad they will never learn.

It had to be my turn.

I smash my palm across the page to iron out the creases as if the force of its press could change the shape of the letters on the page. A poem. August had written a poem. Never in a million years would I have reasoned she cared enough about *anything* to express herself in rhyme.

I knew about her journal. She'd kept one for as long as I can remember. She'd scribble something fervent in it, secret to everyone, her back hunched protectively over the page. Then, she'd hide it away, God knows where, until her next hailstorm of emotion.

I suppose I had always assumed the journal was just another manifestation of my mother's self-inflicted drama. I mean, really, what could she possibly have to hide, this ill-willed, cranky librarian and drunk of a mother? No story there seemed worth telling.

But now this preposterous poem, which gives me pause to reconsider some of my forgone conclusions about my mother.

I wake the next morning disoriented, my numb limbs dangling off a kid-sized bed, but the scent of freshly brewed coffee hovers in the air. When I consult the bathroom mirror, it confirms how I feel—tousled, tired, and tempted to run. I *am* a flight risk here, for sure.

"You look like you could use a drink," Gregor snickers when I shuffle barefoot into the kitchen. He offers me a steaming cup of coffee, and it may be the best cup of coffee I have ever tasted, the caffeine soothing and stabilizing. Much like the cocktail at Clifford's last night, reminding me I'll have to go back and get that damn umbrella.

Gregor quickly sets about attending to August, who has just woken up but seems unable or unwilling to speak to anyone this morning. I can see it settled in her eyes, the smoke of her anger. *But it's just smoke*, I think, *the fire is gone*. Her eyelids appear heavy. Something seems to have slipped out of her focus in the night.

I watch from the doorway as Gregor expertly lifts and rotates my mother's arms and legs, then massages her neck and chest and all of its flappy folds with oil that smells of lavender and mint.

The torn pages from August's journal litter her bedside table, and I make a mental note to retrieve the whole book once Gregor finishes with his therapy.

After a hot shower, I call John to check in.

"She's still alive?" John chuckles, but his laughter quickly cedes to concern when I meet his question with stone-cold silence. "Okay, okay. Sorry. But seriously, how are you holding up?"

"Oh, I'm fine, really. I mean, I think." I sigh, a long overdue exhale. "I'm trying to stay positive."

The comfort of John, of confiding in him, has always eased my panic. His voice across the line lifts some measure of the burden. It was one of the reasons I fell in love with him, I suppose.

"You know, Jan, you've got to take care of yourself, too," John says. "Your mother has always had a way of sabotaging you and your well-being. It's still happening now, you know, even in her weakened state."

"I know," I reply, not missing his insinuation and growing defensive. "You don't think I have put that together myself? I'm just trying to get through this, okay?"

"Okay, okay. I can see you've learned well, young Jedi," he responds. "So, she's holding on. Is she eating? Talking? Does she have any mobility?"

"No, she won't eat, and she's completely bedridden. She seems barely able to lift a finger. And she's not talking a lot. She's sleeping, and there's the oxygen mask…but she's had a few choice words for me."

John clucks sympathetically on the other end of the line.

"Last night, she had this moment," I continue. "I don't know, maybe she was dreaming or something. But there was all this moaning and carrying on, and I go in there, and she's sitting up, or trying to sit up, and she's ripping pages out of her journal. It was all very violent and unsettling."

"Something she wants to hide?" John asks. "Details on a lover from her past that she wants forgotten?"

A lover? Of course, though I hadn't even considered that possibility. It didn't seem possible. She's just so…unlovable. But as a younger woman, when she had it a little more together, perhaps. August once owned a unique beauty—fox-red hair, striking eyes, a color that hovered somewhere between lily pad and ancient fern, and her figure full and defiant. Men noticed her. They knew she was single, and maybe even presumed she was looking for a man. I would see them cast curious, needy glances her way. She tended to scare these men, but she intrigued them as well. August had been attractive in a moth to a flame kind of way.

"Honestly, the thought of discovering a secret lover makes me shudder," I admit. "It's like, when you think you know something about your past, you think you understand your history, but then — well, you realize, you just *don't*. I have to say, I'm having a hard time keeping a grip on things here."

John sighs heavily. "Okay, so call me anytime you feel it slipping. Anytime at all. I'm here. And let me know if you want me to prescribe something for you, something to help you deal with everything."

I return his sigh as I hang up the phone, but my shoulders and spine have loosened up. If nothing else, I'll keep John's offer of valium is in my back pocket, as there is no telling what drama the next few days may hold.

I scrub some hard-set rings from August's bathtub later that morning because it distracts me from the reality of my situation. Just as I finish up, I hear a knock on the front door.

Reena's face greets me through the glass windowpane.

"Reena!" I exclaim, glad to see her standing on my mother's step with a large brown paper bag in one hand and a bouquet of flowers in the other.

"Girl, that garden looks terrible. Your grandma must be rolling in her grave. But I brought these for you," she says, thrusting the bouquet at my chest. "Thought you might want to brighten up the place. And I brought lunch."

"You are a godsend, my friend. There's only old-people food in these cupboards. Lots of oatmeal and Campbell's soup."

"Oh, I know all about it," Reena says, unpacking the brown bag. "Many days I leave the hospital smelling like orange Jell-O. Did you know you can *smell* like orange Jell-O?"

Her paper bag holds chicken salad sandwiches, pasta salad, fancy little cakes for dessert, and, of course, sweet tea. "Wine of the south," I say with approval, pulling out glasses and some of my mother's chipped China plates.

"How is she doing?" Reena asks.

"Still alive," I answer, scooping pasta onto her plate. "And still a pain in the ass." I pause for effect. "Because she's still my mother."

"I take it distance has not made the heart grow fonder."

"I don't know, Reena. I mean, honestly, I feel terrible that I've abandoned her and haven't visited in all these years. I am literally the only family she has. But it's like we live on two different planes of existence. She never asks me about my life, not to mention her only grandchild. I feel…kind of like she died a long time ago."

Reena gives my bicep a sympathetic squeeze, her long lacquered nails cool against my skin. She hesitates for a minute, hedging on her thoughts before proceeding gently.

"I will say," she starts, "that your mother has come to be known as a bit of an eccentric about town."

"Oh, that would kill her if she knew that," I reply. "All that has ever mattered to her is appearances—what people thought about her, how she was accepted, and did she fit in."

"Oh, I think she knows," Reena says. "I didn't fill you in on a lot because, well, it's been a while since we've talked, and I knew the two of you were estranged. But Miss August, she's been a bit of a spectacle this past year."

I look up from my pasta salad, intent to hear more but not wanting to hear more.

"First, she decided to give it good to Mrs. Lackey at the grocery store," Reena continues. "I'm not sure what caused it or what the outburst was about. But she told her, and anyone within earshot, to go straight to hell if she looked at her 'like that' one more time. And she threw a cantaloupe at her."

"Oh my god! A cantaloupe?"

"Then, apparently, there were some kids going door to door, selling baked goods for their church." I brace myself for what could be worse than a hurled melon. "The way Sally tells me it happened," Reena explains, "your mother snatched their Bible right from their little elementary school hands and took to yelling at them. She said it was full of lies, and they might as well just have fun in life. Worship the devil because they were all going to burn for their sins anyway."

My eyes grow wide, my forkful of salad freezing in mid-air. "Damn" seems like the only appropriate word in response, so I settle my fork and hang my head with familial shame. I knew it had been bad, but not *this* bad.

"You ask me," Reena says, reaching across the table to refill her tea, "that eclectic front porch is also her way of giving the finger to the town."

I cradle my forehead in my hands. "Oh, Reena, eclectic is such a polite way to say that she's batshit crazy."

"I know, I'm sorry," she says, clearing the dish I had pushed away, helping in any way she can even while laying it on the line for me. "I'm not telling you these stories to hurt you."

"I know, I know," I reassure her, grasping for the phantom locket around my neck, then nervously folding and unfolding the napkin I'd tucked in my lap. "It's just always been so complicated with August. I've obviously known her my whole life, but I cannot tell you who she is. I don't know why she's so angry either. Gregor says the pain can make people crazy. But we both know it started way before the pain. You should have heard her last night, Reena. Wailing like a baby, tearing up shit. She seemed so confused…I mean, she thought it was my *birthday*." I roll my eyes and Reena chuckles. "I think I'm just realizing I don't know very much about her. Her childhood, her friends, her parents…"

"Oh yes, Miss Patty," Reena says, gazing around the outdated kitchen that used to be Grandma's. "You know, I came to this house with my Grandma Lou before you and your mom moved into town. Our grandmothers were friends. She'd bring me here sometimes when they played bridge. I'd hide out under the table with crayons and marbles. Probably this very same table." She gives a solid knock to the surface. "The place actually hasn't changed that much."

"Huh. You knew my grandmother?" I ask, surprised Patty dared to socialize with a woman of color back in the 70s. It suddenly occurs to me Reena might be able to help fill in some of the holes in my own story.

"Well, I was six, so I'm not sure how well I *knew* her. But I do remember her shuffly little husband. He looked just like Mr. Magoo."

I laugh out loud, almost spitting out my mouthful of iced tea.

"I remember he would come around when the grandmas were playing cards," she continues. "Shuffle in, shuffle out, asking where dinner was. I remember being under the table, watching those brown slippers just sliding back and forth across the floor."

"Ha! It's funny the things we remember, isn't it?" I say, wiping the tea off my lower lip. "He actually wasn't my real grandfather, you know. At least, I don't think so. I never met him. But I remember August saying that Patty had taken in a man to support her and keep her living within her means. He apparently disappeared before Grandma Patty died. Not sure if he ran away, or maybe he just died, too.”

Reena nods as if she has always known this, and so I continue.

“August hated her mother, hated this town…I was pretty shocked when she told me we were moving back here. I’d only met Grandma Patty once when she flew out to California and took us to stay in a hotel. I remember her saying that a girl needed a proper bed to sleep in. Oh, and the swimming pool! It was the first time I had been in such a clean body of water, not some dirty-old watering hole! I absolutely fell in love with the chlorine, the smell that stayed in your hair and the squeaky clean on your skin. They couldn’t get me out of that pool!” I laugh at the memory. “But I would have liked a chance to get to know Patty. Maybe it would have helped me to understand my own mother a little more.”

“Well, my friend,” Reena says, settling the dish towel she had used to clean the dishes while we talked. “Just be grateful that you are the apple that fell far from the tree.”

My thoughts cut to Cliff, asking me if I was still an apple farmer, and a small smile escapes the corners of my mouth. I push back from the table to help pack up the leftovers before stumbling on a thought.

"Reena, do you happen to know someone named Geraldine?"

Her brow knits together, and her mouth twists quizzically.

"Because there was a Geraldine in August's journal. Someone in her life…"

"Well, let me think," Reena starts, tucking her chin over her clasped hands. "Now that you mention it, there was this one lady who I saw your mother with a bunch. Not recently, though. A year or two ago, maybe? I never knew her name, but they would shop for groceries together, or I'd see her drop your mother at the post office. I just assumed she was a friend or cousin or something, staying with her for a while."

A cousin. August had never had any friends, but perhaps Geraldine could be distant family.

"And you haven't seen her recently? No way for me to get in touch?" I ask.

"Sorry, Jan, I haven't. I can ask around, though. Bill—you know, the custodian you met at the hospital— he's actually my cousin. I think he knew your mother back in the day, so he might know. And I can ask Grandma if she remembers anything that might help."

"Grandma Lou? The one who played bridge with Patty? She's still alive?"

"Ninety-six, can you believe it? Good genes, I guess."

"Well, maybe I could meet her?"

Reena looks surprised as she pulls on her coat. "Sure, I guess so. She lives with my uncle over on Sullivan Street. I'll call over there later." She gives me a quick hug as she heads out the door, and I finish my sweet tea in one long, satisfying gulp.

Chapter 14: Seeking

Reena calls over to Uncle Joe's not once but twice later that afternoon. Both of them are hard of hearing, Reena decides, and if they're not standing right beside the phone, there's no use in calling again. Instead, she detours on her way to the night shift at the hospital and gives a quick knock on Joe's front door.

"Reena!" Uncle Joe says, surprised to see her. He eyes her medical scrubs. "You just getting off work?"

"No, I'm on my way," Reena says, stepping into the front foyer. In Uncle Joe's house, an open door equates to an explicit invitation to come inside. She can smell something crispy and fried in the air, and she sniffs the scent in dramatic fashion, raising her nose in appreciation.

"You want some dinner?" Uncle Joe asks. He turns back toward the kitchen.

"No, thanks." Reena smiles. "I just need to ask Grandma a question. Is she awake?"

"She should be." Joe chuckles. "It's time for *Jeopardy*, ain't it?"

Joe heads into the kitchen to finish cooking, and Reena turns down the short hall toward the living room.

Grandma Lou sits pinprick straight on the edge of her seat with half a bowl of orange slices at her side.

"Who is Wallace Stevens?" she shouts at the TV. Someone on the screen offers a different answer, and the *Jeopardy* buzzer scolds them. "It's Wallace Stevens!" She turns to acknowledge Reena as she enters the room. With a dismissive click of the remote, the TV goes dark. "Hey there, baby. Some fools on that *Jeopardy*."

"Maybe we should get you on the show then, Grandma." Reena chuckles, settling on the couch across from her.

"No, I'm too old to be flying cross the country for a damn game show. But tell me, to what do I owe the pleasure of this visit?"

"I just have a quick question for you. It's for a friend of mine. You might remember her. She moved out before we finished school, but I think you knew her grandmother…"

Mary Lou raises the remnants of her eyebrows in an inquisitive manner and selects an orange slice from the bowl resting by her knee.

"Miss Patricia? Littleton?"

Grandma's mouth flips into a quick smile before she reconsiders, letting the corners of her mouth fall into a frown. "Aah, yes. I remember Patty. What's this about then, honey?"

Reena reaches across to grab a slice of orange for herself.

"Well, you see, Patty's granddaughter, the one I went to school with, she's back in town for a few days because her mother, August, is not well. She's dying, actually."

Grandma Lou nibbles on the skin of the orange.

"And well, Jan—that's Patty's granddaughter—is trying to connect her mother with any long-lost friends who might want to say goodbye. She's specifically looking for a person named Geraldine. Does that name ring a bell to you? Maybe someone you remember from the bridge club or something?"

Mary Lou shakes her head and turns her attention back to the bowl of oranges. "'Fraid not, honey," she answers, clearing her throat in polite finality.

"Okay." Reena wipes a piece of pulp on the thigh of her scrubs. "Worth a try." She gives her grandmother a quick kiss on the cheek and hurries back to her car, aware she's dangerously close to being late for her shift.

Grandma Lou watches her granddaughter through the window, still so young and fit, full of energy and questions. Shame she hasn't met a husband by now.

Mary Lou scratches the whiskers on her chin in reflection. When she had been young and free, she couldn't stay away from the boys. Friday nights down at the boardwalk at Shell Beach, a clapboard walkway lit by sand torches, and vaudeville all around. The sweet smell of crispy cornmeal, and the men strutting by in their dapper suits and bowler hats. Everyone making eyes at one another while the waves crashed and the seagulls circled for scattered popcorn, it all felt like an elaborate dance.

She recalls that she actually took Patricia down to Shell with her once, and she was a conspicuous redhead with freckles bobbing through a sea of ebony. It made Mary Lou giggle at the time and even now.

"*Why* is everyone staring at me?" Patricia had whispered, panic rising in her voice. Mary Lou remembered the way she wobbled down the boardwalk in her high heels, awkward and uptight like a chess piece in enemy territory. It had been too much for Patty. Mary Lou had walked her home. It was a bad idea to let anyone as white and frightened as Patricia Littleton into her own world of glorious color.

Chapter 15: Partying

A few hours later, Brian honks his horn from the curb in front of August's house. I grimace and reconsider my decision to go to Tara's party. But considering the state of my mother's home and porch, I wonder if Brian feels too intimidated to venture further, and I decide to give him the benefit of the doubt. I grab a jacket and slide into his passenger seat.

"Your mom's place is looking good," he jokes. I reward his sarcasm with a laugh and relax into the deep bucket seat of his old Jeep.

"That's what my husband said, too."

Brian nervously clears his throat at my clumsy attempt to reinforce that the evening isn't a date. Since it's a shitty thing for me to do, I quickly change the subject.

"So, Tara's party is the cool place to be tonight?"

"Jan, this is Seaville, not New York," Brian replies with an edge of resentment as he pulls away from the curb. "Tara's party is the *only* place to be tonight."

A few moments of uncomfortable silence pass between old friends, who are now, clearly, virtual strangers.

Brian tries again to break the ice. "So, how *is* your mom?"

"Crazy," I respond. "And pretty sick. The hospital sent in a hospice nurse, so it's just a matter of time, I would think."

"I'm sorry, Jan," he says, his resentment softening to sympathy. "My mom passed two years ago. She had lung cancer. Lifelong smoker."

"Oh, wow. Now, *I'm* sorry. I didn't know." Brian had one of those mothers I'd always envied, the kind that set the table for dinner and sat front row at her kid's soccer games. The kind who sang "Happy Birthday" with unapologetic volume at birthday parties.

He nods in acknowledgment, and the car falls quiet again. We pass Sally's house and the old McCready house on the corner. I can hear the loud *tick, tick, tick* of the turn signal as Brian patiently waits for a slow sedan to pass, then navigates the old Jeep toward Main Street.

"So, whatever happened to McCreepy?" I ask, recalling my conversation with Cliff as the rundown home recedes in my side-view mirror.

"Uh, I think he still lives there," Brian says.

"No way," I reply, the doubt evident in my tone. "He was such a social pariah. You'd think he would have turned tail and beat it out of here."

Brian shrugs and cruises slowly over the bridge. "Well, you make a home somewhere, and it's hard to leave."

I think of August. Why did she choose to stay here all these years when it seemed to make her so miserable?

"Well, he's just an old man now," Brian continues. "Still mostly keeps to himself, though. I've seen him from time to time walking his dog. He always has on this weird long coat, even in the summer. Yeah, he's still a little creepy."

As we pull in front of Tara's house, one of the ostentatious Victorians on Main Street, holiday chatter and music reverberate out the open front door. I brace myself for forced merriment and questions that require polite answers.

Inside the tinseled entryway, we're greeted with a tray of cranberry punch precariously balanced on the fingertips of our hostess. Tara's hair curls in blonde ringlets, and she shimmies toward us in her sparkling red dress, looking just like a Christmas ornament. I glance down at my jeans and boots and realize I had not dressed appropriately for the party.

Tara notices my discomfort and puts me at ease with a dismissive wave of the hand. "Oh, never you mind, you. Come over here, and give me a hug, Janus." She passes off the tray to a young server in a white shirt and bowtie.

Tara came from old money, and the home she inherited must have once been a grand plantation. A sweeping, trellised oak staircase curls around an intricate crystal chandelier, leading its descendants into a velvet-draped front hall. Beyond lies a proper sitting room with stiff-backed embroidered couches and a grand piano. And the biggest fireplace I have ever seen boasts a barn burner tonight.

"How is your mama?" Tara asks, properly painting her face with sympathy while reaching her empty hands to my shoulders to take my coat.

I shrug the thin jacket off and try to blend into the merriment. I feel stuck on the threshold of this scene, trying to understand my role. These people never made it out of this town, and I find myself wanting to scoff at their simplicity. Almost instantly, I regret accepting Brian's invitation, but I try hard to hide that I'd rather be anywhere else but here.

"She's not doing well, Tara." I sigh, letting the part of me that is a daughter worthy of condolences win my internal struggle. "But we expected it. She has congestive heart failure. We knew this time would come." I'm beginning to accept the script written for me, and with practice, I think I can master the scene.

"Bless your heart," Tara says, taking me by the elbow and leading me deeper into the throngs of revelers, toward a small bar set up beside the fireplace. "Let's get you a stronger drink." She replaces my cranberry punch with a bourbon on the rocks, which I gladly accept.

"And how is the acting going?" she asks. "I heard you were going to be a regular on *One World, One Life*. I saw you on a few shows, and then *poof*—you were gone."

"Oh," I say, peering down at Tara's peep-toed high heels, then at my scuffed city boots. "We had some professional differences, you could say."

"Too bad. That was always my mama's favorite soap." Tara motions to a waiter passing a tray of shrimp cocktails. Released from my inquisition as she begins to detail which hors d'oeuvres she'd like passed around next, I take a quick survey of the party, hoping to see Reena, before I realize the event seems like a whites-only crowd. Some things never change in Seaville, and I'd be fooling myself to assume a descendant of slaves would ever get invited into the plantation house. Not even in the twenty-first century.

I spend the next hour or two making small talk with forgotten friends and shaking the hands of people I'll likely never see again. I nibble on ham pinwheels and spicy cheese straws, and I answer a hundred stupid questions about New York City and the soap opera. It's still better than being cooped up in that house with August. Yuletide jazz plays from cleverly hidden speakers, and drinks are poured liberally by a heavyset man wearing reindeer antlers, whom I presume to be Tara's husband. Everyone gets smashed.

By ten thirty, the party starts to wind down. Brian had more than a few bourbons and looks nowhere close to planning his leave, so I resign myself to one last drink beside the fire.

Lisa, someone I vaguely remember from high school, leans on the back of the sofa, chatting animatedly with a lady named Connie, who I met earlier. Connie's dressed from head to toe in crimson velvet, including pumps her feet ooze out of.

"My feet are killing me," I hear her say. "Let's sit down." She then wobbles around the couch. I check my phone for any emergency texts from Gregor, and I catch fragments of the ladies' conversation.

"Cannot believe how much that street has changed since you moved in…" Lisa says, her words slightly slurred.

"I can't *wait* until they start tearin' down some of those older homes. Did that old lady who lives at the end of the block, the one with that terrible porch, croak yet?" Connie asks, sliding off a shoe and rubbing her swollen foot.

Noticing my presence, Lisa stops short and throws a panicked glance my way. "Uh…" she mumbles.

Eager to see Connie try to dig out of her hole, I join the conversation. "It's okay, Lisa." I pause to accept her audible sigh of relief. "That's my mother in that house." I turn to Connie, who seems busy evaluating her swollen foot. "And yes, I agree. The house is a disaster."

I can see the blood drain from Connie's face, then quickly return as bright-red spots on the apples of her cheeks. Her complexion winds up a suitable match for her outfit.

"It's her heart," I explain, feeling slightly less burdened as I share the story with strangers. "And I don't think she'll live much longer. I'm here just for a bit to… help?" It comes out as a question. I'm not really sure why I'm here. "Yes. To help," I reaffirm, hoping to convince myself.

Connie gulps down her drink and whispers, "I am so sorry. I didn't mean anything by it."

I offer her a polite smile, silently commending myself for walking the high road. "But to answer your *real* question," I continue, "I'm not sure what will happen to the house. It was my grandmother's home, and she lived there her whole life. Seems a shame to tear it down. But I'm an only child, and I don't want it."

Behind Connie and Lisa, the logs in the enormous fireplace are burning low, settling. There's a soft hiss from the dying fire.

"I mean, how do you *stay* here?" I confront the two ladies with the question that had been percolating inside me since I'd headed south on Thanksgiving Day.

They recoil at the inquiry, then look to each other for help.

"Well, what I mean is…what *keeps* you here? Lisa, you've lived here your whole life, am I right?"

Lisa nods, slow and cautious, still wary of my attack.

"I mean, really," I carry on, well aware I've shifted gears and run off the high road, ready to plow into a ditch. "Aren't you *bored* of everything that's been the same your entire life? Don't you feel *trapped* here?"

Lisa hiccups, which turns into a slight giggle as her relief at my offense takes over. "Well, that's just what we were talking about when you sat down, Jan," she counters with her own drunken insistence. "It's *not* the same here, not anymore. This town has changed *so* much from when we were in school. Why, just in these past few years, folks from out of town have been pouring in, buying up all the old houses that have fallen by the wayside, tearing the shit down and building something shiny and new. Honestly, it's keeping the island afloat. If you'll excuse the pun. They're coming in from Atlanta and from Richmond. People want to escape the cities. You know how that is."

I don't respond to the implication that I must want to escape *my* city, which I very much do not. I've only been gone a few days, but it feels like weeks. I miss my tiny apartment strewn with Laney's worn sneakers, borrowed books, and dirty coffee mugs. I miss the honking and bellowing from the street below, the drafty windows, and the way the air feels electric when I step out into the night.

Lisa continues, intent on providing proof of life for our hometown. "There's a shopping mall now just outside of town. You can get there before you even finish your morning coffee. And if you do finish your coffee, well, they've got a coffee shop! And there's a gym, too. A real gym with treadmills and a tanning bed that will keep you tan in the *winter*." Lisa shows off her bronze forearms with boozy pride.

"And we also have that new restaurant in town," Connie offers, the embarrassment beginning to recede into her pale cheeks and the pattern of her freckles reemerging. "Clifford's. It's a really nice place. You should go. This gorgeous man swooped into town last year and opened up a fabulous restaurant. Nicer than this town has ever seen. I swear, it's the best pasta I've ever had. And y'all, you'd never know he's from up North. He is hot *and* friendly."

Brian settles into a chair beside the couch, a fresh drink in hand, convincing me I will indeed be walking home tonight. "Cliff's place?" he asks, leaning in eagerly, his drink sloshing just a little. "You found it last night, Jan, right?"

"Yes. Right where you said it was," I reply, making another mental note to go get that damn umbrella first thing in the morning.

"Didn't you love it?" he asks with a big whiskey grin.

"Oh, I just had a drink," I answer. "But you're correct, ladies, it's downright fancy for Seaville. And that Cliff…he's something else. All sorts of crazy ideas about this town." I swirl the brown liquor over my melting ice cubes.

"What do you *mean,* Jan? What ideas?" Lisa asks, somewhat bothered and defensive.

"Well, he's like some big-city sleuth here to solve our town's mysteries." I laugh as I hear myself saying *our* town, and I almost correct my statement to relinquish any ownership of the place. *Your mysteries*, I want to say. *I belong to New York City.*

Brian takes a long pull on his drink, pondering my words.

"Okay, I'll bite," Connie says. "What mysteries?"

"You know what I'm talking about, Brian." I turn to him for reinforcement. "Why, we just passed his house on the way here…McCreepy?"

"Oh yeah, right." Brian nods. "McCreepy and the dead girls."

"*Dead* girls?" Connie straightens abruptly. Another log crumbles over the grate, and she startles as it snaps behind her.

Brian scoots his chair closer to the couch, his drink sloshing and landing with a splash on Connie's discarded pump. He's close enough now I can smell his whiskey breath.

"So, my dad told me that when he was in high school, must have been '67 or '68, this guy, McCready—you know, we used to call him McCreepy when we were kids—went crazy and walked into Pop Gray's with a gun and shot the two girls who were working there."

"Oh my! That's terrible." Connie twists her red lips.

"And they never even caught him," Lisa adds in between hiccups.

"Well, Lisa," Brian scolds, "they actually *caught* him, but he was acquitted. He never did the time. He got off as a free man and has been haunting the streets of Seaville ever since."

"Oh, come on, that's like a horror movie," Connie breathes. "You mean, the strange, tall man who lives in the big dark house on the corner of Chestnut? With the trench coat and the yappy little dog?"

"Yeah, that's the one," Brian says, turning to me. "But what does Cliff know about McCready? Isn't he from Boston?"

I shrug. "I was wondering the same thing. He seems a little preoccupied with it. Says it's one of the reasons he came down here. I guess he used to live here, and his dad worked for the county sheriff or something like that."

"Oh, this is just so awful. A child killer living right in our own community. We *need* to do something about this." Connie stands up and stumbles, then tries to regain her indignation. "Lisa, how come you never told me about this?"

Lisa giggles drunkenly, handing Connie her missing shoe and staggering to her own feet. "Because I forgot all about it, that's why. It all happened years before I was even born. Don't worry 'bout it, Connie. Just some town folklore, that's all."

The two friends hook arms and sway over to the punch bowl.

"Hmm." Intrigued, Brian's expression looks like that of an amateur sleuth. "We should go ask him."

"Who? Cliff? What, now?" I look at my watch, and the hour is late. Gregor remains at home, tending to the needs of my mother, hopefully withstanding the insult and fury she is likely slinging his way.

Don't get sidetracked. Focus, Jan. Go home. Tend to the matters that brought you here.

But Brian pulls me to my feet, shoveling through a pile of coats in the hallway to find ours, cheek kissing Tara goodbye. I wave to the hostess over my shoulder as Brian pulls me out the front door.

"All right," I reluctantly agree. "But we're walking. No way I'm getting in a car with you."

"Fair enough," he says, offering his elbow to guide me down the front steps. The cool earth and the warm air have collided in a conspiracy of fog, and it settles low, draping our shoulders and whispering in our ears.

The lights are still ablaze inside Clifford's, and as we step inside, the room feels warm with smoky jazz and hushed conversation. Cliff stands behind the bar, chuckling over a joke someone told and drying glasses. Brian and I grab two stools at the end of the bar.

"Hey!" Cliff waves and hollers at us. "What can I get you two?"

"Club soda," I shout back.

"Whiskey neat," Brian answers, slow and sloppy.

Cliff brings our drinks and props his elbows on the bar in front of us, dish towel appropriately slung over his shoulder. "Brian, where you been, man? It's been a while."

"C'mon, Cliff," Brian replies, clearly tickled to be on a first-name basis with the town's flashy newcomer. "Just working, just doing my thing. Can't spend every night in here watching hockey with you." I find it entertaining to watch Brian working so hard to be cool. It ignites flashbacks to the high school lunch table.

Cliff has already shifted, however, and I can feel him studying me with those battleship eyes. "Have I seen you somewhere before?" he asks.

Once again, he catches me off guard. Surely, he remembers me. I stammer, "Umm, I, uh, I was just here yesterday."

"Oh, yeah, yeah. I know that. Sorry. I didn't mean last night…" He cocks his head to the side as if to absorb my profile from another angle. "Somewhere else, though…"

"The commercial," Brian volunteers. "The soap commercial you were in, Jan." He grabs his cocktail napkin, rubs it over his armpits like a bar of soap, and pitches his voice as high as he can go. "As *clean* as you want it!"

I roll my eyes, snatch the napkin, ball it up, and throw it in his face.

"That's it!" Cliff snaps his fingers and smiles broadly. His deep laugh fills the room again.

I can feel the flush of embarrassment creeping up my neck despite the part of me that still *yearns* to be recognized.

"Ahh, a star has graced our presence," Cliff announces as strangers down the bar start to stare.

"Hardly," I respond. "That commercial was filmed years ago, and I'm afraid there haven't been a lot of takers since then."

"Well, you had that part in the soap opera. It's more than most folks in Seaville can lay claim to," Brian says. "You're the one who got away and grabbed the spotlight."

"A soap opera? Whoa, that's real Hollywood," Cliff teases.

I notice the angle of his chin sharply contrasts with the curve of his smile. He has a way about him, this Cliff. Something that seems to make people *crave* his attention. I find myself shifting and clamoring to be the focus of those dark eyes. And it's been *years* since I've pulled that kind of shit.

"So, Brian." I nudge him with my elbow. "Didn't you have something you wanted to ask Cliff?"

"Ah. Yes, indeedy," Brian says, leaning forward with conspiratorial importance, half of his drink now a puddle on the bar. "McCready. You got something on him? What do you know, my friend?"

Cliff wipes away Brian's puddle with a quick snap of his dish rag. "McCready? Ah, yeah, right, Jan and I were just talking about that whole business." His eyes find mine, and it feels like a rescue from the bottom of a dark mine. "McCready didn't do it," he says.

"Bullshit," Brian retorts. "I mean, I know he wasn't convicted, and I don't really know why. But that dude is strange. And scary."

"I *know* why he was acquitted, Brian." Cliff holds forth without hesitation. "Because he didn't do it. He was never even in that ice cream shop that night."

"Never in Pop Gray's?" Brian protests in disbelief. "My dad said he went in there with a gun and that people saw him—"

"Read the court records, man." Cliff clearly had. "McCready was merely a witness. He was camped out in a phone booth. Told the cops that he saw some men running away from the scene."

"And were *they* found?" I jump into the fray now, my curiosity piqued. "The men?"

"No," Cliff replies, pulling glasses from a shelf beneath the bar and stacking them in neat rows. "And in fact, McCready ended up recanting his claim about the men running away, which is suspicious, I'll give you that. But he didn't do it."

"How are you so sure?" Brian asks, his drunken eyes narrowing, just slivers of doubt.

"No forensic evidence points to him. No one saw him actually in the shop or even on the sidewalk outside. The guy's just a loon. He was in the wrong place at the wrong time. And maybe he liked the attention. He was making up stories so fast that he had the police spinning in circles. Not to mention, African American in the '60s—well, he was an easy scapegoat."

Cliff turns to the register to run the bill for the college kids a few stools away. "Be right back," he promises.

Brian looks down at his thumbs twiddling in his lap and thinks a moment. "Nah, I still think McCreepy did it. I mean, all these years, someone would have said something by now. Someone would've started another rumor, right? I mean, this is Seaville. The whole town talks when someone's skirt is too tight."

I chuckle. "I see your point, Brian. But I don't know. It seems like they would've hung it on him if they could, and it's a good point that Cliff makes about the police in that era. This certainly was not a Black man's town."

Cliff returns holding our check. "No rush, guys, seriously. I'm enjoying the chat. I just have to give it a last call, or they'll shut me down."

The last patrons at the bar, other than Brian and I, slip out the front door.

"Oh shit! The time! We should go, Brian. I've already been gone far too long." I push back from my stool and yank on my jacket.

"Whoa there, Cinderella! This is just starting to get good," Brian says, but he obligingly throws back the rest of his whiskey and slaps a twenty on top of the check.

"Come back anytime," Cliff calls after us. "I'll share some more of my theories with you. And you can try the pasta. It's as good as any in New York." He waves at me—at *us*?—as the glass door swings to a close at our backs.

Brian is crushingly drunk, and I am too tired to care. Slow and unsteady, we make our way back to Airlie Gardens on foot through a milky fog. We bump and stumble, ricocheting off each other and the steel hand railings of the tall bridge, colliding with the corners of the November night.

Chapter 16: Wishing

Gladys had insisted on a night walk, and so Nelson snapped on her leash and obliged, though he normally didn't venture out this late. It's warm for the last week in November, but he wears his long raincoat and hat anyway. Gladys trots ahead of him, puffy tail wagging, and turns the corner toward Main Street, their usual route.

Tonight, music drifts from the big stone house on the corner. *Someone's having a party*, Nelson thinks wistfully. It had been so many years since he had gone to a party. He used to love to dance, and he was good, too. Mama always said he could've been one of the Commodores.

He stops in front of the house, just distant enough that he can see inside but not close enough so that anyone looking out can catch sight of him. Last thing he wants is trouble.

A man and woman stumble out the front door, tugging on their coats and tripping down the steps. They'd probably had too much Christmas punch. *But they look easy*, Nelson thinks, cool with whatever direction the night wind might blow them. He envies them—their freedom and the careless way they slouch off the blanket of fog that has descended from the dark.

Nelson hadn't felt that kind of freedom since April of '67, the night that gashed open his future and left him here alone, nursing the wound that would become this scar of a life.

He had spent two long years whiling away in Mr. Tucker's attic. He'd tried to move out, to make it on his own, and to take his burden—the heavy chain of his existence and all he represented—off the Tuckers. But nobody in town wanted any part of him. No one would give him the time of day much less a job. He'd spent a few months working up at the corn mill in Jacksonville, but the brutal bus ride to get there took an hour each way. The work was hard, and the pay was poor. But at least they didn't know him up there, and he didn't have to hang his head and wear his repentance like an ugly shirt he could never take off.

Sometimes, he'd offer to be a help around the house, maybe run to the store to pick up something Mrs. Tucker needed. Though when he did dare to show his face around the good people of Seaville, the crowds, well, they'd part like the Red Sea. He could hear the mutter of their whispers, their baseless accusations, and the names they'd call him under their breath, but he chose to persevere—to buy the gallon of milk or the cough syrup or whatever Mrs. Tucker wanted. Then he'd be on his way.

He would never respond, never reciprocate, never stoke their angry fires.

He knew he had to somehow move forward, but he felt stuck in the cobwebs.

When Mrs. Tucker got the diagnosis, the bad news, Mr. Tucker sat him down and offered him a cup of chicory tea. Any time the Tuckers wanted to fix him some tea, Nelson knew something more serious than tea was brewing.

"Son," he said, "Mrs. Tucker and I were never able to have children." He cleared his throat. "And I'm not sure if she has ever forgiven me for that."

Nelson fidgeted uncomfortably at hearing the family secret, something that didn't belong to him. He hadn't seen his own mama in more than two years, and for someone to share with him their truth, it felt a little like a betrayal to his kin.

"But since you came to live here," Mr. Tucker continued, "you have been such a comfort to her. Well, to us. She loves listening to your feet stomp around this attic, and she can't wait to make you bacon and eggs for breakfast every morning."

Nelson squirmed some more, dismayed and flattered all at once.

"I guess what I'm trying to say, son is that I feel… we know…that Mrs. Tucker might not make it through the cancer." He stopped to choke back a sob. "But no matter what happens, I want you to stay on."

Nelson remained through the last days of Mrs. Tucker's life, even lending a hand to Mr. Tucker with the house and the yard after his wife had passed. Mr. Tucker had to sell the convenience store after he started having heart problems, and Nelson moved down from the attic into the spare room and took over most of the household chores. His mama had never taught him how to cook, but he could read a recipe as well as anyone, and Mrs. Tucker had a great big handwritten cookbook of her family's secrets. Nelson would pick out the easy things like chipped beef on toast, baked chicken, and anything that resembled a soup. He fed Mr. Tucker as he grew weaker, kept up his house and garden, and cleaned the gutters, and mended the fence. As he always did, he carried on.

When Mr. Tucker passed of a massive coronary, Nelson learned the house, which had been fully paid for, belonged to him. He soon gained a new understanding of the soul-wrenching concept of solitude. But with a roof over his head, and a little bit of money he inherited from the Tuckers stashed under his mattress, he could make do for a while.

He hadn't seen Mama since that last semester at school, the one nobody allowed him to finish. A letter arrived from his Aunt Ida stating Mama wasn't doing so well. She had been laid up in bed due to her failing kidney was failing. When he talked to Mama on the phone, she sounded in good spirits, but she missed him, and she wanted him to come see her.

"Come on up here, Mama," he'd said to her the last time they talked. "I got this whole house, and I own it. It's mine. There's even a bedroom just for you. You can stay here. You can live with me."

He heard her long sigh on the other end of the line, and at the time, the shame that burned within him made him believe she didn't want to stay with him because of his incarceration. But after the letter from Aunt Ida, he knew her health kept her in Roanoke Rapids, and she just didn't want him to worry.

So, one early fall day, sometime in the early seventies, he decided to pack a suitcase and head to the bus depot on the outskirts of town. He didn't leave the house much, so on this particular day, he took his time and his care, strolling down the sidewalk, breathing in the crisp, salty air rising from the sound, and enjoying the crunch of the beach car's wheels as it rolled down the sandy street.

It wasn't that he didn't notice the people who stared at him as he walked by, his small suitcase tucked under his elbow. It's more that he had learned to live with the whispers and looks. He'd accepted his fate.

And indeed, he had adapted. He'd learned if he needed to run to the market for groceries, he'd better be the first one there when the store opens. No other customers to bother with—just him, his little basket of groceries, and Jimmy, the regular cashier. Jimmy always acted polite, nodding hello, and ringing him up without any fuss. Jimmy was colored, too, and that helped matters.

Nelson had also revived Mrs. Tucker's vegetable garden, which had gone to bramble when she took sick. He'd found a shovel and hoe and some old seeds tucked away in a backyard shed. He'd grown potatoes, carrots, lettuce, and beans. Tomatoes in the summer, too. So much fruit he'd had to prop up the drooping plants with chicken wire. If it came down to it, he knew he could self-sustain if need be.

But without a job and without any friends, he just had too much time on his hands, and the one place he knew they wouldn't ever deny him entry was the town library.

Once a week, he visited with Ms. Mavey, who always seemed happy to have a chat over her lunch break.

She routinely had a stack of books waiting on the corner of her desk for him, and he savored the idea of someone anticipating his arrival. The stories in Ms. Mavey's books offered Nelson their own kind of salvation: lands to which he could travel, characters he could meet, and happy endings he could pretend were his own.

"So, how are you holding up, Nelson?" Ms. Mavey asked every week, taking a bite of her sandwich or a sip from her coffee mug.

"Oh, it's the same," he always replied, and then maybe he'd change the subject and tell her about the garden or ask her thoughts on one of the books he'd just finished.

"But, are they getting any kinder, then, the people 'round here?"

"No, ma'am," he'd say. "I reckon it's just hard for them to forgive."

"Forgive?" The color would rise in her cheeks. "There is nothing to forgive, Nelson. You've done nothing wrong!"

Ms. Mavey was both a friend and a defender. She'd always been on his side since the first day he stumbled in the library, covered in blood and shame. But after she had her baby girl, she had lots of important things

to keep her busy. So, Nelson just enjoyed the hour he got
with her each week.

The grit on the sidewalk turned from sand to red
clay as Nelson left the steel corridor of the bridge and the
bay in his wake. The bus station lay a mile further inland,
and he'd walked it many times to get to the corn mill. But
this trip felt different. By the time he'd reached the ticket
window at the station, word had clearly circulated
throughout town that Nelson McCready had packed a
suitcase and planned on going somewhere.

Like a predator lying in wait, a black-and-white
cruiser rolled down the street, passing Nelson at the ticket
booth and parking in the small station lot.

"How much for a ticket to Roanoke Rapids?" he
asked, fishing in his pocket for some cash he had retrieved
from the mattress. But before the lady with the big
bouffant working behind the counter could respond, he felt
the shadow of police officers encroaching. In the glass of
the ticket window, he could see the reflection of their
navy-blue hats and the determined chisel of their chins.
One fat, like a roll of white bread, and the other hard-set
and thin. Before he could turn about to face them, he felt a
tight hand grip his shoulder.

"Mr. McCready," the one handling him said, his voice booming, announcing his arrival on the scene. "We got some reports that there was some trouble down here."

"T-t-trouble?" Nelson stammered, whirling around to face his accusers and shaking off the officer's hold. "I ain't causing any trouble, sir. I'm just up here buying a bus ticket."

"A bus ticket for who?" the other officer asked. A chunky block of a man, he wore a nameplate that reads "Bellows." His stubby fingers rested on the holster of his firearm.

"For me, sir, for myself," Nelson responded. The tension at the ticket bay built, the October air still and full of suspense.

The lady behind the window leaned in closer to her side of the glass, her nose almost pressed against it.

Nelson sighed. "I need to go home to see my mama. She ain't well."

"Well, Mr. McCready, you know now that's not going to be possible," the tall officer said, pulling a small notepad and pencil from his back pocket. He looked younger than Bellows, but clearly, he was in charge.

"Date and time?" he asked Bellows, who snapped to attention and consulted his watch.

He cleared his throat. "Uh…it's October 5 at 1:28 p.m."

"Okay, then," the officer scribbled on his pad. "Our report states that at 1:28 p.m., October 5, the suspect, Nelson McCready, was detained in violation of the court order reprimanding him to this jurisdiction."

Bellows began to reach around Nelson's back with his pair of shiny silver handcuffs.

"Wait, wait, wait!" Nelson shouted, stepping away, his hands held high in the air to avoid their capture. Of course, no way Shorty could've got them up there even if he jumped. "You're going to arrest me for trying to get on a *bus*?"

"Son, you are attempting to leave this county, which is forbidden under the terms of your release from jail."

"No way! You can't handcuff me for trying to buy a ticket!" Nelson objected, certain he had to think fast. "Why, I've been taking this here bus for weeks to get up to Jacksonville to work. No one bothered me then! Just 'cause I got a suitcase, you tryin' to *arrest* me?"

The officers looked dubiously at one another because it was obvious Nelson had a point.

"Why do y'all want me to stay here so badly, anyway?" he continued. "If I am such a criminal, why don't you want me gone? Let me go! I won't come back, I swear. I don't *want* to ever come back!" He thought for a moment about the Tucker's house—*his* house—but he still wanted to go. He'd be fine to get on that bus and never return, just for a slice of Momma's buttered cornbread.

The two officers looked at one another again, unsure of how to proceed.

The cop in charge finally conceded. "Boy, go home," he said. "We won't take you in *this time*. But make no mistake. You try to leave this county again, and you will be arrested, you hear me? And if we get you behind bars again, you best be sure you'll see a trial for that other Neal sister."

The woman with the bouffant hairdo behind the glass nodded her head in agreement. The officers turned in unison and headed back toward their patrol car.

Nelson heard Bellows whisper to his partner, continuing his complaints all the way to the car. "Why didn't we nab him, Junior? What will the chief say?"

Junior shouted back to Nelson before climbing in the driver's side. "Go home now, McCready, you hear me?"

Nelson, still standing dumbstruck on the station platform, limped away from the ticket window, which now had a closed sign hanging from a hook on the other side of the glass. The lady with the big hair was nowhere to be seen.

Defeated, he began his sullen return to the Tucker house, the police cruiser following at a watchful distance.

Nelson knew he was a captive here. A prisoner of their convenience, even as he walked freely down the street. He'd need to call on Mr. Dorian again to try to find a way to clear his name. First, however, he had to consult the funds stashed beneath his mattress.

The next afternoon, Nelson sat in a lopsided office chair, pleading with Mr. Dorian across a metal desk strewn with candy wrappers and empty cartons of cigarettes.

"You want them to do *what*?" Mr. Dorian asked, rising quickly from his desk chair so the napkin tucked on his lap tumbled to the ground, crumbs scattering.

"Put me on trial again, sir," Nelson said. He retrieved the stray napkin and passed it back to his former lawyer.

Mr. Dorian had left the public defender's office and had situated himself in a cozy, cubby-hole law office behind the town library. His lunch, a turkey sandwich, and coleslaw, lay half eaten on his cluttered desk beside two empty mugs stained with coffee rings. A small box fan whirred in the window, but his office still felt insufferably hot.

Dorian mopped sweat from his brow with the crumpled napkin. "Why would you want to go back to trial, son? They could hang you this time." His thick drawl softened the blow of his words, but Nelson shuddered anyway.

"B-b-but…" Nelson stuttered, "I th-th-thought you said there was no way they could find me guilty of the second murder if they couldn't find me guilty of the first?"

"No, I said they didn't have the evidence to bring you up on the second trial. If we push them, they're gonna find a way to get you."

"But…*why,* Mr. Dorian? I didn't do it."

"Because, well, it's still an unsolved crime, Mr. McCready, and they have closed the case. They are not out there looking for a killer, and they are not about to open this thing back up. You're their guy. They just couldn't prove it when I took you to court. But you get a different judge, wind up with a few friends of the chief's on your jury, and it could be a different story this time."

"But, sir, I just don't understand. I mean, if *I* didn't do it then there's someone out there who killed two girls and got away with it. Don't they want to know who that person is?"

Dorian sighed and sat heavily on the corner of his desk. There was a mustard stain on his tie. "Look," he said. "Somebody out there knows what happened that night at Pop Gray's, and for whatever reason, the police in this town don't care enough to find out. Cracking this case back open would just raise a lot of eyebrows. It would scare people."

"They're already scared. Of me."

"Nelson," Dorian said, sighing again. He then paused to take a bite of his turkey sandwich. Another squirt of mustard landed above his lip. "This will pass, I promise you. People are just still on edge. Give it another year or two, and everyone will forget about you. Lay low, find a hobby, get a dog or a cat…they make great companions."

Nelson nodded and passed Dorian another napkin.

"But whatever you do, don't ask for another trial. I promise you, they will find a way to make it stick this time."

A cold wind snaps against Nelson's trench, and he shakes his head, chasing these memories away. Gladys has stopped to do her business, and she always picks the same spot, the corner of Sullivan and Main. The roads are quiet at this hour, and the lights on the arc of the drawbridge twinkle in the distance.

"C'mon, girl," Nelson says with a gentle tug on the leash. "It's time to head home."

Chapter 17: Protecting

When I tiptoe in, well after midnight, I find Gregor asleep on the cot stashed in the corner of the defunct dining room.

"I'm so sorry," I whisper as he startles awake at the sound of the door latching behind me.

"No, it's okay." Gregor wipes his tired eyes with the back of his hands. "I wanted to speak to you anyway. Your mother…I think she's in a lot of pain, and she's not telling us."

Typical August, I think. Rigid and stubborn and always in some sort of pain.

"Mm-hmm," I say, unsure of what response he expects.

"Miss Jan, there is the option of giving her more medicine now. That is, if you provide consent."

I sit down on the couch with the gravity of a torpedo. "The sedation thing?" I ask, exhaustion dripping from my voice. My hair, saturated by the fog, clings to my neck.

"Yes. But you should know that this is serious sedation. What we are striving for is a state of light unconsciousness," Gregor continues, his soft voice filling the quiet house. "Your mother should still be somewhat aware of the presence of others. She may be able to communicate a little, but none of it may make sense. It's also possible that this sedation may induce deep sleep, not unlike a coma. And it is possible that she will never wake up from this coma."

"So, you're saying if she wakes up at all, she'll be crazier than she already is?" The bitter bite in my voice is hard to hide, and I scold myself. There's no need to pull Gregor into the drama of my family history when he's just here to do his job.

He lets me off the hook with a polite half-smile. "So, then, do you want to proceed?"

"Maybe." I feel myself hedging. "Let's see how she is tomorrow?"

"Of course. Good night, Miss Jan. And get some rest." He reaches to turn off the lamp he had clearly kept on in anticipation of my return. "Oh, and there is one more thing…"

I turn back at the foot of the stairs, suddenly so tired my bones ache.

"Tonight, your mother was groggy, half awake. She kept asking for a 'Matty.'"

I frown, digging both thumbs into my throbbing temples.

"Do you know this Matty and how to reach her?" he asks.

I don't know anyone by that name, just as I don't know any Geraldines.

"She said 'tell Matty,'" Gregor continues. "I assume she wants this Matty to know that she's not doing well."

"Okay," I try to reassure him, "I'll see what I can find out." I drag my body up the stairs to August's half-open door, where I slump against the frame and watch her struggle for each shallow breath.

The wearied path that has led me to this place in time began with that cautionary glint in Ms. Devere's eyes when she angled her rearview mirror to find me so many years ago. "Has it always been like this?" she asked.

I can reason now that while August has certainly never fit the part of "mother", in all honesty, she doesn't fit well for any part. Like a spinning top, she's always tried to land upright, but it's never going to work.

Her understanding that she was an outcast is one of the things that kept her moving all those years up and down the West Coast, baby and belongings in tow. But I believe she *did* try her best to make it work here in Seaville, at least for a while.

We moved back here in early spring, '75 or '76, I can't exactly recall. These are the things that my memory holds onto: the end of a long journey, the orange van winding down Chestnut Street, big homes with manicured lawns. The scent of fresh cut grass, perfect hedges of tulips and iris, beckoning with a come-hither grace. Cherry blossom petals settling on the windshield, gathering on the wiper blades, a kind of sinful snow. I had grown up surrounded by desert and dense forest, cactuses and ferns, and the hard scramble of seaside cliffs, so the lazy green sprawl of Seaville, as we drove towards Grandma's home, struck me dead center. I was enamored with the clean, quaint beauty of it all.

But when we pulled into Patty's driveway, I remember August gasped. Angry, she slammed her palm into the steering wheel.

"What is *this* fucking disaster?" she shrieked. "No. This is not what I came home for…"

Indeed, the lawn had grown up to our knees, and weeds decorated the cracks in the sidewalk. A few withered daffodils swooned by the front steps, and August stooped to their level, trying to resuscitate them.

"We will need to fix this yard right away," my mother announced, but I didn't see the cause for such concern. "I'm sure the neighbors have already summed us up as no-good, white trash anyway, but Janus, you hear me now, a first impression is everything. They will take one look at this, and they will *know* we are not good enough."

Her conviction startled me.

Back in California, August couldn't have cared less about tending the crops at Riverskeep, the miles of apple trees, or the field daisies the other ladies would gather to sell at the market. Yet there, in those first days back in her childhood home, August seemed to be reborn as a master gardener, dedicating all her daylight hours to weeding and digging, elbow-deep in roots and earth.

Since August hadn't taken the time to enroll me in school, I had nothing to do but slouch around those porch steps as August whittled in the earth. My dirty clothes and knotted hair probably screamed of disrepair and neglect, louder than any overrun garden ever could have. I still remember the gnawing emptiness in my stomach, and there being nothing in the pantry except coffee grounds, whiskey, and a box of stale Wheaties.

I decided in that first week I detested that stupid garden. I would resent every flower that lived and died in there, and when no one was looking, I'd take pleasure in stomping out a peony or hacking off the pompous crown of one of those irises.

And I hated our new home. It felt like someone else's lonely, unkempt world we had just barreled into. It also may have even been the beginning of my hatred for my mother.

I finally sleep after days of restlessness, and my dreams are vivid, swollen, and bruised. I see a faceless man, who I know to be Nelson McCready, though he's nothing more than a shape. The man in my nightmare carries a long machete, the kind used in the jungle, and he approaches through the wavy storyline of sleep. Slowly, methodically, he slashes the air between us with his piercing blade of nothingness.

In my dream, I'm a huddled victim alone in a dark house. No, a cave, and I can just see the opening, the beckoning of light, like a mythical salvation.

As my dream self uncurls, her body ready to crawl toward the light, her arms, thin as twigs, collapse, and rivulets of blood drip to her wrists. Then, I can see it—the knife in her back.

I awake on the other side of the dream, sweaty and drawn, and my back actually does *ache*. Reaching for my shoulder blades, I gingerly assess for wounds. Finding none, I rub the remnants of the nightmare from my eyes and wrestle out of the tangled bedsheets to sit on the edge of the twin bed, staring down the bare walls of my childhood room as if they could offer me a purpose for the new day.

"Matty," I say the name aloud because it rests, fat and heavy, on my tongue. In August's last days, I know the responsibility will fall to me to help her find this Matty.

Gregor attends to August with bedpans and balms as I muddle toward her room. Just outside her door, I muster my brightest morning smile, though certainly my acting convinces no one.

Low moans escape into the hallway like a ghost the daylight cannot chase away, and as I enter, August strains forward, attempting to sit upright, only succeeding in raising her head an inch off the pillow. Gregor moves quickly to support her craning neck with the pillow.

"August, you're awake." That's all I can think to say.

"Well, that's obvious, Janus," August sneers in her usual way, though her voice escapes as no more than a raspy whisper.

"And how are you feeling?"

"I feel like…shit. Like I am dying," she says, grunting through her exhale.

"Well, that's obvious, August." My retort seems to have earned the crack of a smile across my mother's lips.

Gregor greets me. "Good morning, Ms. Jan. I was just getting ready to ask your mother about her pain. How is it today, Ms. August? On a scale of one through ten." He skillfully removes a bedpan from underneath his patient.

"No," my mother says curtly, a blatant refusal of his question, punctuated by spasms of coughing. Gregor doesn't flinch but instead makes a quick note on his chart, then he backs out of the family battleground, bedpan still in hand.

"He's just trying to do his job, August. And to help you. He's trying to make your life better."

"Life?" My mother coughs and snorts. "What do I have left of life?" As if to prove her point, another fit of coughing racks her body. "No," she says weakly after it subsides. "He can't do anything to help. He's just trying to *kill* me quicker. That's what he's doing. So that you can take *the house*."

I smirk at the idea I'd bring in a henchman to kill my mother. She's not of sound mind, I reason, adding these assertions to August's delusional ramblings yesterday, her snarling insults and her ill-fated poems. August's journal rests on the corner of her bedside table, and as I reach down to turn on the lamp, I let my fingers drift to the cover of the book.

With an unexpected ferocity, my mother's bony hand shoots from the bedcovers and grabs my wrist. "That's *my* diary," she growls, low and primal. "Mine. You can read it when I'm gone, but while I'm still breathing, it is *mine*."

I'm stunned by the speed and agility with which she still seems capable of moving and by the clarity of her intention. "Of course, it is yours, August," I say, recovering. "I was just hoping…Well, Gregor mentioned you were calling out for Matty in your sleep last night."

Trepidation flashes like fire, burning across the brittle timber of August's face.

"Oh, I don't know," August says, her grip on my wrist easing, the flaccid arm falling back to her side like a rain-starved weed.

"You don't know *what*, August?"

"Don't know…(cough, cough)…why I would've said anything like that," she mutters.

"So, you don't know a person named Matty? A woman? A man? A dog? For Christ's sake, August, I can't help you if you're not honest with me." Frustration grows inside me like a wave I'm riding to the crest. "And how about Geraldine? Who is she?" The swell of my anger fills the room.

August coughs again. "I don't *want* your help, Janus," she answers, hot and wet. "I've never…asked for it…Just leave again. Leave like you always do." She tries to catch her breath, struggling for wheezing gulps of air. Just when I think she can't carry on, that her physical capacity can't support her, she still does not relent. "Do you *know* what this pain is like, Janus? It doesn't help… what he gives me…it doesn't help…(cough, cough, cough)…He's trying to finish me off with one of those bags of (cough) slush he keeps hooking up."

"*No one* is trying to kill you, August!" I shout. The wave crashes over my head, the rush of it in my ears, and my own breath releases short and quick. "You *owe* me some answers before you go. There are things we never talk about. My father. Your secrets. Your poetry. Your goddamn poetry!"

August rolls her bloodshot eyes and licks her dry lips.

"But now, here we are, and time is running out!" I raise my voice and grit my teeth. "Running. Out." My mother glares through my outburst, but she holds her tongue. "Okay. Okay. You know what, August? Maybe I *will* just go!"

I pivot to leave, and my elbow collides with the bedside lamp, sending it tumbling to the ground. The crunching disintegration of the lightbulb causes the dim room to grow even darker.

I storm into the kitchen, ready for a fight with anything that moves. Gregor stands there, quietly leaning against the countertop, sipping coffee from a mug that reads "Sunshine and Sarasota'" and features a drawing of an enthusiastically smiling sun.

"Okay, Gregor. So, my mother is all bent out of shape because she thinks I've hired you to kill her." Gregor laughs, nearly spitting out his coffee. "And she's fighting like a champ to have it her way, always her way… I am so done with this." I shrug, a futile attempt to shake off my anger. "So, can we talk about this sedation thing? What *is* it, anyway? What would you actually give her?"

Gregor pauses, considering the situation and measuring the heat of the moment before he answers. He takes one more long, pondering sip of his coffee, the sunshine mug winking at me, before he finally says, "It's phenobarbital. That's what we give them for palliative sedation."

I know enough to understand it's a big drug, a powerful force on the body. The drug killed Michael Jackson, after all. I find myself unable to meet his gaze, and instead, I fixate on the cup's beaming face.

"I think it's time," I say, hoping Gregor can't see my hands trembling as I reach into the cabinet, looking for my own smiling mug.

A few hours later, as the sedative slowly drips into my mother's veins, a disquieting sense of culpability simmers within mine. Her graying body slumps and releases like a droopy rag doll, and my internal skirmish between sensibility and sympathy escalates into waging war. Not knowing what to do with this new agitation, I dig out my running shoes and headphones and venture out for a jog—my therapist's orders for dealing with the panic.

Yesterday's muggy warmth has been vanquished by brisk November winds, and the afternoon sky has become clear and blue. *High pressure moving in*, I deduce, thanks to my weather-lady training at the TV station.

I'd only packed one T-shirt and one pair of leggings, so I shiver down Chestnut Street until my adrenaline kicks in. I turn on running music, something hard and metallic to match the clanging gears of my mind.

My pace quickens as I turn toward Main, but I stop fast when I see him, and I scoot to hide behind the base of a large elm. He's huddled low to the ground on the corner of Chestnut and Airlie, wearing a long, brown trench coat. As if culled from my dreams last night, before me crouches Nelson McCready, though he doesn't look like a menacing villain. Unless his disguise is his thick, goofy sunglasses hanging lopsided over the arch of his brow and an oversized double-breasted raincoat.

He rises slightly from his crouched position and shifts his weight to reveal a bright-purple leash attached to a small white poodle that seems to be deciding where it would like to pee. As McCready waits, he examines the contents of his fingernails.

Peering from behind my tree trunk, I feel a little silly. He doesn't seem dangerous or deranged. Rather, just a man waiting for his dog to finish its business. When the poodle finally leads its owner up the sidewalk, I take note of McCready's distinct gait, his habit of stepping heavily with one foot while dragging the other. I resume a slow jog behind the pair, keeping a watchful distance, but I can't correct my impulse to follow.

When they arrive home to the old two-story clapboard badly in need of repair, McCready lets his dog off the leash at the gate. He looks over his right shoulder then his left, seems to mumble something to himself, and then limps away, his long frame trailed by an even longer shadow.

I watch him disappear up the winding sidewalk, and before closing the front door behind him, he surveys the street again—searching, wary. I wonder if he senses being followed.

Shivering off the odd encounter, I resume my run, which quickly becomes a manic sprint, my mind moving as fast as my legs, a tumbling spiral of distraction and doubt. I race past the entrance of Airlie Park, its hallmark dogwood trees now brown and bare, and turn the corner onto Main, where the arc of the bridge rises before me. Seagulls swoop and chatter. Thin cirrus clouds drape the sun, drawing gray stripes in the blue sky and casting shadows on the ground. I speed past the old Southern Baptist Church, its tall steeple leaving a pinprick in the blue sky. I have to weave and dodge parishioners in their solemn stream out of the place of worship, which reminds me it's already Sunday, and I've been trapped here in Seaville for three days.

Everything around me, from the sandy sidewalk grit beneath my shoes to the closing call of the church bell, feels both familiar and foreign, like a puzzle I've already solved and discarded. But it's scattered before me again, the box torn apart, pieces lost, and I cannot make them all fit together again.

Drained and a little disoriented, I stop on the corner of the island square to catch my breath, hands on my knees, inhaling greedily. I decide to turn home, resolved to confront August once and for all, deathbed be damned. It's time for me to bend my mother until she breaks—until she gives me what I came here for.

Running with purpose again, I cross the bridge and turn into Airlie Downs. But watching my pounding feet instead of the path ahead, I plow with force into a warm, squishy body. I bounce off the collision and land on one knee, the scrape of the pavement finding its way through my leggings.

"Girl, are you okay?" The boisterous voice above me belongs to Sally Mavey, who appears to be considerably rounder than the last time our paths crossed. She scoops me up under both elbows and helps me back to my feet.

I take in the sight of my old friend.

Everything about Sally is big and full. Her mane of curls, currently scrunched into a high, messy bun, her fleshy figure swaddled in a bright shift blouse, and even her resounding laughter that fills the space between us.

"Why, Janus, have mercy! Fancy running into you this way." Sally howls at her own joke, complete with a requisite thigh slap.

I chuckle politely, massaging my aching knee. "Sally. It's good to see you again."

"What brings you to town, sweetie?" She unloads the trunk of her car. With lamps and pillows and blankets, her hands quickly fill up, and without waiting for my response, she drapes a patterned area rug over my empty arms and reaches back inside the trunk to retrieve another treasure. She's talking the whole while, her voice muffled from within the trunk.

"I heard about your mama. They say she's really going to die this time."

"This time?" I ask, juggling the ungainly rug, feeling a bit foolish.

Sally appears from the far reaches of her car, holding a large pink ceramic elephant and puffing heavily from the stretching and contorting required to retrieve it.

"Well, it's just that most people already thought she was dead and all."

I frown, but Sally continues. "She just kind of holed herself up, I guess. Shame, too. She was a damn good bridge player."

"You played bridge with my mother?"

"Used to," Sally says, dusting off her hands and closing the trunk. "It's been many years since the ladies have gotten together."

I nod and smile, trying to hand her back the rug, but her arms still appear full.

"So, I'm redecorating my place," she says, pointing to the Victorian house at the top of the drive. I see the front step littered with pumpkins and gourds and a small scarecrow on a stake. "Want to come up and see it? Have a coffee? Or a Band-aid?" She laughs at her own joke while trying to balance the ceramic elephant, lamps, and a bag stuffed full of pillows.

I know I should head home, my impending confrontation and all, but Sally doesn't typically take no for an answer. Resigned, I scoop up the lamps dangling precariously from her arms and trudge up the driveway.

A gaudy assortment of faux international accessories fills Sally's home. Wooden giraffes of various sizes stand at attention in the corner. Asian art in jewel tones cascades down the walls, and Bavarian beer steins line the fireplace mantle.

"Wow, you must travel a lot," I say, perhaps too sarcastically, surveying the living room.

"Oh, honey, no," Sally corrects. She grabs the lamps from my arms. "I just shop at Pier 1. All. The. Time."

Sally leaves a signature scent in her wake, and as she bustles into the kitchen, I catch the unmistakable aroma of jasmine. She measures out the coffee and pulls out two mugs, peeling the Pier 1 price tags off the bottom.

"You still acting?" she asks, yanking a jug of milk from her refrigerator. Before I can answer, she pushes on. "And how is the family? Your daughter must be a teenager by now! Tom is good? Haven't seen him 'round these parts in years."

"Tom is good," I answer, not mentioning the divorce, leaning against her counter. I shift my weight off the aching knee. "My girl is in middle school. She's thirteen. So yeah, I guess she is a teenager. Huh, makes me feel kind of old."

"Girl, I can't believe it. You don't look a day over twenty-one."

"Well, thanks, Sally. I feel about eighty-one right now."

"Stuff with Mama wearing on ya, huh?"

"I guess so. Also, I've got to be honest, it really feels bizarre to be here like this. I mean, not in your house. That feels lovely. But being back at home—at August's, I mean—I'm just sitting around, waiting for her to die. It sounds awful, I know. Every second I'm in that house with her, I'm planning my escape."

"Oh yeah, I remember that closed-in feeling when Mama was sick," Sally agreed. "Although I wanted to be there with her, I guess I still felt kind of helpless. And hopeless, too."

"And then, *when* she dies," I continue, airing my grievances, "all the work that will be required to upturn that awful house, going through all her stuff…I guess I'm trying to say I'm pretty overwhelmed. And just being in this town where, you know, everything has changed, but I still can't help feeling just like the kid who was trapped here so many years ago. The kid who I thought broke free…"

Sally hands me a warm mug, and we sit facing each other on a fluffy coral-colored chenille sofa.

"Oh, I'm sorry to keep carrying on like this. I guess I needed to *run into* an old friend," I joke.

Sally laughs at my attempt to poke fun at our unexpected collision

"This town feels like it gets its claws into you and doesn't let go," I continue, sipping the hot coffee. "Funny…I actually just saw old McCreepy on the street right before I ran into you."

"Oh?"

"Yeah, I never really knew the whole story about the murders at Pop Gray's, but just seeing him out there is unnerving. He has this horrible, violent past, and yet he's just walking his dog down Chestnut Street."

"Oh no, honey, he's not violent. He didn't kill anyone," Sally says, picking at a pull on the couch cushion.

I'm surprised at Sally's conviction, and it makes me think, fleetingly, of Cliff's similar assurances.

"McCready. That poor man," Sally continues, leaning in too close. I can smell the coffee on her breath and the jasmine escaping the creases of her neck. "All these years, that's been hanging like a cross around his neck. Hasn't been able to work in this town. He had to go find a job over at a corn mill near Jacksonville 'cause no one would hire him here. And do you know, he was trying to get his teaching degree when he was arrested?" She shakes her head. "Humph, it's a crying shame. No one will talk to him, really, except—well, you know what? He and your mama, they were friends."

I choke a little on the coffee sliding down the back of my throat. "What the…were they…did they?"

"Date?" Sally giggles. "No, I don't think so. I'm pretty sure McCready was not your mama's type." She looks at me sideways. "But I did see them taking long walks together. Almost every day until your mama stopped showing up. I expect they were both just lonely souls, looking for a piece of the past to hold onto."

"Well, the only thing that is becoming clear," I say, shaking my head, "is that I have no clarity at all. Who *was* this August?" And then, I correct my tense. "I mean, who *is* she?"

"Don't feel too bad," Sally says. "I'm not sure any of us really know who our parents are deep down and what their lives were like before we came along. Hell, my momma was so liberated back in the day that I'm not even sure if the milkman might not be my daddy."

I laugh, which I hope was the intended response, though, for a change, Sally delivered the line with a straight face.

"Well, Sally, I have to admit, I never really paid attention to the rumors around here, but I'm curious now since it seems he's become August's new best friend. Why are you so sure that your neighbor there is an innocent man?"

"Because I asked him about it," Sally replies, and of course she did. "We've never really talked too much. A nod and a wave from time to time. But then, one day a few years back, I saw him at the grocery store, and that was a rare sighting, for sure. Just standing there, looking at the eggplant. I mean, you hardly ever see this man out and about, except when he's walking his dog. So, I stroll right up to him in the produce section, and I asked him why everyone still thinks, all these years later, that he did it."

I can picture Sally's confrontation, leaning in too close, only the space of an eggplant between her and McCready.

"And he said that the only thing he's guilty of is standing by and doing nothing. He said he *was* there that night but never even went into Pop Gray's," she concludes.

"Well, of course, he's going to say that to protect himself," I suggest.

"I don't think so, Jan." Sally drains her coffee with one last gulp. "Do you know that he was charged with two counts of murder? He was acquitted on one because there was absolutely no evidence, and they never even brought him to trial on the second count. Why do you think that is?"

She doesn't give me a chance to offer a guess before she soldiers on.

"Because they *wanted* it to hang over this man's head like a dark cloud all these years. They *wanted* a scapegoat. And if he was *charged* but not *tried*, well, technically, they could close the case. No further investigation needed." She dusts her hands in the air as if ridding her palms of cards she'd been holding in a magic trick.

"But he was tried, wasn't he? And found innocent?" I ask.

"Aha! There's the wiggle room," Sally muses. "He was tried on one count only of the murders. They didn't have the evidence, so boom! Acquitted. And then they *chose* not to try him on the other count of murder."

"But *why*? And then, if McCready didn't do it, wouldn't they need to keep looking? Why wouldn't they want to find the real killer?"

"Exactly," Sally says, leaning close with her long-lashed, beady-brown eyes. "*Why*?"

Later that afternoon, I sit beside August, listening to her shallow breath fill the vacant space of her bedroom, when I notice the blue leather journal still clutched in her clawed hand. With the help of the sedative Gregor has administered, I'm confident I can wiggle it out of her grip without waking her. But first, I feel the need to register my complaints to the relative silence.

"So, what's your story anyway, August? The real story. You've been out there living your best life, haven't you? Playing cards and pissing around town with a pariah—with the *one man* in this town standing accused of murder. Wow, you sure know how to pick the good ones… So, what happened to the lady who cared *so much* about what everyone else thinks?"

Only the quiet hum of the respiratory monitor attempts a reply.

"And I hear that you're cussing out the children selling girl scout cookies? That can't be very good for appearances. Oh, and the garden looks like shit, by the way. Your mother would be *so* disappointed. And don't get me started on that porch. You know they're *all* talking about the porch, right? They are talking about you, August. And believe me, not in a good way…

"So, I hope you're happy. You're officially the witch they always teased me about. But your powers…

Poof! They're gone. And you're going to die a lonely old crone."

August remains still, but I have a sense I'm being heard. I can feel a certain shift of power in the room, and I'm emboldened by my mute audience.

"Well, you always wanted them to notice you, didn't you? Well, they did. Great! You got everything you wanted." I sigh and bury my head in my hands, the exhaustion of my anger draining my accusations.

"I guess I don't blame you, honestly…letting the dark win. In some ways, I get it," I confess. "I know it wasn't always easy being a single mother, paying all the bills alone, and dealing with me when, really, all I ever wanted to do was leave. I'm sure I wasn't always the best daughter, but, August, I tried. I *tried*. You were all that I had, too. All those years. I wanted you to like me. I wanted a *mother,* like everyone else had, who baked shit and told stories at bedtime, who took their daughter shopping for jeans and hair clips and whatever it was people shopped for…I just wanted my equal share of what everyone else seemed to have."

I gingerly place my left hand on top of my mother's, which rests on the journal. I then slide my right palm underneath the book and pull it free

"But now," I say under my breath, "I want some answers."

*****

You don't even know, Janus, how the anger eats at me from the inside out. I tried to spare you the worst of me all these years. You may not realize it, but I did.

When we lived out West in the yurt on the apple farm, or just driving around when we had nowhere to call home, we were lost, Janus. Two lost souls.

But I was free. The anger, the expectations, they all disappeared, and finally, I could just be. I could live in the skin I was born in.

So, when I had to come back here…well, it was never going to be good for me. I knew it at the time, but there were no real choices, were there? Mama was gone. We had a house with no strings attached and maybe a chance to start again.

And yes, maybe I drank too much or didn't tuck you in bed like you needed me to, but I got you out of here in one piece, didn't I? For all my failings, you think you've made something of yourself now, don't you, Janus?

The people in this town don't understand me. They never have. I should have left town when you did, I could have gone to Broadway, maybe I still had time left to see my name in lights. And maybe I could have escaped it all. But now the reckoner, he comes for his keep...I can hear him calling in the distance.

Chapter 18: Investigating

I shuffle into the kitchen, simmering but spent, and begin to rifle through the pages of August's journal, each consumed with words or the equivalent acreage of scribbled, nonsensical doodles. The last entry in the book appears ripped clean, and I assume it's one of the crumpled pages I retrieved yesterday. I scrounge through the messy kitchen drawers for a piece of scrap paper and sit down at the table to make a list of all my unknowns:

- *Geraldine? Cousin?*

- *Matty?*

- *The farm?*

- *McCready? Friend?*

- *Where is the cat?*

When Gregor enters the kitchen to fill his empty water bottle, I jump in surprise. He moves so quietly and carefully it's hard to hear him coming.

"I'm sorry to bother you," he says, his warm accent filling the tired kitchen, something softening and settling.

"Not at all, Gregor. I'm just going through a few of my mother's things, trying to see if I can help solve some of the riddles she's been throwing at us these past few days."

"Matty?" he asks.

"No idea," I reply. "She denies even saying the name out loud, so I think I'm going to have to keep digging. This is a pretty small town, but still, you've got to find the right people to ask."

He peers over my shoulder at the list.

"Did your mother lose a cat?" he asks. "I've seen a cat in the backyard several times. A tabby. I gave it some milk this morning."

"I don't think the cat is hers. I saw something in one of her notes," I explain, flipping through the journal. "Sounds like she was feeding it."

Gregor moves to the kitchen window, surveying the overgrown backyard. "Don't see it out there anymore, unless it's hiding in the weeds."

Turning my full attention back to the journal, I decide it makes the most sense to attack it in reverse chronological order.

November 19, 2016

No one is calling for Thanksgiving this year. Janus has clearly abandoned me. She could care less that I'm sick. That's okay. I can't stand to celebrate this year, anyway. Not thankful for this disease or for this life. I don't think Geraldine will come either. She said she will stay in Boca to see her grandchildren. Just an excuse, I'm sure.

I scribbled a note on my list: *Geraldine Littleton? Boca Raton?*

June 4, 2016

I know I am running out of time. I see it on Dr. Spencer's face when he looks at my test results. I see it in the mirror. The people on the street whisper when I pass by. They are talking about me again. I don't know if they know I'm sick or if they're just talking about me. They always talk. They don't believe that I belong here. Mama was right. Of course she was, she was right about everything.

I wish I was still wandering. Is it too late, I wonder? Can I pack up and go back to California, stumble into Riverskeep, and die beside those apple trees? Wonder if Fred is still alive?

I shudder at the mention of Fred and close the cover of the journal. It seems clear August still *aches* to belong somewhere, to be accepted. This has been her Achilles' heel for as long as I can remember.

It was the reason we never went to church like all the other God-fearing citizens of Seaville. We couldn't afford the *right* clothes for Sunday's finest, and she wouldn't dare give the other parishioners something to talk about. And though she always needed a steady paycheck, August refused to take any sort of secretarial work or any job she considered "blue collar," though a town like Seaville offered little else for someone with August's lack of education and experience. Librarian was as low as she'd go, justifying it by claiming it to be a scholarly occupation.

Gregor pops his head back into the kitchen. "I see the cat," he announces.

I hurry to the window and spy the scrawny orange cat slinking through the tall grass, a tiger through the jungle. As I crack open the back door, the hungry cat turns toward the sound, then runs over in the hopes of more milk. I stoop to offer it my hand to sniff, but the cat has no interest unless I have something to eat in the offering.

"Grab me something from the fridge," I ask Gregor, urgent now to lure this stray into my clutches, eager to solve any part of the puzzle within my reach.

Gregor pulls a bag of stale cheese from the refrigerator, and I pour the shreds into my palm. The cat returns to me, purring.

As it nibbles, I scratch behind its ears and notice a collar and a nametag. As the cat lifts its face in pleasure, I see the plate of the name tag hanging around its neck: McCready.

In the evening, just as the sun's light begins to trickle like melted honey behind the horizon, I hatch a plan.

"Brian, I want to pay a visit to McCready."

"What?" Brian asks. I hear a muted crash in the background. Something dropped or someone stumbled.

"I said I want to pay a visit to McCready."

"I heard you, Jan," he says, a bit breathless, recovering. "But why?"

"Well, since I've been home, I've been learning all this new information that I never knew about my mother. And she won't talk to me about any of it. I think she and McCready were actually friends. So, I want to see if he can help me shed some light on *any* of these questions."

"Whoa," says Brian. "And you want me to come with you?"

"Well, the man was accused of murder, so yeah," I say, "if you don't mind. I don't think it's a great idea for me to go in there alone."

I have the cat in my lap, and it's softly purring as I scratch its belly. Despite its lankiness, the animal appears clean and well-kept, clearly loved by someone.

An hour later, Brian and I knock on Nelson McCready's front door, the cat tucked in the crook of my arm.

The heavy oak door opens just a crack. Dim overhead light illuminates McCready's sharp profile as he peeks outside, barely enough space for his brow and nose and chin. "Yes, can I help you?"

"Uh, Mr. M-McCready," I stutter nervously, reverting to that schoolgirl in the witch's cape, running in fear. I take a breath and continue. "You don't know us, but I, uh, think we found your cat."

"My cat?" McCready asks, opening the door wider and shifting his wary eyes to the cradle of my arm. The hard creases of his brow relax when he sees the tabby. "Briar!" he exclaims, clapping his sinewy hands together in delight.

"She was at my mother's house in the backyard." I relinquish the cat to its owner.

"Thank you, thank you." McCready's voice softens to a warm Southern rasp. "She does tend to wander off. Always comes back, but it's been a while since I've seen her. Figured someone must be feeding her turkey leftovers."

"My mother was feeding her for a while. I think you may know her. August Littleton?" I drop her name like a test missile to see how it lands.

In the hallway shadows, I can see McCready's face rise, then fall ever so slightly.

"How is she?" he asks in his hoarse whisper. He steps back and throws the door open. "Please, come in, come in. Any friend of August's is a friend of mine."

Brian shrugs. We step inside.

The only overhead light in his cramped home burns in the hallway, making the place feel gloomy. A small table lamp lights the room beyond, where stacks of books pile in corners and spill off shelves. The air smells as I would have imagined—closed in, musty, forgotten.

Holding tight to his cat, McCready motions for us to follow him to a small sofa and easy chair clustered around a coffee table piled high with magazines. I glance at the copies on top, the free AARP publication that also comes to my mother's home, and a few worn, decades-old copies of *Time* magazine.

"So, how is August doing?" McCready asks again. "I've been worried."

"Well, she was sent home from the hospital with hospice care," I answer carefully, watching McCready's wrinkled face continue to cave. "You were friends?"

"Friends." He rolls the word in his mouth as if savoring the taste of it. "Yes, I guess we were. Not too many of us left anymore from the old days."

Brian sees his opportunity to jump in. "Did you and August go to school together, then, uh, over at Lee High?"

"Oh no," he replies, "I'm a bit older than she is, and I didn't grow up in these parts. I'm from up Roanoke Rapids way. She and I actually just connected a few years back when she brought me Briar, much like you did tonight, you see." He pauses to survey the two of us. "You her daughter?" he asks.

I nod.

He turns to Brian. "And…her son?"

"Oh, no," I interject. "Brian is just a family friend. He, uh, gave me a ride tonight. Helped me with the cat…"

"I see," McCready says, weighing his next words before he speaks. "Well, you clearly know who *I* am."

I feel my face flush and loosen the scarf I'd wrapped around my neck. "Mr. McCready," I begin, moving to my agenda, "I am trying to help August, my mother, get her things in order before…well, you know… and I'm having a hard time communicating with her. She seems to need some closure in a few areas, and frankly, I don't know where to begin."

"And you want to know if I can help?" he asks, a bit incredulous. He regains some of the animation he had shown over the cat, surprised and happy to be of use. "Well, I'm not so used to visitors, you see. When your mother brought back my cat that first day, she was all in a fit. Carryin' on ever so about animals needin' proper owners, and did I know how much money she had spent on feedin' my cat? She was a sight, too. That long, crazy hair, thin as a whippet, mad as hell…" McCready smiles at the memory. "I think I calmed her down by offering her some of my chicory tea. Oh no, my manners! Would either of you like a cup of tea?"

We both shake our heads, and so McCready continues. "And it turned out, August and I had quite a bit in common."

I loosen my scarf a bit more and clear my throat. "Mr. McCready, I'm not exactly sure how to ask this, but were you and my mother ever an…item?"

McCready's laughter bounces off his wood-paneled walls and shakes the room. He laughs for a full minute, maybe more.

"No, my dear, we were not lovers."

I'm awash in relief, but my mouth feels dry, and I wish I had accepted some of that tea.

"What we had in common, you see, was we were both drunks. Lonely drunks. We'd be trying to quit, and we'd take long walks together to keep the other from pickin' up the bottle," he continues. "I feel like I probably did most of the talkin' though. Your mother never had too much to say, at least not about herself. But if you want more information, you should probably talk to Geraldine."

"Oh, good, you know Geraldine?" I reply, feeling calmer by the minute. "Is she a friend or a cousin?"

McCready clears his throat. "No, not a cousin. Geraldine was your mother's—how do you all say it nowadays—partner?"

Brian draws in a sharp breath.

"Partner?" I ask. "As in…"

"Yes," says McCready. "I assume *they* were lovers."

The only sound in the room is the soft purr of the cat.

"But I think they ended things a while ago," McCready inserts into the quiet. "I think it ended rather badly, actually."

I nod in understanding, although I comprehend nothing. My mind plays white noise, my shoulders lock, stiff and hunched, and a temporal pulsing begins at the top of my spine, the pain encroaching the base of my skull like an invading army.

"Do you know how to get in touch with this Geraldine?" Brian asks, sensitive to my stunned silence.

"I do not," he says, and then pondering a thought while he strokes his cat's ear, he offers, "but I *do* know that she lives in Florida. She would come up here for the summer and stay down there in the winter. You know, how old white people do."

"Maybe we could look at your mom's phone records?" Brian suggests, nudging my shoulder with his, trying to snap me back to coherence and my greater mission.

"Mr. McCready," I blurt out. "Do you know Matty, too?"

"Matty, Matty…" McCready rubs his lightly whiskered chin, the sound grating like sandpaper. "No, I don't recall August talking about Matty. Maybe someone from her past?"

I quiver at the thought of August's sticky, murky past, which was quickly becoming a chasm of the unknown, and perhaps unknowable, elements of her life.

"I can see I've thrown you for a loop, Miss Littleton," McCready says. "I apologize for giving you information that might be hard to deal with. But your mother was a very complicated woman. I know because I, too, am restless and complicated. She never really found her true happiness, did she?"

I agree with him, shaking my head. Tears settle in the corners of my eyes, and the base of my skull throbs with insistence.

"Neither have I," he responds. "But for entirely different reasons."

He lets the cat free, and it jumps to the floor. He leans in toward his guests. "Do you have any idea what it's like to live your entire life in exile?"

Brian and I both shake our heads again in timid silence, scared schoolchildren facing down the bully at recess. Somewhere in the house a floorboard creaks, and another cat, thin and black, scuttles around the corner.

"Forgive me, Mr. McCready," I say finally, finding breath in my lungs and will on my tongue. "But why did you stay here? Why didn't you pack up and leave and start over somewhere else?"

"Please, call me Nelson," he says with a curt smile, his fingers fidgeting on his knees. The black cat slinks against his bony ankles. "Well, my dear, it was against the law for me to leave the county. I was—I still am—under indictment for a crime I did not commit. A *murder* I did *not* commit. And a Black man, running from the law at the end of the Jim Crow era? No, I did not want to be that man. If they caught me alone at night, I would have been lynched for sure. Anytime I tried to leave here, they knew. Somehow, they always knew."

I shudder again, ashamed I chanted with the other children outside his home on Halloween night. Guilt folds itself into my percolating emotions, and I notice Brian also shifting uncomfortably on his side of the sofa.

"So, I stayed here," McCready goes on, gesturing around his living room, his palace of well-worn furniture covered in cat hair. "Safe in this home. Alone. Doors locked, shades drawn, for all these years, with Gladys. And my cats. I call them the Pips." He chuckles. "I have not had many choices, you see. I'm living out a life that was dealt a poor hand, but I'm determined to play until the game ends."

I admire the way Nelson owns his circumstance and embraces his solitude. So unlike my mother, who blames both of those on everyone around her, determined to be the victim.

"Mr. McCready, Nelson, forgive me for asking," I say, because now I *needed* to know, "but as you say, you were not involved in these crimes in the sixties. We have no reason not to believe you, but why do you think you were blamed? What were you doing there?"

"Ah yes, the question. Why I was there?" he asks, stroking his chin again. "You'd think after all these years, I would have come up with a good answer. The truth is I don't even remember anymore why I was there." He pats the pillow beside him, asking his cat to return. She obliges with a leap onto his lap.

"The memory is murkier with each passing year, y'all," Nelson begins, with slow methodical strokes down the furry stripes of his cat. "I just remember that I needed to call my mama that night. And, well, I didn't have my own telephone in those days. No one did. We were just struggling students, trying to make our way. So, I had to make all my calls from Southern Bell's finest, the phone booth downtown. And there was only one booth, you see? So, when I got in there, I tended to stay until I had finished my business."

I nod my encouragement, hopeful Nelson's about to reveal something new, something we need to know. Brian perks up and leans forward, absentmindedly petting a white cat that is bathing itself on the arm of the sofa.

"Now, I know I called Mama that night, but I can't remember why I stayed in the phone booth. Maybe for no good reason. Maybe a storm was coming. Maybe I had some other calls to make, or maybe just because I was a poor student with nothing better to do on a Sunday night. Can't recall all those details now. But I was still in there when the police showed up with their lights blazing, sirens screaming, askin' me to step out, put my hands in the air… just plain arresting me, right on the spot. I had no idea why."

Gladys the dog approaches the couch with trepidation and sniffs at the strangers in her home. I scratch behind her ears, knowing I cannot risk Nelson getting distracted from his story.

"I don't know what I did or said next. I just know I was scared. *Real* scared. A Black man gets pulled out of a phone booth by police with guns drawn. Never gonna turn out well. I don't think I knew, at that point, what had even happened in Pop Gray's that night. I never saw anything. I swear to you now. But the police, they started asking me all sorts of questions. Why was I there? How long had I been there? What did I see? And I panicked, I did. No other way to say it. Probably just made up some story on the spot that I thought might get the handcuffs off me. It was dumb—dumbest thing I've ever done. And y'all, I've paid the price every day since they locked me up."

Brian catches my eye, and I nod my silent assertion that he should press the matter.

"But you said there were others, right? Other men, or boys, you saw running away from the scene?" Brian asks, eager as a squirrel trying to crack its first nut.

"I don't know what I said," McCready replies. "I may have said something like that. I just know I was really scared."

Brian exhales loudly, his jaw clenching and unclenching as he tries to work out the facts. "So there never were any other suspects?" Though I presume he knows the answer.

"Those cops took me into the station so fast. Pressed charges like the world was ending tomorrow. There was no time for them to even think about any other suspects," McCready says, his resentment cutting like a dull knife, edging his words. "I ain't got no money for no lawyer. I had just moved to town, so I didn't know too many people, really just the kids at the boarding house. I was in a real pickle."

"So, Cliff was right," Brian says under his breath.

"And Sally was right," I agree, a little louder. "For what it's worth, Mr. McCready, there are quite a few in this town who believe in your innocence."

"Believe, believe…" McCready knits his brow. "I don't really care what they believe anymore. I gave up on that a long time ago. I'm dead to them all…" His voice trails off, sensitive to the thought of my dying mother. "You see, I was blamed for it all. And I never really knew what I was up against. I didn't fight because I couldn't fight. I was one Black man drowning in a sea of white." He stands then, Briar tucked in his arms and Gladys obedient at his heels. "Please, give your mother my best. Tell her that I do miss our walks together."

I remain still on the sofa for a moment too long—until I feel Brian nudge my knee. We're clearly being shown to the door. But I have to try one last time, just for a little bit more.

"Nelson, if you don't mind me asking, what did you and August talk about on those long walks?"

"Oh, just old people stuff," he says, opening the front door, ready for us to leave. "The weather, the way it shook our bones. The old days, the new days. Where life had taken us before we ended up here to die."

As I move begrudgingly to the door, I want to ask more questions, needing to hear from someone, anyone, who knew more about the person my mother had become.

"Yes, indeed, those long walks helped me quit the drinking. And Aggie stopped drinking, too. But that's when she fell really sick."

Something about the idea of August finding the internal willpower to control her vices actually irks me. It seems like too little, too late.

"Did she ever talk to you about her family?" I ask with some hesitation, loitering on his threshold. "Her mother or father…or me?"

"Well, Miss Littleton, I think your mother was very proud of you, though I'm sure she didn't know how to show it. It did always seem like she carried a sort of regret around with her."

It isn't much of an answer, but I surrender, shaking his hand. "Thank you for your time, Mr. McCready."

"Thank you for bringing back my Briar cat," he says. As he closes the door, he adds, "A good day to you both."

Brian and I stand on the doorstep, speechless, assessing the damage.

"Whew," he says first, "that was intense."

"Yeah," I agree. "My mom is gay."

Brian smiles despite the gravity of the moment. "I did not see that one coming."

"You and me both."

"What are you going to do?" asks Brian. I look over my shoulder at the dark house behind us, and I can see Nelson watching us from his window, willing us to take leave.

"Well, I guess I will need to find Geraldine."

Chapter 19: Folding

Geraldine, who lives alone in a thatched-roof cottage in a cove near the shores of Boca Bay, drinks coffee and daydreams out her window on the Monday after Thanksgiving.

Patterned, yellow light dances through the still-green leaves of the lemon trees. There's a cold wind sweeping down the coast, always unusual in Florida, but the leaves are persistent. Maybe in their mind, it's still summer. They, like her, invest in hanging on.

She'd picked the last fruit from her orchard a few weeks ago with a little help from some illegals on the side and had already sold her seasonal stock at the farmer's market. She made enough cash this year to buy her grandchildren something nice for Christmas, and though they'd all just left this morning, the house seems far too quiet. She misses the pitter-patter and smeary mess of them all.

But she's glad Thanksgiving has come to an end for another year. She's getting too old to manage all that cooking and those pies. So many pies required now! Troy wants pumpkin, the twins will only eat apple, and Suzanne —well, she only ever eats one bite of a slice—always brings Geraldine fresh pecans to make pecan pie, so she must make that, too. Geraldine prefers sweet potato pie, but she's the only one who does, so she never even makes it. She only serves the other's demands.

Thinking maybe it's time to scratch the itch of that craving, Geraldine starts rooting around in her pantry for some of those sweet potatoes just as the phone rings in shrill defiance of the silence. She gratefully snatches it up with a quick hello.

"Um, hello. I'm trying to reach a Geraldine Lynch who knew my mother, August Littleton. Do I have the right number?"

Geraldine drops the sweet potato she's holding. It makes a loud thud on the ground. The lady on the other end of the line seems to be speaking about August in the past tense.

"Well, yes, I know August," Geraldine replies, her heart suddenly feeling seismic. "Is something the matter? Did she die? Please, Lord, tell me she did not die."

Geraldine has been dreading this call, though she knew August was not well. They hadn't talked in months, but that last time, she could hear it in her voice like air slowly leaking from a tire, thin and worn.

Before the lady on the phone can answer, Geraldine follows up with, "And who is calling, may I ask?"

"Ms. Lynch," the lady replies, a calm relief rounding out her words. "This is August's daughter, Jan."

So, the daughter had found her. And did she know about it all?

"You see," Jan continues, "August, well, she's at home with hospice care now, and I'm afraid…well, she doesn't have much time left."

Geraldine stares hard at the warty sweet potato on the floor. She kicks it lightly with her big toe and watches it roll and stop under the ledge of a cabinet. That's how she feels now. Like a battered sweet potato.

There must have been a long moment of silence because the voice on the other end of the line says, "Geraldine?"

The daughter sounds a lot like August, calling her out like that. Insistent, impatient, eager for more of everything—information, time, attention, love.

"I'm here," Geraldine says finally, as a layer of sadness settles between them.

"Oh, good," Jan says in a soft voice. "I'm sorry. I know it's a bit awkward to hear from me and to hear such bad news. I just feel like I need to, you know, help August tie up some loose ends. She seems to really be struggling with letting go."

"How did you find me?" Geraldine asks.

"Well, Mr. McCready told me your first name, and I had to do some digging to find your last name. My mother has a few old boxes lined up in the spare room, and I've been going through her things. Anyway, I found a few of your letters. To her."

So, she knows, Geraldine resolves.

"Even then, it wasn't so easy to find your number," the daughter continues. "You're the third Geraldine Lynch I called."

"Well," Geraldine says, trying to gather herself and collect her thoughts. "I truly am very sorry to hear about August's poor health. And I'm sorry for your troubles, I am. But it has been a while since we've been in touch, and I'm afraid my friendship with August didn't end on the best note. I'm not sure she would even want to see me."

The daughter inhales sharply on the other end of the line.

"I understand, Geraldine, maybe more than anyone," Jan says. "North Carolina is an awful long way for you to come, and I can't even say if my mother will still be alive if you make the trip. But perhaps, if you're able and you're willing, you could help me understand a little bit more about August's life these past few years? I mean, it seems she has been off…a bit more than usual."

Geraldine's fist closes tightly around her coffee spoon, and she stirs it with vigor, without awareness. "She would not want you to know," she whispers into the phone line.

Jan stays silent.

"It was very important to her that others were not aware of our relationship…"

"Aware that you and August were a *couple*?"

Somewhat uncomfortable, Geraldine lets out a burst of nervous laughter. "Well, we were a couple of old geezers, that's for sure."

"I must admit," Jan says in a measured voice, "I was shocked when Mr. McCready told me about your… friendship. But even then, a part of me was just grateful that August had found a companion."

Geraldine clears her throat. "Well, I'm sorry to say that it did not end well, and I can't be of more help to you." She taps her foot impatiently and stares out at the tossing trees.

"Oh," Jan responds, sensing the conversation might be coming to a close. "I see. Before you go, maybe I could ask one question. Do you happen to know who Matty is?"

"Oh, I…I'm not sure I do." Sadness sits heavily on Geraldine's shoulders, an old lady shawl she cannot shrug off, and she's unsure how much she can confide in this persistent voice on the other end of the line.

"Oh," Jan says again. "Well, that's okay. It's just someone else August has asked about, and I'm just trying to do what I can do to—"

"I cannot come," Geraldine interrupts, her hands nervously folding and unfolding, folding and unfolding, as was her way.

"I understand, Ms. Lynch. I do, really, it's not a problem. Sorry to have bothered you."

"I just can't. Goodbye." Geraldine throws the receiver back on the cradle as if it had caught fire. She puts her head in her hands.

She knows she will have to go to August.

Chapter 20: Arriving

The call to Geraldine had been uncomfortable at best but also unproductive. August's journal amounts to more questions and no answers, and I still have no lead on the identity of Matty. But I did get the cat back home, so I feel perhaps my efforts aren't entirely in vain.

August remains in deep, sedated slumber, and I take the found time to call John for moral support.

"Your mother has preferred ladies all these years, and you never even knew?" John asks, incredulous.

"How would I know, John? It's not like we got on the phone and gabbed about our sex lives."

"Well, do you think she went both ways?" There's a snicker in his voice, and I know some part of him enjoys this fodder for gossip. "I mean, she must have liked men at least a little bit because, well, *you* were born."

"I don't know, John. You tell me how to account for the sexual persuasions of a bipolar misfit."

"Okay, okay, you made your point. But do you remember her ever having a girlfriend?"

Our nomadic life in the orange VW didn't lend itself to making friends of any persuasion. My earliest memories, the ones I try to hide from but inevitably always find me, are only of my mother and me. No other man, no other woman. And they went something like this: empty campgrounds, dry riverbeds, swatting away mosquitos, and scrounging for food forgotten by campers who came before. A half carton of warm milk, some crackers, or brown bananas. Nights spent on a stranger's sagging couch with only my old ratty doll for company but unlimited access to cartoons on a black-and-white TV. The crowded yurt on the apple farm where, I suppose, I had been old enough to realize August was one of Frank's chosen conquests.

I grew up amongst the wanderers and the squatters. August and I made our way without having any idea where we were going or why. Those days with just the two of us—ambling, lingering, departing—may have been the best days I ever spent with my mother. Before her brow became permanently pinched in judgment. Before her hands clutched for a life she could never grasp, and before time and disease took away her beauty. Before contempt became her language.

August was never a good mother, and I knew that even then. I'm not sure if she ever saw me as a real person or simply more of an appendage. Back then, however, I had a somewhat intangible understanding of neglect. I had no other view of life to which I could compare my own.

"I don't know who my mother may or may not have slept with, John," I counter. "And unless she's going to give me the name of my father, I don't actually care. But the point is…I *found* her."

"Who?"

"Geraldine! Try to keep up, John."

He snickers on the other end of the line.

"I found her last name on a letter in one of those boxes I told you about in the closet. I paid for one of those internet name search things, and I called a few numbers until I found her."

"Wow. Nice work, detective. Did you learn anything from her?"

"Unfortunately, no. Sounds like a bad breakup."

"Ugh. Can you imagine having to end a relationship with August?"

"Actually, I can," I say. "I've been trying to do it my whole life."

"Jan, I'm sorry this is so shitty," he says. "Let me ask again. Do you want me there? I can come tomorrow. I just need to unload a few things at the office."

Mentally, I review the list of daunting tasks that lay before me—a funeral, sorting out the house, the bank, the debt August would undoubtedly be leaving in her wake —and I admit I'm overwhelmed. Still, I feel these are things I need to take care of on my own,

"No, not this time," I reply with as much certainty as I can sell. "I've got this under control. Thank you, though. How is Laney?"

"Oh, she's fine. Knee-deep in basketball practice and the new boyfriend," John says. Then, with a pause for consideration, he continues. "Jan, don't you want her to be able to say goodbye to her grandmother?"

I sigh. Preserving the distance in place and time between my mother and my daughter somehow feels imperative. "John, we've been over this. Laney doesn't even know her, and that's really for the best. She doesn't look good, she's not even talking, and when she does, nothing makes sense. It's all nonsense. In fact, right now she's just sleeping all the time." I neglect to mention the sedative I had Gregor administer. "I mean, what would she even get out of it?"

"Okay, okay. Your call. I'll give her your love when she gets home from school. And you hang in there, kid."

As I end the call, Gregor walks into the kitchen, frowning and holding August's medical chart. "Jan, I am sorry to bother you."

"No bother, Gregor. What's up?"

"Your mother's blood pressure is up this morning, and it's quite high. I know you know this, but because of the DNR, we won't give her blood pressure medication for this. It's a very normal reaction to the phenobarbital."

He gently pulls a kitchen chair from the table and sits down beside me, intent to meet my eyes.

"But we also see this, usually, as a sign," he says. "It's one of the body's ways of telling us it's tired of fighting."

I nod my understanding. "Is she awake?"

"I honestly cannot tell," Gregor replies. "You can see for yourself. She lies very still. I don't think she is uncomfortable. Her eyes stay closed, but sometimes, when I have my back turned, I think they're open, and she's watching me."

"Story of my life, Gregor." I rise from the table, grabbing the sweater I had flung over my chair. "I need to run to the store. There's no food in this house, and we'll both feel better if I can make us a proper lunch."

"A proper lunch sounds good," Gregor agrees. "Go ahead. She'll be fine while you're gone."

I hurry out the door, afraid my chances to escape the confines of August's house grow slimmer as she declines.

Dark clouds blanket the horizon, and thunder echoes beyond the marsh grass, telling me a storm brews out at sea. The morning air feels thick and sticky, the promise of rain prompting me to turn back to grab an umbrella. But then I remember I never retrieved it from Cliff's bar. My watch reads 10:30 a.m., and I'm not sure if the restaurant is still closed, but I walk briskly in that direction.

When the sky opens up, I'm at the crest of the drawbridge. The raindrops have mixed with small pellets of hail that bounce off the railing of the bridge with resounding clanks and pings. The air turns colder, and my sweater is not enough, so like a refugee escaping certain doom, I run the distance and pound urgently on the restaurant's locked front door.

I can see Cliff inside, filling large carafes of water from the sink at the bar. He waves and hurries to open the door.

"What happened to you?" he asks with a devilish grin, taking in my drenched clothes and the hair plastered to my face.

"I'm sorry. I know you're not open yet," I apologize, gratefully stepping into the warm dining room. "But I think I left my umbrella in here a few days ago." I look down at my wet boots and notice water pooling at my feet onto the clean wood floors. "I'm sorry," I say again, regretting I had come.

"Ah, yeah. No apologies needed, Jan," Cliff says. "You want some coffee?" With unexpected familiarity, he reaches over my shoulders and peels off my wet sweater, hanging it on a brass hook beside the bar.

I did. I wanted coffee, and I wanted company. I wanted to stay here in this warm place that smelled like oregano and freshly baked bread. A place where there was no looming death, no passing judgment, no unknown history.

"I can't stay long," I reply, sliding my wet jeans onto a barstool. Cliff steps through the swinging gray doors that lead to the kitchen and returns with a hot cup of coffee.

"Fresh brewed," he says, setting it in front of me. Steam rises from the mug to meet the occasion. Then, remembering my stated quest, he stoops below the bar, rummages for a minute, and comes up with my umbrella.

"Guess I could have used this on the way here." I laugh, throwing it on the empty stool beside me.

"What *really* brings you out in this weather, anyway?" Cliff asks.

"I need to get some groceries. Literally, there is nothing left at my mother's place but canned goods. I didn't expect I'd be staying in town this long, but since I'm still here, well, we've got to eat. And honestly, I had no idea it was going to storm."

"Your mother…is she going to be okay?"

"No. No, she's going to die. Maybe not today. Maybe tomorrow. Maybe next week. Maybe in a month. It's kind of hard to tell."

"God, I'm sorry, Jan," Cliff says, the condolence I have now become accustomed to hearing. "I remember those last few days before my dad died, and you really just feel the futility. Like there's nothing you can do to ease their pain."

The tension in my shoulders begins to ease, and I nod appreciatively, but I'm eager to move on from the very subject I had been fleeing.

"Oh!" I snap my fingers. "But I did want to tell you that I think you were right about McCready."

Cliff blinks at the abrupt change of subject, but then offers one of his 'I'm interested' lean-ins. "What do you know?"

"Well, I guess I don't *know* for sure, but I just kind of feel like he's telling the truth. We met him—Brian and me. We found his cat." I sip the hot coffee loudly, and it sounds like a slurp. Fidgeting on my stool like a nerdy teenager tripping over herself to talk to the varsity captain, I smile.

"You and Brian are—" Cliff's jaw tightens with the question.

"Just friends," I insert quickly. "Old high school friends." A bit self-conscious, I pull my fingers through my wet hair and fumble for the chain missing from my neck. "I do think McCready was set up, though."

"Yeah, the fall guy, for sure," Cliff agrees. "I mean, whoever did it could still be out there. Killed two young girls in cold blood…Why do you *need* a fall guy?"

"A Black man in the sixties…easy way to close a cold case?" I offer.

"Yeah, I get that." Cliff picks up a pen from the bar and twirls it in his fingers, pondering the evidence. "But the thing is, the case wasn't cold. They charged him with the crime *the next day*. Like they had solid evidence implicating him when in fact, they had nothing but his location at the scene. Why do you do that if you still have all these questions about what happened?"

I watch Cliff's pen twirl while I sip my coffee, feeling slightly silly as if I'm acting a part on a team of ragtag detectives. But I'm enthralled all the same. Nelson was my mother's friend—something I had never known her to have. Perhaps one way I could ease her pain would be to try to ease his.

"So, you know what I think, Jan?" Cliff leans his long torso across the bar again, so close I can smell him, ripe with cedar and spice. "I think one of the cops did it."

"Ah, a cop cover-up. " I stir a coffee that didn't need to be stirred. He's too near, and I have to distract my hands and steady my mind. I'm attracted to Cliff for sure, but in a way I have never *known* attraction before, an odd yearning to be *close to* him, more comfort than come-on.

"It's the only way I can make sense of it," Cliff expounds on his theory. "Maybe one of them had a thing going with one of the girls. Jealous rage kind of violence. Then, when his cop friends show up on the scene, they see his gun or some other tip-off it's their friend, and they start to figure out who to pin it on. They see a Black man in the phone booth, and they say, 'That's our guy.'"

There's a loud clatter from behind the swinging kitchen door, breaking my reverie and bringing me to the present. No longer a ragtag detective, I morph into a sad lady with wet hair and a dying mother, sitting at a bar well before noon and hanging on this bartender's every word like a schoolgirl crush.

"My produce delivery guy," Cliff explains, straightening up. "He's kind of clumsy. Let me go check it out."

"Of course, of course." I shoo him away and try to refocus. Umbrella, groceries, then back home. Now is *not* the time for flimsy excuses and flirtation.

When Cliff returns from the kitchen with a heavy box of citrus, I button up my damp sweater and retrieve the umbrella. The rain pounds on the windows and puddles form on the sidewalk, and I dread leaving this bar and facing the errands before me.

"Heading out in this?" Cliff asks, raising the beacon of his dark brow while hoisting the box on the counter. "You can stay. I'll make you some pasta. I swear, I really can cook."

I laugh. "So I hear. But really, no, I have to get to the store and get home. It's just…it's not a good time."

"Okay," he says, extending his hand. "But if you want to talk any more about this 'cold case,' come by tonight for a drink. I usually start closing up around nine."

I shake his hand, trying hard to come off as cordial, friendly, and appreciative. But an electric reverence creeps up my forearm as our hands connect, and goosebumps crawl up my spine. It's definitely time for me to leave.

"We'll see. My mother…but thanks for the coffee." I wave over my shoulder and head out into the drenching gloominess of the rest of my day.

As I load my shopping cart with groceries, I replay my visit with Cliff. The warm café, his strong hand clasped with mine, the way he leaned in close and listened attentively. I have never met anyone like him. Though I've only known him for a few days, I feel a sense of trust, almost as if we're old friends.

Strolling absentmindedly through the produce section, I recall Sally's story of her inquisition of McCready beside the vegetables. Cliff's theory — that the cops were in on a decades-long cover-up to hide the actions of one of their own — starts to resonate. I grab a bag of apples (grateful to have fallen far from the proverbial tree) and consider the possibility that, if true, Nelson's name could be cleared once and for all. He seems like a nice man, someone who obviously cared for August, despite all her warts.

I head home with three full brown paper bags, more than I can easily carry. I have to keep stopping to juggle the load, but at least the rain has passed, and I have tucked my umbrella away. Pausing to readjust a failing shopping bag, I realize I've stalled in front of the town library.

Despite the cold, the library's front door appears propped open, and the familiar, stale smell of old books and harshly used upholstery wafts out to the sidewalk. I find it strangely nostalgic and inviting.

I venture inside, and not much has changed. Several dusty couches, a shade somewhere between orange and brown, sit in the middle of the room, surrounded by magazine and newspaper racks. A new "Kid's Corner" has been created with patterns of balloons on the wall and some bright bean bags in the center of a rug covered with pictures of dogs and cats. I'd spent so many afternoons holed up in this place, and for better or worse, it feels like an integral piece of home.

After we'd moved back to North Carolina, it became clear to August that her wandering days were over, and she settled for a job behind the shiny librarian desk. Her days became filled with shelving, stamping book-return cards, and silencing all patrons who dared raise their voices above a whisper. At night, she'd complain her feet hurt or her back ached, but I knew, in reality, she sat on her ass in a swivel chair for most of the day.

The librarian at the front desk today seems young, maybe early thirties, with horn-rimmed glasses, trying hard to look the part.

"Can I help you?" she asks when she notices me studying her from just inside the front door.

"Oh, no. S-sorry," I stammer, propping a grocery bag on my hip. "It's just…my mother used to work here. She was a librarian, and I—"

"Oh, you mean Miss August?" The young librarian smiles now. "You look just like her. Yes, I know Miss August, know her well." Her smirk intimates maybe she knew her *too* well. "Would you like to put those behind the desk while you look around?" she asks, gesturing to the groceries.

"Oh, no, thanks. I just happened to wander by on my way home. For old time's sake, you know?"

"Okay, then," she says, rising from her chair, and picking up a stack of books off the desk. "I heard August was not doing so well. In fact, and I'm sorry to say this, but I thought she had already passed."

"She's pretty sick," I say, starting to feel like a broken record, "but she's still with us."

"I'm so sorry to hear that. I mean, I'm glad she's still alive…Anyway, you know what I mean. She was a bit of a legend around here."

I nod my agreement and shift the weight of the bags to get more comfortable.

"Well, we'd love to send her some flowers from all of us at the library. Would you mind giving me her address?" The librarian hands me a Post-it note that she ripped off from a yellow pad, and I have to put down the groceries to write the address. "Give your momma all our best. Tell her that Beth sends her well wishes." She then proceeds to a rack of books to restock the collection in her arms.

"Will do, Beth," I say, turning to leave the lonely library. "Say, one other question. Does the library still have back copies of newspapers on microfilm?"

Beth smiles her best bless-your-heart smile. "We have a database now."

"Oh, of course. Does it…Would the records go back to the late sixties?"

"I'm not sure. I guess it depends on which publication you're looking for and how they ended up converting their back copies."

"Wilmington," I say. "*The Star*."

Beth's brow crinkles behind her horn rims. She's clearly annoyed at being derailed from her shelving task. With a sigh, she puts down her books, clips back to the desk, and scribbles something, then hands it to me. "There is online access to this database through the county central library site. We don't actually manage any of the records here."

I accept the paper, noticing she gave me the same Post-it on which I had provided my mother's address, but I slip it in the wet pocket of my jeans anyway, and with a grateful wave, I haul my groceries out the front door, my squeaky, wet shoes declaring each step of my departure. Guess August won't be getting that flower delivery, after all.

That same afternoon, I turn my attention back to the stacked closet in the spare room. A box layered with memories and junk remains on the floor in the corner of the closet, albums askew, pink hat poking through. I reach in for the hat, smooth out the wrinkles, and place it on the windowsill.

Hoping to find more of Grandma Patty's belongings, I dive to the bottom of the peeling cardboard, my fingers searching for treasure until I feel the smooth gloss of a photo under the palm of my hand. I slowly pull it from the bottom. It's a faded black-and-white image of August and Grandma Patty, standing side by side in the front yard, framed by a spotless front porch just behind them.

My mother's face, round and cherubic, betrays a hint of a genuine smile, and though her pigtails show no color in the picture, I know they would have been blow-torch red. She wears a summer frock, lacy socks, and patent-leather shoes, and a small stuffed bear dangles from one hand. The other hand holds tight to her mother's.

Patty poses with a similar subtle smile as if a secret had just been shared between mother and daughter. She's dressed sensibly in a slim pencil skirt, a small clutch, and sensible heels. Her hair appears short, stiff, and coiffed, as always. They look happy, but photographs tell the story they want to tell.

I wonder if Grandma Patty had been a good mother to August—whole, available, and compassionate—or had she been the beginning of a ragged generational chain of bipolar mania? I carefully place the photo beside the pink hat on the windowsill and decide to dump out the remaining contents of the cardboard box.

And there it is, on the floor, scattered amongst cassette tapes and wrinkled report cards, like a treasure pulled from the rubble: my long-lost locket, its chain broken and frayed. I'd worn it around my neck from the moment August gave it to me in that white box with a silver bow. She'd said the locket once belonged to her, and she'd found it as she rummaged through Patty's old jewelry chest.

"Mama would want you to have this," August said, her green eyes shiny and sad. "It was a piece of her, and now you can carry her with you."

And so, it had stayed with me and became a part of me—until the moment my mother ripped it away. I rub my neck as if the pull of the chain still burned my skin.

I lost the locket on the day I left for New York. August sat on the armrest, smoking a Marlboro Light as I headed to the front door, Ms. Devere's station wagon idling in wait.

"Where do you think you're going with that necklace, darlin'?" Her words oozed through the cigarette smoke, threatening and insidious. "That was *my* mother's! If you leave this house now, that makes you a thief. That locket stays *here*!" She'd lunged off the armrest, clawing at the nape of my neck for the clasp.

I remember clutching the chain in desperation because it had always been more than just jewelry to me. Though a thin trinket of cheap metal, the locket made me feel connected to something bigger and broader, validating

I belonged *somewhere* because I carried a piece of the past with me.

August fumbled unsuccessfully with the closure before grabbing the chain and ripping it clean from my neck. The ties that bind unfurled and collapsed at our feet.

Now, retrieving the neglected necklace from the floor, I finger the broken chain, digging a fingernail into the slit of the locket to pry it open. Inside, I find a small, yellowed picture of a horse against a bright blue barn.

I close my hand around the locket, hug it to my cheek like an old friend, then place it on the windowsill beside the other found belongings.

I sift through the upended contents like a child on the beach, searching the sand for seashells. Graying paper with a raised seal catches my eye, and I carefully extract it from the pile of scattered papers. The type is faded, but as I hold it up to the overhead light, I can see that it's a birth certificate.

Janus August Littleton, Born November 28, 1967, New Hanover County, North Carolina

Mother: August Patricia Littleton

Father: Unknown

The date of birth is wrong. My birthday falls in December. I grapple with the confusion for a moment before I realize the lie I've been living with. It blooms salty and acrid on my tongue. I want to spit it out, right onto the wilted carpet beneath my feet.

The lines of lineage begin to pull me, taut and painful, dragging me down like an anchor. Fiercely clutching the tattered paper, I barrel with purpose and fury straight into August's room, questions barking like a rabid dog in my mind.

"Mother, can you hear me?" I shout.

August does not respond. Slow and guttural, her breath leaves her mouth in a sickly snore, but no other signs of life arise to acknowledge my anger.

"August? Mother? If you can *hear* me, what do you know about this?" I shake the certificate in front of her closed eyes, a futile rattling amidst the beeping and whirring of the monitors.

"Miss Jan, is everything okay?" Gregor approaches from the hallway, his innate sense of calm belying the temper of my outburst.

"Can she hear me, Gregor?" I prod, breathless and flustered, tears running furiously down my face. "I need her to wake up now. I need her to be able to speak again. I need to know. There are things I need to *know.* Can we… can we stop the sedative?"

Before Gregor can respond, I pivot back to the inert invalid, searing the fire of my breath into her ear. "August," I whisper, "if you can hear me, and I think you can, I want to know the identity of my father. And you *know*! You've known all along, haven't you? I have my birth certificate here. I'm holding it! It says my birthday was yesterday. Why does it say that? It says I was born right here, in North Carolina, not out in California, like you always told me!" I shake the paper beneath her nose again like a jar of smelling salts with the power to rouse her from a medically induced semi-coma.

Gregor treads carefully, taming my flailing arm and the angry flap of paper and guiding me by the shoulder away from August's bedside.

"I do not think she'll be able to answer you right now, Miss Jan," he says, easing me into the armchair in the corner of the room. August's folded laundry still sits stacked, crumpled, and disheveled beside the foot of the chair, and I mentally scold myself for not putting it into the drawers. But what's the point? I'd just have to dump it all into Goodwill boxes in a few days anyway.

"I can see you are upset," he continues, "and if there's some way I can help, I will do so. But my goal is to help your mother ease through the transition from life to death, and I have found that anger does not help that transition."

Poor Gregor, walking into this mess of a family.

"The sedative," I squeak, hiccupping away my tears. "Can we stop it?"

"That is not typically the course we take in palliative sedation, Ms. Jan. She should have a dose every twelve hours to continue this therapy."

"But do we *have to?* I mean, could we just skip a dose for tonight, and see if she wakes up?"

"At your discretion, yes, I can do that, though I'm not sure if it's the most ethical course we can take here. And even if we skip this dose, I cannot say if she'll wake up. Sometimes, a patient will stay in this semi-conscious state until they pass on, regardless of the administration of the drug. Your mother's journey is very different from your own, but you're both trying to find peace. You're seeking closure, and perhaps she is seeking forgiveness…"

I confirm I understand with a shameful nod.

"So, in the meantime, what can help you to relax?" he asks, trying to mollify me with his slow Caribbean calm. "Talk to a friend? Is there someone else in the family, maybe an aunt or uncle, who could help you with your questions? Maybe a cigarette?"

We have a laugh while Gregor hands me a box of tissues. I blow my nose loudly and let the Kleenex fall to the floor.

"I don't have any family other than her." I confide as I slump against the back of the chair. "I mean, I knew my grandmother a little before she died. She visited us in California once or twice, but it was pretty superficial. Still, I guess I wanted to *really* get to know her, you know? I dreamed of some connection to family, but I knew I was never going to get it. And I had these ideas about what a family should be. I don't know…catching lightning bugs in a jar, bedtime stories beside a crackling fire. You know, all that corny shit? Ha! Maybe I watched too much TV, but that was what I wanted."

"And you feel like your mother denied you this?" Gregor asks.

"I guess I do…" I say. "You know, when we lived out West, and it was just the two of us, I didn't feel like I was missing anything. I guess I didn't know what there was to miss. But when we moved here, life was so different, and *people* were so different…They had all grown up here, lived here their whole life. There were no wanderers like us.

"And there were all these, these strange Southern accents, and social norms and family traditions. All the things that make a small town tick, and I didn't understand *any* of them. I think I knew then that August and I would always be the outsiders. It was a big, dark hole that opened up in our life, and I felt like my mother fell right into it."

Gregor nods his head with understanding. "I never knew my grandparents either, if that makes you feel any better."

"Really? Why not? Did you move to the US when you were young?"

"No," Gregor says. "They were killed in a hurricane."

"Oh." A new layer of guilt—the empathetic kind that shames the selfish kind—washes over me. "I'm so sorry, Gregor. And I'm sorry to keep going on about all this. I know that you're right. I should let go of some of this anger. It's just that…well, I feel like I'm learning so much about my mother, about this, this *life* she had that, honestly, I knew nothing about. And it makes me wonder —was I cheated, or was I spared?"

He smiles, then turns his attention back to August, tucking loose covers under the mattress and gently rolling and maneuvering her fragile frame to avoid bedsores. "My advice would be to call a good friend, Ms. Jan. Call your husband. Call your daughter. Find someone who connects with your soul. You know, you are grieving, too. Whether or not you know it, you are losing something important to you. You're trying to say goodbye to a part of your past."

Gregor, wise beyond his years, has a point, and so I slink into my old bedroom and scrounge through my purse for my phone. I dial Reena and wait for her to pick up.

"Reena, are you at work? Can you talk?"

"I can make the time, Jan. How are you holding up, girl?" I sigh with relief at the sound of her friendly voice.

"I'm still alive, Reena, still alive. And so is August."

"That was going to be my next question. How is hospice working out for you?"

"Amazing," I answer. "I couldn't do this without him."

"Thank God for the hospice worker, truly angels on earth. I hope you've been able to get out of the house a little to try and keep your sanity."

"Uh, I am guilty of escaping without a second thought." Reena truly understands the way I operate. "Hey, have you been to that new place, Clifford's?"

"Well, now." Reena laughs. "*He's* a tall drink of water, isn't he? Thirsty much, my friend?"

"Yeah, yeah." I shrug off the tease. "Let's go there soon and grab a drink."

"You think you're going to stay in town a while, then?"

"Well, it's hard to know how long she's going to hold on, Reena. I mean, I can't pack up and go back to New York when she's like this, can I?"

"You would feel like shit if you did," Reena says.

"Exactly. And it's kind of strange, but the longer I'm here…Well, the more I'm learning, even though none of it makes sense to me. It's like I never even knew my mother…"

"Oh, right, I meant to tell you, I asked my cousin Bill if he knows someone named Geraldine," Reena begins, and before I can fill her in, she continues, "He said he doesn't recall meeting her, and Billy, well, he's kind of like Sally, he knows most everything about—"

"It's okay, Reena," I interrupt. "I found her."

"You did?"

"Yeah. It's a long story. Maybe one I can tell you over that drink. Can you meet at five at Cliff's?"

"Oh, at *Cliff's*? On a first-name basis now, are we?" Reena teases. "Let me see what time I get off…" She rustles some papers. "No, can't do it today, girl. Let me look at tomorrow…Let's see, Tuesday, Tuesday…Can you do it tomorrow at five? Oh, and before I forget, Bill said to send his prayers to your mother. He said to tell you that August was the only one who was nice to the colored kids back in the day."

"Nice?" I balk. "August was *nice*? Did he tell you anything more?"

"No, should I ask? Didn't seem important."

"No, no, that's okay. I'm just surprised, I guess."

"I'll see you tomorrow at five unless I hear otherwise from you?"

"Will do, Reena. Drinks are on me."

There's a knock at the front door, and I'm not expecting company, so I bound down the stairs to spy out the front window, and I see a yellow cab pulling away from the driveway. The sun is setting, and on the front porch, a lumpy figure waits in sepia shadows.

Chapter 21: Flirting

August's daughter looks so much like her, Geraldine marvels, as the front door hesitantly creeps open. The jawline, those fierce eyes, the puzzled brow settling into wrinkles but still so beautiful.

"Hello. I'm Geraldine," she introduces herself, trying to be brave and offering her hand to shake.

The daughter takes a step back in surprise, and Geraldine feels bad she arrived without any notice.

"I know I said I wasn't coming," she continues, "but then…I just had to. I hope you don't mind." Her hand still outstretched, she watches August's daughter's face vacillate between shock and feigned pleasantry for what seems like a long while. She had forgotten how cold it could be up here in North Carolina, and she shivers through her thin trench.

Finally, Jan returns her handshake and invites her inside.

Geraldine rolls her suitcase into the front hall, unwraps her headscarf, and takes a look around. It still feels a little bit like home. She sees the cozy throw she'd knitted over that rainy Fourth of July weekend still draped on the back of the couch. The photos she took on the farm with her old Nikon are still frameless, propped up on the mantle. But the place seems kind of dirty, and it smells a lot like an old people's home—like apple juice and rotting skin. Geraldine hates those places and continues to make her son promise never to put her in one.

"I'm so surprised to see you," Jan says, taking her coat. "After we talked on the phone, I thought that you—"

"I know, dear," Geraldine interrupts. "I know, I thought so, too. But after we hung up, I reconsidered, and then the next thing I did was buy a plane ticket up here. Before I could even understand it all myself, I was in the sky flying."

Geraldine moves with natural ease around the living room, a room she had helped craft, fluffing the couch cushions and tweaking the placement of the lamp that rests on the end table. She can feel Jan watching her intently.

"I loved your mother, at one time very much, and I can't let her die alone."

Geraldine's words fall heavily in the room, and she realizes as soon as she speaks them they may have offended August's daughter, who had also rearranged her life to be by August's side. She begins folding and unfolding her hands, her expression of worry. "I'm sorry, dear, I didn't mean—"

"I know." Jan offers a small smile. "I'm glad you're here, Geraldine. Truly. She will be glad you're here, too. Only—"

"What?" Geraldine cuts her off. "Am I too late?"

"No. I mean, I don't think so. She's still alive, but she's sedated. I mean, they call it palliative sedation. For the pain. She's been in a lot of pain."

Geraldine does not hesitate a moment longer. She bustles down the hallway to August's room, Jan trailing behind her.

"Geraldine, this is Gregor," Jan says, introducing the tall Black man who's carefully rubbing an ointment into the thin, cellophane-like skin of August's arms. August does not object. She's not jawing his ear off either, so she must be in a deep sleep.

"Hello, Gregory," Geraldine says, without paying him any mind, without seeing anything but the crumpled heap of the woman she once loved. On her tiptoes, like a mouse surveying the prospect of a morsel, she approaches August's bed.

Geraldine's face falls as the dim circle of light from the bedside lamp reveals a fragile old woman, who by all appearances has given up on life. This did not look like the same August that Geraldine had once adored, a lady who could hoof up that big hill on the farm with a knapsack of sandwiches, spend all afternoon riding until the horse's hide was chapped, then stay up all night playing bridge and swilling whiskey. No, the August she knew went full throttle. This lady in the bed appears barely able to run on battery.

She finds the courage to touch August's cheek, discovering her skin feels cool and leathery. Tears well up in her eyes, and she kneels on her bad knees at her partner's bedside.

"Aggie, it's Geraldine. I'm here." She reaches for August's hands, which are now damp and slippery from the ointment Gregor has applied.

Geraldine lets the others in the room quietly slip away, and she sits on the edge of the bed for a good, old-fashioned cry.

****

I close the door of my mother's room quietly, like a parishioner sneaking out of church before the closing prayer. Though still bewildered at the unexpected arrival of Geraldine, I feel a profound sense of relief someone who cared so much for August has magically appeared on her doorstep.

"Jan, is that your aunt?" Gregor whispers in the hallway as we both creep downstairs.

I laugh. "No, Geraldine apparently was my mom's *partner*."

When Gregor still looks confused, I clarify, "Her girlfriend, Gregor. *Partners*. You see?"

Understanding dawns on his face. "Yes, I see. Oh…I see."

"And I would have given you the heads up, but I had no idea that she was coming. In fact, she just told me this morning on the phone that she *wouldn't* be coming."

Gregor and I sit down wearily at the kitchen table. My notepad, keeping company beside a day-old cup of coffee, remains propped open to the bulleted list of my familial mysteries. I pick up the pencil and, with some degree of satisfaction, scratch through those that appear to have been resolved:

- ~~Geraldine? Cousin?~~

- Matty?

- The farm?

- ~~McCready? Friend?~~

- ~~Where is the cat?~~

As I mark off McCready's name, I remember Cliff's invitation to return for pasta. Now that Geraldine has arrived, well, maybe it would be okay to skip out again. I mean, it's not like Geraldine had hopped on a plane to visit *me*.

"Wow. You're making progress." Gregor watches me cross out the scribbled notes. "You've only been here a few days, but you've already figured out a lot."

I sigh, pushing away the cold coffee and doodling in the corners of the notepad. "I don't even know what I'm digging for here." I push back from the table and stretch on my tiptoes to reach the top of the refrigerator, where I blindly grope the dusty surface until I find what I seek. I pull down a half-empty bottle of bourbon, August's faithful hidden stash. Raising my eyebrows in invitation to Gregor, I pull two juice cups out of the cupboard.

"I can't." He raises his hands in protest. "I'm working here. It goes against my employment contract."

"Aw, c'mon," I coax. "Who's gonna tell? Not me. I'm the bad influence here. Just a small pour to keep me company. August has a bedside companion now who either loves or hates her. We're not really sure. What could go wrong?"

I pour the bourbon into both glasses and slide one down the table to Gregor. He shrugs, tries a sip, and makes a sour face.

"Yeah." I laugh, knocking back my own glass in one shot. "When you drink one of these bottles every week, you can't afford the top shelf." Yet, I refill my glass.

"So, you said your mother had a drinking problem?" Gregor asks, gingerly pushing the juice glass away.

"She does." I take a thoughtful sip, reconsidering my answer. "I mean, she did."

Nelson told me he had been grateful for my mother's help in gaining sobriety, which amazes me still and makes me think maybe I will ask Nelson over after all. I wonder if reconnecting him with Geraldine might bear low-hanging fruit as I continue to pick through the briars and bramble of all my questions. Maybe the three of us could all have a coffee and share our stories of August. Perhaps there could be something to learn in forcing a collision of these elements of the past, kind of like careless curiosity in a chemistry lab.

"Gregor," I ask, spinning my almost empty glass introspectively on the kitchen table, "is there something wrong with me that all I want to do is get the hell out of this house? Like, all the time? I mean, does that make me an inherently terrible person? That I don't *care* that she is dying." I lower my voice to a whisper. "That a part of me *wishes* that she would die."

"Miss Jan." He evaluates the twisted emotions on my face before he responds carefully. "There is no person who wants to sit idly by as their parent dies. Nobody wants to be in this place. For some, they feel too connected and are upset that they have to let go. For others, the connection is broken already, and all they have are the memories, both the good and the bad."

"Broken connection," I repeat, shooting back the last of the liquor. "That's me. Don't judge me, okay? But yeah, I need to get off the beaten path. I'll be back in an hour or two. Just call me if there are any changes in, well, in anything. Okay?"

It's unfair to ask Gregor to absolve me of my guilt, but he just smiles and pushes his untouched glass my way. "Just don't drink and drive. Walk where your path leads. Okay, Miss Jan?"

Unsurprisingly, my path leads me back to Cliff's, and I arrive just as the dinner rush winds down. Half the tables inside are full, couples wiping clam sauce from their chins with red napkins and toasting small life celebrations with the clink of stemless wine glasses. A family with young children straggles out the door as I step through, the mother pulling coats from her stroller as the chill of the night settles in.

Cliff stands behind the bar, and he catches my eye with a slow, satisfied wave, gesturing to an empty stool at the far end of the oak expanse. I slide onto the empty seat, hang my coat on a hook beneath the bar top, and before I can even pick up the menu, a glass of red wine and a heaping bowl of pasta appear before me.

"Glad you came back." Cliff smiles, the corners of his eyes crinkled, and then he works his way down the bar, settling bills and pouring cocktails from slender liquor bottles.

The pasta tastes as good as promised. Buttery angel hair, crescents of tomato, and delicate shrimp. I breathe in the warm aromas, garlic, and something peppery, lick the cool wine from my lips, and congratulate myself on this latest, greatest escape from Chestnut Street.

As the evening's crowd dwindles, Cliff pulls a server from the floor to take over the bar and finds the stool beside mine. He brings a scotch on the rocks, and his eyes, a reflection of silvered stone, warmly meet mine. The cuff of his shirt rests just high enough for me to make out the word emblazoned beneath his dragon's wings: *Truth*.

"So, what did you think?" He gestures to my empty bowl.

"Terrible." I scoff.

"Ugh. New Yorkers!" Cliff groans, and I playfully throw my napkin at him.

I have forgotten what this is like, this kind of ease with a man. All these years since the divorce, I'd become a head-down-on-the-streets, order-in-Chinese-on-Friday-nights kind of woman. I reasoned it far too complicated to start all those dating games over again, and instead, I'd focused on Laney and on scraping together just enough work to keep paying my rent on the Upper West Side.

Somehow, these past few years, I'd been able to compartmentalize my need for anything sensual, avoiding liaisons and lust, pursuit, and pleasure. I'd decided to lock it all away in that same dark vault of denial and dysfunction where I'd buried my history. But now, the thrill of the chase comes racing back, like a wild horse broken free from its stall. Here at this bar, where the lights dim, and the jazz plinks and plunks its promises, and Cliff sits too close, my left elbow *almost* touches his right. And he seems interested, too. *Doesn't he?*

Our proximity feels a little too bold and ostentatious. *Wildly inappropriate,* I can almost hear my mother's voice chiding me. I'm aware that this—whatever "this" is between Cliff and I—is about to become the primary subject of small-town gossip, something I'd desperately tried to avoid in all the years I'd lived here. August's strident voice bleats in my head. *Folks will say you're nothing but a tramp.*

But the wine has made me voluminous, and I find myself unfolding for Cliff, starting with the story of the knock at the door that turned out to be Geraldine.

"So, your mother likes women, and you had no idea?"

"No idea."

"And she and McCready were *friends*?" Cliff asks, a bit incredulous.

"Sounds like it. She helped him get sober, as he tells it."

"Huh. I wonder if he ever confided in her. I mean, if she ever talked to him about that period in his life. You said she grew up here, right? So, she would have been here around the time that he was arrested."

"I guess she was. She would've still been in school. Though we've never talked about it," I reply. "I'm not sure what Nelson knows. Maybe more than he's willing to share. But I guess I don't blame him. You know, he's just a harmless old man, looking for a friendly face.

Someone he can talk to. Sounds like people around here have been real assholes to him for the past fifty years."

I think about Nelson clutching his lost cat, rubbing the soft inner portion of her ears with his long, thin fingers. The poor man's life has been built on the foundation of loneliness and fear.

"Maybe," I continue, grasping at the idea that had been formulated earlier that evening, "I should bring him up here for a coffee, and I could introduce you. You could put on your old detective hat and dig for some of your answers."

"Hmm. Yeah, that's a good idea. I probably should have never given up that old hat. I was good at it, you know?" Cliff sips his whiskey and gets lost, just for a moment, in a former life and a different version of himself. "But the beat will wear you down," he says, snapping back to the present. "And when my Pops passed away, it was really his dying wish that I come down here and take the house, take over where his younger self left off. I think he thought I'd just roll right onto the police force down here. But then, with the money I made from selling my place in the city, and this space being open…Well, I just had to take my chance with the restaurant. It was now or never, you know? Anyway, no regrets."

He raises his nearly empty glass in salute, and I meet his with mine.

"No regrets," I agree, and the clink of our drinks feels like an unanticipated announcement. We smile at each other, linger in the flirtation, and consider the possibilities.

"Listen, I've gotta get this place wrapped up," he finally says, standing abruptly and breaking the moment. "You want me to give you a ride home?" The question rides the line between chivalry and suggestion, that runaway horse of hope and hazard.

"Sure," I reply without hesitation, my confident smile hiding the fact I'm completely unsure of what comes next.

Suddenly, it all feels as if Cliff and I are characters who have stepped into a scene of a play, and I prepare myself to give my best performance. Cliff locks the front door to the restaurant while I survey the set. The large spruce propped in the center of the island square has been strung with lights, casting their glow across the empty sidewalks. The moon above us resembles a wounded eye, swollen with the bruises of the night. A biting winter wind blows in from the sea.

I shiver and move closer to Cliff, drawn to the warmth of his body. I hear only our footfall and the cadence of our breath as it leaves us in puffy, white wisps of cold air.

Cliff's old Ford pickup, the kind with dents and scars cowboys like to keep around, sits parked just down the block. I climb inside, both reluctant and ready, and Cliff revs the engine and cranks up the Rolling Stones. Middle-aged rebels, we peel away from the darkened storefronts that line the town square.

"You said Chestnut Street?" Cliff nervously clears his throat. His sleeves still rolled up to his elbows, he spins the steering wheel in the direction of August's house. I watch slants of streetlight dance across the dragon etched into his forearm. I'm intoxicated, not only from the wine but also the moment and the man.

"No," I reply, still teetering pleasantly off-balance, unwilling to relinquish this escape. "I mean, yes, that's where my house is. But no. I don't know. Maybe we could just…take a drive? Look at the stars? Something like that?"

Every cell in my being rejects the notion of returning home to August, to the cramped cubby of my childhood bedroom, the bare kitchen cupboards and creaky, splintered floorboards constantly announcing comings and goings.

Here in Cliff's old, beat-up truck, I'm a cowgirl going home with the hottest cowboy in the saloon. And if I'm a cowgirl tonight, then I'm not a daughter, I'm not a caretaker, and I'm not a watchtower for trouble. No, I'm just a cowgirl in this imaginary play…

Cliff raises his eyebrows, surprised at my change of direction. "Okay then. Where to? The beach?" I can almost feel his pulse quicken, but he just keeps driving, my chivalrous cowboy, awaiting further cue.

You know what this will do to your reputation, young lady. I can almost hear August's scolding, the echo of her voice in my head so loud I look over my shoulder to the empty backseat.

Cliff steers the truck toward the beach, his headlights cutting through a thin veil of fog escaping from the cool, wet streets.

The Rolling Stones on the truck's radio sing about wild horses, and the song's refrain leads me to a sudden notion.

"No, not the beach," I direct from the passenger seat, trying to sound calm and cool. "Do you happen to know if there's a farm around here? One that has a blue barn?"

Disappointed, Cliff takes his foot off the gas and thinks for a moment, the truck slowing to a crawl and the crease in his brow deepening. "Yeah, I think I do," he offers. "There's this old dirt road a few miles from here. I discovered it one day when I was racing to beat the drawbridge. It cuts off a few miles from my house."

I exhale. "Can you take me there?"

"What? Now?" He laughs. "Oh…you're serious. Okay. Yeah, I guess I can."

Cliff turns the truck around, and we drive in relative silence. The anticipation of something unknown tickles my fingertips and rings in my ears. Cliff shifts gears into four-wheel drive as he turns onto the rutted dirt road, thick with stones and brambles.

"I hardly ever go this way at night," Cliff says, flicking on his brights. "It's too damn dark, and there are cattle roaming around all over the place. And deer, and fox, and a million other animals I don't want splayed on the front of my truck."

The thin glade of trees off the main road gives way to harvested rows and mown fields as the truck rumbles up a slight embankment, a hidden hill in the middle of this coastal plain. Moonlight ricochets through the cab of the truck as the road jerks and tosses us forward. We crest the small hill, and I can see the domed silo and the crumbling arch of another building, its wood worn and wilted.

The blue barn.

My hands rise instinctively to my neck, hoping against logic the locket will be there, resting in the hollow between my collarbones, but I'm frustrated at the touch of my bare skin.

The truck rolls to a stop just past the barn, the only sound in the air a drafty guitar from the dashboard as the Stones play on.

"Well, you got your stars," Cliff says, rolling down his window and pointing up. Indeed, stars spill from the night sky, every constellation demanding recognition.

I throw open the passenger door and jump out onto the dirt road, my gaze fixed upon the fieldstone foundation, the crumbling wood, and the barn doors barely hanging onto their hinges. Someone had sprayed graffiti up one side of the building, a high schooler's celebration of the class of 2012.

"What is it, Jan? You look like you've seen a ghost."

"Sort of feels like I have." I spin in a wide circle, taking in the fields of high grass, the expanse of the barn, the impossible stars above us. "You see, we had a picture of this very barn hanging in the hallway. And, well, the locket I used to wear as a kid…my mother gave it to me for my twelfth birthday," I try to explain, suddenly breathless. "There's a picture of this barn in the locket. I mean, it's a picture of a horse but here in front of this barn."

"This barn?" Cliff asks, leaning out of his car window. "Why?"

"I don't know. A blue barn and a horse in front of it. I never asked her why that picture mattered. It's just another thing that didn't seem important at the time."

"And you've never been up here before?"

"No, not that I can remember," I reply, rifling through my memory, hoping to seize a clue or sense a trigger. But I only find confusion and a sense of loneliness, sheltered here in a field of starlight. Unsure of my goal or my intention in coming, or why my heart is beating with such ferocity, I consider moving in closer. A part of me is aching to excavate the ruins of this place, maybe to find a relic of my past. But it's dark and late, and I'm alone on a remote hillside with a stranger, and so instead, I numbly climb back into Cliff's truck.

"Well, it must have some significance. Could the farm have belonged to someone in your family? Your mother maybe? Your father?"

I shrug my shoulders and watch the barn retreat in the side-view mirror as Cliff drives slowly away, the truck's rear tires spewing grainy red dust into the dark.

"I never knew my father," I state quietly, a sad piano from the radio providing accompaniment. "And I don't think my mother's family ever kept a farm, though I've been wrong about a lot these days, so who knows?"

The farm road subtly descends and turns back to sandy gravel and then pavement as it approaches its intersection with Main Street.

"Should we head to the beach now?" Cliff asks hopefully. In the moonlit sky, I can see the sharp steeple of the Baptist church on the other side of the sound, slicing through the canopy of bare trees.

"No," I reply. "Just take me back home, if you don't mind." All the wild horses of this night feel as if they've run their course. I'm suddenly tired and done playing the part of the cowgirl. The earthy scents of farm and pasture give way to marsh grass and oyster brine as we drive toward Airlie.

"Well, maybe I could help you find out more. I mean, about the farm," Cliff offers in suggestion. He glances my way cautiously, easing the truck onto Chestnut Street, trying not to disturb the balance of connection and curiosity that hangs on weighted scales between us. "And also, you know your suggestion from earlier about inviting McCready for coffee? I think we should do that."

"Oh, right," I agree, somewhat distracted, not realizing Cliff had turned into my neighborhood until we drive past Nelson's house, all its windows dark at this hour. "Yes, we should invite him."

The truck slows as Cliff eyes the McCready cottage. Our flirtation at the bar suddenly feels like a nostalgic memory instead of something that happened less than an hour ago. I try to recalibrate my focus, like a photographer adjusting her lens and angle to sharpen the view and capture the picture. But seeing the old barn had left me flustered, and I couldn't regain any semblance of cool composure.

We pull in front of the house, and I watch Cliff's eyes examine the sagging porch and its junkyard collection, the haggard limbs from the old oak littering the front lawn. A shadow passes across his face, something I can't quite decipher and he tries to hide. Shock, pity, or perhaps revulsion.

"No place like home," I joke, a cover for my shame, and I fumble for the passenger door.

"Wait," he says, reaching across my body to catch my hand before I can open it. "Could I… could I maybe come in?" His voice has an edge to it, and his eyes flash with an unexpected urgency.

"Oh no, Cliff," I answer quickly, worried about the mixed signals I've undeniably been sending. "I mean, it's just not a good time. My mother…I mean, who knows what's going on in there? I couldn't. It's just, it's not a good time."

He withdraws his arm, rejection creasing his brow. "Oh right. Yeah, of course. Maybe another time."

Unsure what else to do, I lean across the front seat and kiss him on the cheek. "Thank you for getting my mind off all of this," I say with a flourish toward the porch as I climb out of the truck. "And thanks for the ride home."

I ascend the porch steps and turn back to wave. From the cab of his truck, Cliff watches me leave, but his expression seems troubled. His smoldering confidence has burned and crumbled like the last embers of a camp fire. It's not until I'm back inside the house that the truck rumbles away, and I collapse on the worn couch with a sigh of relief.

I fall fast asleep, still wearing my coat and boots, and unexpectedly, I sleep in this disarray through the night. I wake in the morning to a stiff neck and the smell of toasted bread, the snap of something frying on the stove.

In the kitchen, Geraldine hums a show tune. "Good morning, dear. Have you had breakfast?" She greets me as I plod into the kitchen. Her eyes linger on my mangled mess of hair and last night's wrinkled clothes before she turns back to the stove, prattling on. "There's coffee, and how do you like your eggs? Your mother always liked them scrambled, but I prefer over-easy."

"Um, any way is fine. Thanks," I answer. "How is August doing?" I can hear Gregor's gentle voice rising and falling upstairs.

"Oh, she's awake," Geraldine says, wiping her hands on her flowered apron.

I'm surprised August has come out of her sedation, and the news should spur me to action, but I'm stuck, transfixed really, watching Geraldine prepare breakfast. She moves so naturally, so at home in my mother's kitchen. She knew exactly where the extra salt lived, and she rummages through the right drawer for a clean dish towel.

"I'm glad you came, Geraldine."

She smiles over her shoulder, stirring the pan. "Me too, dear. It has seemed to do your mother a world of good. Now, to see if I can get her to eat these eggs…"

Gregor takes August's blood pressure as I make my way upstairs. A candle flickers on the corner table, and the room smells like lavender. Geraldine's touch, no doubt.

August's hair has been brushed, and it hangs over her shoulders in strands of gray silk. She looks revitalized, calmed. But I scold myself not to be deceived and to remain prepared for war.

I offer an opening salvo. "Hello, August."

She does not smile in return, but her reciprocal nod appears soft, even compliant. "So, you found Geraldine." Her voice sounds full of sleepy gravel and barely registers above a whisper. But still, I think I can detect a note of gratitude.

Gregor removes the pressure cuff from her thin arm, then meets my eyes with a nod toward the door. I follow him out into the hallway.

"Did you skip the dose?" I ask, keeping my voice low.

"No, I didn't. She awoke, despite the sedatives, and as you can see, she's very tired. But the good news is she no longer seems to be in much pain, so perhaps we stay the course with this therapy."

I nod in agreement and return to the chair beside August's bed.

"August, you know you didn't have to hide Geraldine from me. I'm actually glad that you found someone you enjoy being with."

I can see August stiffen under the bed covers, her weakened joints creaking to attention. "Well, it didn't work out anyway." She coughs and tries to raise her arm to wipe the spit off her chin, but she's too weak. "She left— like they all do." Deep grooves around August's mouth turn down into a frown, painted with sleepy drool.

"But she's back now," I counter. "Making eggs for you."

August releases a noise somewhere between a chuckle and a snort.

"There *is* something else that I need to talk to you about." I tread lightly, knowing the ground beneath my feet could be riddled with land mines.

August's groggy eyes suddenly snap open, willow and wild, the eyes of a forest animal deciding between fight or flight. Her gaze darts around the room to the foot of the bed, the floor, and the dresser.

"My journal!" she squeaks, her raspy whisper becoming loud and shrill. "Where is it?"

I feign a casual survey of the room, unwilling to admit I have taken the book. "Relax," I say, gently touching August's elbow, feeling the tremors of her agitation through the thin bedclothes. "I'll find the journal, but it's not about that. I want to ask you about something else."

August's shoulders tense and strain as she tries to raise her head off her pillow. Her breath comes in big, wet gulps, and the heart monitor begins an incessant, wild beeping.

"Relax," I repeat, attempting reassurance, trying to sell the part of the compassionate daughter. "August, what I'm trying to say is I found my birth certificate. In that box in the closet."

August's anger deflates like a popped balloon. Her shoulders slump, and her head rolls back deep into the valley of her pillow.

"Oh, *that*." She exhales, her eyelids surrendering.

"*Oh, that*?" I dig in, irritated, and I grab onto her elbow, a bony projectile sticking out from the sheets. "That's all you have to say? No father listed, but I guess that's not a surprise. But what about the birth date? Why does it say I was born in November? And why does it say I was born here in North Carolina? I thought the story was that you left home when you found out you were pregnant and drove out to California. What am I missing here, August? *What* is the truth?"

Geraldine comes clambering into the room with a heaping plate of eggs.

"I don't think," I begin, holding a hand to stay Geraldine, but then I see August's eyes snap open as her old partner settles onto the bed, holding a forkful of buttery eggs. To my surprise, August takes the bite and chews slowly and deliberately like a cow relishing her cud.

Geraldine gives a satisfied smile and pushes a stray lock of silver hair back from August's face. Rolling my eyes, I stalk out of the room.

I find Gregor downstairs at the kitchen table, patiently notating charts.

"Okay, what the hell is going on here?" I demand. "I mean, one minute she's dead to the world, and you can't shake her awake, and the next, she's up and eating an omelet. Is this normal?"

"Ah, Miss Jan," Gregor says, putting aside his charts to assuage me. "I have found that nothing about the process of death is 'normal.' Each patient takes their own journey, each story unfolds a little differently. But yes, it is okay. If she wakes, she wakes. If she wants to eat the eggs, then she should eat them."

"But Gregor, she wasn't eating at all for days. Or so I thought. And now…I mean, how long can she hang on?"

It's not a graceful question but a practical one. I envision my empty apartment back in New York, and how this quick overnight trip has stretched on now for five days. I need to connect again with Laney, to feel the crook of her arm through mine as we stroll toward the subway. The plants on my windowsill require water, though they may already be dead. I missed that audition, and I probably already lost my new job at the TV station after sending a vague email this morning, citing a family emergency.

And yet, I need to settle matters here. For the first time since I drove over the drawbridge on Thanksgiving night, I feel like I'm being pushed in an undeniable direction, a swimmer seeking shore in a wildly thrashing sea.

After a hot shower, I find Geraldine sitting at August's bedside. Sleeping deeply, my mother seems to be once again under the spell of her sedative. Geraldine has pulled the armchair tight beside the bed to read a tattered paperback novel.

Having nowhere else to sit, I awkwardly settle cross-legged on the carpet at the foot of Geraldine's chair like a toddler cozying up for story time. Geraldine lowers her book, an old Agatha Christie, and she surveys me over the brim of her spectacles.

"I love her mysteries," I say, pointing to the book jacket.

"Oh, this? Yes, me too, dear. I've read this so many times I know who the villain is. I just grabbed the first book I saw lying around as I was running out of the house yesterday. I hate to fly without having something good to read."

"You live full-time in Florida now?"

"Yes. My son just had a daughter, and I wanted to be closer. Also, the mortgage is all paid off on my home, and it was just sitting there empty. I decided it was all just…easier. To stay down there, I mean." Geraldine folds and unfolds her hands, kneading her palms like a loaf of doughy bread, a nervous habit she summons often.

"Oh, I understand." I encourage her to continue by scooting closer, intent on helping her recognize my appetite for her story and my yearning for connection in this quiet break in the battle.

Comfort oozes from Geraldine like a warm pair of mittens worn against the wind. The bedroom blinds have been opened and slants of filtered light dance through the dusty air and settle, like sustenance, at my bare feet.

"Your mother, she just had so many needs," Geraldine pushes on, "and I…well, I wasn't sure I was the right person to be taking care of those needs. And she changed. She did. The way she used to embrace life—our long walks, the card games, and good conversation—it all seemed to disappear. Poof! In an instant, the lady I knew, the lady I thought that I loved, well, she just seemed… gone. She was angry. All the time. At everything." Geraldine presses and folds her hands, twiddles her thumbs, and adjusts her spectacles. Her gaze rests on August, lying feeble in the bed, but her mind seems to linger with the memory of the whirlwind my mother once was.

"Was this all…did this all happen after she got sick?" I ask quietly.

"Oh, yes, I guess her diagnosis made things worse. But I don't know. Maybe she really stopped trying even before that. It was like she had lost all empathy. It was all about her all the time. No consideration for others. It had to be her way. Also, I guess I knew that her physical condition would not improve. I had seen heart failure before. I…I wasn't sure if I could handle all that."

"You seem to be handling it pretty well right now."

Geraldine modestly casts her eyes down to her paperback. "Well, I didn't handle it so well last year. I mean, I ran back to Florida as fast as I could. But yeah," she stands slowly from the armchair and stoops over August, planting a soft kiss on her forehead. "Yeah, I'm here now."

She straightens and clears her throat. "Rise over run. That's the way I was brought up," Geraldine continues. "You know, my daddy—he was a math teacher—he always liked to say that. Rise over run, Gerry! Of course, he was talking about algebra, but I knew he really meant something more." She eases herself back into the soft chair. "And whether or not you realize it, Janus, you, too, chose to *rise*."

"Please, call me Jan," I suggest. "August is the only person who ever calls me by my full name."

Geraldine smiles in her easy way. "Your mother has all your commercials taped on the VCR right over there." She points to an old cassette recorder tucked under the television. "And that time you were on that soap opera, we watched those episodes about a million times."

"Hmm," I muse, disheartened by the idea of two old ladies fast-forwarding and rewinding to find my bit part as a bit player.

"I didn't know she had those on tape. But clearly, there's a lot I didn't know about."

"You didn't know about me, I assume?"

"No. Not until this week. So, if you don't mind my asking, how did you and August meet?"

"At the library," she says.

Mention of the library reminds me of the slip of paper with the address for the periodical database. *Where had I put that? Coat pocket?*

"I was checking out a few books," Geraldine continues, holding up her Agatha Christie in demonstration, "and your mother was working that day. It had been years since I had seen her, and back then, I was a married woman."

"Oh, you knew her before? From where?"

"Why, from high school, of course."

"You're *from* Seaville?" I ask in surprise.

"Yep. I grew up here, then went off to college at East Carolina. Got married and moved down to Florida because Chuck got a job with Amtrak down there. We moved back here in '95, after my youngest graduated. You wouldn't know the kids. They never lived here. But Chuck and I lived over off Airlie Road for, oh, almost twenty years. When he died, I got one of those small apartments they built up by the sound. It was just me, you see. Only needed one bedroom. A place to store my knitting needles. That's when I met August. I mean, met her again."

"Were you friends in high school?"

"Oh, I don't know if you would call us friends. I was a senior when she was a freshman. I'm not even sure if she knew I existed. But I always thought she was so pretty. She and her mama, Patricia, looked alike. That red hair and the seafoam eyes. I guess I had a crush on her, but back in those days, we were never honest with ourselves. I just assumed I liked boys like a normal girl, and that I just hadn't found the right one yet."

"Your husband Chuck—was he the right one?"

"He was." She pauses, pondering the question, hands folding and unfolding. "He was a good man, and we had a happy family for many years. I didn't let myself entertain the idea of being with a woman. It just wasn't practical, and I was a mom, so I had to set a good example."

"But after he died?"

"After he died…I guess I kind of lost my sense of place. I sort of had to figure everything out again. When I ran into August, it was kind of like…like finding the lock for the key you always had, but it'd been buried under the couch for forty years. It was a chance to be a new me."

I watch my sleeping mother, wondering if any of our conversations will seep into her subconscious.

"And how did you know she would be interested? I mean, how did you know you could pursue a romantic relationship with her?" I ask, though I'm not sure I want to hear her answer.

"I don't know, Janus. Sorry. Jan. It all just happened. I guess, if I think back to high school, maybe there had been rumors that August preferred girls. I don't think she ever had a boyfriend, and maybe in those days, if you were a pretty girl with no dates, people just assumed?"

I tuck my wet hair behind one ear, swallowing hard to find my courage. "Geraldine, since you and August were, uh, close…did she ever talk about my father?" I search Geraldine's eyes behind those thick glasses for a flicker of knowing, a spark of veracity, but Geraldine only returns my imploring gaze with steady sympathy.

"Jan, honey, I don't know anything for a fact. I mean, she didn't really talk about it. And I was long gone at college when you were born. I never asked your mother, and she never told me, but I know that she did, of course, have relationships with men." She pauses and thumbs at me. "I mean, obviously, you're here, right? But I never heard her speak of a great love."

"I was thinking about the timing. I mean, wouldn't it have to have been someone she knew here in Seaville? I don't know that for sure, but it seems she left North Carolina after I was born. That Grandma Patty turned her out. And as she told it, she just kept running across the country until she ran out of land."

My desperation is palpable, and I can tell Geraldine would like to reach out and crumble it to powder. She wants to have the right answer.

"That may be, dear," she says, choosing her words carefully, like a painter with her final brushstrokes. "Maybe you could ask her when she wakes up again?"

The burden of that task settles heavily on my shoulders. I'm not sure how many more confrontations I can bear, how many more starts and stops. I don't understand August's wide, fearful eyes every time I ask her a hard question.

"I was trying to speak with her about it earlier when you were making the eggs," I mumble, feeling dejected. I pick at the peeling polish on my toenails. "But she seemed so…alarmed at my questions. Then, she got agitated, and her heart monitor was going crazy. I don't know. These questions might kill her."

"Well," Geraldine says with a sigh, "she *is* going to die anyway." She states it with such matter-of-fact truthfulness I almost laugh out loud. "And you need to know before she's gone, don't you, dear? Or how will you ever know? The secret dies with her, I would imagine."

She's right, of course. I need to keep trying. Time seems to be vanishing as quickly as the light in August's eyes.

"Geraldine," I ask, marching the conversation to a less painful battlefield, "how well do you know Mr.

McCready down at the far end of the block? He's the one who led me to find you."

"Ah, yes," Geraldine says, folding and unfolding. "I know Nelson. He's a good man. Nearly got run out of town a few times, though."

"Yes, I've heard he's had some troubles, though I never really knew the whole story until I met him recently."

Geraldine leans in, keenly. "And do you now, dear? Know the whole story?"

"Well," I wiggle uncomfortably in my Indian-style position, still feeling a little like an impatient kindergartner at circle time. "It sounds like he was wrongly accused and maybe even set up to take the fall by the police."

Geraldine nods, the wise schoolmarm, her loose bun bobbing up and down, white wisps drifting down to her cheekbones. "Yes, I think that's right. And that may be one of the reasons your mother wanted to befriend Nelson. Because she knew Matty was the one who had him arrested in the first place."

Matty! The name at the top of my list.

"Oh, do you know where I can find Matty?" I jump in. "She was mentioned in August's journal, too. And Gregor overheard August talking about her in her sleep."

"Well, she's a he," Geraldine explains. "And you can't find him anymore. I'm afraid he died years ago."

"Oh, no. That's too bad. So, how did August know him?"

"Well, as I recall, Matty had a horse farm a few miles inland."

The horse by the blue barn.

"He was, oh, I don't know, kind of a family friend?" Geraldine continues. "August loved those horses. She'd go to the farm every chance she could to groom them, give them food and hay, take 'em out for a ride."

I swallow hard. "And so…I'm sorry if I'm not following, but what does that have to do with Nelson?"

Geraldine appears caught off guard. "Of course, how would you know? Why, Matty is Chief Matthews. He headed up the Seaville town police for years. He was the one in charge of the whole investigation into those girls' murders at Pop Gray's."

"Oh, Lord!" I gasp. "But McCready—uh, Nelson, I mean—I asked him if he knew someone named Matty, and he didn't."

"Your mother was the only one who called the chief by that name. Everyone else just called him Chief.

McCready wouldn't have known unless August gave him the connection. And I don't think she did. She knew that the accusations against Nelson had made his life hell and that on some level, Matty was responsible for it all."

My heart races as I try to digest the information Geraldine serves up, heaping helpings of both comfort and pain.

"When did Matty die, Geraldine? Do you recall?"

"Let's see." She unfolds the clasp of her hands and starts counting on her fingers. "I graduated from high school in '65, four years at school, yep…Oh, I don't know, sometime in the late sixties or early seventies? It was after Chuck and I moved to Richmond. I remember my mother calling me with the news. It was quite the scandal if I remember correctly. Yes, that would be sometime in the early seventies."

"Scandal?" I dig further.

Geraldine lowers her voice and leans down toward my cross-legged space, even though we are the only two conscious people in the room.

"Suicide," she whispers. "Shot himself in the head, he did."

I close my eyes and try to piece together the jagged angles of this southern soap opera unfolding before me, arranging and rearranging fact and fiction, aligning words, phrases, and notions I have been gaining, gathering, and grouping over the past few days.

So, Cliff's theory that this Chief Matthews, or Matty, might have played some role in covering up the murders at Pop Gray's and pinning them on McCready seems to hold up. And if she befriended Matty and spent time on his farm, then what did August *actually* know about the matter?

My limbs feel heavy, and a massive headache threatens, but I haul myself to my feet and balance on the thin slice of mattress available at the edge of August's bed. I place both hands on my mother's cold arm, scaly to the touch. Gregor thought it possible she could hear and understand, even in her sedation state, and we know can rise from her stupor for something as simple as a plate of eggs.

"August," I try quietly. When there's no answer, I follow up with a more forceful voice. "Mama! Can you hear me? When you wake up, we want you to tell us more about Matty. And about Nelson."

I narrow my eyes to study her inanimate face. She's so still—too still. I awkwardly bend to rest my cheek against her chest, where I can feel the slightest rise and fall. I straighten, sigh, and turn back to Geraldine, whose peaceful repose crumbles as I gauge for signs of life.

"Oh God, is she dead?" Geraldine's voice squeaks like the turn of a rusty faucet.

I shake my head, but still, Geraldine scrambles to her feet, and the book resting in her lap drops to the floor with a thud.

"I'll go get Gregor," she says, breathless, rushing out of the room.

I turn back to my mother. "I just need a little more time, August. Just a few answers before you go. I deserve that much, and I think you know this is true."

My heart feels as vacant as a foreclosed motel, so I'm surprised when a tear slides down my cheek. I wipe it away before Gregor hustles into the bedroom, pushed from behind by Geraldine like prodded cattle.

I explain Geraldine's frantic urgency. "She's barely breathing. It's very shallow. And her skin—it's like ice."

Gregor tucks his stethoscope into his ears and confirms a weak heartbeat. He checks her pulse at her wrist and her neck. "Very weak heart rate, yes, but it's still there."

"Well, can't you do *something*?" Geraldine shrieks, the wispy hairs that escaped her bun now glued to the sides of her sweaty face.

"Geraldine—" I begin, but she stays me with her hand.

She forces a calming breath, lets out a small hiccup, and tries again in a more measured tone. "I mean, can you give her some medicine or CPR or *something*?"

"I'm afraid I can't, ma'am," Gregor responds evenly, resting the stethoscope back around his neck. "Ms. Littleton has a DNR."

"Do Not Resuscitate," I explain when it appears Geraldine is not processing the words.

"You can't help her? She can barely breathe," Geraldine pleads.

"My mission, ma'am," Gregor answers politely, "is to keep her comfortable, not to prolong her life. But let's make sure she gets some oxygen." Gregor wheels the cart closer to the bed and affixes the mask around August's nose and mouth. Geraldine dissolves into sobs.

"How long, Gregor?" I ask.

"A few hours would be my guess," he says. "Perhaps another day."

"Okay. No more doses," I state with resolve. "Let the sedative wear off."

"But Ms. Jan—"

"We *need* her back, Gregor. If there's a chance, we have to take it."

Now that the end seems near, now that there's a definitive decline, like the plummet of a roller coaster, I suddenly know I want more time to sort it all out, more time to understand—the person my mother was and the mark she left on me. Maybe I need to try to forgive and find that damn closure. *Could I forgive? Is that what I came here to do?*

Geraldine collapses into the overstuffed armchair, where she sits listless, her chunky legs curled beneath her, too tired to even fidget with her hands. I kneel beside her and encircle her in my arms. When she leans in, I can feel her exhaustion, her body concave, waving a white flag of surrender.

Gregor examines the IV dripping into August's arm, then locates a box of tissues and hands it to Geraldine, who still sobs in my embrace. She pulls out a tissue and blows her nose loudly.

"I'm sorry I lost it," she says, after a deep breath. "I guess I haven't felt this way since Chuck died. It's just hard to know that I'll be so alone again." I don't know what to say, so I just squeeze my arms tighter around her sagging shoulders. "Do you mind if I stay right here beside her until…you know, until…"

"Of course, I don't mind," I reply, relieved at her offer. "I think she would want it that way. Should I make us some tea?"

"Tea would be lovely." Geraldine finds a quiet smile and pats my hand.

Downstairs, I add water to the kettle and set it on the stove before realizing I forgot to ask Geraldine how she takes her tea. I return quietly upstairs to find her holding tight to my mother's limp hand, her face bent close to August's and her whispers floating into the hall.

"You need to tell her, August. If I know what I think I know, you need to be the one to tell her before you go. Otherwise, I guess I'm going to have to…"

I tiptoe back down the stairs, not wanting to disturb the moment or the message. As I pour from the hot kettle, I'm startled by a light rap on the kitchen window. *Goddamit!* Boiling water splashes down the side of my thumb.

Draped in a cascade of colorful scarves and holding a casserole dish, Sally Mavey grins through the chilled windowpane. She holds the foil-covered dish up as an offering as if it were her admission ticket into August's kitchen.

I wrap my scalded thumb in a cool towel and open the back door. A chilly, salted wind propels Sally and her puff of jasmine perfume through the door.

"You brought a casserole?" I ask. "You shouldn't have."

Sally hands me the surprisingly heavy dish and begins to unwrap her layers of bright scarves, peeling off her too-tight overcoat to reveal a lime-green tracksuit beneath. She brightens the dim kitchen as she dumps her belongings in a messy pile on the floor beside the door, just like she used to when we were kids.

"Oh, it was no trouble at all. It's lasagna. Comfort food," Sally says. "Remember, Jan, we do this in the South when someone is," she lowers her voice, "*dying*."

"Yeah, thanks for reminding me because folks don't do that so much in New York City." I slide the token casserole onto the countertop. "I was just making us some tea. Can you stay?" I know full well Sally has every intention of staying for a while.

"*Us*?" she asks, leaning into my space with anticipation. "Who is this *us?*"

"Oh." I stall, realizing for a change I may be holding more information than Sally. "Well, you see, August, it seems, had a—"

"Girlfriend?" Sally finishes my sentence proudly.

"Well, yes. Did you know?"

"I didn't *know*. But I *suspected*. I mean, we all did. Lady with a gray bun?"

"Yes, and she's upstairs, so keep your voice down. Her name is Geraldine." I put the kettle back on the stove to reheat the water and rummage through the cabinet for another mug.

"Geraldine, Geraldine…" Sally rolls the name on her tongue, drumming her fingers thoughtfully on the kitchen counter while trying to place her, scanning her mental archives for a story to share. "Now, isn't that sweet that after all these years, your mama found love? Girl, when you said 'us', I thought you meant you were here with that strapping biker dude who owns that restaurant downtown."

I fumble the spoon I'd just pulled from the silverware drawer, and it drops with a metal clatter to the floor. A balmy blush rises up my neck as I bend to retrieve it. "What do you mean, Sally?" I ask, trying to sound nonchalant, turning my red face away from her and toward the kettle, begging it to whistle.

"My friend, this is a small town. There are eyes everywhere." Sally chuckles. "And people do talk, as you well know. I happened to hear that a certain someone," she points one of her brilliant pink fingernails at me, "left the bar last night with the foxy bartender, riding off into the night in his old cowboy truck."

"Oh, that." I try for a dismissive wave. "No, not what you're thinking, Sally. We're just friends."

"Sure, you are," Sally replies with a wry smile as she helps me unwrap the tea bags. "You know, he's from good southern stock, too. He may have that bizarre Boston accent now, but his family was one of the first to settle this part of North Carolina. Real good stock, if you ask me."

Makes him sound like a farm animal, I think as the kettle begins its low moan. I grab it from the stove and fill Sally's cup with the steaming water.

Sally bobs her tea bag, watching the liquid cloud to brown, when suddenly, her sunny optimism dissipates. "Wait a minute," she says, mid-bob, her face sober and serious. "That Clifford…his family…well, he's a *Neal*. Jan, *they* were the ones who were murdered in Pop Gray's. I wouldn't have put it all together if you and I weren't just talking about it. About McCready…If I've got the family tree right, those girls would have been his *cousins*."

My heart lurches inside my chest. "W-why didn't he tell me that?" I blindly put the empty kettle back on the hot stove. "I mean, we've thoroughly discussed his whole back story. He told me he used to be a cop. That his dad worked for the county sheriff. His mission to pursue justice and all that. I knew he was oddly invested in it all and that he had some theories. But I just thought he was clever and curious."

Struggling to make sense of the connections, I search to find reason in Cliff's intent. My fingers and toes have gone numb, as if I'd been left out in the cold too long.

Sally reaches over and drops a tea bag in my mug, and I realize I've been fervently stirring nothing but water.

"And Cliff, well, he said that he wants to meet McCready," I tell her. "He asked me to introduce him and set up a time for coffee. I guess now I understand why…"

"Well, if he thinks Nelson killed his cousins," Sally speculates, an eager reporter leading her subject to a foregone conclusion, "do you think he's looking for some kind of revenge?"

"Revenge?" I wonder. "No, not revenge. He doesn't believe that McCready committed any crime. At least, that's what he told me. I'm honestly not sure what to believe anymore."

I sag into a kitchen chair, forgetting all about Geraldine, who waits patiently for her tea at my mother's bedside. My legs feel weak, and my head buzzes like an angry beehive. I wrap my fingers tightly around the warm mug as if it can help me get a firm grip on reality. The burn on my thumb begins to blister.

"But why wouldn't he tell me all this?" I plead with Sally. The rickety wooden chair groans under her large hips as she joins me at the kitchen table.

I consider Cliff's sudden turn to urgency as I tried to leave his truck last night, wondering if he had known all along about August's connection to Chief Matthews and perhaps baited me to get closer to the source of his true intentions.

"Well, if you ask me," Sally says, "knowing what I know now, he came back to Seaville with a mission—redemption, or whatever, for whoever killed his cousins. Does he know that August and Nelson were friendly?"

"Yes. I mean, he does now. I just told him about that last night. But it bothers me that he didn't share his connection with me. Isn't it strange, Sally?"

"Strange, indeed." She blows on the rim of her mug.

The dry kettle sizzles and pops.

"Forgot to turn off the burner." I sigh, jumping to my feet to save the scalded teapot.

Geraldine bustles in from the bedroom. "Jan, did you burn up my kettle?" she asks before noticing Sally, reclined at the kitchen table in all her lime-green splendor.

"You must be Geraldine," Sally says, hauling herself to her feet and giving the old woman a squishy hug. Geraldine, unfazed, accepts the stranger's affection.

"Sally Mavey. Pleased to meet you," she carries on. "I live just down the block, if you ever need anything. And I brought a lasagna." Sally hikes her thumb over her shoulder to the casserole dish on the counter.

"Sal and I went to school together," I add, watching Geraldine take in Sally's unapologetic brand of brazen.

After two cups of tea, Sally agrees she has overstayed her welcome and heads home. But the information she provided has changed the trajectory of everything, and there's work to do.

First, I have to find that Post-it the librarian gave me, the one with the periodical database address scribbled on the back. I fish in the pocket of my jeans and sigh with relief that I haven't lost the scrap of paper.

Chapter 23: Digging

August doesn't own a computer, and I left my laptop back on my desk in New York. There's no way I can leave again and head back to the library to search the news database, so I call Brian, explain what I'm searching for, and ask him to bring over printouts.

Brian would come, I figured. No matter what, he would drop whatever meaningless task he was about to embark upon and rush to my aid. I know I'm taking advantage of his affection, but I don't care. I have needs, and time appears to be of the essence. So, I'll need to get by with a little help from my friends, as the song goes.

A sweaty and eager Brian arrives on August's doorstep an hour later with a fistful of printouts as anticipated.

"I got the *Star News*, and I found a few articles in the Raleigh paper, too." He breathlessly barrels into the living room, spreading the articles out on the coffee table. A light film dampens his brow, and I wonder if he actually sprinted the distance.

"Thanks, Brian. You don't know how much this means to me." I offer a friendly hug, and he beams.

"This one." He points to an article as he plops himself square in the middle of August's couch. "It seems to be the first crime report, though I'm not exactly sure what you're looking for." He looks up at me, hopeful I'll settle in beside him.

"I'm not exactly sure either." I settle cross-legged on the living room floor and begin with the article Brian suggested, a two-column piece from the Wilmington paper.

Small Town Murder Leaves Town Shocked

By Len Garvey

Sisters Kimberlee and Louise Neal, ages nineteen and seventeen, were killed in cold blood while working the late shift at Pop Gray's in Seaville the night of Sunday, April 23, 1967. Both victims were shot at point-blank range and died on the scene.

Robbery is the suspected motive, but no suspects have been identified.

Seaville Police Chief, Dillard Matthews, interviewed several witnesses who were near the scene that night, although there are no eyewitness accounts to the crime. The murder scene was discovered by Mr. Reginald Robinson, owner of the Dixie Theater, also located in the Seaville island square.

"I saw the lights were on, but the front door was locked, so I peeked in. I didn't see nothing at first. It was just, no one was at the front counter." Mr. Robinson said. "I called out 'hello, is anyone working?' No one answered, which kind of got me worried. But when I went around to the colored entrance, I looked down and saw the blood coming from under the kitchen door. I knew someone was hurt, so I started to go back there, and I saw them, before I went in. Through that little window on the swinging door, you know?"

The chief's incident report includes a note that Mr. Nelson McCready, 21, was using the town phone booth when he saw a white man and a colored man running with "something sharp, maybe a pipe" in their hands. Mr. McCready could not be found for further questioning.

Residents of Seaville say they are dismayed that this violence can happen in their small town. "It scares me to death," said Mrs. Millicent Barber, who was interviewed as she was leaving Robert's Market on the day after the murders. "To think some dangerous man is running around the streets, shooting innocent girls. In Seaville. What is the world coming to? This is what you get when you let that beach car bring all types onto the island."

The deceased, both students at Seaville High, are survived by their parents, Mitchell and Mary Neal. Services are planned for Sunday at 11:00 a.m. at the Seaville Baptist Church.

The article does not specifically identify Nelson as a Black man, but the implications are there, and I could read it no other way. A snapshot of Pop Gray's, its chrome facade gleaming even through the old, black-and-white photo, appears at the bottom of the page.

The wooden storefront sign in the picture has since been replaced with neon letters. And in the space where Pop Gray's offers a small patio today, it appears there used to be a thin alley. In the old photograph, a sign hanging in the alley reads "Colored Entrance."

Brian watches me scan the article, looking for signs of progress, hoping he can be the source of a breakthrough, a savior in my search.

"What else have you got?" I ask, setting aside the first piece.

He hands me another article. "This is from the next day, April twenty-sixth also from the *Star*."

Arrest Made in Ice Cream Murder Case

By Len Garvey

Seaville Police have detained Nelson McCready, 21, and have charged him with the double murder of sisters Kimberlee and Louise Neal. The siblings were shot inside Pop Gray's, an ice cream store in Seaville, on the night of April 23. The victims were employees of the store and were the only two working the closing shift.

McCready has been charged with robbery and second-degree murder, as it is believed the suspect entered Pop Gray's with the intent to rob the store of the daily bank deposit, which led to the ensuing violence. It is reported that $138 is missing from Pop Gray's prepared and accounted daily bank deposit.

No murder weapon was found on the scene, and none have been recovered.

"Mr. McCready was arrested at his home at 9:30 a.m. this morning without incident," Chief Matthews said in a statement earlier today. "He is our only suspect, as he was near the scene before, during, and after the crime, and we believe he gave a false account of his actions during that time."

McCready, originally from Roanoke Rapids, NC, is enrolled at a local college and has resided in Seaville for the past year. He is being held without bail in the town courthouse, awaiting arraignment on these charges.

Below the text there's a picture of Nelson in his early twenties, sporting a neat afro and a thin mustache. His eyes look out at the reader complacently, even then in the wake of his peril.

"Less than twenty-four hours later, they make the arrest?" I ask. "With no weapon and no motive."

"Well, there was the $138 dollars taken," Brian suggests.

"But even that doesn't make sense," I counter. "Was the whole day's revenue only $138? That seems unlikely. It's pretty paltry for a booming business, even back in the day. And the article doesn't make it sound like it…I mean, why would he enter with a gun with the intent to steal money? Say things go south, and he kills someone, maybe even by accident. Even in that case, you take *all* the money or *none* of it. You don't grab a handful and say, 'Yeah, this was worth murdering for.'"

"Well, Jan, that's a fair observation," Brian says, shuffling through the articles. "It all backs up McCready's story. But, uh…I gotta ask. What *is* going on? Why all this urgency? Why are we frantic for this information about a decades-old crime right *now*?"

He nudges the crown of his head sideways, toward the stairs that lead to the bedroom where August lies in repose. I sigh deeply and reach across the coffee table, placing my hand on top of Brian's.

"It's complicated, Brian," I begin. "But I think August may somehow be mixed up in this…in whatever cover-up may have happened back in the sixties."

His mouth falls open. "At Pop Gray's? My God, why do you think that?"

"Well, you already know she's a friend of Nelson McCready, and I'm not sure if that friendship was a coincidence. Knowing August, I'm wondering if it was a calculated acquaintance."

Brian becomes an easy audience, following along, taking me at my word, and buying in.

"And I've come to learn, just today actually, that August *also* had some sort of relationship, back when she was a kid, at least, with the man who arrested McCready. Chief Matthews."

"Uh, what kind of relationship, Jan?"

"I don't know for sure, but I'm trying to put the pieces together."

"So, you think the chief had a reason to cover it up. August knew about it, and then she felt bad McCready was implicated, so she wanted to make amends or something?"

"Maybe something like that," I say. "She knew the end was near for her. People make lots of choices that are normally out of character when they are staring down the barrel."

"Wow." Brian exhales. "That's kind of an unexpected turn of events, Jan. I thought we were just gossiping when we were at Cliff's the other night, and now, well, it's hitting pretty close to home. I bet he'd be interested in hearing all th—"

"Oh, I think he already knows," I interrupt.

"You told him?" Brian asks, crestfallen.

"No, I didn't tell him that August knew Chief Matthews, but I'm pretty sure he's known all along that my mother was somehow connected to the case. I think that's why Cliff has been so friendly to me."

"How would he know?"

"Brian, he's *from* Seaville. He moved to Boston when he was a kid. His cousins were the ones who were, you know, killed…"

"His *cousins*?" Brian's jaw drops even wider.

"Yes. His cousins were the Neal sisters. Sally Mavey put two and two together, even though Cliff never let on. And well…did *you* know his last name?"

"No. I guess I thought it was Clifford, but you're right. I mean, Cliff Clifford? What was I thinking?" Brian clucks under his breath. "That Sally Mavey…that lady has her nose in everything. Always has. So, okay, let me get this straight—you think Cliff *knew* you were August's daughter and all along had his suspicions your mom knew about the police cover-up?"

"Well, not at first. I think he started to put it together as we got to know each other, and then last night when he dropped me off—"

Brian looks like he's been punched in the gut, and the last thing I want to do is tread on his affections.

"I know it sounds bad," I quickly continue, hoping to soothe the wound I had just inflicted. "But it's not like that. I just had to get out of this house last night. I thought Cliff and I were making a connection, I guess. I've been out of the game quite a while, Brian."

"Oh yeah, right," he says, collecting his heart off his sleeve, trying to tuck it safely back into his chest. "No, I get it, Jan. He's a pretty smooth dude. But now do you think he was—"

"Yes. I was being used," I state. "But now you know the reason for the urgency, Brian. Pieces of this puzzle have been dangling in front of my face for the past few days, and now they're starting to drop into my lap, begging to be put together. And if it all comes back to August, if she's the last one alive who knows something about what happened…And look, we may already be too late. She's been in and out of consciousness for the past two days. And Gregor says she doesn't have much longer."

I can hear the quiet whirring of the heart rate monitor from upstairs, the constant backbeat of my days.

"Well, can't you just ask her when she wakes up again? I mean, if she wakes up again?"

"If she wakes up again, I want to be ready. I want to know as much as I can. She's cagey, Brian. She only looks out for herself. I won't let her play games with me anymore. There's not enough time. I plan to demand the truth, which will be easier after I've uncovered all this shit."

"Well, let's keep reading, then," Brian says, seemingly resolved to be a shoulder to lean on, a Watson to my Holmes.

Raleigh News & Observer

Horror in Seaville Claims the Lives of Two Girls

April 26, 1967

By Marshall Tucker

Two sisters were brutally murdered on the night of April 23 in an ice cream store in downtown Seaville. Kimberlee Neal, 19, and Louise Neal, 17, both employees of Pop Gray's, were shot to death inside the store while performing their nightly closing duties. The suspect, Nelson McCready, 21, has been accused of armed robbery and murder. He is being held in the Seaville Courthouse jail with a trial date set for May 1.

Eileen Conway, 17, also employed by Pop Gray's, was not on duty at the time of the crime. "I am so sad for the Neal family," said Conway. "And I am also a little bit frightened. I know that some people hold grudges in this town, but none of it makes sense to me." Conway told the reporter she would not be returning to work at Pop Gray's.

Brian reads over my shoulder. "Grudges?" He finishes the paragraph. "That's an odd quote, for sure. What is she talking about? Could there have been some sort of relationship between McCready and one of the girls?"

I hurry to my notepad on the kitchen table and scribble down the name Eileen Conway.

"Oh, there's a page two for this one," Brian says, holding it up. It includes a photo of a smiling young lady in a frilly apron and a pillbox hat. The hat is monogrammed with a P, and it looks like the same hat I pulled from the box stashed in August's closet. My heart skips a beat as I scan the photo for a caption.

Eileen Conway of Seaville, employee of Pop Gray's. Photo courtesy of the Conway family, taken one week prior to the incident.

The hat was part of a uniform for employees of Pop Gray's. What had Reena said on the phone? Something like, "August had been kind to the colored kids." Without a word, I drop the article and bolt upstairs.

"What's going on?" Brian calls from behind. He grabs the printout I just discarded and follows me into my old room.

"Holy shit," he says, stopping cold when he sees the array of treasures propped on the sill. "Why do you have her hat?" He gestures to the paper in his hand.

"It's not *her* hat," I say as I yank the article from Brian's grasp. "It's *her* hat." I give an aggressive nod toward my mother's bedroom. "August must've worked there, too, at Pop Gray's."

"Well, shit," Brian mutters.

I'd left August's stolen journal in the crumpled covers of my bed, and I snatch it and head down the hall to August's room. Geraldine has nodded off in the large armchair, but Gregor is beside the bed, finishing an IV drip.

"Gregor," I whisper, mindful of our exhausted guest, "do you think August will wake up again? Ever?"

He consults his watch, scribbles the time on his notes, then joins me in the doorway where I wait, fidgety and agitated.

"I cannot say for sure, Ms. Jan, but I find it doubtful. Her heart rate and blood oxygen levels tell me she's really battling just to keep breathing, I'm afraid. Sometimes, in these situations, the body gives up the hope of wakefulness, just trying to stay alive."

I nervously caress the spine of August's journal. Brian still stands behind me, unsure of his purpose other than to follow along, curious and awkward on this threshold of death.

"It might be a long night, Jan. How about I put on a pot of coffee?" Brian asks, finding a task but forgetting to whisper.

With a start, Geraldine awakes. "Ouch," she says, rubbing her sore neck. "I'll take some of that coffee," she calls after Brian, who already started toward to the kitchen.

Geraldine hauls herself to her feet and shuffles to August's side, listening for her breath with her back arched like a defensive cat. "Well, she's still alive. That's good. Your old lady is a fighter." She turns back to me, noticing my clutch on August's journal. "Anything good in there?"

"I-I don't know," I stammer. "I haven't really had time to go through it all."

"Well." Geraldine holds her lower back and nods her head at the book. "I'm not sure you'll find what you're looking for in there. The stuff you want is buried in history. That thing is just full of the woes of a geriatric old lady in the throes of depression."

It's as if I'm standing at the edge of an abyss. It feels dangerous, but I'm impetuous, a renegade with nothing to lose, so I push forward. "What do you know, Geraldine?"

"I guess I don't know anything for a fact, Jan." Geraldine sighs heavily. "I was hoping your mother would tell you all this, but I think there is something, and she never stated this in so many words—"

"*What*, Geraldine? Tell me what it is you think you know."

"I think that the chief may have been, well, less of an 'uncle' than I previously implied." My heart begins to tumble. I can feel it falling down into the void. "He's likely your father, Jan."

My heart plummets, rolls and lurches past Geraldine's words. It lands heavily at the bottom of someplace dark.

"I *do* know that your mother had some affection for him," she continues. "She often talked about going up to his barn and riding her horse. I guess he kept a horse just for her. Did you know that?"

I shake my head as realizations begin to drift up from the depths, the truth rising like ghosts. It was *his* farm. The locket, of course, must have been a present from him, and not handed down from Grandma Patty as August had led me to believe.

"But the chief was a married man," Geraldine states. "And a pillar in this town. I think it just burned inside August all those years. I mean, she had known him her whole life. Since she was a child. And really, I think, when she was of a certain age, he probably groomed her to be his mistress."

I collapse to the floor, sobbing, pieces of my broken heart scattered around me. Geraldine kneels beside me, stroking my hair like the mother I never had.

*****

Oh, I remember those days up on the farm, riding bareback on Jo for hours. Tacking up old Daisy, whenever Alice fancied a ride. The water pail fights with Junior when it got too hot, and always teasing him because he was still too small to get up on his pony without a stool.

All those years, Mama had no problem with my visits up to the farm. When I was a girl, she would even come along and ride one of the mares alongside me. We'd laugh and gallop in the sunshine like we hadn't a care in the world.

Matty would come round on Sunday afternoons and pick me up in his cruiser. If Mama didn't come along, I'd sit in the front. Mama and Matty had been friends their whole life. Mama even said they'd dated for a while in high school. They still had a lot in common, and they'd always exchange pleasantries. Mama would ask about Miss Alice or how the kids were liking school.

I loved those rides in the front seat of the cruiser. We'd roll the windows all the way down as the island grew smaller behind us, and I'd stick my head out the front window to breathe in the air as it lost its brine, the scent turning to hay and manure.

It was that way for years, and I looked forward to Sundays the same way the church folk did. It was the day of my salvation.

But then, on my sixteenth birthday, Matty came round with a gift—some real nice farm boots for when I'd ride Jo or go work with Junior up at the barn. He gave them to me wrapped in a red bow with a kiss on my cheek. After that, Mama started to mind. Something palpable had shifted. Mama said now that I was older, I shouldn't be spending all my time riding ponies, I should be getting serious about school, helping around the house, maybe get a job. She said I was too mature to be running off to the farm like that, and people were starting to talk.

I didn't care, though. It was worth the scorn.

Mama came out to meet us one night, her hair in tight curls and her mouth grim and set, as Matty pulled in the drive.

"Go on in the house, Aggie," she instructed, and after I scampered out of the passenger door and made my

way up the front steps, I saw her lean in low through the open car window.

"You listen to me, Matty," I heard her seethe. "It's time for you to stop coming 'round here. This is not a game, and I know you too well." Mama didn't know I could hear her, and I never let on I was listening from right inside the screen door.

"Oh, Patty, lighten up." Matty laughed. "I'm just playing. I'm just trying to get to know the girl."

Mama said something stern and strong I couldn't quite catch because just then, the wheels on Matty's car kicked up the gravel in the driveway as he sped away.

But Matty, he came round for me again and again. Sometimes, he came by so late Mama was asleep, and she didn't even know I was gone. And yeah, he had his intentions. Eventually, there was a lot less horseback riding, and a lot more horsing around. But I knew I loved him, and as Matty once told me, he was a church-going man. God never frowns upon love.

****

Brian hears my wailing and rushes back upstairs, preceded by his pounding footsteps and the jiggle of coffee beans still in their bag. He appraises the monitor behind August's head and the two women huddled dejectedly on the ground.

"It's okay, sweetie," Geraldine says softly, "we just need another minute."

Brian backs away, and we can hear the coffee beans retreat back down the stairs.

"I know she wasn't always the easiest. I'm sure there were times when you felt like she wasn't there for you," Geraldine says, her voice full of balm and cure. "She carried around some deep shadows, and I think…Well, I think it all just got in the way of who she wanted to be. But it's never too late to understand that broken people…they have a story, too."

"Thank you, Geraldine." I raise my face to hers. "I can try. All I can do is try." And for the first time in as many years as I can remember, I do want to try. I don't completely understand why, but I want to try to feel *something, anything* for my mother.

I brace my weight on the frame of August's bed, and I pull myself off the floor and into a seated position at the foot of the mattress. Taking a moment to find my breath (*always find your breath*, I can hear John lecture), I sniffle and wait. I'm hoping something that feels like love washes over me with its assuring waves.

But it doesn't, and so I try whatever form of connection I can offer.

"I want to forgive it all, August," I choke out. My words sound hollow and empty in the still room. "Those years I felt so alone, not worthy of love. Your anger, the drinking, all the arguments…but I don't think I ever even knew you."

I place my hands on hers, which Gregor, staging her final scene, has gently folded and draped over her torso. Her skin holds a deathly hue, mottled with the color of rotting plums. I pull a deep breath into my lungs in an attempt to capture enough air to fuel a soliloquy.

Still, "I forgive you" is all I am capable of, and I hope my futile message seeps into her sleep and finds her in the vacancy. I carefully trace the deep line that runs a rivulet down August's dry cheek, the mark of time and memory. If awake, she would recoil from such affection, from the intrusion. She would reject this presumption of familiarity.

"I *do* forgive you, Mother," I say it a third time, hoping the litany makes it so.

August doesn't awaken. She doesn't acknowledge me, and no tearful absolution ensues. I can only see the slumber of her downturned face, pale and starved of life, her closed eyelids that refuse to even flutter with a passing dream. I watch and wait for some sort of recognition, for the end point of this end point, the punctuation of the sentence. But all I get is another trailing ellipse.

"There, dear, now how did that feel?" Geraldine speaks from her armchair, where she has again taken residence. "That was a nice try, sweetie. I bet she heard you. Now, give yourself a little break, and why don't you go get some coffee. Bring me some, too. That boy in the kitchen is probably scared to death to come back in here again, what with all this carrying on."

Brian does look shaken when I return to him, his face ashen and grim, so unlike the Brian willing to put things up his nose to get a good laugh. I regret the Littleton saga appears to have broken him.

"Is she?" he asks, gingerly handing me a mug.

"No, not yet," I say with a swallow of coffee, which has turned lukewarm. My mouth feels dry, like it's been rubbed with sand. I head to the refrigerator for a bottle of water and guzzle it before speaking again. "Let me take a cup of that to Geraldine. I think she was up all night."

Brian pours a cup fresh from the carafe, and when I return with Geraldine's sustenance, August's room seems brighter, as if my forgiveness alone has chased away its shadows.

Geraldine is raising the blinds on August's window, letting in the filtered light. "I can't take this darkness any longer," she says, accepting the warm mug. "And I hope I didn't speak out of turn by giving you that information, Jan. It's just, well, I'm sure she wanted to tell you herself. I mean, I think she did, at least. Before I left for Florida, she was puttering around a lot, cranky and sort of off her rocker. Mumbled about 'making amends.' I think, honestly, she was just waiting for the right time."

"Well, it looks like she may have waited too long."

"Not necessarily, dear," Geraldine says thoughtfully. "Perhaps there is a way you could help her, and maybe help yourself along the way."

"You mean right her wrongs?" My thoughts shift to Cliff and his quest for familial reparation.

"Hmm." Geraldine considers what I said. "Maybe just set the pieces straight."

"But how would I even *begin* to do such a thing?"

"Well, you've already started with the most aggrieved person: you. And you worked at it, you found some answers, you dug deep to find a way to try to forgive her. So, who else has she done wrong? What kind of closure can we bring this woman, teetering here on the edge of death?"

Closure. I sigh. There's that damn word again.

"What's going on up there, Jan?" Brian asks when I return to the kitchen. He's pacing back and forth on the worn linoleum, small solo journeys of concern and suspense.

I take a deep breath. "Well, Geraldine thinks that Chief Matthews is my long-lost father."

"Woah," he replies, and then, in need of something to do, he grabs the carafe and tops my mug off. "Look, Jan, you've had an awful lot dumped on you in the past twenty-four hours. I honestly don't know how you're holding up. Why don't you go lie down for a bit and try to get some sleep? I can stay here and wake you up if anything changes with your mom."

He's right, though I don't feel tired. In fact, every nerve in my body seems like it's on fire. My arms and legs need to move, and my mind is reeling like a fishing line that just hooked the big one.

"No," I say. "I can't let down my guard. Not now. Not until this is over. Especially with all the coffee you've been pouring me."

Brian chuckles and hands me my phone that's been charging on the countertop. "Someone's been trying to reach you."

A text message from Cliff flashes brightly across the screen. Resentment wells in my throat, bitter and burning, but I click it open.

Had fun hanging out last night. I'd love to see you later. When can I come over?

I slide the phone into my back pocket without replying, unsure whether to commit to my affection or to my anger.

Brian rubs his temples. "Okay, well then, maybe I'll go lie down…Just kidding, Jan. Really, how can I help? Want me to heat up the lasagna?" He grabs Sally's tinfoil-covered dish, just wanting to be of use.

"No. I mean, sure, if you're hungry. But wait a minute, Brian, that actually gives me an idea…Can you reach out to Sally and see if she knows how to reach Eileen Conway?"

Brian raises his eyebrows. "That girl from the article?"

"Well, she wouldn't be much of a girl anymore, would she? Let's start by figuring out if she's still alive. I'm going to go see if Nelson would like to pay his last respects to August."

"Roger that." Brian pats his pockets to find his own phone, relieved he has a mission.

"Geraldine?" I pop my head into August's room. "Can you sit tight here while I run out for just twenty minutes? I promise it won't be long. I just…like we talked about, there is something I can do, I think."

"No problem, hon. Her breath sounds better now. Not as shallow. She's hanging in there. Maybe she heard you." Geraldine sits at August's bedside, folding and unfolding her hands over August's, pausing only when Gregor lifts August's hips to check a bedpan.

Part 3: 1967

Chapter 24: Fighting

The lights are low inside Hank's Saloon, dimmer and darker than the street-worn clientele who scuttle through the front door, trailing the scent of whiskey. Chief has been here too long. He'd settled at the bar in the early afternoon, and now the sun angles low in the sky, sending shards of hot-pink sunset through the lowest slats of the blinds.

It had been a bad day at the station. The paperwork had started to pile up and morale was low. He'd asked his deputies to join him for a drink at the bar, but everyone had politely—no, politically—brushed him off.

His bourbon nearly dry, he can see the bottom of the glass with this last sip when the boys from county police amble in, one just as scruffy and disheveled as the next. They'd been down at the river, tying one on, and now they stumble and slur their way up to the barkeep.

It's Mitch Neal who sees him first.

"Chief." He nods, his tone dangling somewhere between surprise and aggravation.

Neal has always been a righteous bastard, acting like deputy sheriff for the county is, somehow, more of a noble cause than working on the town force. But Mitch looks broken now, his eyes dark and hooded, his shoulders slumped.

"Mitch," Chief responds, apathetic and emotionless. He grabs his hat, prepared to leave.

The bartender serves Mitch a shot, and he throws it back hard and fast. His eyes set like metal forged in fire, and he pivots from the bar, advancing confrontationally close to the chief's unshaven profile.

"Chief. I *know* what you did." Billy spits out the words, toxic and teeming, and they land without remorse in the narrow space between the two men.

Chief cocks his head sideways, surly, drains his glass, and sets it with a loud thud on the bar. "Son, I don't know what you're talking 'bout right now, but this might be one of those times you want to back the fuck up and mind your own business."

"My *family* is my fucking business!" Mitch shouts, loud above the din of the bar. He shoves Chief hard enough on one shoulder that he slumps down further into his barstool.

Matthews, a strong whip of a man, slowly unfolds himself to confront his younger rival. He's like a linebacker in farmer's clothes, but Neal serves the business of redemption, and he lands the first blow clean across the chief's chiseled chin.

Matthews strikes back, but too many bourbons make him slow, and he misses high and wide as Mitch ducks and weaves. The other guys from the sheriff's office gather behind them, knee slapping and laughing, and now Chief gets really mad. Before Mitch can even ball up his fist, Matthews has him around the neck, lifting him off his toes, smiling like a comic book villain as his rival gasps for air.

The sheriff's boys stop laughing and rush in to save their friend in distress, but the chief just grunts and releases his grip. Mitch falls backwards and tumbles to the ground. He grabs his neck, sputtering and coughing, but the chief just throws a ten-dollar bill on the bar and saunters to the door. He rubs the throbbing welt on his chin.

"You got nothing to say for yourself, Chief?" he hears Mitch yelling behind him. "They were *just kids*!"

The swinging brass doors of Hank's Saloon clip closed as the chief steps out into hot air. It feels like the breath of a dragon. He dusts off his hat before placing it back on his head, reminding himself that, no matter the word on the street, he remains the man in charge in Seaville.

Chapter 25: Snooping

"Boy!" The loud bellow comes from the back of the barn. "You better get on out here before I start shoveling this hay myself!"

Junior wipes the last toast crumbs on the leg of his pants and races to the side porch to find his shoes.

"Junior!" Chief hollers again, impatient and unreasonable. "I mean it. If I have to lift up this pitchfork myself, swear to God, there will be a price to pay. You better *git*, son!"

Junior slips on his work boots without lacing them up, anxious to quell the angry beat his father drums. He races out the screen door, hearing its loud bang as it swings back hard behind him.

"Junior, watch yourself." The gentle scold comes from his Mother, who's cooking bacon in the kitchen. But he pays her no mind and keeps running toward the barn. Better to have an ornery momma than a daddy who will whip the tar out of him.

Junior arrives, sweaty and heaving, just as Chief picks up the pitchfork. Just in time.

"Dang, boy," Chief says. "It ain't summer no more. You can't sleep past sunrise when we got chores to do." He tosses the fork at his feet, where it lands heavily on Junior's big toe. He winces but doesn't complain. Chief won't hear it, and he's already walking a thin line.

"Yes, sir," Junior mumbles, bending for the pitchfork and digging into the large stack of hay.

"All this," Chief instructs, pointing at the golden straw, "needs to get into the barn loft this morning. Got that?"

"Yes, sir." He shovels with intent now, ready to show his father he's up to the task.

"Don't come in for lunch 'til it's done, you hear?"

"Yes, sir."

Satisfied, Chief nods at his boy, then wipes his brow with a handkerchief he pulls from his pocket.

Out of the corner of his eye, Junior watches him walk down the hill as he digs the pitchfork deep into the bale. Chief's still a young man, not past his mid-forties, Junior guesses, though he doesn't know the ages of either of his parents for sure. His father has strong bones, and Junior likes the way his own chin and nose are broad and sharp like Chief's. Chief's dark hair grows black as coal, and he has a grin that could shame the devil (as Mother liked to say).

Lately, though, Chief had been awfully sour, extra cross with Mother if she burned the biscuits, and lashing out at all his kids, not just Junior, drinking whiskey every night. He'd sit out on the side-porch steps until late at night and the entire bottle was gone. He'd overheard Chief and Mother having an argument about it one night this summer when she was trying to get him to come to bed.

"Goddammit, Alice." Chief's voice, slow and heavy, echoed across the porch and into the open windows of his bedroom. "I'll come when I am good and ready. I got some things I gotta work out."

"And the whiskey helps you work it out, Chief?" his Mother had dared to counter, her voice thin and irritable, like fragments of a hornet's nest.

"Damn straight it does, Alice. Or maybe it just helps me forget about it. Forget about all of this…and all of you…"

"That's real nice, Chief," he heard Mother mutter as she walked back into the house, slippers shuffling angrily across the kitchen linoleum. "Real nice to want to forget about your family. Maybe you got someone else on your mind. Is that it?"

Mother must have gone to bed after that because the arguing stopped.

The next morning had been just like all the others. Mother and Chief up drinking their coffee before any of the kids even opened their eyes. Mother, with a smile, asked Junior how he wanted his eggs when he tumbled into her sunny, morning kitchen.

Junior starts to make a good dent in the hay, so Chief must have decided he could move on to his other responsibilities. Junior can see him wandering in the direction of the horse stable, up behind the big barn. Even at twelve years old, some part of Junior feels sorry for Chief, who never seems to be truly content. He's a hard-working man, for sure, managing everything at the police station all week long, then keeping the farm running on the weekends.

Their old farm is tucked away from the coast on a small hill of good soil, hidden from the highway by tall pines and a winding dirt road. They keep mostly just the horses now, though they have a few small crops like corn and green beans they can harvest in the summer and a crop of sweet potatoes in the fall. Junior's sisters, and sometimes that Littleton girl, help out with the horses: grooming them, mucking the stables, and keeping them fed and exercised. But most of the hard labor falls to

Junior, the hauling and lifting and digging. Now that school has started back, he spends most every Saturday—and Sunday, except for time spent in church—working in the fields or the barn.

Before those murders happened, Mother would take them all into town for ice cream at Pop Gray's on a Saturday night, a reward for labor paid.

But a lot has changed since those girls got killed. The whole town's in an uproar about that colored man getting away with it. Chief, he's been working overtime, never really sleeping and can't hold his temper. And Junior's best friend, Shep, said his father told him that Chief had gotten into a fist fight over at the saloon with a guy from the county sheriff's office. Nobody knows what it was all about, but Junior has his own suspicions.

He stops scooping the hay long enough to wipe the sweat off his forehead with the back of his hand. Junior decides, right then and there, it might be best to get out of Seaville after he graduates high school, find someplace to start over. Otherwise, he thinks, I ain't ever gonna get out of Chief's shadow.

Chapter 26: Reopening

Denny smacks the palm of his hand hard against the Whitehouse steel churner. "Piece of shit," he mutters under his breath.

"Denny!," his mother admonishes. "Is that the kind of language our customers expect from the Confectioner?"

"Awww, Mama," Denny groans, "no one can hear me back here in the kitchen. Besides, this new churner *is* a piece of shit. One of these here loopy wheels keeps getting jammed!"

"Hmmm," Mrs. Gray ponders, "maybe that colored boy, Billy, can help you fix it when he comes in tomorrow morning."

His mama was right, Billy did know how to get things going again. Just last week, he'd helped Denny wrench open the dishwasher and pull out all the silverware that had gummed up the works in there.

Besides, it's late summer already and Denny had already churned so much ice cream that the walk-in freezer is stocked to the brim. They aren't selling as many scoops this summer, because business was kind of slow to return after Kimberlee and her sister got whacked back here.

Denny remembers Kimberlee fondly, the nights he took her to the drive-in across town. She wasn't the sweetest girl, but she was good to look at, and in his own shallow way, Denny misses her.

He scrapes the last of the unchurned cream out of the large metal bowl and turns the churner off for the night. Mopping his brow with the hem of his apron, he peers out through the small window of the steel swing doors that separate the kitchen from the parlor.

Most of the booths and counter stools are empty now, except the corner booth in the back, where he sees his father having a serious conversation with Chief Matthews. Fred Gray twists his tiny mustache in concern as the Chief leans across the table to say something.

The two men nod in agreement, then rise from the booth to shake hands in parting. Denny watches Chief saunter up to the ice cream counter, a wry smile cracking the corners of his mouth. He tips his hat and leans forward, like he's whispering something, to that girl Aggie. Denny watches her shoulders roll through a giggle, the pink bow on her ponytail bob up and down, and the chief reaches over the counter to squeeze her hand.

Denny wonders briefly about the strange acquaintance, the exchange he just witnessed, then he shrugs his shoulders and decides to call it a day. Tommy

Wilson is throwing a keg party out on Lumina Beach tonight, and Denny needs to head home and grab a shower so he can be ready for all the ladies.

Part 4: 2017

Chapter 27: Aligning

I grab my jacket and forge into the scene, cast in shades of brown and blue, that has been set for this late November day. Clouds gather in the east, piling up on the horizon like layers of a cake. An offshore wind whips fiercely, driving rain off the water. It has dropped twenty degrees since last night. My light jacket is not enough to shield me from this unexpected winter onslaught, and my lips tremble with the cold. I tuck my chin deep into the collar and hustle the two blocks to McCready's.

Lights are blazing warmly inside Nelson's home, and from my vantage in the cold, I now recognize its certain clapboard charm, it feels more like an unkempt English cottage than a haunted house. I barge up the walk, uninvited but unwilling to relent on my current course, delivering a hasty knock on the front door.

Nelson answers with a cat draped over his arm—not the same cat I'd returned days earlier but a butterscotch cat with enormous ears, another one of the Pips.

"My goodness," he says. "My favorite visitor. Come in, come in. It's cold out there. They say a storm is rolling in."

Inside his front foyer, the aroma of vegetable soup blankets the smell of must and litter.

"I can't stay, I'm afraid." I shiver, breathless. "August's barely holding on, but it occurred to me that she might want to say goodbye to some of her old friends."

"Oh?" he asks apprehensively, putting the cat down and pulling his brown cardigan close around him.

"I thought of you, of course. I was wondering… well, would you be willing to come by, uh, sometime soon? Like maybe now?"

"*Now?* Oh, I don't know. I don't really go out very much." He timidly eyes the encroaching darkness outside his window. "And this weather."

"I know," I agree. "Indeed, it's miserable out. But I think it would mean a lot to her…and to me."

I can see him hedging on indecision, and so I quickly offer more enticement. "Geraldine is here, too. She came into town yesterday."

He smiles now. It's the cherry on top he needed.

"She is a sweet soul, that Geraldine," he says. "I sure would like to see her, too."

"Come on, then, grab your coat. Your scarf, too. It's freezing out there. I'll make sure I get you back home before this storm hits."

Nelson pulls the soup off the stove and finds his keys to lock the front door. As we're leaving, he remembers a forgotten necessity and runs back into the house to retrieve it. He returns with a tall, white prayer candle, the kind that lines the altar at a Catholic mass.

"Let's go." Nelson tucks the candle inside his coat pocket, and together, we battle the whipping wind and the lowering sky for two long, frigid blocks.

"Mama always used to say that you can feel a storm coming," Nelson intones as we walk, breath escaping his lips like cold smoke. "Feel it in the ache of your bones, you can, and in the pulse of your veins."

I think Nelson's mother may have been correct. As the clouds thicken above us, my senses seem to sharpen and saturate, as if the Earth intends to give us fair warning of the fury she's ready to unleash.

"I learned something similar from my job," I tell him. "Well, a job I *used to* have. Not sure if they'll have me there anymore. But you're right. Science tells us that our bodies do *feel* the drop in barometric pressure. The atmosphere is, in fact, weighing us down." As we trudge against the wind, I can feel it pressing close on our shoulders, as if the roiling clouds themselves have mass and heft.

"Huh," Nelson replies.

We stumble in from the cold to find Brian stooped over the fireplace, trying in vain to get a fire started. A plastic bag of dirty ash lays at his feet. The damp wood hisses, and the living room fills with wood smoke.

"Are you sure that chimney still works?" I cough, unwrapping my coat and scarf and pulling off my stiff boots. Brian shrugs and rises to shake Nelson's hand. He wears a long smear of soot across one cheek like a boy scout with war paint.

"Oh, it will be fine," Nelson reassures Brian, grateful for a face he recognizes. "I used to light fires here all the time."

"Well, well, well. Who do we have here?" Geraldine croaks, the shuffle of her slippers announcing her entrance.

Nelson embraces her warmly. "Hello, sweet lady. I'm so sorry this is the reason you've returned to us."

"Well, I'm glad I came, all the same," Geraldine replies. "You look well, Nelson. Wish I could say the same for Aggie…" Nelson nods sympathetically, and Geraldine takes his arm and pulls him down beside her on the saggy couch, attempting to explain the sad state of affairs.

"You see, she's not really awake. She's hardly breathing at all. It's hard to see it, but Gregor tells me that she can probably still hear us, and she's aware of what's going on around her. At least, on some level…"

As Geraldine spouts on, I pull Brian aside. "What did Sally say?"

"Yep, she knows Eileen Conway," Brian confides, his breath stale with coffee. "But she thinks she may have moved to a retirement home in Wilmington. She was going to try to find the name of the place. She said her cousin is friends with the family and was at their wedding or something."

I smile in spite of the tension dragging down the corners of my mouth. There wasn't a connection east of the Mississippi Sally couldn't make. "Is she going to call us back?"

"Yeah. Or she might have said something about coming over…"

"Jesus." I sigh. "I guess we're hosting a party now."

"Yep," Brian says. "I'll put on more coffee."

"Fuck the coffee, Brian," I call after him, "pull out the bourbon."

The wind moans uncomfortably and presses in on the house, and the flimsy panes of glass in the tired old windows rattle in protest. I do a double-take as I walk past the front window. "My God, I actually think it's snowing!"

"Hah, look at that!" Gregor laughs as he heads down the stairs with a stack of dirty towels.

Dime-sized flakes drift and dart past the window, swirling around the trunk of the old oak tree. "This is the first snow I've ever seen," Gregor says, his Caribbean accent slipping through in defiance of the weather outside.

"Jan, are you seeing what I'm seeing?" Brian barrels into the living room, holding a bottle of liquor. "Is that *snow*? Must be quite a cold front blowing through."

Behind us, the fire has finally caught, and it begins to crackle and snap.

"They said on the radio it's a Nor'easter blowing up the coast," Nelson offers, gazing out at the charcoal sky, the dendrites drifting slowly to the ground. "Heard we might get six inches, maybe more. Didn't think it was gonna start until later tonight, though."

"We might want to get you back home, Nelson," Geraldine says, "with Gladys and the Pips and all. Let's go upstairs and see August."

The two friends rise from the couch, Nelson favoring his bad knee. They lock arms and move in solidarity. I follow discreetly behind them, careful not to encroach, yet needing to witness any sort of communication they may be able to get out of my mother.

Nelson stands slack-shouldered by August's bed, unsure whether to speak or touch or get too close to the fragile inconvenience of a dying friend. "I'm sorry," he finally says to Geraldine, clearing his throat when she clutches his elbow. His fingertips dab the corners of his eyes. "It's just that the August I know is such a pistol, like the kind that you get whipped with. That kind of pistol." He chuckles to himself and sniffles a bit. "I guess I'm not so good with things changing…"

"None of us are, Nelson," says Geraldine, looping her round, fleshy arm around his waist. "Why, I've been cryin' my eyes out since I've been here. It's okay, though. Sometimes, to just sit with her is enough."

Someone thought to bring in the two folding chairs that were stashed in a cobwebbed corner of the front porch. Gregor, maybe? Geraldine grabs one and moves it beside the bed with a metal clunk, and she motions for Nelson to take a seat. The rusty chair creaks as he unfolds it and tucks his long body onto the seat's edge.

"Hey, remember that time August, you, and me played poker at my house?" Nelson begins, turning to Geraldine with his color commentary. "She thought she had it won, remember, had a hand of two pairs? I went and pulled out a flush at the last minute…Dang, she got so mad! I didn't know anyone could get that mad about cards. Didn't talk to me for two days, do you remember?" Nelson's eyes look alive with the memory, and Geraldine nods and laughs.

"And what about that time she tried to make a pot roast, and it all went horribly wrong," he continues. "I had to grab the fire extinguisher, and you were about ready to call the fire department."

"Oh, my goodness, yes." Geraldine giggles. "I had almost forgotten about that. I had to let all of your cats outside, worried they couldn't breathe. So much smoke."

"We were swatting at that charred hunk of meat with wet dish towels like that would make a difference!"

Muted laughter fills the room for the first time in days as snow drifts serenely past the bedroom window. I take the time to remember to breathe. Bringing them together was the right thing to do, and I'm patting myself on the back when the vibrating pulse of a text message arrives in the back pocket of my jeans.

It's Cliff again.

Everything all right there? I didn't hear back. Getting worried.

I don't respond, but I notice the battery on my phone is running low, so I head into my room to find a charger. Outside the bedroom window, the ground begins to whiten, a crusty layer on top of the fallen leaves. A lonely red cardinal hops along a bare branch of the old oak in the backyard, and a peaceful lull has settled on the house and those taking refuge within it. The calm before the storm.

Down the short hall, I watch as Nelson lights his prayer candle, summoning the sharp and sour scent of church incense, and he begins to bargain with his God, a murmur of faith harmonizing with the unforgiving beep of August's heart monitor. Geraldine tucks herself into the big armchair and knits threads together with the slow, methodical rhythm of a metronome, a careful click of the needles.

Gregor drifts in and out of August's room like a summoned angel, adjusting a pillow here, taking a pulse there. I can hear the rattle of dishes echoing throughout the house as Brian gathers cutlery and courage in the kitchen

I stand alone, hollow and ineffectual, in the middle of my barren childhood bedroom, staring out the window as the day rapidly gives way to night and snow piles on tree limbs and settles on roadways.

A knock on the front door implodes my mirage of calm, and I head downstairs as the jasmine scent of Sally whisks back into our gathering. This time, her offering looks like a plate of brownies. Breathless, she peels off her winter coat and places the plate of treats beside the casserole presently waiting for the oven.

."Y'all, I think I found Ms. Conway up at the Springwood old people home." Sally steals a brownie for herself, munching through her words. "Her daughter married my second cousin back in the nineties. They got a divorce a few years ago, but the split was amicable. Bobby gave me the address, and I tried to call. But when they put me through to her room, no one answered. I left my cell phone number with the front desk and asked them to have her call me as soon as she could. Told her it was of the utmost importance." Sally talks with her mouth full, and now has brownie crumbs scattered down the ample front of her green tracksuit.

"Thank you, Sally." I brush off some of her crumbs. "You really do know how to come through."

"So, did you talk to him yet?" she asks.

"Who?"

"Cliff. Does he know that you *know*?"

"Oh, no." I'm embarrassed. "I haven't talked to him yet. I'm just too pissed off."

"I get it," Sally says. "But, hon, if it's answers you want, he may have more than anyone. He has clearly been after this for a while. Maybe you should play his game? Don't let on that you know he has an agenda."

I nod, reaching for one of Sally's brownies before I spot the bottle of bourbon Brian had obligingly retrieved from the top cupboard. I pour myself a short glass, pondering Sally's suggestion as I peer out into the hurling dusk. The alcohol slides down the back of my throat, warm and welcome.

Nightfall reminds me I had a plan to meet Reena at 5:00 p.m. at Cliff's, which for many reasons seems to be out of the question now. The analog clock hanging over August's stove had long ago run out of batteries, but I retrieve my phone and check the time and see the text from Reena.

I'm here, but don't come out. The roads are bad already. Cliff says he's closing the restaurant because of the weather and will give me a lift home in his truck. Unless you want us to come to your place? (His idea, btw)

Without a rational pause, I respond. *Okay, come here.*

There it is. The scene has been written, the score composed, and the curtain will rise. Nelson, Cliff, and Geraldine, all under one roof, while my mother's time onstage dwindles with the daylight. Now, I just need our antagonist to rise from the edge of death to play her part.

Sally pours herself a bourbon, too, and Brian puts the casserole in the oven. They find an old Coltrane record and turn on August's dusty turntable. They entertain one another by bickering about the best way to keep the fire going. "You've got to *blow* on it," I hear Sally complain.

Character actors, I think. Both of them. Not integral to the plot but here to create the mood and support the backstory.

Reena and Cliff arrive ten minutes later, the growl of the engine and crunch of snow beneath the truck's tires audible through the thin windows of the old home, even over the brassy jazz. I watch from the window as they pull to the curb, and I can see Reena chatting away gamely in the passenger seat, her blue knit hat bobbing in the middle of some story.

I brace myself, breathe my way to mindfulness, smooth down some unruly hairs, and try to find my character.

This is *my* show. I am the star, after all, and this production…it's the culmination of so many years of sacrifice. If Cliff still believes he can lead the opening dance, then goddammit, I'll have to put on my tapping shoes.

Cliff and Reena pick their way carefully up the snow-covered front steps, Cliff offering his arm for support and Reena side-stepping a limb from the old oak that had come crashing down in the wind. I open the front door before they can knock, confident with my behind-the-scenes knowledge, solid in my character study, and ready to perform.

"Hi, come on in." I accept a quick kiss on the cheek from Reena, and then, playing the part, the same from Cliff. My heart races as our bodies briefly collide, and I wonder if he can feel it beating, galloping, through my sweater. Less desire, more fury, though the two emotions battle inside me, so I pull away with haste.

Cliff tries to keep his trademark cool, but I can see the intention in his eyes as they sharply survey the scene, the lens of a detective scanning for his clues.

"Man, it got bad out there fast," Reena says, peeling off her hat and coat and hanging them on the coat rack behind the door, the same one she had hung her Guess jean jacket on thirty years ago. "Oh hey, Sally, Brian." She plops down on the couch and yanks off her snow-slicked boots. Flakes fall onto the worn rug and instantly begin to melt.

Cliff, decidedly less comfortable, advances warily into my personal space, searching and inquiring, "So how's your mom doing?"

I take a long stride to the side, seeking my mark. "August is still hanging on, for better or for worse," I reply. "Cliff, you already know Brian. Have you met my friend, Sally Mavey?"

As Cliff extends his hand, Sally swoops forth like a bird of prey and snatches him close for a robust air-kiss on both cheeks. "So nice to finally meet you, Cliff. I've been to your restaurant, oh, many times. The white clam sauce could not be better."

Cliff, flummoxed by Sally's intimate pleasantries and close talk, quickly recovers his scattered charm. "Oh, that's great to hear. Yes, the sauce, it's my mother's old recipe…"

Brian brushes the soot off his hands and offers one to Cliff. "Good to see you, man."

"We're having bourbon, Cliff," Sally announces as she flits into the kitchen for the bottle and glasses. "Would you like some?"

"Uh, sure, I guess." Cliff shrugs. "On a night like tonight, seems appropriate."

Cliff definitely appears on edge, his polished veneer transparent now, his eyes wandering the pictures on the walls, and his boots lightly kicking at the stains on the carpet.

"Ah, the secret stash," Reena says, still rubbing her cold, sore feet when Sally returns and starts clumsily sloshing the brown liquor into five short glasses, errant drops beading on the old, wooden coffee table.

Sally clears her throat. "Ahem. To August…" she offers, holding up her tumbler. The rest of us join her toast with a respectful clink of our own glasses.

"I'm going to want one of those!" Geraldine shouts as she descends the stairs.

Brian laughs. "Man, she's got great hearing for an old lady."

Geraldine sticks her head into the living room. "You bet I do," she says, before noticing the newcomers. "Oh, hello. I'm Geraldine." She waddles into the front room, greeting them with a wave. "Sorry, I need this drink." She grips her lower back as she chugs the bourbon. "I've been sitting up there too long."

"Who is it, Geraldine?" Nelson calls, trailing behind her. "Who's here?"

Enter pivotal character, limping into the denouement.

Cliff's exploring eyes snap into hard focus, then divert into mine like heat-seeking missiles.

I nod, mouthing, *Yes. It's him.*

As Sally refills empty glasses, Nelson slowly emerges, his cane poking and prodding in front of him. An awkward smile spreads across Cliff's face as his long-awaited person of interest stands before him.

I inhale deeply and plunder on with introductions. "Geraldine, Nelson…These are my friends, Reena and Sally. And this is Cliff…oh, I'm afraid I don't even know your last name, Cliff." I toss my line to the audience, anticipating its effect.

"Neal." Cliff drops his surname like a boulder. "Cliff Neal…and it's nice to meet you."

Nelson blanches, his dark skin fading to a sickening gray. His bottom lip quivers and droops. "What is this business? What is this all about?" he barks, a spark of anger instantly igniting behind his gentle eyes.

The air in the room, already tempered with the subtext of death, intensifies and gathers in pitched waves and dark currents.

"Nelson thinks you brought him here to corner him," Reena whispers in my ear. "He thinks it's an inquisition."

"No, Nelson—Mr. McCready," I plead, "it's not what you think."

Nelson limps over to the coat tree and rummages furiously to find his belongings, unwilling to allow himself to be trapped in the spider's web once again.

"Please, sir, if you would just hear us out…" Cliff moves toward him carefully, aware we are collectively balanced on a tipping point. "I *know* that you are an innocent man. No one believes that more than me, I swear. I was just hoping to meet you someday, hoping that we could…talk."

Nelson spins toward Cliff, his hands trembling as he tries to wrap his scarf, fumbling and failing. "You their kin?"

"Yes," Cliff says. "They were my cousins." He glances my way sheepishly. "But I didn't actually know them. They died before I was born. But, you see, when they were murdered, well, it left a *stain* on our family, one that no one has been able to scrub out, all these years. No one ever recovered. My aunt…she left here, and she never looked back. She's a broken woman, a recluse. She always just wanted…answers."

Brian, Sally, and Reena stand in a stupefied line in front of the couch, watching the drama unfold, front row at the theater. Brian bites his nails, and Sally slurps her bourbon.

"But I *know* it wasn't you," Cliff continues, eager to convince Nelson to stay. "My father said it from the beginning. You didn't do it. You were set up. You see, he knew all those cops on the island, but he didn't work with them. He was a deputy at the county sheriff's office, and there was always bad blood between the two forces. But my Pops, he said the evidence wasn't there to arrest you, that something was up from the very beginning."

Nelson seems to relax, loosens his scarf a bit, and uses it to mop the beads of sweat rising on his brow.

"But I really would like to talk with you to learn more about what you know and to see this whole thing from your view. I told my Pops before he died I would get to the bottom of it all, see it through, try to find some justice for Aunt Mary…"

Nelson turns to me with accusing eyes. "You brought me here for *this*?" A sob escapes his throat before he speaks again. "I've said it so many times, but I will say it again now." Tears brim in his eyes, and his body shakes. "It wasn't me. I'd nothing to do with it. I was just…there. And I made up that stupid story just trying to get out of it, any way I could. I was *twenty-two*. And I had *no one* on my side."

"We know, Nelson, we know." Geraldine steps forward, her motherly instincts in high gear. She settles her arm protectively over Nelson's bony shoulders.

"And Jan," Cliff edges in, spinning to face me. "I'm sorry I didn't tell you about my connection. At first, I didn't actually realize that your mother was August Littleton. And then, well, when we started to get to know one another, and we went to the barn…well, it all sort of seemed too late. And I know the timing is terrible— actually, beyond terrible—but I believe, I think we *all* believe, that your mother may know a thing or two about this whole debacle."

I'm ready to respond with something bitter and biting, but Nelson interrupts before I can get a word out.

"What do you mean?" he asks, his voice now a fire alarm to match the heat of his anger. "What would August *know*?"

Geraldine reaches for my hand and gives it an encouraging squeeze.

"Nelson." I gulp for courage. "I don't have any proof, and I haven't been able to ever get a straight answer out of my mother, but I think August and Chief Matthews may have been…together. I think the chief may have been my father."

"Ah, okay. Yes, now I see…" Nelson considers it all as it dawns on him his friendship with August may have had an intent and purpose of which he was never made aware. He clasps his hands together, palm to palm, then raises them to his pursed lips, beleaguered and betrayed.

"Well," Cliff starts, "there's a lot we still don't know here, and—"

"There is something else I *do* know, though," I interrupt. "Something that I figured out just today. August worked at Pop Gray's. She was a waitress. I found part of the uniform in the closet. So, it's not a stretch, I guess. She probably knew your cousins, too."

Geraldine scowls and drops my hand. "Well, that must have been after my time. I don't remember that."

"You think August knows something about what happened that night?" Nelson's eyes burn with intensity. They dart amongst us, pleading for answers, for absolution.

"I don't know," I answer honestly, realizing this page of the script is completely blank.

"Mr. McCready." Cliff, still fiercely clutching his empty glass, tries again. "I've had this theory for a while now, and I'm wondering…is there anything you can tell me about the police presence there that night? I mean, *before* the murders. Was it a normal night, everyone going about their business, or did you see any cops—or anyone or anything suspicious—poking around downtown that night?"

Nelson sighs and leans his long body against the mantle, the fever in his eyes breaking. The memory of that night rises before him like a bad movie he'd watched a thousand times.

The phone at the other end of the line rang and rang.

"Dammit, Mama, pick up."

He let it ring five more times. "Must be at church," he muttered to himself, placing the receiver back on the cradle inside the cramped phone booth.

It was hot in the booth, a damp spring night pressing on the glass from all sides. He could see a sliver of sunset dangling over the blue water in the distance. Back home, there were hills and valleys but no view of the end of the world like this. No place to watch the day fade away like God's magic, even if from inside a phone booth.

The shiny blue-and-white police car cruised past the phone booth and began its deliberate circle around downtown. This was the second time the cruiser had slowed to a crawl in front of him. Nelson could see the bulge of the chief's Adam's apple as he craned his neck out the car window to see what was happening inside his phone booth.

"Ain't breaking no law," Nelson muttered to himself from inside the rectangular confines. He didn't want to leave because he really needed to reach Momma tonight, and he worried someone else would get in there. If he didn't get her tonight, she wouldn't be able to send him the money in time, he couldn't pay for school, he'd have to drop out.

He did not want to drop out, no sir, not after two whole semesters and getting his big break in the white college. Only the third colored man they'd ever accepted, he desired to make them all proud.

Two young boys with crew cuts tumbled out of the ice cream store, one of them throwing a jab at the shoulder of the other, who held a chocolate cone. The cone dropped on the ground with a splatter, and the boy who lost it got an angry look on his face and started shoving at the other, who laughed as hard as could be. Nelson saw the chief's car slow again in front of the boys, then saw the chief's wide-brim hat leaning out the window, giving them some words.

"Now that you mention it, the chief *was* there that night, driving up and down," Nelson reveals. "Doing laps around the town square, eyeing everyone up."

"Okay. Do you recall if you saw him go into Pop Gray's?" Cliff asks, hopefully.

"No," Nelson says, crestfallen.

Brian, trying to busy himself by poking the fire, shuffles up behind Cliff and inquires in his low whisper, "So, you think the chief really did it?"

Cliff makes a shushing noise over his shoulder to Brian as if silencing a nagging child before he continues. "Mr. McCready, did you know any of the cops who worked for the town police back then? I mean, know them personally?"

"No, I tried to keep my head low, Mr. Neal. Black men didn't really make friends with cops back in those days…or in these days, for that matter."

"Understood," Cliff says. "And did you ever meet either of my cousins? I mean, maybe you were even their customer at Pop Gray's?"

Nelson shakes his head sadly. "Not to my recollection. I didn't really have a lot of spare change to be going 'round getting ice cream."

"I guess what I'm trying to understand is," Cliff continues, "well, had you ever heard rumors about any sort of relationship between either of my cousins and someone who worked for the police force?"

Behind them, Sally puts down her empty bourbon glass with a heavy thud. "Oh, you want to know if it was a crime of passion," she says loudly.

Cliff turns to her with a bemused smile. "Yes, I think that's where I'm trying to go here. It just seems like one of the possibilities. Or perhaps…did Ms. Littleton ever share anything like this with you while she was…you know, up and about?"

"No, we never talked about it. I mean, I didn't even know she used to work there. She never let on. And I'm afraid I wouldn't know anything about no crime of passion," Nelson's voice wavers, sounding far away and lost.

"Oh, I can find that out, no problem," Sally speaks up, her green tracksuit swishing as she hurries to her bag to grab her cell. She pours another bourbon and begins to climb her phone tree.

I move silently away from the conversation to lay eyes on August. Gregor sits bedside, a small notebook in his lap, writing something in short strokes, immersed in his own world. Nelson's prayer candle burns mightily on the bedside table, and August continues her drug-induced slumber, her breath ragged and shallow. Chaos spins around her like an angry tornado, but she remains resolute, unscathed within her own selfish center.

"Mama," I poke, a slight nudge on her arm. "Mama, you have visitors here. We want you to wake up."

"You called her Mama," Gregor says, looking up from his notepad with a questioning smile. "It's the first time I haven't heard you use her given name."

"Huh," I reflect. "I guess I did."

Cliff must have watched me slip away and quietly followed. He waits for me in the hallway just outside my mother's room, his dark head hung low, and his broad shoulders humbled.

"Jan, I'm so sorry I didn't tell you," he says. "I don't tell many people—anyone, really. And I didn't know you were a Littleton until yesterday after the barn, and then, for sure, when I dropped you home. But I wasn't…I didn't try to—"

"Use me?" I finish his sentence with a sneer, indignation swelling in my chest.

"No, it had nothing to do with getting to know you, I swear. I liked you, from the moment we met. I don't know. I guess I felt like we had a connection."

I cross my arms tightly in defiance, and yet, I can still feel the pull of this man. Resourceful, resilient, and repentant, Cliff pleads for my forgiveness here in the unforgiving hallway of my childhood home.

Sally scurries up the stairs, full of resolve, but sensing the tension, she starts to back away.

"No, it's okay, Sally," I beckon to her. "Did you learn anything?"

"Well, it's *something*, I think," she says, looking back and forth between Cliff and I, unsure where to drop her next bombshell. She clears her throat, looking a little bit ill at ease. "So, you know it's just a rumor, right?"

"Sally, what is it?" I press.

"My mama's best friend Leanne from Bridge Club said, sure enough, there was a story back in the day about Chief Matthews and a girl from the high school. Nobody knows for sure who it was, but now I guess we know it was your momma, Jan. Leanne said the chief liked to hang around Pop Gray's too much, especially for a man of his age."

"So, maybe there is something to it." Cliff throws me a timid glance, seeking my endorsement.

"And there was a rumor of a baby," Sally continues, breathless. "That the chief had an affair and had fathered a child, but no one really knew *who*. But Jeanne said, once Alice found out, it was all sticks and stones for their marriage. The beginning of the end. When Alice was ready to leave the chief, that's what Jeanne said, well, you know. He shot himself."

"So, you think the chief was trying to contain it all?" I ask, the tremble in my voice undeniable. "That maybe *August* was the intended victim that night at Pop Gray's. A way to fix his mistake?"

"But why?" Cliff challenges. "If your mother was the object of affection, or the one carrying his child, however you want to look at it, and she walked away alive, why did the other two die? Did they get in the way? Something go wrong with the chief's plan?"

"Oh, God. Hell if I know!" I throw my hands into the air, overwrought with the idea the father I'd been seeking my entire life had *finally* been revealed, and after all the anticipation, he's a monster. "I mean, I didn't know the man. I can't defend him. He may have been a psychopath. Maybe he murdered them. It's the only thing that makes any sense. Maybe he went in there one night, had a milkshake with his mistress, knocked off her friends, took the $138 dollars, and blamed it on a Black man. That seems about right since, clearly, I was born into a family of crackpots."

"Jan," Cliff whispers, stepping in to wrap his dragon-winged arms around me, as a heaving sob, like a cannonball, explodes from my chest.

"Jan, honey, I know it's a lot," Sally says, "but I have something else for you, too."

I brace myself in the circle of Cliff's arms, accustomed by now to the required posture the body must assume to absorb crushing blows to its identity.

"I heard back from Eileen Conway. Well, really from her nephew," Sally says. "She wants to talk to you. She says she remembers your mother."

I breathe a sigh of relief.

"But here's the thing," Sally continues, "the nephew says she's not so good in the memory department. She has the Alzheimer's, Jan."

"Shit." I throw an exasperated glance at Cliff. "But you said she remembers August?"

"I know it sounds kind of tricky," Sally says, "but maybe it's like she remembers things from her distant past but not the more current stuff. My Aunt Edna had the Alzheimer's, and that's how it was for her, at least. But Sam—that's her nephew—he said that if you come visit her, it might help jar some memories. Sometimes, face-to-face interaction helps her remember. And Jan…"

"What?"

"Well, you *do* look an awful lot like your mother."

I nod, inhaling the worn comfort of Cliff's flannel, the sharp scent of oregano that never seems to leave his skin.

"What do you say we go and pay a visit to Ms. Conway right now?" Cliff asks. "The Springwood is not far from here. Less than a half-hour drive."

"But the roads…" I protest, feeling certain I will break if one more secret comes tumbling out of the closet.

"Four-wheel drive, Jan. I'm from Boston. This storm is nothing I can't handle, and we're in this together now. Ms. Conway actually *knew* your mother back then. She may have even been there that night. So, she may be our only chance to corroborate." He then softens his tone, the context changing everything. "Our last chance to understand."

Chapter 27: Remembering

A half hour later, I'm back in the cabin of Cliff's pickup, all loose threads and jagged seams, skidding around icy corners toward the next disaster. A soft blanket of snow, pierced by blades of marsh grass, drapes the banks of the sound and lays heavy on the boughs of the tall pines. The streets are empty, and the visibility is low, and the truck seems to cruise into another plane of existence. No Rolling Stones serenade us tonight, just the quiet crunch of snow beneath the tires.

"Tell me more about August, Jan," Cliff suggests gently. "I mean, you've already told me she wasn't really a great mother, but was there, I don't know, *anything* redeeming you can remember? Was she *ever* a good *person*?"

"Well…" I dig deep, struggling to find my inner balance, wobbling and tipping. "Okay. The beach. She loved to take me to the beach. We'd walk down to Lumina almost every day."

Cliff nods, and I carry on.

"So, in my "good" memories, I can see her flip flops slapping ahead of me over the bridge. And I'm dragging my beach towel on the ground behind me, like Linus and the blanket."

I laugh, and Cliff politely joins me.

"And the *best* days," I say, "were the days that she wasn't drinking, or angry, or crying quietly beneath her sunglasses. The days that she remembered I was there, when she and I would sit at the shoreline digging for sand crabs and building drip castles."

"*What* kind of castles?" Cliff asks, turning into the Springwood parking lot.

"A *drip* castle," I explain. "You build them with the dark sand, the wettest, right in that spot that the waves have just abandoned." Cliff is a good listener, affirming that my story is one he wanted to hear.

"You just grab a handful of the wet sand, and slowly let it drip through your fingers onto the dry land. Over and over again until you have, well, you have an ugly castle."

"Sounds to me like a pile of mud," he teases. "A mud pie?"

"Well, she called it a castle. And I believed her. Because in those days, I needed something to trust. Even if that something was just a pile of mud."

"Yeah, I get that." Cliff eases into a parking spot. "We all need something to trust." His words sound bitter, though, like he wants to spit out a bad seed.

"The thing about those days," I continue, uncertain why I need to share more, though I do. "August seemed so *content*. I still remember her, sprawled out on her beach towel, wearing that bright-orange bathing suit of hers that I hated. But we just sat there, watching sand drip from our fingers, no other agenda. We were at peace. I was happy, you know…" I wipe away an errant tear. "Because *she* was happy."

He parks the truck in front of a lumbering building with a Greek Revival facade, Roman columns, and a classical wrap-around porch.

"Jesus." Cliff kills the engine. "Was this place a plantation?"

"Probably. C'mon, we've got to be quick." I sniffle, climbing out of the truck and heading for the entrance, determined to find a way to heal the wounds of the day.

Overheated air envelops me as I swing open the heavy front door, stepping into a grand entrance hall adorned with chandeliers and plaid armchairs. A stooped gentleman straggles down the hallway beyond the main foyer, holding the elbow of a frocked lady with a bobbing yellow bun. The lady makes me think wistfully of Geraldine, currently at home twiddling her thumbs and willing my mother to stay alive.

Cliff joins me at the nurses' station that's discreetly tucked in the corner of the foyer, and we wait patiently until the woman at the front desk finishes her phone call.

"Well, tell him I said to finish his homework before he goes, do you hear?… Mmhmm, all of it." She puts her hand over the phone mouthpiece and whispers, "Just one sec, y'all…Jimmy, what did I tell you this morning? No, you cannot ride on that ATV in the snow… No. Is your homework done? What did I *say*?"

Cliff clears his throat impatiently, brash and Bostonian, and just then, a young man in a corduroy blazer steps forward.

"Miss Littleton?" he questions with some hesitation and a thick Southern drawl.

I don't bother to correct the mistaken last name as I approach the earnest man. He's nervously rubbing one of the tweedy patches on the elbows of his blazer.

"Mr. Conway, I presume?"

He nods with a slow smile. "Call me Sam, please."

"Jan." I shake his hand. "And this is my…" I trip over the label, uncertain how to explain the presence of Cliff. "Uh, this is Cliff."

"Thanks for meeting us here, especially in this weather," Cliff says, clearly sensing no need to explain further as he shakes Sam's hand.

"It's not a problem." He gestures for us to follow. "I live right down the street, so when your friend called, it was easy to pop over since it sounded quite important."

"Yes, it is," I answer quickly. "My mother—well, she may not make it through the night. And, well, she used to be friends with your aunt years ago. And I just…Well, I have some questions I'm hoping Ms. Conway can help answer."

"Oh, well," Sam empathizes. "I'm so sorry to hear about her poor health. You can follow me this way to Eileen's room."

The hallway is lined with IV poles and discarded wheelchairs. The stale smells of age and antiseptic fill the air, and the quiet hum of someone's TV plays a game show in the background.

"Did Miss Mavey tell y'all about my aunt's mental state?" Sam asks as we stop in front of a closed door. The gold-embossed placard outside reads *Conway*.

"Yes," Cliff replies. "Her memory is failing, right?"

Sam chuckles. "Well, it has pretty much already failed. She doesn't know me anymore, not really. She thinks I'm one of the doctors here." He laughs again. "Or sometimes, a gentleman caller." Cliff and I politely smile, anxious to get what we came for.

"But it is funny what the memory can do," Sam continues. "She does seem to recall quite a bit more from her past—her school days, even when she was a child. Not sure how much of it she's making up, maybe just imagining things she wished had happened, you know?"

We nod in unison, hopeful that our agreement will hasten the opening of the closed door.

"Anyway, come on in," Sam says, finally turning the knob and revealing tiny, blue-haired Eileen Conway. Wrapped in a yellow robe on the end of her bed, her rapt attention focused on the local evening news, she clutches a mug of something warm and steamy and doesn't bother to look toward those incoming.

"Y'all see this?" she asks, her voice high and thin, sweetly tinged with enough southern lilt to match her nephew's. "Someone broke down the windows at the Walmart." She screws up her face in disapproval before turning toward us. She gasps audibly, and the mug goes crashing to the floor, tea splattering across the rug and wall.

"August." She chokes on the name.

"Ms. Conway," I say quickly. "I'm August's daughter. My name is Jan."

"Why are you here, Aggie?" she asks me, rising gingerly from the edge of her bed, all the color draining from her face. "And who are all of you?" She waves a trembling hand at Cliff and Sam.

"Aunt Eileen." Sam rushes to the spill with a handkerchief he pulls from his pocket. "These are some old friends from Seaville. Do you remember Seaville?"

"Of course, I remember it. That's where we live, isn't it?" she spits back, irritated, yanking the tie on her robe. "But I thought you were planning to leave town, Aggie?" she asks, pivoting back to me. "After what you did…" Eileen raises a scolding finger and holds it inches from my face.

I swallow hard, my confidence oozing like syrup down my spine. "*What* did I do, Eileen?" I ask in a reluctant whisper.

"You *know* that Chief is married. You even keep acquaintance with his wife," Eileen fumes. Turning to

Sam, she adds, "Y'all know that Ms. Alice comes in for ice cream all the time, always orders strawberry…"

Eileen has regressed to a distant time, where her younger self scooped a frothy pink confection into a glittering dessert dish, smiling as she handed over the silver spoon.

"What about the chief?" I ask, timidly stepping forward and into the wavy lines of Eileen's historical relapse. She takes a step backwards, retreating from my advance.

"Well, you *said* the baby was his, didn't you? Why, that's what you told me just the other night when we were closing at Pop's…"

I feel Cliff gripping my elbow, the extra support keeping me on my feet.

"Ms. Conway," he starts, "Eileen. I'm, uh, a friend of the family. My name is Cliff Neal."

Eileen narrows her eyes suspiciously and turns her gaze on Cliff, studying his face, his hair, and his clothes until she's satisfied with her recognition.

"Oh, you're here, too, then? It took me a minute, but I know you now, Chief," she says.

Cliff looks over his shoulder, certain she's speaking to someone standing just behind him. I shift my weight, find my footing, and throw a soft elbow into Cliff's ribcage.

"She means you," I whisper. "She thinks you're *him*."

Eileen's apprehensive eyes transform to coy, twinkling, and she's once again the schoolgirl with the shy smile who had gazed out from the black-and-white photo in the *Star News*. "Well, it's awful nice of you to call on me, Chief." Her frail fingers quickly go to her hair, where she begins to smooth and primp the fine gray strands. "I must look a sight. I haven't had a chance to get ready for school yet…or was I going to work?" Her eyes dart around the room, seeking her textbooks or maybe her pink pillbox hat.

Cliff shoots me a nervous glance, which I return with a slight shrug. He lightly reaches for Eileen's hand, offering something between an affectionate squeeze and a handshake. He, too, seems rattled, but he plays along.

"Miss Eileen, a pleasure to see you again," he says. "You were saying that you know about…that Jan…I mean, August and I…are having a baby?"

Eileen's wiry hands drop back in her lap. She looks flustered now. "Well, I try not to gossip about these things, but those girls, they were always teasing you, Aggie. Remember how they were always making fun of you about being a *lesbian*." She lowers her voice to a whisper with the last word, leaning toward me with a shared secret. "I wasn't sure if you were or you weren't, but boy, it sure did seem to bother you."

"And then you and Chief started up," she continues, "and those girls, they were threatening to tell Ms. Alice when she came by for her scoop of strawberry. And then, you told me about the baby, that's what you said. And you said you were going to go away. Why, I thought I'd never see you again. But here you are." Eileen eyes my stomach for signs of a baby bump. I cross my arms protectively over my torso, inhale deeply, and continue.

"Eileen, remind me, if you will. Those girls who teased me—they were the ones who we worked with at Pop Gray's, right? The Neal sisters?"

Eileen purses her thin lips now and puts her hands on her tiny hips to think, to search for something she had once known. After a long moment, the memory arrives. "Of course, Kimberlee and…well, something…yes… something happened to them, though. What was it?" She pauses and turns to look out the window, as if the answer lies just on the other side of the frosted glass. "And what was it you said about that gun? Someone has a gun…"

She wheels back to us abruptly, but her face appears startlingly blank. Void of expression and aspiration, it's as if she has turned into a ghost.

"Who are you?" Suddenly, her voice sounds startled, high and brittle. "And what are you doing here?" Eileen's eyes flash from my face to Cliff's and back again. Without warning, we have become strangers and potential enemies.

Sam steps forward, a calming hand finding his aunt's shoulder. "Aunt Eileen, it's okay. It's Sammy. It's Shep. You're in your new apartment, remember? You're safe. Nobody here is going to hurt you. These are friends." He pulls her into a stiff hug, a scene that had been rehearsed many times. "It's okay that you don't remember. It's okay."

"Oh, Shep." Eileen's distraught reply muffles as she buries her face in her nephew's shoulder.

Sam, still with his arms around Eileen, nods toward the door, giving us a dismissive wave.

We still have many questions, but we have no choice but to respect the request.

I tremble as I close the door behind us, searching Cliff's eyes for the bloodhound detective, eager for someone to chase down these questions and capture the answers.

An old man in a squeaky wheelchair ambles by, intent on inspecting the young visitors. Cliff offers him a curt nod and heaves a heavy sigh. "That was unreal. I've gotta tell you, I'm totally freaked out right now. I mean, the memory plays some mean tricks, but that was something else…Now we know why Matthews was a regular at Pop Gray's."

"Jesus Christ," I swear. "According to the high school version of Eileen, his wife hung out there a lot, too. Maybe she knew what he was up to?" I'm wringing my hands, yearning down the hallway for a bathroom since I feel like I might vomit any minute.

"So, my cousins *knew* about the affair, and August *knew* that they knew…"

"And *he* probably knew that they knew…and his wife, too."

"And August knows what he did with the gun," Cliff hypothesizes. "So, any way you slice it, you have at least one parent who is a sociopath."

"Thanks, Cliff," I mutter scornfully. "But yeah, that's what it's starting to look like."

A nurse in pink scrubs holding a small paper cup full of pills scoots past us, gingerly pushing inside Eileen's door. A moment later, Sam tumbles out of the room, relieved of the burden of comforting the kin who didn't seem to know him.

"Sorry about that, folks." Sam ushers us away from the closed door. "When she has a moment of clarity, well, it can fade real fast, as you just saw. She gets real upset, and they like to give her some sedatives to keep the blood pressure down."

"No, of course. We understand," Cliff says. "I would feel bad if we caused her any stress…"

"Oh, no." Sam gives another wave of his hand. "She's all right. She won't even remember you were here." Sam navigates us back to the foyer of the complex, and he motions for us to have a seat on one of the plaid couches.

I fumble with my bag, forgetting we brought Cliff's truck, digging for car keys as I'm anxious as hell to get out of here. "We really should be going, Sam. We've already taken up too much of your time, and the storm, and my mother…"

The smell of decay seeps into the pores of my skin, and the heavy, overheated air makes it hard to breathe. Panic rises in my chest, and the pulse of trouble grows at my temples. I know I need to escape this place of death in perpetuity.

"Oh." Sam, clearly disappointed, must have thought our visit had just begun. "But there *is* one more thing I wanted to talk to y'all about. Can y'all stay for a cup of coffee?"

Cliff snaps to attention, following Sam's lead like a dog on his scent. "Sure, yeah, I'll take a cup," he answers decisively, before I can object.

I force a smile. "Maybe one for the road."

Sam disappears around a corner.

"I just want to go, Cliff, I have to get back before August…you know…" I whisper through clenched teeth. "This was a bad idea to come here now like this. I thought I could handle it, but it's just too much."

Cliff calmly raises his thick brow and presses the palms of his hands toward the ground, giving me a look that says, *Settle*.

Sam returns with two Styrofoam cups and a granola bar, which he has already ripped open. His mouth twists with worry as he hands over the lukewarm coffee and stuffs a large chunk of granola into his mouth. He sits down across from us in an overstuffed armchair upholstered in pinks. He chews busily for a minute and then looks up, ready to talk.

"At first, I didn't put it together," Sam says, a crumb falling from his lower lip onto the chair. "But when Eileen called you August, it all started to make more sense, and I think I have figured it out now."

Cliff slurps his terrible coffee and leans forward in an attentive, all-ears way, propping his elbows on his knees and waiting patiently for Sam to continue.

"When Ms. Mavey told me some friends from Seaville were coming by, I guess I didn't realize that August was your mother. You see, my aunt didn't have any kids of her own, and well, I guess I kind of played that part for her, even though she's not that much older than I am. So, as you can imagine, I got to hear all her stories. And there was this one story she'd tell about her friend Aggie, who I now assume was your mother, August."

I nod in agreement.

Sam hesitates, the way people do when they don't want to be the bearer of bad news. "I heard it more than once before her memory started to stray. And, I mean, how many people can have that name, right?"

Sam looks uncomfortable and repentant, like a choir boy late for church. I tuck my fidgeting hands beneath my thighs and calmly survey the room for the nearest exit, ready to bolt as soon as he finishes his speech.

"You see, Aunt Eileen told me that when she was a girl…a teenager … she and this Aggie were close. I guess you know they worked together as Sundae Girls?"

I just nod again obediently, ready to be on the other side of whatever punishing blow lands next.

"So, this Aggie would tell her things…things that maybe she didn't tell other folks." Sam shoves the rest of the granola bar in his mouth, chews fast, swallows hard, and then loudly crumples up the wrapper. "My aunt had a car, a blue Chevy Impala. We just sold it a few years ago. She said she would drive Aggie places she needed to go— to work, around town, whatever. I guess your mom didn't have her own car in those days?"

I shrug. I had no idea.

"Eileen told me that she felt like maybe Aggie fancied her. You know, in *that way*…" Blotchy red embarrassment rises from Sam's collar. He looks around nervously and clears his throat.

"It's okay," I reassure him. "Turns out, August does indeed prefer ladies."

"Oh, okay then. It's no harm to me, anyway," he states. "As she tells it, one day, they were parked in the Impala outside the ice cream store, getting ready to go into work. Aggie leans over a little too close, and Eileen said she got nervous that she was going to try to kiss her, and well, she just didn't feel the same way. My Aunt Eileen, you see, she definitely liked men. But instead, she said Aggie whispered in her ear that she was buying a *gun* and that two of the bullets in it were intended for those girls who ended up getting *shot*."

My hands clench into fists beneath my legs, the fluorescent room grows dim, and my breath sputters out in shallow gasps. Beside me, I can feel the muscles in Cliff's body tense, a buzz of anticipation radiating from every one of his pores.

"Sam, you say August told your aunt this *before* the murders?" Cliff asks.

"That's what she said. And that after the girls were killed, she said that Aggie brought it up again like she was bragging. She even told Eileen what happened to the gun…"

"Oh yeah?" Cliff thrusts his chest forward, bursting at the seams. "So, she *had* the gun. What did she do with it?"

"Aunt Eileen said that Aggie asked to borrow her car the next day, and she was acting strange and all, but she still said yes. I guess Aggie told her she drove out to some farm somewhere to get rid of the gun, and well, she told Aunt Eileen that she gave the gun to the chief of police."

A sound escapes my lips, somewhere between a choke and a chortle.

"Well, I'll be damned," Cliff murmurs.

"When I heard this story at first," Sam continues, "it made me wonder: if the police chief had the 'smoking gun,' so to speak, why wasn't Aggie charged with a crime? It was such a sensational story, as she told it, well, I'm not sure if I ever really believed Aunt Eileen. I thought, you know, surely, she had mixed up some of the facts. But now, witnessing her little relapse in time tonight, her seeing you…well, the story sort of makes more sense."

"Did Eileen ever tell *anyone*?" Cliff asks. "I mean, other than you? The police, maybe?"

"I don't think she did. She said that, at the time, she just thought Aggie was pulling her leg. You know, like trying to get a rise out of her or trying to get her attention. But I think over time, she may have realized there was some truth to it. But by then, she'd moved out of town, lost touch with everyone from here, and it sort of just became part of her past, I guess. Folklore."

Cliff inhales sharply and dares to look my way. I sink into the lobby couch, defeated. I'm done. All of my emotions have been spent down to empty. Cliff thanks Sam again, shaking his hand, then pulls me to my feet, carefully leading me out of Springwood and back into the known world of his old blue truck. It's not until we're close to the island that either of us utters a word.

"So, either she was covering for him…" I begin.

"Or he was covering for her," Cliff finishes.

Neon streetlights that line the roadway flash like warnings in the darkened cab, the tires beat like a drum, and Cliff and I drive through the falling snow toward the beginning of the end.

Chapter 28: Directing

"Anyone hungry?" Reena calls from the kitchen, the sound of her voice a relief as we walk back through August's front door. The warm aroma of cheese and garlic greets us, a welcome contrast to the antiseptic smell of Springwood.

"Here, here," answers Nelson as he and Geraldine straggle, arm in arm, toward the kitchen.

They stop short when they see Cliff and me standing inside the threshold, dazed and disheveled, like defeated soldiers returning from foreign territory. The expressions on our faces tell them we had just been to battle.

We'd decided on the way home we would keep Sam's story to ourselves, at least for a while, until we could find a way to reason through the madness of it. So, Cliff and I shrug our shoulders and report we visited with Eileen, but nothing much had come of it.

We join the others at the dining room table, where Reena had found a way to present a meal by adding a few cans of tomato soup to Sally's lasagna. She ladles a bowl of soup for Gregor and takes it to him at August's bedside as the rest of us pile our plates. We pass around the bourbon bottle, almost empty now, small sad splashes in the bottom of our glasses.

"Too bad it's snowing so hard out there, or I could go and get a refill," Sally says, eyeing the dregs of the liquor.

"Oh, I have a case of wine I ordered for the restaurant in the back of my truck," Cliff offers. "Should I grab a few bottles?" No one protests, so the wine, a vintage Cabernet, much fancier than the cuisine or the occasion demands, winds up retrieved and poured.

We sit with the quiet, save for the slurp of soup and the mournful song of the cold wind against the windowpanes. We try to make small talk, the kind that's uncomfortable but necessary to get through the meal. Every sip, each bite, just seems like a way to kill time until August awakens. Or until August dies.

At some point, Reena turns up the old stereo, and a soft, hollow jazz fills in the empty spaces between us.

I watch Nelson across the table, nodding politely as Geraldine rambles on about her daughter-in-law, who *may* have a shopping addiction. But he isn't really listening. His eyes scan the room for signs of friend or foe, seeming to settle on Sally.

"Excuse me, miss," Nelson says across the table, interrupting Geraldine's story.

Sally, surprised, rests her fork and replies, "Who, me?"

"Yes, I'm sorry. I know your face, and I, well, I think that we're neighbors, but I don't remember your name," Nelson says, his voice wavering.

Sally, not accustomed to being forgotten, bristles. "It's Sally Mavey. We've met before. And yes, I live just across the street."

"Mavey, Mavey…" Nelson reels back thoughtfully in his chair, trying to place the name, searching the blank space in his mind that yearns for a memory, before keening back on Sally. He snaps his fingers, yanking the idea out of empty air. "I've got it! I know who you remind me of…Yes, that's it!" He chuckles to himself. "A very old friend, many years ago, she used to work at the library…What was her name? Oh yes, yes. It *was* Mavey."

Sally warms up like melted butter. "Why, yes, that's my momma."

Nelson draws in a quick breath of revelation, his memory clicking into focus like the lens of a camera. He leans across the table to Sally, tears unexpectedly welling in the corners of his eyes. "You know, Sally, your momma, well, there was a day that she saved my life." The rest of the table stops chattering. Everyone stills their clinking utensils and tunes in to the exchange between Nelson and Sally.

"Now this," she says, sliding her chair closer, "is a story I need to hear."

Just then, however, Gregor emerges from the doorway. His eyes are set and serious, framing a new urgency. "Miss Jan," he says, his tone still measured. "I think she's waking up. There is some talking…some words. Can't really make it out, but you should come."

My spoon splashes into my half-empty bowl, tomato soup splattering on Brian, and without a glance or word to the others, I bolt for August's bedroom, my long-awaited stage entrance. I find August steeped in the shadows of the room, lit only by a dull bedside lamp and the flicker of Nelson's prayer candle burning on the dresser.

August is indeed mumbling, wheezing, coughing —wet and furious—and I have to lean in close, searching for coherence. I breathe in my mother's scent, musty attic and seeping sour, feeling like it could be the last time I do so.

August's eyes flutter open, startlingly lush against her bloodless pallor. They drift idly, waking from a dream, and then, with a remembered urgency, her eyes dart around the room. She seems to be looking for something or for someone.

"No. Nooo," she moans. She pants for each breath, fighting against a force that pulls her from within.

"August," I begin gently, enunciating my words as if speaking to a toddler. "Are you with us? Can you hear me?"

She blinks, her witch eyes fierce and fevered as she searches my face. "Mama?" she asks, confused.

"Umm, no. August, it's me, Jan…your daughter."

Dismay burrows into the crevices on August's brow and the crow's feet around her eyes. Her parched lips tremble as she fumbles to find words, but only incoherent sounds escape. I take my mother's limp hand, not because it feels right to do so, but because it seems the right thing to do. It's what the scene requires.

"And Geraldine is here, too," I remind her, beckoning to her partner, who hovers expectantly in the doorway.

Geraldine swoops in. "Oh, you've just been resting for a good long while, Aggie." She caresses

August's shoulder gently. "It's all right now. It's all going to be all right. You just keep breathing. That's all you gotta do."

August's face softens with recognition, and her panicked breathing eases as she finds her place in the present.

"Where heeee?" August's words barely sound like words. Slurred with the effort of speech, saliva drips from the corner of her mouth.

Gregor steps into her field of vision, offering a cup of crushed ice. "I'm right here, Miss Littleton," he says respectfully. He gently wipes August's chin, props her head up with the flattened pillow, and holds out a spoonful of ice chips. She moans but cannot or will not open her lips.

"You know who else is here?" Geraldine chimes in, trying to sound chipper, as if she'd just dropped by to borrow a cup of sugar. "Why, one of your old friends came to pay a visit."

August's eyes cut to Gregor, confused. She ignores Geraldine and chokes out the words.

"*He knows*," she whispers. Nostrils flaring, August attempts to lift her head from the pillow, the tendons in her neck straining valiantly but to no avail.

I bow my head, crouching lower to meet her face to face. "*Who* knows, August? Who knows *what*?"

August doesn't answer but instead darts her wild eyes at Gregor, who stands patiently beside the armchair, waiting with his cup of ice.

"Nel-son (cough, cough, cough) *knows.*"

"Mother," I begin, feeling the pulse of patience slipping away from me. "That's not Nelson. That's Gregor. He's here to help. He's been keeping you comfortable with medicine and massage, and he's been here for *days.*" I smile apologetically at Gregor, who waves it off and holds out the ice cup for someone else to try.

Geraldine takes the ice chips and assumes the bedside position she had claimed upon arrival. A few pellets make it across August's lips and dissolve on her tongue before she speaks again.

"Where's (cough, cough) the boy?"

I'm suddenly struck by the understanding August has been, on some level, completely aware of her surroundings, even as she tumbled through the altered consciousness of her deep, drug-induced sleep. She'd been listening to our conversation, making note of our comings and goings.

"What *boy*, August?" I hedge, irritated that she's going off script. "You mean, the *men* who are in the living room? Those are just some friends of mine here to wait out the storm. No need to worry."

A fit of coughing racks her body, and as it subsides, each intake of air seems more desperate than the last.

"Mama," I try again, easing myself into an uncomfortable position at the foot of the bed and trying to shake off my aggravation and sound conciliatory. "There is something I wanted to talk to you about, and there is no need to get yourself worked up. Just listen, okay?"

August stares back at me coldly, her chest heaving, indignant and unrelenting. I know time runs short, and I need to proceed with my line of questioning. The show must go on.

"I need to know…" I falter a bit. "About Matty. About my father."

August winces like my words are razors, but still she shakes her head, a difficult sway against the dent of the pillow.

"I c-c-can't breathe." She wheezes and coughs. "The b-b-boys…I need to seeeee…"

I catch Geraldine's eye, trying to decipher the eccentricity. August seems to be weaving in and out of coherence. Geraldine, with no answers, just shrugs.

"You mean Nelson, Aggie? Is he the boy you want to see?" Geraldine suggests, offering August the oxygen mask.

Crimson circles rise in August's cheeks. "No!" she snarls, turning her head away from the mask, wavering for a second to gather what breath remains. Then she continues. "The boy…who was taaaalking."

"Okay, August." I try to sound soothing. "I can get him."

I hurry downstairs to the dining room where everyone is still conversing in awkward, hushed whispers around the table.

"Um…okay. Strange request, I know, but August says she wants to see 'the boy.' I don't know what she's talking about but, uh, I think she was able to hear us—everything—while she was sedated, and maybe was processing some of it. She's really confused, but would you guys be willing to come up to her room? Maybe she wants to place faces with the voices she's been hearing? I honestly don't know…"

"All of us?" Brian gulps.

"Yeah, I guess," I respond. "I'm not really sure who she means or why she wants to see you."

Brian stands sheepishly and Cliff with eager anticipation.

"Nelson, would you come up, too? I mean, if you're willing…" I ask.

Reena, sitting beside Nelson, gives his hand a reassuring squeeze, and so he resolutely nods and rises from his chair. I lead the three men up the stairs and down the short hall to August's room, where we all stop, ill at ease, on the threshold.

I take Brian by the arm and lead him in. "Okay, August, this is Brian. You may remember him. He went to high school with me."

Brian gives an uncomfortable wave. "Nice to see you again, Ms. Littleton. If there is anything I ca—"

"No," August cuts him off, the roll of her eyes swatting him away like a fly.

Dismissed, Brian turns on his heel and hurries back down the stairs with palpable relief.

"Sorry," I whisper as he rushes past me.

"Him," August rasps, finding the bodily strength to raise one trembling, bony finger and point toward Cliff.

His thick brows rise in arched surprise, but he steps forward when called, all at once a strapping hero and a scared little boy.

"Okay, then" I interject into the strained silence. "August, this is my friend, Cliff Neal."

"I *know* who…this is," she huffs, spittle flying again. "Come here, b-boy. Let…me look."

Cliff shuffles further into the room, his hands thrust in his jean's pockets, heeding my mother's abstruse bidding.

"So…you (cough) f-found me," August mumbles, her pointer finger wilting and a tear smearing her parched cheek. "I never m-m-meant to (cough, cough, cough)…"

"Um, Ms. Littleton, it's a pleasure to meet you," Cliff replies, uncertain of the appropriate response. I ease back onto the edge of the bed, lost in my own rattled reticence, watching this scene, so different from the one I thought I was directing, unfold.

"And *you*." August, weaker now, limply nods her head toward Nelson, who still stands in the hall.

"Hello, my old friend," he says, reluctantly stepping in and creating a distraction for Cliff to gracefully retreat.

"It's *you*," she says faintly as Nelson approaches. Her eyes slide sideways toward Gregor as she calculates her earlier mistake, then they drift back to Nelson. "I'm s-sorry…it's all…'cause of me." Her words are reverential, almost a whisper.

"Whatever you're talking about, August," Nelson says, flustered, "I still appreciate the friendship that we've had." He picks up her listless hand, which I notice has now taken on a bruised, purple hue.

With an unexpected energy, August heaves back into her pillow, writhing her head back and forth, silver hair swirling like Medusa's snakes. "No! *Listen!*"

But before we can comply, she begins to cough violently, as if her ailing heart wants to escape her body. The room fills with the sounds of phlegm and despair, and she struggles to regain her breath.

Nelson releases her hand and steps away. Her body seizes and thrashes and barks. The incessant beeping of the monitor quickens, its sporadic heart line rising and falling dramatically.

Gregor moves in to check August's pulse, and as the coughing subsides to a slumbering snore, he keeps his finger securely on her wrist.

"She has very little left in her, Ms. Jan. You can see the mottling on her hands. This is a sign that the organ of the skin is losing its oxygen. It usually indicates that our patients have only a few hours left."

****

Only. Hours. Left. In that case, I'm gonna let myself go on back to the things that really matter ...

Stepping out from the old Cadillac onto the frozen dew of the Neal family's front lawn, I was sure I could hear the tree frogs singing. Can't be, I chided myself, it's December. And no trees grow this close to the sea for them to hide in.

The Neals had a large white house with blue shutters and an ocean view. Whole family must be stuck up, I decided, rubbing the early morning out of my eyes. I'd never been so exhausted in my whole life. My head ached, my back throbbed, and my breasts felt like swollen fists of fire.

"Get those babies outta there," Mama hissed.

She looked a mess, too, though she'd tried to clean up that morning with a brooch on her blouse and a little slipshod lipstick. Her red pin curls stuck out in crazy coils all over her head, and there was a long run in one stocking.

I yawned and stretched down into the back seat where my twin babies lay swaddled and still, asleep side by side in matching blankets on the baseboard of the car.

Janus and Jefferson I'd named them, the boy after the wisest of the founding fathers. That name I'd picked out for Matty, thinking maybe he'd take a little bit of pride in his newborn son.

Mama warned me not to name the babies and not to get too attached because she said she had a plan. A plan which, I'd learned that very morning, would result in this very errand.

She rolled out biscuit dough with her old wooden pin and told me, "You're gonna give one of those babies to the Neals after what you've done to that family."

I glared across the kitchen table at my mother as I tried in vain to get the girl to suckle.

But there was some relief in the idea. Two babies were too much, and Mama and I, we'd been holed up in the house for months, no one to help and no chance of escape.

Mama had run herself positively ragged, and our home and the garden were in shambles. I was fat and lonely, and the girl baby, she cried all the time. I couldn't get her to feed, so I'd been thinking maybe I'd keep the boy.

"For Christ's sake, August," Mama had scolded as I'd mulled my choice this morning over breakfast, "cover yourself up and give that baby a bottle. This is a kitchen, not a whore house."

I knew I was failing at motherhood just as I knew Mama probably felt the same way.

Jefferson was the good baby, for sure, calm and steadfast like his daddy. He wasn't more than a few days old when he started sleeping through the whole night. And he only cried when he's hungry, and when I fed him, he was so grateful for and satisfied with my milk.

So, when Mama reached out for Jefferson in the cold morning light of the Neal front yard, I instinctively pulled my son to me, wishing I could tuck him back inside my womb where he would belong to me alone. I clutched his warm little body in the crook of one arm and offered up the girl with my other.

"August, what in the hell do you know about raising a boy? Nothing, that's what. A boy needs a father, and you can't give him one now, can you?"

I was foolish to ever believe the decision would be mine.

Mama snatched Jefferson from my aching arm, and quick as a wink, marched toward the Neal's front door, her low heels clacking up the front steps. She knocked loudly, suspecting they may still be in bed, but I could tell it was of no consequence to Mama. She just wanted this to be done and over.

After a very long moment of shivering apprehension, the door opened just a crack, and Mitchell Neal's tousled head peeked out.

"Who's there?" he demanded, too early for pleasantries.

"It's Patricia Littleton. May I have a word, Mitchell?"

"Why, it's very early, Patricia," he muttered before noticing the tiny baby swaddled in his blanket. The door opened a bit further to reveal Mrs. Neal in a blue bathrobe and curlers, concern wilting her lovely face.

"You probably have no knowledge of this," Mama began, deliberate and straightforward, as there was no other way to be in a trying time such as this. "But my daughter recently gave birth to twin babies, a boy and a girl."

Mr. Neal scratched his whiskered chin with a puzzled expression. He nodded to me as I stood at the bottom of the porch steps, trembling with the other baby in my arms. "Yes, I see, Patricia. It's cold out there. Would you both like to come in?"

"No, Mitchell, thank you, and we don't want to take any more of your morning. What we are here to say," she paused to inhale bravery from the crisp morning air, "well, after your tragic loss this spring, and seeing that it left you childless, and we now have more children than we can handle, we'd like you to take this baby boy to raise as your own." She held out her offering, the baby squirming and ready to wake with cries of hunger.

"But I d-don't…" Mr. Neal stammered. "I won't… we d-don't have any…"

Mrs. Neal pushed her way into the foreground, nudging her husband aside with the force of a linebacker.

"I'll take him," she breathed, her words cold smoke in the damp morning air. She gathered the child from Patricia's grasp, tucked him in the nook between her shoulder and neck, and without another word, pivoted into the dark corridors of the house.

I could hear Jefferson's cry echo out from the foyer, then recede into the silence. My heart died a small

*death, and I shed a tear, the first and only that would fall
down my cheek for many years to come.*

* * * * *

Geraldine and I decide to take turns sitting
bedside, and I volunteer for the first shift while Geraldine
and Nelson sit beside the fire. We are all shaken by the
events of the evening, carrying confusion and grief in
varying measures.

August continues to slumber through her rattle-
chested sleep, each breath potentially her last, while I pace
beside the bed, trying to solve the riddle August has set
before us and struggling to decipher her intention.

When Geraldine relieves my watch, and I return
bleary-eyed and dazed to the living room, I notice right
away Cliff has disappeared. I wonder briefly if he has
high-tailed it out of dodge until Reena, seeing the question
in my eyes, nods toward the front porch.

The snow blows fiercely now, an angry retort to
the island's summer splendor. I find Cliff somberly
rocking in one of the rickety chairs.

Gasping, the cold stealing my breath, I ask, "What on earth are you doing out here, Cliff? What's going on?" I can tell from his ashen face something has derailed, something fundamental has changed. He stands up stiffly and turns to face me. His eyes, normally alive with questions and wildfire, deaden, admitting their own surrender.

"Can we talk inside?" he asks, his voice cracking in the cold. "It's freezing out here."

I lead him back into the house, through the living room where Reena and Nelson have dealt a pack of playing cards and into the kitchen where I put on the kettle for tea.

Cliff angles rigidly into a kitchen chair like a man who has forgotten how to sit. I move to him, but he doesn't reach for me—in his way or any way, in fact. It seems he's being careful to avoid contact altogether.

"What is it, Cliff? You're scaring me." I don't know how much more drama my psyche can handle before it dissolves just like those drip castles from my memory.

"I just spoke with my mother, Jan."

"Okay?"

"I called her to tell her what was going on down here, but also because I couldn't shake that weird feeling I got when Eileen confused me for…well, you know." He can't even say the chief's name. "And then, I don't know, it was so unsettling with your mom in there. I guess my alarm went off."

"Well, what do you think is going on?" I grab his hand, attempting to offer him the same comfort he had provided me earlier today.

"My mom gave me some answers," he continues, his voice wavering and his eyes cast to the ground. "Some shocking answers, and it's important I tell you about them."

I'm entirely thrown by his demeanor and sudden sense of utter dismay.

"I wanted her—my mom—to know about what we had learned," he explains. "You know, about my cousins and the chief. Maybe we'd decide together if we shared it with my aunt or not." He pulls his hand away from mine, tucking both into his jacket pockets.

"My mother…she broke down on the phone. 'I should have told you sooner,' she said."

"Told you what, Cliff?"

He sighs deeply and looks out the window, distant and unfocused. "She said that your mother *gave* me to her…or rather, to my aunt." His voice cracks like a mirror afraid to reflect the truth.

"What are you talking about? I'm not following. I don't…I don't understand."

Cliff looks as if his gut has been punched right out of him, but he swallows hard, locks his eyes with mine, and continues. "I guess your mother, when she got pregnant, had twins. A boy and a girl."

"*What?*"

"Apparently, she and your grandmother showed up at my aunt's door one day with two babies, and they handed one to my aunt. Handed *me* to my aunt."

"Oh my God. What are you saying?" My face has lost its feeling, and my stomach lurches and heaves.

"My mother was crying a lot on the phone," Cliff says. "It was hard to understand everything she was saying, but I guess my aunt was in shock, and so she took the baby. She took *me*. And then, well, my aunt and mother decided they would keep me. But my aunt, who was older…she had just lost her teenagers…and so, my mother would raise me as her own."

"But that means—"

"Yes," Cliff says, meeting me dead in the eye. "It means that you're my sister."

"But how can this be?" I wail, the question bouncing off the man sitting beside me, who clearly had no answers and so many problems of his own. "I don't get it. She had twins, and she gave one away. But why would she do that? And how did no one know?"

Cliff's eyes water with grief.

"Mom said that your grandmother did all the talking…that she was sorry my aunt had lost her children and that her own daughter couldn't care for us both. Then they left…without me."

"Oh God," I breathe, instinctively throwing my arms around Cliff's neck. My embrace suddenly and thoroughly platonic, all embers of attraction extinguished and replaced with an unexpected familial affinity. "So, that's why she acted so strange with you tonight. She knew who you were. My God…unbelievable. Even when she was sedated, she must have been listening and processing everything. Everything."

"I never imagined, not in a million years," Cliff says, cradling his head in his hands, "that this could all turn so upside down. I mean, when Aunt Mary suggested that I move back down here to poke around and see what I could learn…I mean, did they *want* me to know? Did they want me to discover *this* truth?"

My eyes drift to the tattoo emblazoned below his elbow. "You're my brother," I say it out loud to see how the words feel. They bubble up my throat, race across my tongue, and escape my lips before anyone can stop them. Both foreign and familiar. Cliff and I had shared a womb, bloodlines, and a birthday. We shared a *birthday*. "Um, wait. You just had a birthday, right?" I ask him.

"Yeah," he says, looking up, "Last week."

"Well, then the birth certificate I found must have had the correct date."

"And I suppose we can't hope there's another birth certificate stashed around here somewhere?" Cliff cracks a small, wry smile.

"I doubt it," I say. "But I promise you that someone in this town knows more than we do about all this."

"Sally?" Cliff asks, demonstrating he's a fast learner.

Chapter 29: Confessing

Sally has had one too many bourbons, and we wake her from an inebriated couch nap, so she moves slowly into the kitchen when we ask her to join us.

"How're you holding up, Jan?" she asks, plopping down across from Cliff, the thud in the chair unforgiving.

"I gotta tell you, Sally, my life just keeps getting more complicated by the minute. I feel like I've been asking this a lot, but I need your help with something. Do you mind?"

"I live for this kind of shit, Jan. Better to spend my time helping an old friend than buying another candle at the Pottery Barn. This is the most drama to happen in Seaville in years! What can I do for you?"

"Well, Cliff just introduced a whole new wrinkle into our Greek tragedy."

"Don't keep me waiting, y'all. What's the wrinkle?"

"It seems—well, I guess there's no way easy way to say it—August gave birth to twins." Sally gasps, her long manicured nails flying to her lips in shock. "And, well, one twin was me, and the other was…Cliff."

"Sweet baby Jesus!" Sally exclaims. "Color me backward, I did not see that one coming."

"I know. Neither did we. But I was wondering—I mean, *we* were wondering—if you had any idea how we could find out more about all this? Who around here might know more?"

"God, Jan." A breathless Sally stares at me, dumbfounded. "That's one wily genie you just let out of its bottle. I mean, yes, I can hit up the Bridge ladies again, but Lord…gossip like this? If they knew about it, well, there's no way it would still be a secret after all these years. We should ask Reena."

"Reena? How would she know?"

"Well, she may not, but weren't your grandmothers friendly?"

"That's right, Sally. She did tell me that just recently. I actually hoped to meet her grandmother. She's still alive, you know."

A furious fit of coughing echoes down the stairs like an omen.

"Jan!" Geraldine calls, her tone filled with dread.

I hurry back up the stairs, Cliff close at my heels, and we barge into August's room. Geraldine stands beside the bed, squeezing August's purpled hand, and Nelson kneels below her, bowed in prayer with his flickering candle.

As the wheezing and hacking subside, August slowly opens her eyes, eyes that hover on the edge of sightless death, the witch rising from the flames of her own burning stake.

Her focus settles upon Nelson. "It was me," August whispers.

"What was you, Aggie?" Nelson raises his head, and his face remains serene, but his tone prickles with betrayal. "What're you talking about, August? What do you *mean*?"

"Those *girls*…and their (*cough, cough*) damn pink ribbons…" she rasps, the words sliding from her lips, oily and thick. The heart rate monitor's sonorous beeping intensifies, competing with the hacking explosions coming from August's chest.

I hear Cliff's sharp intake behind me and Nelson's defeated sigh, but all other effects surrounding me are lost to this very instant, the one I had been both seeking and evading.

"August, what on earth are you saying?" I take one step forward, my question primal and wounded, the angst of knowledge crushing my chest.

"They *knew*," August groans as a slight angling of her chin turns her face toward me. A gurgle rises in her throat like some intrepid underwater monster gulping for air. "I *had*…no choice." Her words dissolve in the froth escaping from her lips.

With a trembling hand, her clawed fingers flex and clutch the air, grabbing for the past. They land around my wrist like a vise, her grip unexpectedly strong and tight, a shackle both visceral and surreal. Her eyes, unhinged and desperate, lock onto mine.

"They *knew*, Mama," August whispers, "I *had* to…"

And then, as if an unseen hand has reached out from the corner shadows to strangle her, she chokes. Flails. Suffocates. I'm uncertain if this is the last gasp of the fluid in her lungs or the revolt of her very soul.

"Dear God," Nelson mutters, turning away and hiding his face in his hands.

Geraldine throws herself dramatically across the foot of August's bed, sobbing. "She can't breathe! Someone *do* something!"

*****

It's all happening so fast, now, but it's okay, because Mama is here, and she knows these secrets. Her forgiveness is pure and clean, I can feel it washing over me, as I go back to that Sunday evening long ago, curled up on my bed, just me and my diary.

I wasn't going to be able to cover for Kimberlee for the Friday shift because Matty said maybe he could come around that evening, and I wasn't about to miss a chance to go up to the farm with him, just the two of us.

But I had to go into Pop's to tell her, so, I stashed my diary back under the pillow and headed over to the island just before closing time, knowing I had to beat the drawbridge before it opened at nine.

The wooden sign hanging at the front of Pop's was already flipped to "Closed," but the lights still burned brightly through the windows facing the square.

I knew there's going to be trouble even before I entered through the side door, but I didn't know I would catch the sisters right smack in the middle of mocking me.

There was Louise with her pink-ribboned ponytail, prancing around the kitchen with a wad of napkins stuck up the front of her shirt. "So, Chief, do you think it's

YOUR baby? Or maybe, could it be someone else's?" she snickered.

Kimberlee took her voice down to baritone. "Why, Jan," she mimicked, not sounding at all like Matty, "I guess it could be my baby, but ain't that awful strange because I thought you were a lesbian!"

The girls dissolved into giggles, and napkins come tumbling out of Louise's shirt front. It wasn't until she bent down to pick them up she saw me standing by the alley door.

"Oh." She's caught by surprise, and I could see an instant flame of shame, which she quickly replaced with annoyance, saying to her sister, "Look who's here, Kimberlee. Why, Jan, we were just talking about you."

"I know you were, Louise," I seethed. "I saw your little show just now."

"C'mon, Jan, lighten up." Kimberlee breezed by me to grab the broom and dustpan.

"We know you're knocked up. We've heard you puking in the bathroom over and over again. Really, it's disgusting."

"Yeah," Louise agreed, tucking the napkins back into their box. "And we know the chief has been having his way with you. I guess someone forgot to tell him that you

really like girls." The sisters slapped each other a high five.

"And look at your belly," Kimberlee prodded, "I mean, it gets bigger every day. It won't be long before everybody knows. Before Alice Matthews knows. Guess we'll have a little something to talk about next time she comes 'round."

I clenched my fists and wrapped my arms around my torso, hunching over to try to make it all go away.

"I can't work for you on Friday, Kimberlee," I blurted out, anger scalloping the edges of my announcement. My face burned and my eyes watered, and I turned back to the alley door to beat it out of there before I let this boiling rage get the best of me.

"Hold it right there, you little slut," Kimberlee said, stepping in front of me and blocking my path to the door. "What do you mean you can't work for me? I have plans, so you've gotta cover that shift."

My eyes narrowed to angry slits. "Well, I have plans, too, and I will not be here on Friday night!" I pushed her aside and cut to the door, but she grabbed my arm so hard I was sure it would leave a mark.

"If you don't do it," Kimberlee fumed through clenched teeth, "I will tell everyone in this town about *your affair and your bastard child. A bastard child having a bastard child. Everybody will know, and they will shame you right out of this town."*

I yanked my arm out from her grip. "Oh, it's going to be blackmail now, is it?" I shouted, shoving her forcefully out of my way.

As Kimberlee stumbled to the side, her sister rushed in, pushing me from behind, and I was propelled into the wooden frame of the alley door, where my head knocked loudly. For a moment, all I could see was black. Clutching my forehead, I stumbled out the side door and collapsed onto the paved alley, hunched beneath the dangling sign that said "Colored Only."

I could hear the sisters laughing again inside, and I thought long and hard about what Mama said. Take care of the problem, she told me. So, I fumbled with the clasp on the small purse I was carrying and confirmed the gun was still in there. I gripped the handle and pulled it carefully from my bag. Streetlights from the island square caught in the shine of its barrel, illuminating its powerful beauty. I released the safety and slowly rose to my feet.

With a deep breath, I pushed the alley door back open. The laughter had ceased, and I could only spot one Neal sister, Kimberlee, who had her back turned and must not have heard me come in. She was sweeping crumbs into a tray when I came up on her from behind, placing the cold barrel right between her shoulder blades.

"Guess this might get in the way of your Friday plans," I said. I heard her breath draw in sharply, and I pulled the trigger.

Blood and guts exploded onto my hands, across my face, and over my clothes, and her body tumbled like a rag doll onto the black-and-white-tile floor.

"Who looks like Raggedy Ann now?" I couldn't help but taunt.

I was disgusted by the mess I'd created, but I was moving like a machine now, operating without emotion. I was just trying to take care of the problem.

It took me a second to figure out that Louise, who was nowhere on the floor, must have been loading ice cream in the walk-in freezer. She likely had not even heard the shot I fired. I knew if I could get there quickly, I could trap her in there, maybe without her even seeing me coming. But then I remembered the freezer door didn't have a lock, inside or out.

I ran over with my gun still drawn. The freezer door remained closed, and knowing how the handle sticks, I took the extra time to wriggle and turn it just so, yanking it open to find Louise inside, wrestling to get a heavy container up on a high shelf. She screamed when she saw me stooped inside the low frame of the freezer door, blood splattered on my face and gun in hand. Knowing she's cornered, she turned and lunged at me, the vat of ice cream like a shield of armor in front of her chest.

She knocked the gun out of my hands, and it spun around on the freezer floor like a game of spin the bottle, and for the first time that night, I felt fear rise up my throat. I managed to push past Louise, then I dove for the weapon because I couldn't let her get away.

I grappled for the gun, secured it in my grasp, and then raised it high to shoot her once as she ran out of the open freezer door. The bullet lodged in the side of her neck. She dropped the ice cream, a dull, creamy thud, and clutched the wound, where a river of red had begun to flow. She then fainted to the ground, half of her body still trailing into the freezer. I shot her again in her chest just to make sure it all took, and then I stepped over her twitching body and out of the freezer.

Panic brewed and bubbled inside of me as I took stock of my violence. I grabbed a damp dishrag from the kitchen sink and wiped the blood from my face and neck, then scoured my hands and arms with the abrasive dish soap we used to wash dishes at Pop Gray's. I hoped to

God I didn't have blood spattered in my hair, but since my hair was red, I took the chance it might not be noticed.

I slipped quietly back out the alley door before I realized that my boots must have left bloody footprints across the kitchen floor. I cursed to myself but knew it was more important to get away from the scene of the crime, so I tried to collect myself in the dark of the alleyway.

I was careful no one saw me emerge back onto the sidewalk that ran beside the island square. Time was on my side because this town closed shop early on Sunday nights, and few people were out and about.

I hurried back toward home, dodging the glow of streetlights, sticking to the shadows, before I recognized the drawbridge was still raised, the 9:00 p.m. opening.

"Goddammit." I cursed the heavens for my bad luck. That's when I noticed the full moon riding high in the spring sky, and I knew what I had to do.

I hurried down the small sandy embankment beside the bridge, kicked off my farm boots, and filled them with sand. Then, quickly and quietly, I waded into the sound, the muddy bottom squishing beneath my bare feet. The cold salt water saturated my clothes, weighing me down as I trudged in deeper.

When I was chest high, I let my boots drop with a plunk and made sure they each settled on the bottom. Then, I swam away to the farther shore, the cold water of the sound baptizing me, forgiving my sins. I was born again.

The full moon became my savior, keeping the tide low so I could make it across the waterway without concern of depth or current. I ambled up the sandy shore on the mainland side and from there, a shortcut took me through Airlie Downs to get back to Chestnut Street.

It was not until I arrived home I realized I should've dropped the gun into the sound, too. I felt its weight heavy at my side as I lugged the wet purse up my front steps.

Mama opened the door slowly, her face a mask of disapproval and dismay. She must have heard me coming. Standing on the porch, I was barefoot and dripping wet.

"I'm not sure I want to know." She sighed and stepped back from the screen door as I entered. I just shrugged and headed for a hot bath, leaving my purse and the gun inside on the kitchen table. I wasn't really sure what I planned to do do with the gun or, for that matter, with my life from that point forward. But, in my heart, I said a silent prayer that Matty would help me figure it out.

I poured a whole bottle of bubble bath into the tub because I was feeling dirty. As I slid my trembling body into the suds, I thought only about Matty.

My scattered mind began to calm as I envisioned my hopes for the future: standing onstage at the Academy Awards, accepting my trophy. Matty will, of course, be part of my big speech, I vowed, he'll be the one I thank, for the gifts he has given me. I rested my hands gently over the rise of my stomach, closed my eyes, and sank deeper into the warm water.

*****

Outside August's dark bedroom window, the clouds begin to lift and separate, and they propel through the night sky, shepherded by the back edge of the swirling storm. Glimpses of the moon scatter fleeting illumination through the open curtains.

The grip on my wrist reluctantly relaxes, and I watch the embers of malice burning in August's eyes slowly begin to die. My mother's last breath is stolen by the howl of the moonlit wind, the ambush of a storm no one expected but was always destined to be.

Gregor checks her pulse, consults his watch, and records August's time of death.

Without another word, we file out of her bedroom, a procession of confusion, doubt, and loss.

Reena stands at the foot of the stairs with open arms, which I fall into. The sorrow descending on me weighs heavy, but it has little to do with my mother dying. I mourn for all she destroyed in her living, her passing merely a scab encrusting our wounds, and the scars that these wounds will become—well, those would be with us, forever.

"Jan, look at me," Reena says firmly, her voice echoing into the void in which I had fallen. She takes my head in her hands, challenging me to abandon my panic for some brand of perseverance. "Your mother has passed. Take some time with this, and let yourself feel the grief. It is real. Even after all the shit you two went through, she was your mother. If you don't take the time to feel it now, it will hit you like a bag of rocks when you least expect it."

"I know, I know." I sniffle, mopping my runny nose on the sleeve of my sweater, though I'm afraid I cannot cry. That I won't cry anymore. "You're right. I just…Reena, she wasn't making any sense. The things that she said…"

"I don't believe it. Any of it." Geraldine's voice rises resolutely from the kitchen, where she's propped over the counter on her elbows, her brow knit in sorrow and indignation.

"Neither do I," I say as I move toward her words of absolution. I nod, absorbing her denial, even as my mind begins to reconcile the parallels of August's confession with Eileen Conway's version of the past. "I mean, she was clearly confused. Mentally *gone,* right? Reena, she thought *I* was Grandma Patty. She was just out of her mind, right?"

"Yes, clearly her mind was not straight. That was it," Geraldine concurs. She wrings her hands, pacing her small portion of the kitchen linoleum, a rootless, solo journey. She grabs a cup of tea someone has discarded on the counter, but her hands tremble so much the cup clatters against its saucer.

"I've seen this before on the hospital floor, y'all," Reena says in her quiet voice of reason. "Remember, I was a nurse for ten years before I took the job behind the desk. I've seen how ugly death can be—how confusing. For the dying and those sharing the moment with them. Sometimes, people say things they don't mean, things that don't make any sense, and it's all mangled up in the emotion of those last words. It's like their mind is trying to process every thought that is important to them all at once, and it all just gets garbled up somehow."

"Miss Jan?" Gregor approaches carefully. The air itself feels dead, and I find myself missing the distant pulse of the heart monitor, the shallow assurance of time left. "May I call the coroner now, or would you like to wait?"

"No," I reply hastily. "I mean, no need to wait. Call them. Have them come as soon as they can." Gregor nods and disappears with his dispatch.

"Why don't we go sit by the fire?" Reena suggests, and I let her guide me like a small child to a seat on the sunken couch.

Sally sits in stunned silence, an unusual manner for her, at the other end of the sofa, and Brian sits crossed-legged by the fire, the poker and puffer by his side.

"Holy shit, Jan," Brian offers. "I'm so sorry."

Cliff, who had propped himself upright against the mantle, head in hand, looks drained and exhausted, and he finds the empty couch cushion between Sally and me.

"You okay?" he asks, the warmth of his hand on my shoulder both confusing and comforting.

I look down at the floor, the threadbare rug with the green and gold pattern, the same rug that rested here when I was a kid. There's a stain in one corner, an ornery stain as August had called it, and she had stooped over it for hours with a wire-bristle brush. The brown smear never budged, no matter how much she beat it and scrubbed it.

"No," I reply, "I'm not okay. Nothing about this is okay."

"I know. I know." He attempts a wan smile, though he's clearly shaken, too, by the proximity to death and the unexpected admission.

"Do you think…" Cliff begins, hedging.

"That she just confessed to murder?" I reluctantly finish the question for him. "I don't know. I think she was talking out of her mind. I think she must have been subconsciously privy to all the conversations floating in and out of the hallways of this house."

"But why would she fabricate *that*?" Cliff asks, and I know, especially given Eileen's details about the gun, he has a point.

"Well," I say, "August was prone to histrionics. Perhaps that was her last gasp at notoriety. It was one of her many character flaws. She always just needed to be *seen*."

Gregor creeps back into the living room with trepidation, the soft jangle of his beaded cross the only noise announcing his arrival. "I'm so sorry, Miss Jan," he says, distressed. "But the coroner's office is closed because of the storm. They said they cannot come until the weather breaks."

"That's ridiculous," Reena pipes in, "have them send an ambulance. The hospital should have at least one on standby in a storm like this."

He apologizes. "I'm sorry, I tried. They said too many accidents from people driving on the snowy roads. They'll let us know if one becomes available."

"Let me give them a call," Reena huffs, snapping her phone out of her handbag and marching out of earshot.

"Okay," I respond. "In that case, I'm going to need a little time with her, then."

"Of course." Gregor offers his arm to help me up from the couch.

Everything feels so heavy—the weight of my head on my own neck, the bulk of my sweater across my shoulders, the sad steps that lead me to my mother's bedroom.

But here, in the room that death holds, nothing much has changed. Tangled swirls of August's flannel-gray hair rest against the pillow, and with her waxy pallor, her eyes shut tight and her mouth hanging open, it seems as if she's just sleeping.

But everything *has* changed, suddenly, and with a macabre twist and an absurd finality. I have more questions than answers now, and the cliffhanger of August's last scene hangs like an anchor around my neck.

"What did you do, Mama? What did you *do*?"

It had been five days since I had slept, really slept, so I abandon my plans, my pride, and my purpose. I peel the blanket off August's lifeless body, and I wrap it around my own, a swaddle of sorts. Collapsing on the floor beside her bed, the moon pours her maternal love through the parted drapes, and I surrender to a selfish, senseless sleep. Dreams arrive with mercy, visions of drip castles swallowed by the raging tide and kingdoms ravaged by the sea.

Chapter 30: Investing

I wake the next morning, feeling every bit the abandoned orphan, like a bird toppled from the nest. My heart beats its furious wings, hunting and pecking through the notion of loss. And yet, the sense of relief is palpable. Day had slipped into day until the tomorrow I'd dreaded and longed for had finally arrived.

I uncurl my aching body from the blanket I'd stolen from my mother, and I pull myself upright on the floor. Beside me, the corpse has grown pale and rigid. I stare at the lumps and angles of August's dead body without feeling any emotion, numbed by shock and a love lost so many years ago.

The house seems entombed in its own unexpected quiet, and I wonder if everyone has found their way home. It feels fitting, somehow, to wake up this morning so very alone.

But there, tucked in the corner of the room, Gregor sleeps on his bedside cot, which he had moved in from the dining room. I'm touched to know he had probably been there all night, and the loneliness ebbs a little.

Cold drafts seep in from the old windows, so I cover Gregor with the stolen blanket and grab a sweatshirt from the pile of laundry that's still stacked beside the armchair. *Yosemite Park*, it reads in large yellow letters. As I pull it over my head, I wonder if August had ever visited Yosemite. Or perhaps, she had stolen this shirt straight off someone's back.

Outside, the storm has finished. Needles of sunlight pierce the snow-blanketed lawn. Tree limbs, coated in an armor of ice, begin their slow, methodical drip, drip, drip, and I can hear the rumble and groan of the town's only snowplow, bearing down on a nearby street.

On my way to start the coffee, I notice my own bedroom door open just a crack, and a loud snoring comes from within. I can tell from the mop of gray hair peeking over the top of the covers Geraldine tucked herself into my bed.

Nelson is still here, too, a sleeping crumple on the couch, and Reena, Sally, and Brian have sprawled out on the floor in front of the fire, which has burned down to tired embers. They had tucked throw pillows beneath their heads and constructed makeshift beds out of quilts knit by Geraldine.

The only one once again unaccounted for is Cliff, and I find him in the kitchen, fumbling with the coffee maker. He turns at the sound of my footsteps.

"I was trying to do a good thing and get the coffee started," he whispers, so as not to wake the others. "Looks like you finally got to sleep." He brushes my tangled hair behind my shoulder.

He's my brother, I remind myself—an enormous, life-changing, momentous new thing I have no idea how to embrace. *He must feel so lost today. Does he feel as lost as I do?*

I study the contours of Cliff's face, this man who no longer remains a handsome stranger. I shiver in rejection of the attraction I once felt toward him, and I feel a sudden craving for a cigarette.

It's okay, I tell myself as I try to reconcile my anxiety. *Maybe my pull to him was instinctual, like a brotherly kind of love. A twin thing.* Perhaps I can convince myself my gravitation toward Cliff was really all a subliminal search for familiar lines and angles, for signs of myself, like looking in a mirror. The nose, maybe, or the sharp turn of the jaw. I can see our resemblance now as I seek it.

Cliff glances up from the stack of coffee filters he's trying to pry apart, uncomfortable by my gaze. "What?"

"You don't look anything like her. Not really."

"Like August?"

"Right. I mean, maybe a little in the bone structure, but not the obvious, you know, hair color, eyes…"

"Yeah, according to Eileen, I must look a lot like *him*. I can't believe all these years…it's like I've been living a lie."

"Well, that seems to run in the family, too," I say, resentment dripping from my sentence.

But Cliff, wrestling with the coffee maker, seems a shell of himself, and I know he needs something from me that perhaps I cannot give—some comfort or reassurance he's not genetically ruined. After all, his sense of history has just been obliterated in the course of one afternoon, and I feel like he needs me to throw him a rope, a way to climb out of this deep hole we're in.

"Maybe we can find a picture of him?" I suggest, and Cliff nods. The coffee percolates and begins to brew. "So, did we get any word back from the coroner's office last night?" I move to change the subject, determined to begin to confront the matters at hand.

"No. Reena tried to pull all her strings, but nothing was moving on those roads."

"Well, that was quite a storm," I say, since it always feels safe to talk about the weather. My mind drifts briefly to the job at the TV station back in New York, and I laugh to myself since this workweek responsibility feels like it's from another lifetime.

We don't hear Nelson enter the kitchen, but he's suddenly close upon us, dark circles of fatigue puffing his brown eyes.

"You *will* tell the proper authorities, won't you, Jan?" he asks in a low, gravelly voice, the flare of betrayal burning the words as he speaks them.

I'm caught by surprise, and I fumble with my coffee spoon and fidget with the frayed hem of the sweatshirt. "Well, Nelson, I…I guess I haven't thought about what the next step would be."

"With due respect, my dear," Nelson continues, unrelenting, "I know that business last night was hard to hear. But I have lived under this cloud for fifty years. I have a right to clear my name. The next step should be to take this confession to the police."

I lean back on the kitchen counter, dejected and overwhelmed by the appalling choices that now lay before me.

"Nelson," Cliff intervenes, searching for the right words as he selects three mugs from the cabinet. "We all want to see this to its rightful end, and I know that we all have different motivations. It seems now we are equally invested."

Nelson nods in agreement, willing to hear more.

"My concern with going straight to the police," Cliff continues, "with this possibly new information… Well, I guess my concern is that I'm not sure we can trust the police. If we think they covered up the truth about these murders for all this time, how would a vague deathbed confession—unsubstantiated, mind you—convince them to open this case back up and actually clear your name? I guess what I'm saying is we might need more."

The wail of an ambulance interrupts our conversation. In the living room, the others yawn and stretch to life.

"Why would they put their siren on?" Sally complains, rubbing her sore neck. "There's no emergency here."

"And they kept us waiting long enough," Reena agrees, stretching her arms. "They better be watching their manners."

"Do I smell coffee?" Brian asks, the question mangled by a yawn.

"Brian!" Sally swats his arm. "Focus on something besides your caffeine needs. There are other things going on here."

"I'm sorry, but I can't without coffee," he says, stumbling into the kitchen.

Cliff and Reena work together to push aside armchairs and end tables, enabling a path for the stretcher that's slowly being wheeled up August's icy sidewalk. I open the front door and lead them upstairs to August's bedroom, where Gregor, now in action, prudently peels back the bedsheets to free his patient's body for the transport. I watch with something like apathy as the medics carefully lift my mother's rigid frame onto the stretcher.

I search within for an emotion—grief, anger, relief, anything—but I'm unable to summon one. A gutless bystander at the scene of an accident, I watch the whole thing unfold without intervening. Gregor and I then follow the stretcher down the hall, where Geraldine appears in a floral housecoat, her face forlorn. She falls in line behind us.

At the foot of the stairs, Nelson holds his hat over his heart as our disheveled procession passes out the front door. The early morning air embraces us with cold and clarity.

I'm struck by this moment of resolution, by the circular path that a life takes. The first time August was carried down these porch steps in the arms of Grandma Patty, she was just beginning the twisted path of her life. Now, the tired ambulance technicians tuck the stretcher's wheels and carry her down again. They deposit her in the dark cavern of the ambulance, and the finality resounds.

We stand together on the cluttered front porch, survivors of August Littleton, just as futile as the collection of chairs rotting around us. I squint into the glare the rising sun casts on the snow as the ambulance pulls away. I want to turn and run back into the house, but my bare feet have frozen to the splintered wood.

Wearily, Nelson sits down in a rocker. Geraldine begins to cry again, and I can hear her stifled sobs behind my shoulder. A cold breeze blows, and the trees drip, and my mother, the force that created and destroyed me, has gone. This time, the sirens on the ambulance remain silent as they carry her away. The lonely snowplow ambles its way down Chestnut Street.

Geraldine blows her nose loudly, dries her tears, and heads inside to make eggs. Without further purpose, we follow her, and we all eat eggs.

Reena keeps the coffee brewing and quietly chats with Gregor. I can hear her offering him a job at the hospital. Brian and Sally clear the breakfast plates and wash coffee mugs, doing their best to stay busy and be helpful. No one mentions August by name, and by all means, everyone avoids discussing the implications raised in the night.

As Geraldine hands over her dirty plate, she clears her throat, ready for a pronouncement. "Everyone, I suggest we all just forget about what happened here last night." Her voice seems shaky but her intention clear. "These are just ghosts of the past that paid us an unwelcome visit. And Aggie, well, she would want us to move forward."

A moment of careful silence follows before Nelson groans his disagreement and slams his mug down with a thud. "Well, of course she would want that." He balls up his napkin and throws it on his plate, where it immediately begins to soak up grease. "She would want to keep it a secret forever! But these ghosts have been haunting me for fifty years, Geraldine. Fifty years! And I, for one, will not keep quiet any longer." He pushes his chair back from the table with a loud scraping sound and begins to pace the dining-room floor. "I mean, even if she was talking crazy last night, and maybe she was, she still probably knew the truth about what happened that night.

You all said as much yourself. And I've got to find out. I hope to Jesus you will help me, or I will have to do this on my own."

Geraldine lets out a small *tsk* and rolls her eyes in annoyance.

"I think he's right," I agree, somewhat tacitly, and Geraldine shoots me a sour look.

"Yeah, I have to find out, too, Nelson," Cliff agrees. "For my family, for my aunt. It's part of what I came here to do."

"I'm sorry," Geraldine says, rising from the table in a huff. "But I cannot be a part of this. I refuse to help tear down someone I loved." She turns to me. "Will there at least be a funeral service I can attend?"

"Oh…" I pause, surveying the eyes of those gathered around the table, searching for an answer. "I hadn't really thought about it. I guess I should have…"

"Did she leave any last wishes, Jan?" Reena suggests. "Maybe a will? A lawyer?"

I flounder. "I don't know." I'd never even asked her any of this, an obvious flaw in my plan.

"Well, August could not *stand* lawyers, so I doubt she had one lined up," Geraldine says. "But she might have written down her last wishes. Did you check her journal, Jan?"

The journal. I'd forgotten all about the journal, including where I'd stashed it for safekeeping.

"It was here, somewhere." I rise to pick through the cluttered kitchen countertops, opening and closing the drawers. "I was making a list…" With my search coming up empty, I wander up to August's bedroom, where Gregor packs up, unplugging machines and folding cords into his rolling bag.

"Have you seen August's journal?" I ask.

"No, I haven't," he says, "but I was just stripping the bedsheets, and I did find *this* tucked up underneath Miss Littleton's mattress." He holds a page that appears to have been torn from the journal. It's the same shape and size with the scrawling, loopy letters I'd noticed on the pages of her poetry.

For the end:

Give me a gravestone in the cemetery near Mama. Even if they spit on it. But don't bury me in the ground. Burn me like the witch they think I am. Scatter my ashes up beside the blue barn.

Janus gets the house and all my belongings.

When they all act sad, tell them my final words were: Fuck Off.

I sigh. "Well, that does seem like something August wrote of sound mind."

Gregor chuckles. "What will you do now, Miss Jan?"

"I don't know." I think for a moment. "I guess these instructions are pretty clear. I'll have her cremated, sell the house, and tell them all to fuck off."

He laughs his warm, deep laugh again, and I know I'm going to miss this man, so briefly in and out of my life yet an irreplaceable guide through an unfathomable journey. I hug him. "Thank you, Gregor, for everything. You really were a saint."

"Nah, Miss Jan," he replies, "just doing my job." He drags his supply case to the bedroom door but turns back at the doorway. "I can keep secrets, Ms. Jan. It's part of the job. But I would ask that you consider Mr. Nelson's wishes in this matter. It's hard enough to be a Black man here in America, even today. I can't imagine the life he must have lived."

I nod my understanding, then watch him navigate his farewells on the landing below, shaking hands and sharing hugs before leaving us all forever.

I return to the dining room with the torn-out page and share my plans with the group. We will memorialize August at the town's Baptist church as soon as possible. I will put the house on the market, and tomorrow, I will pay a visit to the Seaville police.

"You're welcome to join me," I say to Nelson. "As are you." I nod to Cliff. "Or I can go on my own, and you can just trust that I'll fairly portray what August said before she died."

"Jan, I'm not sure that they are going to listen…" Cliff warns.

"I know, I know, but it's been fifty years, Cliff. Anyone who was involved in covering this up would be long gone. We know the chief is gone. And there's nowhere else to take this information other than August's grave. My family *owes* you that much, Nelson. We *all* owe you that much."

When the roads are finally scraped down to an icy slush later that morning, my friends drift back to their respective homes and lives, except Geraldine, who decides she will take on the funeral arrangements and stay until after the service.

The house, once my grandmother's, then my mother's, and now mine alone, feels empty. I immediately miss the comings and goings and the distraction of it all, including Gregor's calm presence. Strangely, I even miss the pursuit of an unsolved mystery. But surrounded now by the collections of a hoarder's life—the cracked picture frames, stacks of unread novels, and overstuffed pillows and frayed upholstery—I realize I do not belong to this place, and these things do not belong to me.

Geraldine sets to work in the kitchen, scraping plates, drawing a sudsy sink for dishes, and humming a show tune. I wander aimlessly through the house, trying to shake off my sense of shock, drifting without intent or purpose. I find myself back in August's empty room. Gregor has stripped the bedsheets, and he has been so organized I'm certain I'll find them tumbling in the dryer, clean of the death to which they bore witness. Nelson's half-melted prayer candle still sits on the bedside table. I shuffle over and pick it up and examine it like a relic from a long-lost civilization, half its prayers left unspoken.

Anger clogs my throat, like something poorly chewed, and escapes in hot plumes out of my nostrils. I feel the need to destroy, and so I throw the tall glass candle against the bedroom wall, reveling as it shatters into jagged shards and lands with a dull wax thud on the ground. The dishwashing sounds and their accompanying melody cease for a respectful second, then resume with new fervor.

I know I will be the one picking up the pieces later, but damn, it feels good to destroy those prayers.

Chapter 31: Prodding

One week has passed since I answered Reena's phone call in my kitchen in Manhattan, forbearing the news August neared the end. One meager week. Seven days that have taken their toll in decades.

My body feels like I've been to battle, my limbs weak and my ego bruised. Digging through the trenches for truth, uncovering bodies at every turn, dodging exploding land mines. Except the one I didn't dodge, the one that blew up in my face on the night my mother died.

When I call John with the news August has passed, he and Laney are heading home from a basketball game. He puts me on the car's speaker phone, and through the background drone of city streets, my daughter's sweet voice soothes my frayed nerves.

"Mom!" she exclaims. "Guess what? I hit a three to send the game into overtime! And we won!"

"That's the best news I've heard all day. No—all week!" I'm trying to sound stable, trying to step back into the role of the mother this girl deserves. "I'm so proud of you." But then I continue, wavering, "Honey, I've got some news, too. You see, Grandma August…she passed away last night.”

“Oh no!” Laney utters. “Mom, are you okay? Were you with her, at least?”

“Yes.” I selectively answer only her last question as I’m decidedly not okay. “I was with her. And she had a lot of friends here, too.”

This piques John’s curiosity. “Friends?”

“Well, people she knew from her past. I can explain more later when I see you.” There’s so much I won’t tell them now, so much Laney would never need to know. So much, in fact, I would work my damnedest to hide from her forever.

“I’m sorry, Jan,” John says, though his tone belies relief. “Hey, and I heard a big Nor’easter went through there, too. Did you actually get snow at the coast?”

“Did we get snow?” I laugh now, letting it lift my mood. “I’ll say we did. Eight or nine inches, at least. Shut everything down. It was kind of fitting, I suppose.”

“Huh,” John says. “So, how are you *really* doing?”

I choke back my wounded lament, reminding myself the goal is to just get through this call. “I’m good.” I feel my armor cracking but forbid an emotional crumble.

"I'm okay…I miss you guys, though, and I want to come home."

"Then do it," Laney suggests. "Just come home. If Grandma's gone, no reason to stay there any longer. I really miss you, Mom." Her words wilt my resolve. It's been a while since my teenager has admitted she actually wants her mom around.

"I will soon. I just have a few things I need to figure out here. Only another few days, I promise. I'll try to make it home in time for your next game, okay?"

I finish the call with a new determination to set matters straight and get the hell out of Seaville.

I smoke a cigarette on the street corner outside of the Seaville police station, steeling my nerves. I already regret not taking Cliff or Reena up on their offers to accompany me, realizing I could use the mental reinforcement.

This visit to the station, in all honesty, feels shameful. On many levels. And I'd wanted to do it alone to meet whatever judgment or consequence that might befall me or my family with my white flag held high.

The sun shines brightly on the corner. The temperature had risen throughout the night. Though large patches of snow dot the grassy town square, the sidewalks lay bare and dry. Red bows tied to the street lamps droop, limp and wet. Children, home from school for the snow day, run down the block with plastic sleds, hurling handfuls of snow at each other. The freak November Nor'easter would soon become just a memory.

I stub the half-smoked cigarette out on the brick wall and toss it into the sidewalk garbage can. The glass doors to the station swing open, and two officers dressed in blues step out. One nods to me and holds the door as I step inside.

The station is cold and gray, with paper cutouts of Santa and Styrofoam Christmas trees decorating the front desk. It's a festive take on law and order here in Seaville. A desk clerk with tired eyes and an impressively high blond ponytail chews gum and shuffles papers behind the tall desk.

"Excuse me?" I clear my throat, seeking her attention. "Is there someone I could speak to about a, uh, cold case?"

The clerk looks up, amused. "A cold what?" she asks, mid-chew, peering over her glasses at me.

"S-sorry," I stumble. "Maybe that's not the term you use. It's just…well, I have some information, I think. Maybe. About a murder that happened here a while ago."

The ponytailed lady sits up straight, takes off her readers, and leans in. I can smell the spearmint on her breath. "Ma'am, there hasn't been a murder round here in almost fifty years."

I sigh. "Well, then, that's the one I want to talk about."

"Ha! Okay," the clerk replies with resignation, swiveling around in her desk chair to see who she can pass me off to. "Hang on." She makes a beeline for a large, older man dressed in a navy suit. The clerk whispers to him, and they both look my way as if they're trying to decide whether to hear me out or have me committed.

Navy Suit saunters over to the front desk, his big belly and crooked red tie leading the way.

"Well, hello there. I'm the lead detective here at the station, Miss…?" he asks, extending a burly hand.

"Jan Myers," I reply with a handshake. "My mother is August Littleton."

My hand remains in his embrace as I study his reaction. His big, bushy eyebrows rise slightly, and his eyes narrow into small slits of confused recollection. He cocks his head to one side with something like intrigue.

"Yes, of course," he says, motioning for me to follow him through the swinging gate that separates the station lobby from the working desks of the officers. "How is Ms. Littleton doing? I understand she hasn't been well."

"She died." I know that my cold response will land with the shock value of a dead horse, but I don't care.

Navy Suit stops short of his desk, drawing his breath in sharply. "Oh, I'm so sorry," he mumbles, and I hear a perceptible shift in his flippant tone. He motions for me to sit in a clunky metal chair he's pulled to the end of his desk, which appears unruly, cluttered with newspaper, stacks of manila folders, coffee mugs, and a small chess set with the pieces toppled and askew. He rifles nervously through the mess to find a pad of paper. "So, how can I help you today?" He seems eager to turn the subject away from death and toward whatever business is at hand.

"Well, it's about my mother, you see…" I'd rehearsed this in my mind all morning—how I would recount August's bitter last words and how, with chagrin, I would expose this twisted family secret. But now, here in this cold, uncomfortable swivel chair, the words I'd planned refuse to pass my lips. My mouth has become a traitor.

The detective tries to reassure me and put me at ease. "Would you like a cup of coffee? Some water maybe?"

"Yes," I reply, realizing I'm parched. "Some water, please."

Nodding, he heads to the water bubbler sitting in the back corner. I have a moment to collect myself, but the panic in my chest keeps rising, a geyser of doubt. Nothing about this feels right.

When he returns with the paper cone of water, I reposition my approach. "Sir, what can you tell me about your files on the two girls who were murdered here back in '67 over at Pop Gray's?"

"Well, Ms. Myers, we actually don't have an open file on that case. That was decades ago."

"Yes, I understand, but it was never solved. Correct?"

"Well, I was just a kid in high school back then, but if I recall correctly, Mr. McCready was tried for the crime and was acquitted."

"And then what happened? Do you have any records? Did the investigation continue?"

He looks confused. "Ms. Myers, what is all this about?"

"I'm just wondering why there was a suspect, and the suspect was found innocent, and then nothing else was done. I mean, did the police just let it all drop? Did they move on like nothing happened?"

"Well, ma'am." The detective shifts uncomfortably in his chair. "As I recollect, most folks felt that though Mr. McCready was acquitted, he was indeed *not* innocent."

"Based on what?" I challenge, feeling combative now, bravery quelling my anxiety.

"Well, like I said, I wasn't even on the force when that all happened. I would need to look back through those records. But you said this had to do with your mother?"

My face feels like a pot of water set to simmer. Beads of sweat percolate on my brow. "Well, I'm not certain, but…I think my mother worked there at Pop Gray's around the time all this happened. And I think she knew something about it and kept it secret all these years."

"Well, what do you think she knew?"

"I think…" I make a split-second decision to go with Cliff's version of events. "I think the investigator on the case, Chief Matthews, well, he had an affair with my mother."

The detective raises his bushy eyebrows in an impressive arch and reclines heavily in his chair. He did not see that one coming.

"And I think," I continue, "that Matthews, or someone close to him on the force, had a reason to kill those girls and to cover it up."

"Whoa there," the detective says, rearing up now, holding both palms up to stay me. "Ms. Myers, are you insinuating that someone on the Seaville police force had something to do with those murders?"

"Well, I don't know," I say, trying to hide my trembling hands beneath the old metal desk, "but my mother sure seemed to think so. And she knew…she had some information that Nelson McCready was not complicit in this crime. She said as much on her deathbed."

He scribbles some notes on his yellow-lined pad, then looks up at me again with his perplexed face and caterpillar eyebrows.

"And did Ms. Littleton share any evidence of this allegation?"

"No, unfortunately," I say quietly. "It all came out very suddenly. And then she died. But she did work there at Pop Gray's. You can probably find her employment record. And she knew the chief, for sure. She knew him well. She had a nickname for him and called him 'Matty.' I have some of it from her journal. And Geraldine, who was her, uh, partner…she confirmed that August and Chief

Matthews spent time together, back when my mother was younger."

The detective scribbles fervently on his notepad.

"And August," I continue, "well, she gave me a locket with a barn, a blue barn, inside of it. I think it was the same barn over off Delano Road, and I think maybe the property belonged to Chief Matthews at one time."

"Whoa," the detective says again, putting down his pen, breathing heavily. "Okay, Ms. Myers. I get that you have just been through a very stressful time. And I'm sorry about the loss of your mother, truly I am. But Chief Matthews was a revered man around here. Hell, he was the reason many of the folks here joined the police force. And to go around casting aspersions on him without any evidence…"

My fear turns into full-out rage. I stand up abruptly, knocking papers off the corner of the desk. "With all due respect, Detective, it is not *my* job to bring you evidence, sir. It is *your* job to take the information I have provided, and to look for the evidence." The commotion I create turns heads throughout the station, and the detective raises his ridiculous eyebrows at my newfound temper.

"Now, I grew up in this town, too," I continue, "and I know things move pretty slow, and people here protect their own. But this must be enough information to at least open the case back up and to have somebody follow a lead or two. That's all I'm asking. Open the case back up. Give Mr. McCready a chance at real freedom and a chance to take back whatever of his life he has left."

Everyone in the room watches my performance with rapt attention. I had successfully caused a scene. Talk of the town. August would be dismayed. Or pleased.

The detective takes a lungful of breath and with strained effort, rises to his feet. I have worn him thin and bruised his ego, dented it like a rusty tin can. But I don't care. I'd come to play my part, and if my little visit becomes fodder for gossip, then maybe it would keep the pressure on, and he'd put a little effort in.

"Let me look into it, Ms. Myers. I can't promise you this will go anywhere or that there's anywhere for it to go, but I can assure you that the *theory* you've shared is very interesting. I will dig up the old file and give it a look."

I grit my teeth and attempt a smile, then turn to leave.

Behind me, he calls, "Oh, Ms. Myers. What would your mother's maiden name have been? Back in the sixties."

"Her name has always been Littleton," I reply. "She was never married. Because she was a lesbian."

Scene, and *cut*.

Chapter 32: Connecting

Cliff agrees to meet me at Grady's Café after I leave the station, though neither of us can summon an appetite. I tell him about my encounter with the detective and about my outburst and as I fondly recall it, my grand exit.

"Knowing what we know," Cliff says, sipping his coffee, "how are we going to get through this funeral tomorrow?"

"Well, what *do* we know, Cliff?" I ask, exasperated, rubbing my temples. "I guess we know that one, or both, of our parents pinned a capital crime on an innocent man and then colluded to ensure that no one ever dug too deep to unearth the truth."

Cliff exhales. "Well, we also know that the murder weapon was never found, and that Eileen Conway knew *something* about a gun even *before* the murders. If we could locate it, even all these years later, it could be the hard evidence we need to corroborate the story."

"You're not going to let this go, are you?" I ask him, waving down our waitress for the check.

"I can't, Jan," he admits. "I feel, more than ever, that my family sent me here to find the truth. It turns out

I've lived my whole life inside of a lie, and well, if I can bring some understanding to the matter now, maybe we can all see a way forward. Maybe we'll finally get some closure."

There's that damn word again.

As I head out the café's double doors, I recognize the elderly man mopping the entryway. "Bill?" I ask as I approach.

He stops mopping and looks up patiently. "Where I know you from, girl?"

"We met at the hospital last week. I'm friends with Reena."

"Oh, yes, that's it. I guess you can see, I's got two jobs. Sometimes, I's got more!"

I laugh. "I can see that you're a hardworking man, Bill."

He leans on his mop and studies me. "You sure I don't know you from somewheres else? You look awful familiar."

"Well, I grew up here, and I think maybe you knew my mother. August Littleton?"

"Oh, yes, yes…that's it. You Miss August's daughter. Look just like her. Whoo-ee! She a spitfire. Ain't seen her since she left the hospital. She all good?"

I grimace, realizing I'm going to have to get used to being the bearer of bad news. "I'm afraid not. She's passed away."

"Aw, Lord." Bill looks crestfallen. "I'm so sorry, child."

"It's okay…we expected it. But thank you." I pause to watch him process the news. "But, Bill, can I ask you something?"

"Sure, honey. Anything."

"You told Reena a few days ago that you knew my mother when you were a kid. She was a waitress over at Pop Gray's, right?"

"Yeah, I sure did." He leans on his mop now. "Any time we kids gots a few cents, we'd run down to Pop Gray's fast as our legs could carry us. We'd put all our money right there on the counter, and it would be just enough for us to share a bowl of ice cream. You see, it was always just enough, even if it wasn't enough. That's how I remember Miss August. She always good with that. Even if we ain't have enough to pay for it, she scrapes up the change and comes back with a heaping bowl, even if four or five of us." He chuckles at the memory. "That guy who owned the place, he hated it, all these colored kids clambering up on the counter stools, all our faces sticky with ice cream…but Miss August, she our favorite. Yep. Somehow, the change we had was always enough. She'd give us a wink, and we had our ice cream."

The weight on my shoulders lifts ever so slightly, and I offer an appreciative smile. "Did you happen to know any of the other ladies who worked there back then at Pop Gray's?"

"Well, there was those two girls who got shot. They weren't so kind to the colored kids, as I recall. Not that we were happy when they died. That was terrible. It scared us, the whole situation. Because you see, the black folk 'round here, we *knew* 'bout Nelson, and we *knew* he didn't shoot nobody. No sir, he don't got it in him. And he too tall to fit in that damn freezer where they say that girl got shot. Ain't no way! Hell, I'm five inches shorter than him, and I can't even get inside there with my mop."

I make a mental note to tell Cliff about the short freezer at Pop Gray's. I thank Bill and turn to walk away, when I hear him snapping his fingers with the onset of recollection.

"I know where I seen you before—on my wife's story. One World…" he says.

"*One World, One Life*?" I laugh and cringe at the same time. "Yes, that was me. Only for a short time, though."

"Well, I'll be." Bill plunges his mop joyfully into the bucket of soapy water. "Can't wait to tell Missy that I met a real-life TV star, right here at Grady's Café."

Bill's words hang in the air as I meander back home, a cloud of complexities merging into one central character: negligent mother, forgotten friend, winking waitress, hippie vigilante, and now, perhaps, a cold-blooded killer.

Chapter 33: Cleaning

Bill twists the squishy end of the mop in his bucket, the water already a cloudy brown. This storm has got everybody tracking mud into Grady's, and it's his second time today mopping up by the front door.

Funny running into August's daughter here like that. Sure does bring back the memories. How he had to go clean up that mess at Pop Gray's all those years ago. *Yessir*, Bill thinks, thrusting the mop in a corner. *You gotta mess to clean up, better call Billy.*

But he'd never seen nothing like that—the blood and guts, the parts of people smeared all over the floor or frozen solid inside the walk-in freezer. The night after it all happened, he spent hours half in and half out of that damn icebox, his right side frozen solid and his left sweatin' bullets. The freezer door, he remembers, sat low, real low. He'd had to bend in half just to get inside there with his mop.

And later, when he heard they'd arrested Nelson, he knew they got it wrong. Nelson had no mind to rob nobody, and if he did, he sure wasn't going through the trouble to climb into that freeze box to do it.

Besides, Bill figured there was some funny business going on with the police around that cash register, for sure. While he minded his own business scrubbing down the walls—he'd had to use the lye soap to get all the blood out—he noticed the chief and some other bozo wearing blue digging 'round in that register. It looked like the chief slid some of that money into his pocket, and Billy wouldn't have believed it if he hadn't seen it with his own two eyes. He was real quick to look the other way, of course, because what's a Black man got to say about that?

Something wasn't right, Bill knew it at the time, and he'd had a mind to find that reporter guy with the funny hat who he'd talked to the morning after the murders. He wanted to tell him what he saw, what he knew. They even crossed paths —what was his name? Garvey?—the very next day, but the reporter acted like he'd never met Billy. Wouldn't even look him in the eye.

So, he'd let it go. He kept his job at Pop Gray's through the summer and kept scrubbing and smiling and smoking cigarettes with Denny out back when Mrs. Gray wasn't looking. He acted like everything was the same.

But, after all business that went down, nothing was ever really the same here in Seaville.

Chapter 34: Reminiscing

Back at home, Geraldine hustles through the business of a funeral. She orders flowers, daisies and roses, her favorites, since no one knows what kind August preferred. "White and yellow like sunshine," she dictates into the sympathetic ear on the phone. A cleaning service scours the house because Geraldine's convinced friends and relatives will come by to pay their respects. I don't have the heart to argue that there are no friends, and the relatives are all accounted for. All the same, I don't object to the cleaners because it's one less thing for me to deal with, and I'll need to put the house in order for the sale, anyway.

"Going to the store to grab a vegetable tray and some dips for after the service. Maybe a nice spiral ham, too. Do you want to come?" Geraldine asks, pulling on the winter coat she has just inherited from August, which still smells of mothballs from the back of the closet. In fact, Geraldine has already gone through almost all of August's clothes and shoes, tossing anything that fits her into a big cardboard box she'd found in the basement.

"Jesus," Cliff says, when he spies her packings, "where did she find a refrigerator box?"

I don't care, though. In fact, I'm glad someone has the will to go through it all. Someone had loved her and her things enough to want them. In time, I'll decide what piece of the past I want to take with me, what parts I can bear to remember. Right now, I only want to burn it all to the ground.

Geraldine has spent the morning making pumpkin muffins, and they're cooling on the stovetop. She's also just finished tidying up the porch, and all the assorted chairs have been shoved into a stack in the corner. "I just feel better getting things done," she explains, grabbing the broom propped against the railing and chasing some brown leaves off the porch steps. "Maybe you could be of some help, Cliff. Let's get rid of some of this stuff out here. Make it look a little better for our guests?"

I sigh, exasperated. "Geraldine, you don't know the morning we've had—"

"It's okay." Cliff cuts me short. "I can help. But maybe I'll come over tomorrow before the service to give a hand?"

"Perfect." Geraldine breaks into a huge smile. "I'll have breakfast ready for you." She sweeps her way back into the house, seeming to forget about her intended errand at the store.

"Really, Cliff, you don't have to," I tell him. "I can hire somebody to clear all this junk away. After we sell the house, there will be plenty of money to pay it back."

"It's not your sole responsibility anymore, Jan. I feel a sense of—I don't know—obligation. We've got a lot of shit to work through, but here's the good news: we actually have each other. I know all these years you've felt alone. But you're not anymore. Neither of us knew it, but we've been a part of one another since the moment we were born."

That afternoon, Reena provides a full-throated introduction to her Grandma Mary Lou.

"I can hear you, child, no need to shout," Grandma Lou says, raising still nimble fingers to her ears. She sits primly in a lace-collared blouse and large pearl earrings on the overstuffed edge of an armchair in Uncle Joe's parlor. With her walking cane propped beside her, she balances a cup of tea in a saucer on one knee.

Reena, standing behind the chair, shakes her head and silently mouths, *No, she can't.*

"So nice to meet you, Grandma Lou, after all these years," I say, enunciating from my seat across the room.

"Eh, what's that?" asks Grandma Lou, fingers cupping her ear.

"I said, it's very nice to meet you," I repeat, this time projecting with my stage voice.

Reena slides onto the loveseat beside me, throwing a friendly elbow to indicate she told me so. "Do you like Grandma Lou's pillows?" Reena asks, moving several out of her way to find a place to sit.

"Oh, they're lovely," I concur. "Grandma Lou, you made all these?"

Mary Lou smiles, revealing she only has a few teeth left. "Sure did. The embroidery helps me keep the arthritis away."

"Smart lady," I say.

"Grandma." Reena touches her grandmother on the wrist and leans in to make sure she can be heard. "Jan is one of my oldest friends. We went to school together."

Mary Lou nods. "Yes, that's what you said."

"And if I'm not mistaken, I believe *her* grandmother was one of your oldest friends. Miss Patricia?"

"Oh!" Mary Lou exclaims, recognition brightening her face. "You mean Patty? Patty was your grandma?"

"Yes." I'm relieved Mary Lou's memory seems not to have suffered the same fate as Eileen Conway's.

"Oh, that Patty, she was a *strong* woman. Wouldn't take no for an answer. Proud. Couldn't keep her out of that garden. It was her lifeblood. We'd play cards, you see, a bunch of us ladies. Gin or bridge, it didn't matter. Poker, sometimes." Grandma Lou titters at the memory.

"If you don't mind me asking," I say, "wasn't it rather uncommon for Black women and white women to socialize back then?"

"It was, it was." Grandma Lou nods, her thin silver curls bobbing up and down. "But you see, it was more than black and white. It was really about *class*."

"How so, Grandma?" Reena asks.

"Well, you see, I was a nurse. And a darn good one, too. Best nurse in the county. I really knew my stuff!"

"Sounds like someone I know." I throw a friendly elbow back to Reena, who feigns a blush.

"And all the white families knew it," Grandma Lou continues. "They knew I was the best nurse, and all the doctors knew it. You see, they were all white, too, back in those days. So, that gave me and my family not only some money but also a bit of, how would you say it, *status*."

"So did you feel that you were something of an equal to your white friends?" Reena prompts.

"Well, child, *I* always felt I was equal. But I'm quite sure that the white people would have never used that word to describe our relationship. However, for the most part, they were all kind to me and accepted me into their homes, at least for a two-hour card game. You see, I found a way to fit into *their* life, and that made *my* life, well, a little easier."

Reena pats her grandmother's knee as she grabs her empty teacup. "I'm going to get Grandma a refill. Want anything?" she asks. I shake my head and hone in on Mary Lou.

"Grandma Lou, would you say you were close with Patricia until she died?"

"Why, yes, I guess I would say so. You know, I was her nurse, too. And your mother's. And I guess, in a way, I was also your nurse, my dear."

"What do you mean?" I ask, eager for her answer, though I know it before it's even spoken.

"I mean, I was there at your delivery. You and…" She pauses, unsure if she should proceed.

"My brother?" I finish, inviting Mary Lou's sigh of relief. "Yes, I just learned I was a twin only yesterday. So, you were there the day that we were born?"

"Yes, honey. I was the *only* one there. Well, other than your mother. Patricia wanted to keep it all very hush, hush, August being young and unmarried. But, boy, it sure was hard to keep that girl's belly under wraps. I knew it was twins before she even delivered. She was big as a house."

"No one even knew she was pregnant?"

"Not to my recollection. She kept working at that waitress job until her apron couldn't hide it no more, then Patricia locked her up in the house. Wouldn't let her go for walks, go to the store, nothing."

I sit with that for a long moment, the rush of it all almost knocking me over. Mary Lou had witnessed the birth of all the lies that had become the foundation of my life. "You actually delivered both babies by yourself?" I ask again, the tangibility of her answer bound to make it true.

"Patricia would have it no other way. It was very important to her. You know, she cared very much about how she was viewed in the community."

"Do you think…Did Grandma Patty *know* that Chief Matthews was my father?"

"Oh, I think she knew. Or she suspected, at least. She never spoke of it. I assume she was too embarrassed. That's why she devised the plan to, you know, give your brother away and then to send you and your mother off for good."

"That was Patricia's idea?"

"Mm-hmm. And she bought Aggie the ride to California. She gave her money to start a new life, at least that's what she told me. I don't know if that part is true, however. Maybe the girl just ran away from home. I wouldn't blame her, having a child taken away from her like that."

"Grandma Lou," I start, unsure where I'm going to take my next question. "Do you know *why* Patty thought it would be a good idea to roll out this plan? I mean, was it all about propriety — or was there something more?"

"Hmm." Lou narrows her eyes and strokes the soft whiskers on her chin. She looks me over, as if trying to decide if she trusts me enough to let down her guard. "Did you say your momma died, girl?"

I swallow hard and nod.

"Okay." Grandma Lou breathes in deeply. "In that case…" She leans forward from her high-back chair and looks right and left, making sure we're alone. "I swore to your grandmother I would never tell a soul what she told me after you babies were born."

I scoot down the loveseat closer to Mary Lou, and I lean forward, showing my sincerity in keeping the strictest of confidences.

Grandma Lou exhales again and twiddles her thumbs, trying to find the words. "Patty said that it won't right that the Neals lost their daughters, all because of her…"

"What do you mean, Grandma Lou? *What* was because of her?"

"She said she told Aggie to take care of the problem when those girls were teasing her and making fun of her all the time. Then, when they found out about her and the chief, and they just wouldn't let up, and then when Aggie got pregnant, and those girls said they were going to tell Alice and tell everyone…Well, Patty once again told her to take care of things." Lou narrows her eyes again, the bullets of her pupils shooting into mine. "And she took care of the problem."

"All because of an affair with a married man? I mean, it wasn't right, but…"

"No, child." Lou holds some words that taste badly on her tongue, like a pill she doesn't want to swallow. She screws up her face and spits the words out. "Because the chief was your daddy *and* your granddaddy."

And that's when I black out.

Chapter 35: Dealing

Bill thinks being in the janitorial arts is a lot like looking into other people's lives through a dirty window. He gets invited into places—intimate places, secret places—to clean up the mess. And sometimes, folks forget he's even there. It's like he becomes one of the mops or the brooms that don't matter nothing to them, and the folks just go on about their business like they're alone in the room.

That was how it happened on the day Grandma Lou called up Billy's mama, asking if Billy could come over to the Littleton house for a job. Billy rode there on his bike, like he always did, his mop strapped to his back, and went about the job set before him. Baby birthing tended to be a messy business, and when Billy was done, he gathered his bucket and dirty towels and headed downstairs, feeling a little queasy and shaken somewhere in his core.

"Patty, there are places she can go," Grandma Lou said to Ms. Littleton in the kitchen. "Homes that will take her in, churches that take new mothers and their babies…"

"Aggie isn't fit for those places," Patricia said to her, "you don't *know* what she's done. You don't know what she's capable of."

"So, what will you do?" Grandma Lou asked.

"I intend to get her as far away from here as possible. As far away from *him* as possible."

"And the babies?"

Ms. Littleton took a long time to answer. "I have a plan, Mary Lou, that'll take care of the problem."

Grandma Lou met me at the front door with a ten-dollar bill tucked in her fist. "Billy," she said, handing me the money. "You didn't see nothin' here today, you hear me? These people, they been through enough. Ain't no reason to give this town something else to talk about. You keep this to yourself, ya hear?"

Billy promised he would, and he did, all these years.

Chapter 36: Resuscitating

I come to several minutes later, reclined on the very same couch on which I'd been seated. Reena's anxious face, twisted in worry and relief, greets me as my eyes flutter open. There's a cool washcloth on my forehead and a wastebasket by my side, which I immediately use to empty the contents of my stomach.

"There you go, there you go," Reena says, holding back my hair. "It's okay, Jan, your body is just in shock. It's actually kind of impressive that it held up this long." She eases me back down onto the throw pillows when I'm done and gives me a wet towel to wipe my face.

Grandma Lou has retired to her room, regretful her news has sent me to a semi-conscious state.

"Reena—" I whisper, my voice hoarse from bile that burned my throat.

"Jan," she cuts me off. "You don't need to say anything right now. There aren't any words for how you're feeling and what your mind is trying to process. You just need to lie right here, and you need to *breathe*."

But this situation feels way beyond just breathing. The way my mind ricochets and reels, there isn't enough oxygen in the world to keep me stabilized.

"I'm going to call John and tell him what's going on here," Reena says. "We're going to get you some meds to take the edge off, you hear? And then I'm going to make a big pot of tea, and we're going to figure out how to get you through the rest of today."

She squeezes my hand, and I squeeze back.

"Can you tell them to come down?" I whisper. "Have John bring Laney to the funeral tomorrow."

"You sure?" she asks, rising for the task.

"Yeah," I reply. "It's over now, isn't it? I mean, it's all out there. All of the horrible truth."

"Girl, I sure hope so." Reena chuckles as she goes into the next room to make her call.

Someone in Uncle Joe's house has turned on music, a quiet hum of smoky blues. I lie still on the couch, the whir of a ceiling fan drying the sweat that has prickled my whole body, letting the jazzy notes take me back to the Round House theater, to the girl I thought I was and the idea of the person that *she* thought she'd become. I laugh in spite of my misery, realizing that back then, I thought I understood my given circumstances, and my world felt full of possibility, full of that "Magic If."

But no matter the "If" I could have introduced, then or now, it couldn't outrun the circumstance of my history. Mr. Leroy said the "If" was a way we could compromise with fate. But now, I know nothing can change the acrimony and vengeance of those who came before me, those who created me. And there is no path I could have taken into the future that did not lead me here, hopeless and hyperventilating on this dusty old couch in Uncle Joe's parlor. All the guessing games, best intentions, and breathing exercises in the world could not save me from my fate. I close my eyes and let the music play, its tin and brass like a life raft keeping me afloat.

Chapter 37: Understanding

Junior enters the church hall through a side door because he doesn't want to cause a scene. With his fingers, he loosely combs his dark, thinning hair and smooths down the curling edges of his mustache. He gazes across the sparsely populated pews and finds the woman sitting in the front row. Black dress, red hair, the same sense of fire sparking around her she had brought into the station earlier that week. She's seated with a younger girl and some man he's never seen before and then, strangely, the owner of that new restaurant downtown. What's his name? Clive? Cliff? His looks like trouble, for sure, tattoos up and down his arms, though it seems he cleaned up nicely today in his dark suit and tie. Something about that man strikes a chord of memory for Junior. He looks like someone he once knew, but he can't quite place his finger on it.

He decides to sit right here in the back, away from the family and friends, so he can pay his respects to his old pal Aggie without spoiling their day.

After Ms. Myers had appeared at the station, he definitely felt torn. She had been casting accusations and implying Chief knew something or *did* something. Stories like that take like butter on a hot griddle in this town, and it wouldn't be long before everyone started talking.

But then there's also that quiet quest for the truth, and the need to know that had been pricking under his skin just so all these years. So, he decided he could at least pay a quick visit to the Gray's.

When Junior pulled up the wide circle driveway that led to the Gray estate, Denny sat on the front porch, enjoying a Miller Lite. Junior checked his watch, and it read just past noon. He shrugged to himself as he pulled to a stop in front of the walkway and waved back at Denny, who was already making his way down the porch steps to greet him.

Denny had turned into a wide man, no surprise given all the years he had enjoyed as the Confectioner. The mixing, the tasting, the churning, the sampling. It all seemed to add up around Denny's waistline. Now, the thrill of being the most eligible bachelor in a small town long behind him, Denny appeared old and grumpy with a double chin and rim of graying hair encircling a gleaming bald spot.

The Gray's property sat perched at the water's edge, just behind the gates of Airlie Park. Old-money and plantation style, the home had been well-worn through the years, Denny the most negligent of its caretakers. Wind whipped off the cold sound waters as Junior shrugged on his coat to pay Denny this visit. He'd always found it painful to have to make small talk with him since he seemed dumb as a box of rocks, but if he needed to do it to keep his father's name clear, then by God, he would do it.

"Junior, what brings you 'round?" Denny asked, extending his hand, his question both warm and wary. No one ever liked to see the police show up unannounced. He reeked of marijuana and looked as if he had slept in the clothes on his back. Never mind, Junior reasoned, he wasn't there to judge.

"Denny, I tried calling, but seems the number I have for you…maybe it's disconnected?"

"Oh yeah." Denny shrugged. "I switch up my phone lines all the time. That's how you keep the government from tracking you."

Junior raised his eyebrows but quickly determined Denny was sincere in his belief, so he moved along. "Good to know," he responded. "I was wondering if you had a few minutes to help me out with something this mornin'? I got a few questions."

"Questions?" Denny squirmed uncomfortably, probably worried about the pot he had just stashed in the tin can under his front-porch rocker.

"Won't take but a minute," Junior continued. "It's about that old cold case that happened at your family's store in the late sixties."

Denny shuffled his feet but seemed more at ease, and he motioned for Junior to join him in one of the rocking chairs.

"Might seem kind of weird that I'm droppin' in askin' about old news," Junior said, settling uncomfortably into the rickety old rocker. "But I had a strange visit from a lady yesterday who said she was the daughter of August Littleton."

Denny cocked his whiskered head and tried to place a face or locate a recollection.

"August used to work at Pop's, right?" Junior continued. "She was a Sundae Girl about that time. Folks called her Aggie."

"Oh Lord, Junior." Denny chuckled. "So many Sundae Girls come and gone over the years…But yeah, all right. I think I remember her…redhead, real curvy…yeah, that's right. She worked there 'round the same time as them girls that got killed."

"Right. Mm-hmm, that's the one," Junior agreed, relieved he had been able to establish a connection of time and place in Denny's addled mind. "So, this lady's daughter comes 'round to the station, asking all about the case, implying that maybe something untoward went down back in the day. Like maybe there was some sort of cover-up."

Denny hiccupped, looking lost again. "What kind of cover-up, Junior? I thought it was pretty well established that McCready came in and killed those girls?"

"Well, yeah," Junior said. "That's the story that stuck, but Denny, he was acquitted, and in my files, at least, the case remains unsolved. I don't know about you, but someone asking all these questions after all these years…Well, it just makes me all kinds of uncomfortable."

"Yeah," Denny said, casting his eyes around nervously, looking for the solace of something. Another cold can of beer, perhaps.

"Trying to recollect here, Denny, and correct me if I'm wrong, but didn't you…I mean, weren't you having some fun with one of the Neal sisters?"

Denny broke into a cheeky grin then. "Yeah, I guess I was. The tall one. What was her name? Right, Kimberlee…"

Junior could see Denny's mind unreel, maybe latching onto the memory of a backseat on a summer night, windows cracked to let out the steam. "Okay,"

Junior replied. "Can you tell me about the girls who worked there that year when Kimberlee and her sister were shot?"

"Let's see." Denny picked through the bramble in his mind, trying to find some cohesive notion. "Well, now that you mention it, those girls that year, as I recall, they didn't like each other. No sir, not at all. The one you was asking about, the redhead…She had a thing for Kimberlee. She liked her a lot. In *that* way, if you know what I'm saying."

"Interesting." Junior pulled a scratch pad out of his coat pocket and jotted down a few notes. "Tell me more."

"Yeah, okay, I'm remembering now…" Denny continued. "Those Neal sisters, they hated the redhead. I mean, they were pretty relentless poking at her all the time. They'd call her queer, or they'd tease her about being fat or whatever. I mean, I stayed out of it all because, you know, I thought it was kind of hot to think about her liking my girl in that way." He laughed. "Nah, but nothin' ever happened there. And then those girls got shot, and as I recall, it was all pretty terrible at Pop Gray's that summer."

"I bet," Junior replied. "And you never saw this girl, August, retaliate? I mean, did she come back at them? Was she angry they would treat her this way? Or maybe, I don't know, could she have been jealous that you and

Kimberlee were together, assuming that she had a crush on her?"

"Oh, Junior," he said. "I don't know about that. I never saw nothing that made me wonder about that. But are you sayin'—?"

"All right now, I'm not saying nothin'. I'm just investigating, Denny. I'm trying to get answers that someone should have gotten long ago. I'm trying to put something to rest before ghosts climb out of the grave."

"I don't know. Junior, let me get this straight, you're not saying that the Grays had anything to do with those girls getting killed, are you? 'Cause I got a family name to protect here." Denny's eyes darted to the blue waters of the sound, snapping loudly against the shore with the winter wind. He looked like a man bent on escape.

"So do I, Denny." Junior nodded in agreement.

"Say…" Denny said thoughtfully, rubbing his bearded chin. "There was one other girl who worked there that summer. I'm pretty sure it was the Conway girl. Family lived over off Jackson. Maybe you could find her and see what she knows about all of this?"

Junior took a note, thanking Denny for his time.

Driving away from the crumbling estate, Junior wondered if he should just go back into the old case files, dig through the yellowed papers and chicken scratch to maybe find something close to the truth? He had actually thought to do just that after Chief died. It seemed like it would be safe to finally know what happened that night. Because the Myers lady was right—it didn't all add up. Chief had been so positive McCready was their guy, and other than his acquittal, McCready had never caught a break. The police stayed on him like white on rice any time he tried to go anywhere. McCready didn't venture out too much, but when he did, Junior found him polite in passing. He kept out of the way. Even though everyone always wanted to bust his ass for something.

So, it remained a cold case, and no one dared go near it, all these years. When Mayor Deakins asked Junior to step up as lead detective after the chief passed away, the case crossed his mind, though only fleetingly. The stack of petty thefts and cow tippings had piled up after the chief stopped giving a damn, and so the cold case got left on the back burner.

Back at the station, Junior unlocked the storage closet and pulled down the cardboard box that was marked "1967" in thick black marker. It wasn't hard to find the fat manila folder that contained all the police and court records from the Pop Gray's investigation. After all, it had been the crime of the century around here. With worry entrenched in his gut and the protruding folder tucked under his arm, he closed his office door and spread the documents across his already messy desk.

On April 23, 1967, at 21:12 p.m., the station received a call from Mr. Reginald Robinson, owner and proprietor of the Dixie Theater on the corner of Main Street and Ocean Street. Mr. Robinson indicated he was closing up the movie house around 21:00 p.m. when he noticed the lights remained on in Pop Gray's after hours. As this was an unusual occurrence, he went to check it out. He reported the front door was locked with no response upon knocking.

When Mr. Robinson proceeded around to the side door, or "service" door, he found it ajar. Upon entry, he noticed blood on the floor and then the two female victims, who he reported to be deceased upon his arrival.

Mr. Robinson left the scene and immediately returned to the theater to call the police.

Squad 2 (Officer Treman and Chief Matthews) was dispatched to the crime scene at 21:10 p.m.

Officers on the scene confirmed the victims were deceased by gunshot and proceeded to document the scene and retain all evidence.

No weapon was found on the premises. Partial footprints were detected in blood on the floor and appeared to be farm boots. The cash register appeared undisturbed, and no items of value seemed to be missing or out of place.

Suspects could have fled the scene by automobile, though the drawbridge was raised at the presumed time of the crime, per its routine nightly schedule. When dispatch reported at 21:06 p.m., Chief Matthews ordered the drawbridge to stay raised, which would have prevented any vehicle or pedestrian from leaving the island until the investigation was concluded.

There were no witnesses to the crime, though statements were taken from Mr. Robinson and an additional bystander, who was in the vicinity at the time of the murder, Mr. Nelson McCready, age 22. Audio from these witness statements was recorded on Track 279 and 280, respectively, Seaville Station Library.

Junior dropped the report on top of the other clutter and turned on his heel to yank open his office door.

"Greta," he bellowed into the dim, musty hallway. He waited until she raised her droopy head and peered at him over her horn-rims.

"I need Track 279 from the audio storage closet. And 280. And the old eight-track player."

Greta sat still, twitching her pencil, as if deciding whether or not to comply with the request of her boss. He frowned at her, unsure of his next move if she wouldn't go retrieve the tape. Like a battered dog, she rose wearily to her feet and shuffled to the audio-evidence closet, returning a few minutes later, struggling with the heavy machine and a spool of audio tape.

The two exchanged resentful glances but no words, and Junior closed the door on his secretary's pinched face. He loaded the track on the player, fumbled with the knobs and controls, and was relieved to hear a tumble of words from the tape. His father's honeyed voice, a mix of burlap and silk, stern but yielding, filled the room.

"Mr. Robinson, Reggie, is it okay if I record you today?"

"Sure, Jonah, I guess…just talk right into this?"

"Right into the microphone. Yep, just like that… good. Okay, you ready?"

"Sure, go ahead, I guess…"

"Reggie Robinson, can you state for the record what you saw on this night, Sunday, April 23, 1967?"

"Well, yes, sir, Chief." Mr. Robinson cleared his throat. "I was closing up the Dixie, like I always do, right before nine o'clock. I parked my car around back in the employee car lot, so I didn't take up street spaces that our patrons might want to use…"

"Mm-hmm," Chief Matthews approved.

"As I was walking that way, toward my car, I happened to notice that the lights were still on at Pop Gray's."

"And that was unusual?"

"Well, yes. I mean, it was *all* the lights. The ones in the front and the back like they was still open for business."

"Mm-hmm," Matthews said again.

"The front door, it was locked," Robinson continued. "So, I went 'round to the side door, the colored entrance, and I didn't have to knock because the door was already open, just so."

Chief Matthews cleared his throat, a gruff, judgmental sound that made Junior bristle, even after all these years.

"So, I push it in," Robinson said. "I poke my head in, calling out to see if anyone is in there. I says, 'Hello? Hello?' Nobody answers. So, I go in, ever so slowly. Everything looks normal at the front of the store, just as it should. And then I sees 'em. I see their head, one of 'ems head, just sticking out there, right out the ice cream cooler."

"The cooler?" Chief asked, then the sound of scribbled notes.

"The freezer, whatcha' call it…the freezer door was hanging open, and there's a large tub of ice cream spilled out on the floor just starting to melt. There was this…pool of ice cream, and then this…pool of blood. They were starting to mix."

More sounds of scratchy scribble. Junior knew what his father would be writing. The ice cream was *partially* melted, helping peg the time of death.

"Both them girls were lyin' there so still I could tell they'd been shot. I mean, I didn't touch 'em or nothing. But there was a good amount of blood all around 'em. That's when I turned around fast and got out of there. Went back to the Dixie and called y'all."

"Mm-hmm," Chief acknowledged. He then asked, "Reggie, did you notice anything else that might have been amiss? Was the side door that you went in damaged in any way? Any signs of forced entry?"

The man on the other end of the questioning paused to think. "No, Chief, not that I recall. It's strange because I didn't hear nothing either. I mean, earlier in the night. The Dixie's not that far from Pop Gray's, and you would think I would've heard them gunshots."

"Right." Chief seemed to agree, then the sound of a scribble on his notepad.

"Say, Reggie…Did you have a picture show playing Sunday night at the theater?"

"Sure did, Chief. Same show we play every Sunday night. *High Noon*."

"And you had people there watching the show? And no one saw nothing? Heard nothing?"

"Yeah, we had a crowd, a small one because it was a Sunday, but folks were there…and no one seemed like anything was out of the ordinary."

"And about what time did that picture show end?"

"Oh, probably 8:40 p.m. Maybe 8:50 p.m., at the latest."

"Mm-hmm," Chief said again.

The audio recording ended after a few additional pleasantries exchanged between the two men, and Junior sat all the way back in his chair, feet propped up on the messy desk as he liked to do when he really needed to think on something. He groped through a desk drawer, looking for a pack of cigarettes, even though he gave them up two years ago and smoking was no longer allowed in county buildings. He slammed the drawer shut after coming up empty.

What had he learned from the tape he didn't already know from the police report and from his own years of history? The melting ice cream, that was one thing. Chief had clued in on that for sure, but no mention of it in the police report. Junior thought it might have been an important detail, given how it could speak to the timeline.

The chief's line of questioning about the movie playing at *The Dixie* also peaked Junior's interest. Chief knew *High Noon* ended in a loud shootout, guns blazing from every direction. He suspected Chief wondered if the noise from the film could have masked the sound of gunshots at a neighboring business.

Something else, though. He drummed his three middle fingers in the deep creases on his forehead. He liked to do that when he had to think, really think, on something. *What's bothering you, Junior?* he asked himself.

Then, he had it. Relieved, he sat up straight in his desk chair and thumbed through the police report again until he found the phrase dangling in his mind like a worm on a fishhook. *The cash register appeared undisturbed, and no items of value seemed to be missing or out of place.*

If he recalled the case against McCready correctly, the apparent motive had been robbery. McCready had taken some money from the store, but not all of it. Something weird like that. So, if the cash register had not been bothered, where did the money taken come from? Or did he ask the girls to open up the cash register, take out some of the money (but not all of it), close up the cash register, and then shoot them? No, it didn't make sense to him.

Snatching tape 279 off the reel, he fumbled for tape 280 and loaded it up. The grainy quality of the second tape seemed more pronounced, as if it had been played many times and worn from years of review.

"Mr. McCready," the Chief's voice boomed, his tone authoritative. "Can you state, for the record, what you saw when you were downtown last night?"

"Well, yes, sir," young Nelson McCready complied, his voice tense and squeaky. "I went into the phone booth that evenin', trying to reach my mama. She won't answerin', so I had to keep tryin' over and over again. So, I was in there for a good bit"

"And then it says here that you stated you saw two men…" the chief prompted.

"Yessir," McCready continued, doubt seeping into his words. "It was past dusk, pretty much full night, so the light, it was real low, you know? But I coulda' sworn I saw two men just running, just as fast as they could."

"Uh-huh," Chief said. "White men? Colored men? What did they look like?"

"Hard to tell, sir." Nelson's voice cracked, lowered. "Like I said, it was going on dark."

"I see," said the chief, and then the telltale scribble. "And in what direction did these men run? Did you see a vehicle?"

"No, sir, no vehicle. I just saw them running away…running out the square and maybe headed up toward the bridge?"

"Okay, toward the bridge, a clean getaway, huh?" the Chief said. "Even though the bridge was open? And no description on these fellows?"

"No, sir." Nelson's voice was barely a whisper now. "Like I said, too dark to tell."

The recorded McCready cleared his throat and gave a nervous sniffle.

"And this was approximately what time of day, son?"

"T-time?" McCready stuttered. "Oh…I don't know. I don't carry a wristwatch. Let me see…" The chief offered an impatient sigh. "I made the first phone call to Mama before the sun was set, so maybe…7:30 p.m.? But she didn't answer. Not then, not the second time, nor the third or fourth. I was prob'ly in there for more than an hour tryin' to get through. You see, I needed a little money to make ends meet, just to get through the semester. I'm first year up here at the university…" McCready's voice lifted with a pleading pride.

"Ya say you needed money?" Chief intoned with a furious scratch and scribble.

Junior knew the questioner had just gained an advantage on his subject. Rookie mistake. A suspect should never offer more information than what is being solicited. Because listening to the course of the interview, and the high-and-mighty tone that was building in his father's voice, it seemed clear that McCready had, indeed, now become a suspect. A witness who needed money, who just happened to be in the right place at the right time to see phantom figures fleeing into the dark.

The money. How much was actually taken? Junior leafed through the stack of subsequent police reports, carelessly bypassing the yellowed photos crammed into the thin white envelope. He found a report from April 25, two days after the murders, and saw his father's scrawling signature penned at the bottom.

Forensic teams have finished reviewing Pop Gray's, scene of the double homicide on Sunday night, April 23. Partial footprints found on the scene appear to be a man's work boot or farm boot, but positive identification could not be made due to lack of complete prints.

Upon further review of store stock and register, and after interview with the store proprietor, it appears $138 is missing from the daily revenue totals. Mr. Gray indicated hourly register tallies are kept by the waitstaff on a small pad beside the register, and per these tallies, the day's earnings should have totaled $763. However, only $625 was found inside the store's cash register.

Junior stopped reading, the numbers jumping off the page in front of him. Two days later, and then it was discovered the cash count was wrong? Only after the lead suspect identifies he's in need of money? *That* didn't seem right.

Junior thought back to his meeting with Ms. Myers. The lady was rattled, for sure, and he'd had the sense she was holding back, something she wasn't saying. The way she pushed away from her chair, red hair and fury flying, the whole station watching them, slack-jawed. Just don't often see that kind of drama around here. Didn't Greta say the lady worked as a soap opera actress or something?

Junior opened his top desk drawer and pulled out an old cigar. He'd had it in there for ages, probably since his youngest boy was born. He unwrapped it, contemplating and sniffing the open end, stale but still fragrant. He chewed on the tip, lost in his own analysis.

With his free hand, he ruffled through the collected files again, resting on the worn-white envelope of photographs. He dumped them onto his cluttered desk and fanned them out with his fingers. Photos of the victims stared back at him, their point-blank wounds charred from the proximity of the barrel and their faces barren and extinguished.

He also found pictures of the crime scene, the alley side-door gaping open, blood smeared across the tiled floor, the pool of ice cream by the freezer door. Something didn't stick right with him.

"Welp," he said suddenly and to himself, pushing back from the desk so the wheels on his chair sent him spinning toward the back wall. "Got to check this scene out for myself."

He threw the unlit cigar down on his desk and sauntered through the station to the front door.

"Done for the day, Junior?" he heard Greta call sardonically as the door closed behind him.

It was still pretty cold outside, but the sun shone, and all the ice had melted, so Junior decided to walk the few blocks to Pop Gray's. It had been years since he'd been inside. He had never even taken his own kids for a scoop. Maybe the place still left him unsettled.

As he walked there now, he could almost feel Mama holding his tiny hand, his nails still caked with dirt, as they strolled downtown after a long, hot day working on the farm, so many years ago. She'd order three big, colorful cones—one for Junior, one for his sister, and one for herself, always strawberry—and she'd laugh as it dripped down their faces, coming at them with napkins.

He opened the front door of Pop Gray's and found himself warmed by that familiar, sugary-sweet smell, even on this cold day. The sun started to set in the square behind him, and a glimmer of twilight angled in through the front windows, illuminating the chrome and the tight red booths with its soft pink glow. The old jukebox still sat in the corner, and Junior wondered if it still played any tunes.

"Well, hey there, Junior," Lucy Gray said from her stool perched behind the cash register. She flipped through the pages of a magazine since no other customers were in the store. "Can I get you a cone?"

"Naw. Thanks, Lucy, it's too cold out there today for ice cream."

She looked disappointed. "Aww, well we're just getting ready to close," she said, rising off her stool, "so I don't have any coffee or anything made."

"That's okay. I'm all good," Junior said, letting his eyes audit the four corners of the store. As if preserved in time, Pop Gray's maintained its original black-and-white-checkered linoleum floor, and Elvis Presley still smiled at Junior from framed posters on the walls.

"Kind of a weird request for you, Lucy. I'm actually not here as a customer. I'm actually on the job." He registered her alarm as she rolled up the magazine and tucked it away under the counter.

"What's this about, Junior? Denny said you came by his house earlier, too. Kind of freaked him out."

"Well, with due respect, it doesn't take much these days to freak Denny out," Junior said, rubbing his stubbled chin in thought, regretting he forgot to shave that morning. "Say, could I maybe take a look in your freezer?"

"The freezer?" Lucy asked, her brow knitted with confusion.

"Yeah, I know, like I said, a weird request. It's a question I've been trying to answer about…that old case."

"Oh," Lucy said, her face darkening and her age showing through the pinch of her wrinkles. "Well, I guess so. Yeah. C'mon." She beckoned for him to follow, pausing briefly by the front door where she flipped the store's "Open" sign to "Closed." They headed through the kitchen to the far corner where the steel walk-in hummed. It was a small cube of a freezer, not even five feet high, ashen gray, a little rust on the hinges.

"Is this the same freezer from back then?" Junior asked Lucy. He didn't even have to finish his sentence before she nodded. It was all a very unpleasant topic, and Lucy looked to be squirming inside her own skin. She would have just been a kid when it all went down, but she knew, of course, all the sordid details of what happened that night at Pop Gray's.

Junior tried the handle, but it didn't budge.

"Oh, this old thing, it's been stuck like this for as long as I can remember," Lucy said, pushing Junior aside. With a clever flick of her wrist, a jimmy and a twist, the freezer door released, and sub-arctic air billowed out to meet them. Junior shivered.

Tall cylindrical cartons of ice cream were stacked high in the freezer, organized by flavor—vanilla, strawberry, chocolate, pistachio, mint chocolate chip, fudge ripple, and butter pecan. Junior thought again about

Denny, and he wondered who made the ice cream these days.

He stepped forward to enter the freezer but misjudged its height and hit his forehead on the low-hanging doorframe. "Ouch!" he exclaimed.

"Oh, Junior," Lucy uttered from behind. "Should have told you, but you have to really duck down to get in there. Can't tell you how many people have given themselves goose eggs trying to get into this freezer."

He pulled a wilted photograph out of his coat pocket. In the sepia-toned image, one of the Neal sisters lay sprawled across the checkered floor, seeming to have tumbled out from the freezer, almost as if she had just tripped and fallen face first. But a dark bullet hole in the middle of her back and her blood-stained dress belied the truth. She had been shot from behind, point-blank. And unless her body had been dragged, which seemed unlikely due to the proximity of the apparently undisturbed ice cream puddle that had melted beside her, then whoever had shot her had also been in that freezer.

He closed the freezer door with a definitive thud, then tried in vain to wrestle open the stubborn handle.

"Show me again how you got that open," he said to Lucy.

Lucy wiggled and turned the metal handle until the freezer door popped open again. "It takes some practice," she said.

Junior had seen enough to be keen on a theory: someone had likely followed the girl into the freezer, argued with her, and ended up shooting her as she fled. Someone short enough to fit under that little door. Someone who knew how to maneuver the fickle freezer handle. Someone who knew the closing routine. Someone who knew the ins and outs of Pop Gray's.

Junior had the information he had come for. He thanked Lucy and hurried back to the station to write down some notes. Maybe he'd even add them to the file. It would be exciting, after all, to crack a cold case. For Junior had always suspected, from the day his dad came home grumbling about her, that August Littleton had been behind all of it. But the Myers lady, she had opened his eyes to something that had always been right there but he'd never been able to see.

Chief *knew* the Littleton girl was the culprit, and by God, it does seem like he had a mind to cover it all up. Why would he protect a girl who had been nothing but a nuisance to their family all those years, always loitering up at the barn, acting like Jo *belonged* to her, teasing Junior to no end…unless…well, could it be *she* was the one?

Junior remembered one summer evening when he came in from the barn, foul with dirt after slopping the pigs, and his parents didn't hear him creep in. He could still recall his mama's voice, rising low and angry from the open kitchen window. He remembered it like it had been yesterday.

"Chief, word in town is that you've been running around on me. Is what I'm hearing true?"

"Well, Alice…"

"Don't 'Well, Alice' me. Tell it to me straight. I overheard some whispers from the next aisle over when I was shopping at Robert's today. They said there's a *baby* on the way?"

"Oh, Alice, people are just talking. They don't know nothing. Ain't no truth to those lies. People are just upset right now that a colored man got off scot-free. They're mad we couldn't make the case stick, that's all. Just making up lies."

His mama, rest her soul, had given up then. She bought right into Chief's story or enough of it, at least, she could carry on. Mostly above reproach in the town, Chief's sheer self-confidence was enough to make the nasty rumors die down. But after that, Chief took to drinking more, and then he got into that infamous brawl at Hank's Saloon. Junior had heard, many years later, the fight had something to do with the Neal family and the case that had not been resolved, at least not to anyone's satisfaction.

It seemed Chief never really came back from those blows. He spiraled for a few years, and Mama kept talking about divorce. Then, one day, he went up to the barn and shot himself, and well, that put an end to a lot of things.

Junior looks across the mostly empty church pews now and wonders if the redheaded Myers lady might in fact be his half-sister. He's warmed by the idea because, after all, family is family. He slouches back into the hard pew, feeling strangely at peace for the first time in a while. He surveys the scene before him, a bedraggled group of mourners. The old lady with a high silver bun looks familiar, but he can't place her.

Reena is standing strong beside Ms. Myers, and Junior knows she's a good person to have around in trying times. She'd been there at the hospital when his own mama passed a few years back. And Reena's grandmother, Ms. Mary Lou, had been the one they'd called the night Chief died. There was nothing she could do, Chief had long been dead by the time they found him, but she'd helped them discreetly get the body to the mortuary and helped them keep it all under wraps, at least for a while. But a secret like that doesn't hold long in Seaville.

Must be something about being at a funeral that makes it all seem like yesterday. The dark red stain on the back wall of the barn, splattered across the hayloft, and his mama crumpled on the ground. The sad whinny of a horse. Junior shakes the dark thought out of his head. All that has long since passed and doesn't matter now.

He watches from his seat in the back of the church as Sally Mavey, wearing something garishly bright for a funeral, not that it mattered to him, passes tissues down the row, then blows her own nose, the noise echoing through the church.

Then Junior notices his old friend Shep standing in the back of the pews, head bowed. *What in the hell is Shep doing at August Littleton's funeral,* he wonders, feeling his knees creak as he rises off the hard bench to shake Shep's hand.

"Shep," he whispers, creeping up on his friend from behind just like he used to do in the schoolyard. "What are *you* doing here, man?"

Shep, somewhat startled, settles when he turns to see Junior's face.

"Oh hey, Junior," he says. "Just paying my respects. You know, nobody really calls me Shep anymore. It's Sam now." Junior shrugs.

"But anyway, I'm here because my Aunt Eileen wanted to come, but the drive and all was just too much for her. And you know…her memory…"

"Right," Junior agrees, remembering the notes he had taken after talking with Denny. "I had a mind to pay your aunt a visit about this cold case I been workin' on. You say she was friends with Ms. Littleton?"

"Yeah," Shep answers. "A long time ago. They worked together at Pop Gray's."

"You don't say? Huh. I was just over there a few days ago, looking into some things."

Shep fidgets with his tie, uncomfortable, then scatters a look sideways to his friend. "You know," he says, "now that she's gone, I guess there's no harm in me telling you this." He takes Junior by the elbow and leads him to the far corner of the church, quiet as its own collected sins. "Years ago, back when we were kids, that lady in that casket, August Littleton, told my aunt a *pretty big* secret." Shep clears his throat and Junior moves in closer, cocking his better ear toward his friend.

"She told her," Shep continues, "well, that she gave *your* father a gun—a gun that was probably a *murder* weapon, if you get where I'm coming from." Shep's eyes get big and wild, and for a moment, he looks every inch like the boy who would spend hours skipping jacks on the sidewalk.

"My father? Chief? A gun, you say?" Junior asks, his heart beating faster now. The threat of sweat tickles his brow. He thinks of the Smith & Wesson snub nose, its shiny aluminum-alloy frame back at home, tucked safely in his underwear drawer. *A gift,* Chief had said. *Keep it somewhere safe. Don't tell your mama. Don't tell anyone about it. This one is a secret between father and son.*

Junior had grinned from ear to ear, tucked the gun in his waistband, and kept the knowledge of it all these years his and his alone because it was a special gift from his father, who he still loved more than anything in the world, despite it all.

Well, now he knows. Turns out, he'd been hiding a murder weapon in his underwear drawer for fifty years.

Chapter 38: Ending

August is not entombed or lowered into the ground. Instead, she is cremated, turned into an apparition of dust. My mother's life ended dramatically, and those who knew her carry on with its dangling ends.

I walk now with a heavy heart and too many questions to reconcile, but that's what happens sometimes when the truth rises up to meet you, its twisted face unfathomable. But life inevitably moves forward, and I will have to learn how to live in this new skin.

With the funeral service complete, a realtor has been called to assess the house. Laney and John pack up cardboard boxes in August's bedroom, while Geraldine's bags wait by the front door.

"Janus," she says, wrapping her soft body in her enormous trench as she stands by the front door waiting for her taxi. "I know things didn't end up as you'd hoped. But remember, underneath it all, and despite all the things you can't understand, your mother loved you." She offers me a warm embrace, which I gratefully accept.

"And you, too," she says, turning to Cliff, who has come by to help clean out the house and take care of affairs. We both agreed we'd split the proceeds from the sale, with his half going back to his mother and Aunt Mary as a sort of reparation. "She barely knew ya, but you were always her son."

Cliff winces but manages to nod in appreciation, and we both wave Geraldine into her idling taxi.

"Take care of that Laney," Geraldine shouts out the window as the cab pulls away. "She's lovely. And *you* are *not* your mother!"

Standing here on the empty front porch, in the middle of all my beginnings and endings, I let my mind return to the day I'd escaped this very place. How I'd scrambled into Ms. Devere's station wagon with a backpack full of socks and underwear and eyes full of tears. How August had ripped that locket chain clean from my neck, breaking my last connection to what I'd learned to call home. And how I'd spent the rest of my life reinventing myself, willing to play any role but the one into which I was born, dodging questions, and then, in just the past week, digging for answers.

But the answers turned up full of dirty secrets and vile undercurrents, and they have left a stain on me I will never be able to scrub out, just like that unsightly spot on August's old carpet. I'm still standing, though, both broken and reborn.

My eyes linger on the garden, long neglected, covered in moss and the dead leaves of the old oak. One white camellia blossom has tumbled onto the cold ground, its bloom against the brown earth sudden and unexpected. Without a thought, I reach down and gather it in my palm, knowing I'd find a vase inside and give it to my daughter. It would be a promise to her our dysfunctional legacy ends with me—that her future will be as clean and new as the ivory bloom of this flower. And that neither my mistakes, nor her grandmother's, nor her mother's before her, would have the power to define her.

The moment leads me to a strange unraveling, an unwinding of my expectations that feels both consequential and complete. I know now I'm ready to cut ties from the anchor that has been dragging me down for days—the blame, the grief, and my inability to reconcile this world I had stepped into with what I thought were my given circumstances.

I can let all those "Ifs"—those magic, terrible, conflicted fractures in my storyline—fly away into the impressionable blue of this winter sky, which sprawls above me like the rough-sketch scenery of a forgotten play.

Finally, I find my closure.

*****

Nelson lowers himself carefully onto his aching knees, steadying himself with his hands as he descends to the ground. The earth beneath his fingers feels firm and set, having long ago accepted its invited guest. Grass covers the seams of the grave plot, and a dead bunch of daisies nestles against the rounded headstone.

Nelson has brought lilies, which can be hard to find this time of year, but he recalls they were indeed Momma's favorite, so he'd tried each grocery store from Seaville to Roanoke Rapids to see if they had any for sale. With each store he visited, Nelson's confidence grew. Nobody pointed or stared. Nobody, in fact, even noticed him slipping quietly in and out of the floral section. And that was perfectly fine by him.

"Momma, I finally made it home," Nelson whispers with a soft sigh of sorrow, honoring the quiet of the place, though he kneels alone in the graveyard. "Momma…I'm free."

The letter from the Seaville Police came a few days after August's memorial service. It said the charges they'd been holding over him for the second, untried murder had officially been dismissed. He was now free to travel—to live—at his discretion. A small piece appeared in the newspaper, too, something brief and nondescript. The text they used to clear his name was a mere drop in the bucket compared to the headlines that screamed his culpability.

But this afternoon, as the daylight wanes into the evening, Nelson breathes in deeply the pleasure of his freedom. A crisp winter wind tangles its intentions in the canopy of branches above him, and the sun begins to lower behind the trees as if it, too, can respect the magnitude of this moment.

"Momma," Nelson says, "I don't know if I'm too old to try to start a life, to try to make something of myself, and to be a man that you'd be proud of. I don't know what I'm gonna do next. Maybe stay 'round here in the Rapids, maybe head back to Seaville. I've got a real nice neighbor down there watching Gladys and the Pips while I'm gone. Her name is Sally, and she talks too much, but her momma right about saved my life." Nelson softly places the lilies at the base of his mother's grave.

"Yeah, you would have liked Ms. Mavey, Momma."

With concentrated struggle, Nelson rises to his feet and brushes the dirt from his knees. He bends to kiss the cold corner of the tombstone, the way he used to kiss Momma on the cheek when he was saying goodbye.

He shuffles past the graves of lives lost, wondering what stories they had to tell and what secrets slipped loose as they passed from this world to the next. Carefully stepping over the shadows that cross his path, he swings the wrought-iron gate open wide and strides out of the graveyard, onto the bright sidewalk lining the busy avenue.

He smiles wide, his mind set on finding himself a heaping plate of warm, buttery cornbread.

Author and Acknowledgements

About the Author

I grew up in North Carolina but currently live in Arlington, Virginia. I share a passion for writing with the loves of my life, my two daughters, Juliet and Caroline.

After graduating from UNC-Chapel Hill with a degree in Journalism, I spent many years in the rat race before deciding to chase the dream of writing this novel.

Acknowledgments

This book is based on a true story that transpired in Staunton, Virginia in the late 1960s. In 2009, I clipped an article from The Washington Post that covered the tragedy and its aftermath, and ten years later, I found the clipping in the bottom of a drawer. I decided to fictionalize the account, and thus, all characters and events represented in The Epilogue of August are fictional. The town of Seaville is, also, a figment of my imagination, but it is heavily based upon one of my favorite places, Wrightsville Beach, North Carolina.

Now, for the gratitude:

I'd like to thank my sister, Laura Spencer, and my mother, Cheri Spitz, for providing support and encouragement as I slugged through days of doubt while writing this book.

I'd like to thank Juliet and Caroline for being my inspiration, always.

Thanks to Elizabeth Merck for your edits and encouragement, and for helping me understand that writing a book is truly a learning process.

I'd also like to thank Melissa Hackmann for the artwork and design of this book cover. I truly value your talent, creativity, and friendship.

I'd like to thank Lisa, Annah, and Emily for their role on "the sounding board."

And a special shout-out to Ben, Melissa, Whitney, Marla, and Rachael for their support over the past few years.

Book Club Information

I welcome invitations to your book club discussions! I have included some ideas for discussion below, and I would love to join your book club to speak about this novel and answer your questions.

Please contact me at **JJCAuthorChat@gmail.com** for book club inquiries.

Discussion

1. Race seems to be an undeniable factor in Nelson's fate, but where else in the storyline do you find that race alters the shape of a character or event?
2. Could August have lived a different life if she'd had a different mother? In what ways did Patricia influence the course of events?
3. What were the elements in Jan's life that enabled her to grow and succeed, to escape what would have been a very different life had she stayed in Seaville?
4. Secrets, and the lengths we go to to keep them, lie at the heart of this novel. Whose secret surprised you the most, and once the secret was revealed, how did it change how you felt about the character?
5. Did August keep her darkest parts from her daughter out of love, shame, or fear?
6. Each main character in this novel is seeking their own answer, and it's not until they meet and join efforts that they can find some sort of resolution. Are these

characters happier before the storm, or after the storm? Does finding their answers bring the fulfillment they had hoped?

7. Who is your favorite character, and why?
8. At the end of the book, what is one word you would use to describe the character of August?